THE

BLACKSTONE

CONSPIRACY

SYLVAIN PAVLOWSKI

THE

BLACKSTONE

CONSPIRACY

A novel

For my wife Isabelle, her infinite patience and my children: Alexandre, Valentin and Laura. To Laetitia and Stéphanie, thanks to whom two little rays of sunshine, Anastasia and Daphné, illuminate our lives.

Cover: Matthieu Biasotto

Acknowledgements

I'd like to thank everyone who has helped me during the writing of this work, in particular my beta readers. It's always difficult to do this kind exercise without forgetting anyone. I'll give the names in no particular order: Michel Bâton for his quick and constructive feedback, as well as Valérie Laugier and Raymond Lemaire. The incredible group of friends from 123PF: Philippe Guyon, Florence Singaraud and François Vigier. The three companions at Natale, and my longtime friends: François Chiche, Alain Biancardi and Richard Drai. Finally, a nod to my friends from Team Jules who know who they are, in particular: Pierre, David, Ioa, Doudou and JK, for their good mood every day.

Part One:

Chaos Theory

1. SLEEPLESS NIGHT

Elysée Palace - Sunday, September 24th, 11.15 pm

The French president always managed to keep a cool head, even when things weren't going well.

Considering what had happened over the last seventy-two hours, it would have been perfectly understandable he wasn't able to on this occasion. Three days of escalating violence had seen suburbs being set ablaze and mass lootings in many of France's city centers. The security forces had been overwhelmed, leaving the President no other option but to enforce a curfew and place the country under maximum security alert to ensure the safety of the people.

The Head of State was monitoring what was happening from the safety of the Élysée Palace's underground bunker. The high-tech, windowless control room's walls alternated between wooden veneer and raw concrete. There was a glass-topped oblong table with steel legs in the center of the room, around which perfectly-aligned black leather chairs awaited the heads of government.

A giant video screen dominated one end of the room, like an open window looking out onto a world beset by doubt and violence.

The atmosphere was tense, the bunker full of red eyes and tired bodies. President Paul Lavalette and his Prime Minister, Henri du Plessis, were talking quietly. The other government members present were all sweating with worry. The operation's commander-in-chief, General Lartigue, read communiqués that under his orders were brought to him the moment they were received. Lartigue was alert and focused as he questioned the liaison officers, whom he then sent away with his instructions.

Once everybody had taken a seat around the table, the President began to speak. His voice, usually calm and poised, was unable to hide the stress he was feeling:

"Ministers, General, advisers. I thank you all for being here. Earlier today I declared that this country was in a state of emergency and asked for a curfew to be enforced, that would begin at 6 pm.

"I spoke directly to the people in order to give them some sense of reassurance. This is an exceptional situation and as such I've deployed our armed forces to contain the wave of attacks which have been worsening over the last three days."

The President paused, observing the members of the crisis team, before continuing:

"People from the suburbs are armed and roaming the streets. I fear that they may be about to begin an attack the rest of the population. The anger that they've held inside them for so long is about to be unleashed."

He turned to the military man:

"General Lartigue, could you update us on the current situation?"

"Mr. President," Lartigue began as he stood up.

"Ladies and gentlemen, our forces have been mobilized."

He pushed a button on the keyboard that was on the table. A map of Paris and its surrounding area appeared on the giant screen.

"The army has armored vehicles located in potentially vulnerable areas around Paris," the General continued. "The entry points around the perimeter of the city have all been secured. Our concern now is mainly protecting La Défense."

"What's the situation like in other cities?" enquired one of the advisers. "The last communiqué wasn't exactly encouraging."

"It's the same in both Lyon and Lille. It's very tense in the South, particularly to the north of Marseille. Our intelligence services are convinced that attacks are imminent. Gentleman, the suburbs are ready to go to war."

"Thank you, General," Lavalette said as he resumed the lead. "Gentlemen…"

The President was interrupted. An image filled the screen. It was of La Défense, the business district of Paris, in the outskirts of the city. During the day, La Défense is populated by thousands of workers who emerge every morning from its underground train station like obedient little ants. Then, in the evening, it turns into an enormous, silent and lifeless space. Forty percent of France's GDP is generated there; all industrial and financial powerhouses have at least some presence in the area.

The district appeared on the screen, captured in its entirety by a camera on the Pont de Neuilly bridge. A concrete landscape on this cold, early autumn night. The Novotel hotel, with its broken-line architecture, concealed parts of the Tour AXA, in which only a few offices still had their lights on. Further left was the Tour Initiale, the stripped-down rectangle of a construction, whereupon light and shadow danced together to create a playful mosaic of black and yellow. In the background were more office blocks, most of them with all of their lights off. The buildings were huddled together, giving the impression of being one single entity. La Défense, which usually dazzled with a relentless clarity, seemed to want to hide itself. Down the promenade, hardly visible, stood La

Grande Arche, the impressive modern architectural update of the famous Arc de Triomphe.

La Défense, the symbol of French capitalism, needed to be protected.

It was up to the 1st Light Armored Brigade to undertake that mission. Equipped with brand new VBMR Griffon armored vehicles, Commander Blin and his men were ready. Seven thousand soldiers were sent to twenty different locations. Five hundred seasoned fighters positioned at strategic points within the business district. A column of one hundred men had taken up position on the nearby Pont de Neuilly. Their priority was to watch over and defend the passage into Paris via the world famous avenue, the Champs Élysées, an almost mythically romantic symbol of French culture, lined with its fashionable shops and trendy cafés. The other main roads from the west and the north via Saint-Denis and Charles de Gaulle airport were also secured and closed to traffic.

The silence was oppressive on this chilly evening. The curfew meant that the city's noise, usually deafening in its relentlessness, had all but completely fallen quiet. Time itself seemed to stand still; an open bracket toward an unknown future.

A face appeared in the center of the screen:

"Commander Eric Blin, 1st Armored Light Brigade, General!"

"Go ahead Blin," replied Lartigue, eyes glued to the control screen.

"There's movement in Quatre Temps!"

Quatre Temps was a giant, imposing shopping mall made of glass and steel located in the heart of La Défense. It was the largest mall in France, visited by over forty-six million people each year. If La Défense was the symbol of French capitalism, this place was its beating heart.

A violent explosion in the distance made the members of the crisis team jump. The video feed showed debris, illuminated by enormous flames, being blown high into the sky. Nighttime seemed to disappear, the darkness swallowed up by the intense orange glow of the conflagration. Two more powerful explosions rang out, one after the other. The screen showed flaming tongues of fire and dense white clouds of smoke. At least one of the buildings had been attacked.

"It's Quatre Temps! They've blown up Quatre Temps, General!" The pitch of Commander Blin's voice was getting higher and higher as he spoke. "They're informing me that the attacks are near the Grande Arche. They're coming in waves from the West. It seems like it's a coordinated attack!"

The General turned toward the President:

"Sir, what should we do? It looks like we're going to need to engage!" The soldier paused for a moment. The question that he was about to ask, and the answer it received, could change forever how France would be perceived by the rest of the world. This was the country that was famous for its role in the development of universal human rights, for Les Lumières, its role in the Enlightenment. He took a deep breath.

"I ask for your authorization to engage the enemy, Mr. President!"

The Head of State turned to Henri du Plessis, his friend and Prime Minister since May's recent election. "This is it, Henri. This is it," his anxious look seemed to say. He stared at the Interior Minister, a longtime ally of the former president, and with a voice full of sarcasm he uttered:

"Minister, I fear that it we're going to have to clean up my predecessor's mess!"

"General, the enemy is getting closer. They're making ground fast!" Blin regained his calm thanks to his experience as a soldier.

"Mr. President?" Lartigue asked once more.

President Lavalette closed his eyes and lowered his head. His shoulders were hunched over as if someone had just dropped a huge burden upon them. His right leg fidgeted awkwardly, a clear sign of the pressure he was under. Anyone could learn how to be a politician. With a good mentor, a little courage and a keen sense of communication, one might even make a career of it. Paul always wondered what difference there was between being a politician and a statesman, apart from just words and posturing. He was about to find out.

He opened his eyes, composed himself, and nodded his approval to General Lartigue.

"Mr. President, I need your verbal authorization!"

"I order you to engage, General," Lavalette exclaimed. "Defend this country for me. We need it."

"Ordering all units on the ground to engage!" General Lartigue shouted, a little too loudly. "I repeat: I order you to engage!"

Perched on top of his armored vehicle, Commander Blin looked over the scene that was playing out in front of his eyes. The glow coming from the Quatre Temps was increasing in intensity, a sure indication that the fire was spreading. Powerful flames pierced a sky covered by dense smoke clouds that were quickly dispersed by the strong winds. He could just about make out the river Seine, whose black waters intermittently reflected the silver rays of the moon.

He took a deep breath and ordered his troops to start moving in the direction of the boulevard that encircled La Défense. Five other vehicles were to stay on the bridge in order to prevent any attempts by the enemy to cross the Seine and enter from the west, a maneuver that would give them open passage into Paris.

The last video image transmitted to the Élysée control room was a convoy of armored vehicles beginning to move, followed by heavily armed men. In the distance, the first shots of automatic gunfire could be heard.

The civil war had begun.

2. THE ELECTION

Sunday, May 7th – Evening of the election

It had been a memorable night; one that would remain in the public consciousness for a long time to come. The initial results came in at 8 pm precisely.

Candidates' headquarters are generally the first places to receive information from polling stations, whether it be for results or for any recounts that may be required. This time, however, the results were so contradictory that no one knew where this election was heading.

8 pm

The news presenter appeared onscreen. The show was on France 2, a state-owned television channel with a very large audience. Impeccably coiffed, he was dressed in a white shirt and a petrol-blue suit with matching tie. Everything seemed to be in perfect order, except perhaps for his uneasy 'television-smile', that looked particularly awkward when juxtaposed with the guests sat opposite him, who all appeared to be in some kind of catatonic stupor.

"In less than ten seconds we'll have the preliminary scores from the second round of the presidential election," he managed to articulate, albeit in a very nervous manner.

He stared at the control screen in front of him as the seconds ticked by. The countdown hit zero. He regained his composure and began:

"Ladies and gentlemen, the vote count shows that, at the present moment, the candidate representing the Front National has a 2% advantage over Paul Lavalette. This is a preliminary count, with only a part of the total vote accounted for, so it is still too early to start drawing any conclusions. These percentages have been shared with us by the Interior Minister, who informs us that they come only from polling stations in rural areas. As of 8 pm, Paul Lavalette has 49.01% of the vote, while the nationalist leader has managed to accumulate 50.99%. If the results stay as they are, we are about to see a seismic change in the political landscape of our country."

The announcement created something of a shockwave at Paul Lavalette's headquarters. A heavy silence fell over the room, before cries of "Lavalette, Président! Lavalette, Président!" could be heard from the ground floor. Raucous, throaty chants that eventually became whistles and anti-Front National slogans.

The Front National was the second-largest political party in France. The last few years had seen an explosion in the numbers of their followers. At first, they were treated as unimportant; a nuisance or background noise on the political scene. Recent efforts from their politicians and connections in the media, however, had turned them into a party with enough followers to warrant them being taken very seriously indeed. Among their supporters were people who had been left behind by rampant globalization; those who felt that they'd been forgotten by this complex new world. They were the 'have-nots'. Those who have no job, no place to live, no tomorrow and no future. The Front National, cleverly, had put society's most glaring societal problems at the top of the political agenda: unemployment, immigration, security, secularism. They opposed politicians that they deemed to be only self-interested, no matter whether they were Muslim or Christian, rich or poor, believers or non-believers, French of origin or French of heart.

In Lavalette's office were Henri du Plessis, Paul's longtime ally and future Prime Minister, Michelle, his wife, his campaign director and a few friends.

The candidate decided it was time to reassure everyone:

"It's not over until it's over. We know that the rural areas have always liked the Front National. They're anti-Europe. We knew that they would get some support there, and don't forget that these polling stations close earlier than the cities. The urban centers are where we'll find our supporters. There's no need to panic. Keep smiling and let's just keep any communication between ourselves right now. I'm still confident."

"Let's go downstairs," Du Plessis suggested. "Let's join the others and show them that these results haven't done anything to dampen our spirits."

Paul Lavalette, now sixty-two years old, had always leaned to the right of the political spectrum. A man of conviction, a dedicated politician and on many occasions a competent minister, he'd previously occupied various roles within parliamentary assemblies. Capable and well versed in the workings of the state, he presented himself during his presidential campaign as the man to bring the people together. As a liberal conservative, throughout his long journey to the presidency he had pressed home the point of how essential it was for society to develop and evolve, that the necessary reforms would often be painful and that unemployment could be managed without bringing the country to its knees.

He wanted to assemble of group of government ministers who could be trusted; politicians who would be able to design a blueprint for a new society. He knew that he'd have to make some compromises along the way, but he kept this type of thought to himself, at least for the moment. Except for his longtime friend Henri Du Plessis, who would be appointed to the post of prime minister, he had yet to reveal his intentions regarding the make up of the rest of his future government.

In any case, the election had not been won yet, and he was far from being as comfortable as he wished to be perceived.

The presidential campaign had been difficult, at times even nasty, with cheap shots often being the chosen method of dialogue. Paul knew what to expect from his opponents: the leader and other top members of the Front National played their anti-system, anti-monetary union and anti-European song on repeat and in doing so opened up a gaping hole in the current political debate. They offered no solutions. Being against everything seemed to be their policy.

On the night of the first round, the 30th of April, the Front Républicain party were all present for an assembly. The political tenors, with the full support of the tremolos, delivered a chorus of pledges and called for everyone to vote for Paul Lavalette. With all of the ballots counted and prediction reports calculated, he was forecast to gain over 60% of the votes. Victory was just around the corner.

Only one more week.

Monday, May 1st, Paris

3 pm

The Labor Day march left Denfert-Rochereau plaza at 3 pm, as it did every year, and headed for the Place de La Bastille. Labor Day was an important event for the trade unions in France, so political leaders always made sure they were in the front row so they could be seen showing their support. The same pledges and tired slogans were used year after year. Fashion trends had advanced more in fifty years than political ideas here. Parades like this wouldn't have looked out of place in the 1960s.

The confederation of trade unions began to move at 3 pm and was flanked on both sides by policemen. Security was heavy. The usual share of politicians participated, one of whom was the secretary general of the General Confederation of Labour, the largest union in France. Skeptical bystanders watched the protesters from the windows of their cozy Haussmannien apartments.

Having made their way down avenue Denfert-Rochereau, the dense parade of people marched forward down Boulevard Saint-Michel, through the heart of the Latin Quarter. To their left as they marched was the picturesque Jardin du Luxembourg.

It was a gorgeous Parisian day. The atmosphere was good-natured; members of the crowd shouted slogans through their megaphones and held signs displaying the same old slogans: "Capitalism does not pay", "I work therefore I am," and so on. All the while they were accompanied by a team of highly vigilant anti-riot security marshals.

Witnesses stated that the individual was dressed in a large, hooded sweatshirt with white sneakers and jeans. The security forces couldn't explain how he managed to get through multiple layers of their defenses.

As soon as he managed to reach the parade, he detonated his device. Time froze. The blast enveloped all around him. Then came the silence. Eventually wailing and crying filled this empty void of time and space, then spread like a shock wave. The indescribable panic that ensued was captured on mobile phones and played on a loop on all of the news channels. The footage was shaky and badly framed, adding to the drama of the filthy spectacle broadcast on every channel.

Clips showed people running in all directions, with the exception of those that were visibly injured and physically unable to move. In the middle of a road that only seconds ago was filled with people walking purposefully, dozens of bodies lay strewn, moaning in pain as they awaited the arrival of the emergency services. The scent of blood and death hung over the entire scene.

Forty people were killed in the attack, with many more seriously injured.

*
* *

Sunday, May 7th, 8.45 pm – Paul Lavalette's campaign headquarters

The news tickers scrolled continuously on television displaying the current status of the vote count. Supporters of the Front National could be seen dancing and singing in the background. They were nearly there; victory was almost in their grasp. Self-proclaimed experts in television studios explained that these results reflected what the models had suggested, that this was not a surprise at all. The errors of the past meant that the election of a Front National candidate was inevitable. Or, at the very least, extremely likely.

The experienced politicians who had been invited to the studio to comment on the results were slightly more cautious. Prudence, after all, was one of their essential qualities.

Paul's friends, who had come to celebrate with him should he be victorious, were in small groups talking among themselves. The canapés and champagne were nibbled and sipped behind forced smiles. Appearance was everything. It was going to be a difficult evening.

Manipulation or incompetence? wondered Paul.

The whole campaign had proven to be a tough test, but the past week between the two rounds of voting had been particularly challenging. Riding the wave of emotion following the events May 1st, the extreme right party The Front National had redoubled its efforts. The loss of authority by the State, a lack of financial resources, the weakening of the security forces throughout the country and the general incompetence of politicians had all exacerbated the fallout from the attack. The party's leaders, with their belligerent warlord at the helm, began to exploit the situation as soon as they could. Delaying the second round of the election become a possibility that was discussed. A lively debate around the subject took place. The decision not to yield to terrorist blackmailing eventually won out, even though many voices called for the vote so to be postponed so that the tragedy would not influence voters. Paul campaigned for the election to go ahead as planned. Even waiting a few weeks would not be enough to erase the trauma of the attack. It would affect the result and there was nothing anyone could do to change that fact.

They'd just have to deal with the reality of the situation. The incumbent President, dressed in his favorite warmongering suit, which suited him rather well as it happens, arrived at the scene of the attack flanked by his rather pale-looking interior minister. The countless, and, to all intents and purposes pointless condemnations of the events by each of the various political parties had fueled the already strong public perception that politicians could no longer do anything about terrorism. Everything was beyond their control. The loss of trust interfered with the collective unconscious and undermined the status of a government that was supposed to protect its people. The model state was becoming a fading idea of the past, yet it was never more necessary to cling to some kind of common truth that could help maintain social cohesion. The Front National certainly wasn't the party offering solutions to this particular problem.

In just a few days, the Front National had reached a lead of 55% according to the polls, and momentum was propelling their lead higher and higher each day.

The presenter on France 2 began to speak again. The televisions in the Republican Headquarters were at full volume, the chatter around the room faded. Time stood still and the crowd hung on the journalist's every word.

"It's currently 8.45 pm and I'm happy to inform you that we're able to bring you an update on the voting. The two candidates are now neck-and-neck, each of them with 50% of the vote. The leader of Front National however remains just in front of Paul Lavalette of the Republicans with 50.26%, but the lead has been reduced significantly. It is, at this stage, impossible to make any kind of prediction regarding the eventual outcome."

At Paul Lavalette's headquarters, his relieved supporters began to chant as one again: "Lavalette, Président!" They hadn't won yet, but they hadn't lost either. Anything was still possible.

Paul looked at Henri and smiled. He took hold of the microphone and spoke to the one hundred or so people that were stood in the main hall of his headquarters:

"My dear friends, my very dearest friends, the people of France believe in their future. I know we will win! Once again barbarism will be defeated, because the ideas that we offer are born from the virtues of democracy and these ideas will always beat those born from ignorance! France, one and indivisible, will prove once again its ability to remain united."

Applause rang out following his short declaration.

Henri du Plessis' phone began to ring.

"Henri. Hello? Yes? Really? Are you sure? Ok understood, I'll tell him now. Paul?"

"Yes?"

"I have some good news! I've just had the first results for Paris. We've got the lead. They're saying 51%, maybe even 52%."

"Excellent!" Paul felt the tension in his back and shoulders ease up a little. The knots of anxiety in his stomach stuck around for a little while longer, however.

Paul's campaign director, Jacques Saint-Martin, was waving his hand at the other end of the room trying to catch their attention and gesturing for them to come over to him. He was smiling broadly. He seemed to have gotten some good news that he wanted to share.

"Henri? Let's go, Jacques wants to see us."

"Coming."

They headed over to Jacques and went upstairs to discuss in private. Michelle, the potential future first lady, was sat on one of Paul's campaign office chairs having a conversation with one of their friends. She was quite relaxed despite the uncertainty surrounding them.

Paul and Henri sat around the table as Jacques Saint-Martin updated them with the latest information.

"Paul, as you predicted, over the past hour things have improved significantly. I've spoken to a few federations and we're seeing favorable results not only in the region around Paris, but also in the other major cities. With these figures, we're looking at around 52% of the vote, but remember, these are still only partial results…"

Paul breathed a sigh of relief.

"We still haven't received the numbers from the southern and northern parts of the country, but once we know those we'll have a much better idea of where this election is going. What time do you think we'll be able to see the counts from those regions?"

"I'm trying to get them now but so far nothing. Let's not forget it's also possible that good news travels faster than bad…"

"We'll see. In any case, the dice have already been thrown, all we can do now is wait and see how they land."

9.45 pm

The results began to come in one after the other. The needle was slowly but surely beginning to point favorably in the direction of Paul Lavalette.

The lead was almost 2%, with a victory of fifty-one to forty-nine on the horizon. Paul had won the battle of the urban centers with most of the major cities voting in his favor. The counts varied only in the hundreds. Commentators were now proclaiming him to be the victor and his bustling HQ was in full celebration mode, everybody singing and dancing merrily. The moment of doubt had passed, and his supporters were now enjoying the sweet taste of victory.

It was time for him to face the cameras. He gave a short speech to his campaign team before leaving for Place de la Concorde, the capital's largest and perhaps most historic square, where a stage had been set up in preparation for his victory. Michelle, Henri and his campaign director accompanied him.

10 pm

Place de la Concorde was packed with well-wishers.

Paul's motorcade contained dozens of police personnel and members of his security team. Everything had been set up to avoid any violence that could ruin this election night; this fragile symbol of democracy.

His car stopped just in front of the stage. He struggled to get out, with the hundreds of supporters there trying to congratulate him on his success. They reached out to touch him. The fervor of the people was somehow at once reassuring and frightening. Henri was able to get out with a little more ease and climbed onto the stage via the entrance behind it.

Paul had arrived physically, but he hadn't quite arrived in spirit. Henri looked at his trusted battle partner, who seemed to be lost in his thoughts. Perhaps he was beginning to realize that his life was about to change and things would never be the same again.

One can prepare oneself for becoming a presidential candidate. Arm yourself with an electioneering arsenal, create a manifesto and hammer home each day how you're going to implement it. Channel your energy and focus it all on achieving your goal. Endure endless meetings, speeches, rallies and, of course, the occasional betrayal. Overcome each and every difficult moment and hope that you come out the other side somewhat unscathed.

But can one really prepare for becoming a head of state?

Paul made his way onto the platform. It was at this very special moment that he felt the true weight of the presidential office. He suddenly became acutely aware of the millions of people who hoped that he, Paul Lavalette, would deliver them the answers to all of their problems.

He smiled and pushed his way to the front, his arms raised in a 'V' as a sign of victory. The music continued to play in the background. He walked the stage from left to right as the gathered crowd chanted: "Victory, victory!"

The music fell silent. The noise of the galvanized crowd chanting his name was deafening. Paul felt that he should take his time; let the people enjoy the moment as much as he was enjoying it himself.

"Dear friends, companions on this journey. We have won!"

The supporters chanted again, louder this time. "Lavalette, Président! Lavalette, Président!" Paul gestured with his hands to quieten them down. Slowly the noise dissipated and a solemn silence took over the scene.

"Thank you! Thank you! We have succeeded, even though everyone told us it was impossible. We know that the events at the beginning of the week would put a special kind of spotlight on this election. But the brutality of this attack, the disdain for humanity, has reinforced your belief and your determination has not faltered! I will be a president for all of the people. We will put this country back on its feet together, and I am fully prepared to take on this challenge!"

Another round of applause. Paul made his way down from the platform, greeted the organizers and shook many hands.

His mobile phone, which he had judiciously put on silent mode, displayed dozens of missed calls. It seemed that the many people who had lost his number at the beginning of the campaign had suddenly found it again. He took it off silent and it rang immediately.

"Paul Lavalette?", the voice at the other end enquired in an accent that Paul didn't recognize.

"Yes, who's speaking?"

"Stay on the line, I'm handing you over to Chancellor Konrad."

"President Lavalette?" asked the German head of state.

"Madam Chancellor?"

"I wanted to be one of the first to congratulate you, Mr. President."

Paul spoke perfect English and German, which made him one of only a very few French politicians who were able to hold conversation with other world leaders without the need for an interpreter. He was flattered that the German Chancellor had taken the time to congratulate him following the announcement of his victory.

"Chancellor Konrad, I sincerely thank you for your call. You are well aware of my attachment to Europe as well as to our German neighbors."

"I know, and we are grateful to you for that. I hope that we'll be able to see each other before you enter the Élysée. It would be an informal meeting as you won't be president until the official inauguration. But it would send a strong message to our European neighbors and give us an opportunity to discuss urgent and confidential matters."

"Let me think about it, my first outing onto the international scene mustn't be misinterpreted! I'll discuss with my staff who'll confirm the meeting and have everything set up."

"Perfect, Herr Lavalette! I hope to see you soon!"

"Good evening, Madam Chancellor."

"That's a little curious," Paul thought as he hung up the phone, "it seems like there's something urgent that the Chancellor needs to see me about."

*
* *

Chaos Theory

3. THE INVESTIGATION

Tuesday, May 2nd

The noise! She opened her eyes and wondered what day it was. The mobile phone that was sat on the bedside table continued to vibrate and seemed to shake the entire room. She'd slept so little since the attacks that she'd lost all sense of time. The call had just plucked her from the arms of a very rare and very deep slumber.

She tried to get herself together but it felt like she had been underwater for too long and needed to reach the surface for some air. Shimmers of light broke through the curtains in her bedroom. She looked at the ceiling, then to her right where she could sense a cold, empty space in her bed.

"Yep," she thought to herself, "it's Tuesday!" She took a quick glance at her mobile. The large numbers indicated the time was 5.50 am. She picked up:

"Commander Rougier!"

"Hello Pauline. I trust you're on top form? You've had four hours sleep, and in your own bed, no less! We're just finishing the preliminary examinations."

"Hi Pascal. I hope you have a very good reason for calling me so early. A call from the head of forensics must mean that you've made some significant progress with the investigation."

"I'd say it's pretty significant. We've got our man! His name is Oualid Massourd."

"Do we have any background on him? Were we tracking him?" Still feeling sleepy, Pauline tried to gather her thoughts.

"You could say that! He's just returned to the country from overseas where he was fighting as part of the jihad against us."

"Damn it. It was bound to happen one of these days. OK, listen, I'm going to meet up with the Brigade as soon as I can. You can join us, let's say at seven, for a briefing? I'll get the whole team to attend."

Pauline hung up the phone before calling the other six members of the team to ensure they'd also be at the meeting. She knew all of their phone numbers by heart. Since the attack she'd been lost in a whirlwind of activity that hadn't left her any time to even breathe. She'd come home from work at around 1 am and barely slept. She certainly hadn't had enough time to recover from the previous day before she had to get up and start all over again.

Pauline Rougier had been with the Counter Terrorist Brigade for two years. At almost forty years old, she was the youngest commander and the only female director to work at the agency.

An attractive redhead, Pauline stood at five feet six inches and had an oval face with a mischievous, freckled nose that made her look like a student. She had the reputation for being a woman of action; she regularly practiced martial arts, and frequent jogging sessions allowed her to maintain a harmonious silhouette.

Pauline made a habit of being the top of the class in many of the disciplines taught at the National School of Police. She worked within the narcotics brigade for five years after graduating. It was there that she participated in the dismantling of a major international drug trafficking ring that was being used to finance terrorist networks, among various other nefarious activities. It was thanks to that case that she was noticed by the head of the brigade, who wasted no time in fast-tracking her into the CTB.

Pauline had been entrusted with the investigation within minutes after the attack on May 1st. She and her team had been working on the case ever since. Fifteen hours and counting, so far.

The first team of forensic investigators that arrived at the scene found no evidence that could be of use to them. The man, because the terrorist was indeed a man, had detonated his belt as soon as he'd joined the procession. He was vaporized by the explosion. The blast was so powerful that pieces of him had been found one hundred feet away from the point of detonation.

After the wounded and the dead had been taken care of and a security perimeter established, the investigation was able to begin in earnest. Witnesses that were somehow not in a state of shock were able to collaborate with the investigation, but struggled to be truly helpful as the attacker had run into the crowd and immediately activated his deadly contraption. Nothing the witnesses said would be able to provide any kind of reliable clue upon which they could anchor their investigation.

At midnight, after reporting to the director of the agency, Pauline and her team decided there wasn't enough evidence to go on with until the results of the DNA analysis had come through. They would pick up the case again the next morning. There was nothing solid to help them move forward, and they would need to rest before the many hours of sleepless nights that lay ahead of them.

*
* *

Tuesday May 2nd, 7 am

CTB headquarters, northwestern suburbs of Paris

Commander Rougier's team were assigned the 2nd floor meeting room, which would become their headquarters for the entirety of the investigation. Anyone who had a problem with that, and there were a few, would have to suffer in silence.

The room was furnished with typically dull office tables and chairs and lit by fluorescent tubes which diffused a harsh, unflattering light. Their faces, all bearing the hallmark signs of fatigue, were turned toward Pauline. The team of six investigators sat around the table were ready to begin.

The head of the forensic division of the police, Pascal Le Cam, arrived at 7 am sharp. He had been charged with collecting all the evidence at the scene of the explosion.

Pauline welcomed everyone and began the meeting:

"Hello everyone and thanks for being here at such an early hour. Our colleagues in forensics have identified our kamikaze. I'll hand over to Pascal who's going to brief us. Pascal?"

"Thank you Pauline, and hello everyone. I can confirm that we have both a name and a face to present to you. A DNA analysis was performed immediately following the aftermath and it would seem that we've hit the jackpot."

Pascal Le Cam presented a file that contained a few color photographs of the terrorist. "It's someone we'd been tracking," he continued.

"Oualid Massourd, third generation French of Algerian descent, twenty-five years old, he had been categorized as a serious threat to national security. He was convicted for drug dealing five years ago, sent down for twenty-four months but got out after eighteen. After being radicalized in prison, he went to join the jihad in Syria via Turkey in 2014. When Mosul fell, he simply disappeared and we didn't hear anything until yesterday. This means that, for the first time, our country has been attacked on national soil by a French citizen who trained overseas, then returned to wreak havoc."

The officers looked at each other as a heavy silence weighed on the room. The problem of terrorists trained abroad who return to attack their own country, or 'revenants' as they are known in France, was serious. No one knew exactly how many there were nor which ones realistically posed a violent threat to the country. But the threat was there. It was estimated there were at least a thousand. One thousand bombs that could return to France at any moment through the porous Schengen borders and wander freely through the cities.

"Thank you, Pascal. That was fast! We'll continue with the investigation. Anything else you need to tell us?"

"Not right now, but we're looking into the type of explosive used, and we have a part of the detonator. As soon as I have more I'll let you know."

"Any questions before Pascal goes back to the lab?" Pauline watched everyone closely.

No questions. She began to speak once more.

"Arnaud and Julie, I need you to find the CCTV images from Rue Soufflot and around the area. He didn't come packed like that by walking there! She turned to Moussa. "Moussa, you're to go with Yvan. I need you on the ground. Start by questioning the relatives of Massourd. Get all the background you can on him so we start to find some connections. He must have had friends before or after prison. Look more into his family. See if you can establish a link with any Islamist structure via the mosque where he grew up or anything of that nature."

"OK Commander, we're on it!"

"Clara and Kader, you'll review his case file. I want to know everything about his friends at the time, and any contacts he made in prison. If he was radicalized in jail, it may have been there that he made links enabling him to leave and come back."

"Yes boss!"

"I'm going to report back to the director. Let's all meet back here at noon. This is important, I'm counting on all of you!"

Arnaud and Julie took the stairs to get back to their fifth floor office to call the Paris operations center, where all image and video surveillance of the capital were recorded and stored. The Paris 'Video Protection' plan, initiated in 2010, connected thirteen thousand cameras as part of a major security project within the city. Without knowing it, all Parisians were now being filmed and spied on permanently in order to make the streets safer.

The Paris CCTV operations center was a large old building without any particularly distinctive characteristics, located in the south west of the city. It was anything but remarkable. The Parisians who passed by each day could not even imagine the concentration of technology within those digital eyes which analyzed constantly the urban jungle, the road traffic, stop lights and public buildings.

Julie and Arnaud presented their ID badges and entered the command center. It took up an entire floor. In the background was a huge, air-conditioned secure server room, containing computers connected to dozens of screens that formed a digital wall. All of the information they received there was systematically recorded and stored. The images were transmitted in a continuous flow, a feed from each of the Parisian cameras. It was a striking spectacle. One could see the Champs Elysees, the Sacré Coeur and the Opéra Garnier simultaneously, all filmed from every angle. The National

Assembly, the Palais de l'Élysée, the various ministries, the ring road encircling the city. Everything was recorded, minute by minute. Even though they were somewhat used to visiting the center, the two policemen could never quite get over this moving spectacle.

The head of operations was a man in his fifties with a rounded belly and hair as white as his shirt. He greeted them as soon as they arrived with a cordial and vigorous handshake.

"Lieutenants Payre and Lescure? Jacques Radier! I've been expecting you. I spoke to you earlier this morning. We've got an office ready for you so you can start your investigation immediately."

"Thank you!" said Julie, who appreciated not having to waste any time before getting to work.

"One of our specialists is going to assist you. Moving from one camera to another and changing angles is something that requires a little practice! Please, follow me."

Jacques Radier led them to an open door of a glass-walled office that contained a desk with a brand new 24-inch screen on top of it, linked to a keyboard and a type of joystick.

"Wow!" exclaimed Arnaud. "I see you're not lacking any funding here! If we had even half of this at the brigade we'd have achieved world peace by now!" he added, clearly impressed with the technology the surveillance team had at their disposal.

"To be totally honest, it's not like we have dozens of machines like this one, but considering the situation we thought it was best to give you the best of what we have!"

A young man who hadn't yet reached his thirties arrived and joined them in the office.

"Hello!" he said while passing Julie and without so much as a glance at Arnaud. He sat down and began to tap the keyboard.

Arnaud wondered if he or Julie had said something they shouldn't have. Jacques Radier gave him a little sign and they both left the office.

"His name is Nathan, Jacques said quietly. He's a bit... let's say autistic, but he's the most brilliant member of the entire team. Go gently with him and he'll make sure you get the most out of the technology here!"

"Thanks for the advice," Arnaud replied, "we'll go easy on him!"

He opened the office door. Julie and Nathan were looking at images on the screen. He noticed that the young man had deliberately placed himself in the seat between him and Julie, separating them. He took the vacant chair and sat a little bit behind them. Not exactly the best angle he thought, but he wanted to give Nathan some space to breathe.

"Do you have images of the kamikaze?" Julie asked.

"Yes of course," Nathan nervously replied, "would you like to see them?"

"I think that would be a good way to begin."

A few clicks. His agile fingers hovered over the keyboard, and the first images appeared on the giant screen. The specialist brought up various angles of Rue Soufflot, captured by one camera that was attached to the Panthéon, the magnificent mausoleum that contained the remains of some of France's most eminent citizens. They watched as time went by on the screen in front of them. They were staring at the everyday goings-on from the previous day in fast forward.

Suddenly, they saw him arrive. It was precisely 3.22 pm. He was among the crowd on Boulevard Saint-Germain that was walking to join the procession. He seemed stressed; walking in the direction of the parade yet often turning around to look behind him. He crossed the Rue Saint-Jacques and began to run, looking behind himself one last time.

"Stop," said Julie. "Can you zoom in and print this image?"

"No problem," Nathan responded immediately.

He made some adjustments using the keyboard so the terrorist's image filled the entire screen. It was impossible to look away from the determined expression on the face of the attacker. His eyes were red with lack of sleep and filled with an indescribable anxiety. Above all, one could in his face see all the hatred that, in a few seconds, would cause him to spread blood and terror on an unsuspecting crowd.

"Holy shit! That sends shivers down my spine!" said Arnaud, who with this somehow articulated what everyone else was thinking.

A few seconds later the man jumped over the protective barriers without anyone having intercepted him. Then the explosion. The silence was interrupted by the entry of Jacques Radier.

"Did you print this?" he said, placing the photo of Oualid Massourd on the desk.

"Yep, that's him!" replied Julie, "even though it's terrible quality, there's no doubt it's him. Nathan, can you go back a bit so we can try to track how Massourd got there?"

Nathan was switching between various camera angles. The two investigators were both internally thanking the heavens for the young computer scientist, because they knew if they had to do it themselves, it would have taken days. "Technology is useful," Julie thought, "but it's better in the hands of specialists."

They continued their search through the images. They observed their man from a multitude of different angles, making his way down the Rue des Carmes, then walking quickly on Boulevard Saint-Germain.

"There!" said Nathan. They could clearly see Oualid Massourd getting out of a vehicle between Boulevard Saint-Germain and the Pont de Sully.

"What type of car is that?" asked Julie. "Looks like something from the seventies!"

"It's a Golf from the nineties Julie!" Arnaud replied. "I admit it's not exactly one of the latest models, but still. You a rich kid?"

"Can you zoom in on the license plate?" asked Julie

"There you go!" Nathan replied after a few quick adjustments. "234 CV 93!"

"I'm on it," said Arnaud, taking a note of the number.

Arnaud left the office and called the brigade. The answered after the first ring.

"Hello, lieutenant Lescure speaking. I need to speak to lieutenant Clara Rossi or Kader Jaoui. I'll wait!"

"Lieutenant Jaoui!"

"Hey Kader, it's Arnaud. I'm calling from the video surveillance center. We've tracked our man and he's come down in a car. Can you find out the owner?"

"Go ahead, I'm listening. Let's hope it's not stolen."

"It's a Volkswagen Golf, red, license plate: 234 CV 93."

"One second. Got it. 1993 Golf belonging to Yasmina Oufik, address 40 Rue Heurtault, Aubervilliers."

"Thank you Kader, I'll let the boss know."

He went back to the office to ask Julie and Nathan to continue to track the Golf and follow the lead. He left again to call Pauline.

"Rougier," she answered immediately.

"Commander, it's Arnaud. We've got a lead! The video surveillance has helped us to identify the car which the terrorist arrived in. The vehicle belongs to a Yasmina Oufik. We're trying to track its arrival with the cameras."

"Do we have an address?"

"We do. Kader searched the database and the owner lives in Aubervilliers, at least that's what the official documents say!"

"OK, thank you. We'll have a look at the Brigade and call you if we need. Good work Arnaud!"

"Thanks Commander. If I find anything else, I'll let you know as soon as I get it."

Arnaud went back to the office where Julie and Nathan continued to follow the journey of the red Golf. The tech specialist was bringing up different angles, switching between cameras, and the wrinkles on his forehead were indicating that it wasn't easy.

"So?" asked Arnaud, "You guys got something?"

"We lose trace of the vehicle around the ring road," Julie replied. "there's too much traffic. Nathan is doing his best but we've hit a roadblock."

"Ok well in that case I say we should get back to the brigade. Nathan?"

"Yeah?"

"Keep searching and call me immediately if you manage to find anything, OK?"

"Yes, Lieutenant."

"As talkative as ever," thought Arnaud. This young man had indisputable technical qualities, but he wasn't exactly the most engaging colleague on the team. They could trust Nathan, though: if he could get anything from these images that they they could use he would undoubtedly do so.

Julie and Arnaud thanked Jacques Radier for his help and asked him to leave the young specialist as much time as he needed for the investigation. This was no problem for Radier, who was prepared to give the investigators as many of his resources as they required.

They arrived at the Brigade just before noon.

"Perfect," thought Julie, "we'll even be on time for the briefing."

The whole team was present for the meeting that was taking place on the 2nd floor. The electric atmosphere in the room was palpable, you could feel that things were happening. Arnaud and

Julie, Kader and Clara as well as Moussa and Yvan were all sat around Rougier.

Pauline went around the table of partners:

"Julie and Arnaud?"

Arnaud looked Julie, who began to speak.

"We have a picture of the terrorist taken by CCTV cameras at the precise moment he arrived at the parade." She took out the prints that Radier had placed on the desk at the surveillance center and handed them around. "As you can see, the photo is, beyond any doubt, Oualid Massourd. The person responsible for the attack is the man that we have identified with our DNA analysis."

"This is huge," Pauline asserted.

"In addition," Julie added, "by following his movements prior to the attack, we've seen him in a '93-registered red Golf which dropped him at the corner of Pont Sully and Boulevard Saint-Germain. Unfortunately, we then lose him on the ring road. The operational center technician is continuing with the search in case we can somehow find a way around this."

"Thanks Julie. Clara or Kader?" asked Pauline.

"Yes, Commander," said Kader. "Clara an I have identified the owner of the vehicle. Yasmina Oufik, twenty-seven years old. Her address is 40 rue Heurtault, Aubervilliers and..."

Clara interrupted Kader:

"Oufik?" She opened her files and went through the papers contained within. "Here. I've got something from Massourd's trial in 2014! Yes! There was an Oufik that gave evidence. It doesn't tell us much, but there's a link between them."

"Me too," exclaimed Yvan.

Moussa had a look at the attacker's dossier, "and Oufik is mentioned as being someone close to Massourd."

"So who is this 'Yasmina'?" asked Pauline.

"She's Driss Oufik's sister," Clara responded immediately.

"Kader and Julie, seeing as you've been through Massourd's file, I want to see a profile of Driss Oufik as soon as possible. If he's in on this, which seems to be the case, I need to know who he is!"

"No problem, boss!" replied Kader while looking at Julie who nodded in agreement.

"Anything else?" Pauline asked.

She looked around the table. No one had anything to add.

"Keep going and don't let up!" Pauline encouraged her team. "I'm going to see the boss. I'll be in touch."

*
* *

Tuesday May 2nd, 9.30 pm - Aubervilliers

The head of CTB had confirmed that everything they'd dug up on Yasmina Oufik was enough to justify issuing a search warrant. Right now it was just about all the investigators had to go on, and any kind of lead at the beginning of an investigation can prove to be crucial, especially if it's followed up quickly. The more time that passes, the more the leads tend to cool down. In-depth research had failed to find any more specific information about Yasmina Oufik. Her brother on the other hand, Driss Oufik, was also listed as a major security threat and had a record.

The preparations had been quick. The RAID team, the tactical unit of the French police that fulfilled a similar role to SWAT teams in the United States, was mobilized in less than one hour. The ten heavily-armed men were dressed in black assault uniforms with bulletproof vests, hoods and helmets. They waited in front of the building where Yasmina Oufik lived. By their side and ready for action would be the six investigators from Commander Rougier's own team.

Night had fallen over Aubervilliers. Rue Heurtault was calm. The traffic moved only one-way, which meant only a few vehicles drove here, even during the daytime. The neighborhood had been cordoned off and the RAID vehicles parked a little way off, enough to be out of view from Oufik's house.

The old two-story building had a decrepit facade. The bricks of the dilapidated construction, laid bare by whole pieces of plaster that had given up and fallen off long ago, retained old flaps of peeling paint. The only entrance door, in the center of the building, led directly onto the street. A small, poorly maintained garden was visible behind a low red brick wall surmounted by a rusty fence.

To the left, a modern four-story white building with two large windows that made the dimly-lit offices it contained visible from the outside.

To the right there was a construction site surrounded by a tall wooden palisade displaying 'No Entry' banners every two meters. Another sign boasted of the project that offered 'high-quality services' at a 'perfectly-sized scale… located just on the doorstep of Paris'.

The RAID team scanned the facade and the lit windows on the first floor that faced onto the street. The glass used for the windows was three-quarters frosted, the type that allowed residents a little privacy while still letting light in. The second floor was dark; the occupants were probably absent. Yasmina Oufik's apartment was on the third and last floor, where a glimmer of light flickered through the drawn curtains.

The leader of the operation was a large, very well-experienced and long serving member of the force. He had a square face and a solid jaw. Tall, blond, muscular and bright-eyed, he spoke to his and Pauline's teams, both grouped about one hundred and fifty feet from the building, and gave them instructions about the imminent assault.

"We need to get into the apartment situated on the third floor. Two men protected by a shield will position themselves at the front of the group on the stairs. François and Alain, you will lead! Then you, you and you, and you two," he said, pointing at five members of the team. "You'll cover us at the front with assault rifles. Philippe, you're first behind the leading group and you bring the ram. A man will remain on each floor in case anyone comes to help the suspects. Two more on front of the door, and two behind the building," he added, pointing to two pairs of partners.

"Any questions?"

The men looked around, their eyebrows raised as if to reiterate the question to one another. Everything was clear. Pauline came forward and pointed at the building.

"What do we do about the people on the first floor?"

"Commander Rougier, as a matter of fact, I have a mission for you. Can you get them out before we enter the building?"

"Got it."

"Take them out of the danger zone and keep them somewhere warm. We don't know how this could turn out."

He turned back to his men.

"When we're at the door we'll slide a camera in and see what the situation is. If there's nothing blocking us we'll open her up with the ram, then standard assault procedure. Stun grenades then ordered entry as we've done in training. Are we ready?"

Everyone nodded. The police officers were well versed in the exercise; they'd done it hundreds of times before. Each person knew their role perfectly.

"Commander Rougier, are you ready to begin the first floor evacuation?" the operation commander asked.

Pauline nodded and looked at Moussa.

"Let's go?" she said.

"Let's go Commander!"

They made their way to the house as quickly as possible and stood on either side of the entrance. With their weapons ready they pushed open the door. It opened slowly without making any noise. A quick glance inside. They found a small, dim, neon-lit lobby with an old, chipped cement floor and dirty brown walls. On the left were the bins of the condominium; opposite them was the door to the apartment on the first floor and a dilapidated staircase with worn wooden steps. Pauline grabbed the radio attached to her belt.

"Everything's good here! We're entering the apartment."

Pauline made a sign to Moussa and they went to the door of the apartment. They put away their weapons. Pauline knocked and listened attentively. A sound of movement, at first just a little, then a heavy steps dragging on the ground. A man of about seventy years old with all-white hair opened the door. He was wearing an old pair of well-worn jeans and a blue, stained sweatshirt. A beard of several days hid his wrinkled face. He stared at the two policemen suspiciously.

"What do you want?" he asked in a voice that was somewhere between curiosity and worry.

"Police! Sir...?"

"Dalmont! I'm the owner here."

"Monsieur Dalmont, I'm Commander Rougier and this is lieutenant Moussa Zalif," Pauline replied, showing her police badge.

"We need you to follow us. We have a search warrant for the apartment on the third floor. We'd like to keep you protected while the search is being performed."

"I'm in danger?"

"It's hard to say but we'd rather be careful. Do you have tenants on the second floor?"

"No it's empty at the moment. If you're looking for somewhere to stay...?"

"Thank you, but we'll talk about that later."

The old man hesitated, swaying back and forth on the landing. His body expressed his confusion as to whether he should leave his apartment now or invite the police inside. Pauline simplified the situation.

"Put your jacket on and follow us!" We're parked 100 meters down, just at the end of the street. We'll be ok there while the team goes up to the third floor."

"Give me one second" said the old man.

Pauline's radio sounded with a message: "What's happening, Rougier?"

"We'll be out of the building in one minute! We're with the owner. Apparently the apartment on the second floor is empty."

"OK! We'll begin the operation."

"Hurry up Monsieur Dalmont, it's a little urgent!"

"I'm coming, I'm coming!"

The old man grabbed a shabby looking jacket before leaving. Obviously, the renting out of apartments wasn't enough to provide him with a decent pension.

Moussa and Pauline, accompanied by Dalmont, headed back to the operation base where the RAID vehicles were parked.

The ten members of the RAID team ran toward the front door of the building. The thumbs-up from the commander as they arrived to meet the trio indicated that everything was in order. Their quick approach had been almost totally silent; Pauline was wondering how they could run with a bulletproof vest, a shield and armaments weighing at least 40 kg without making any noise.

The troop split, each group had its mission.

Two men stood in front of the entrance door inside of the lobby. Another pair hopped over the garden gate to position themselves at the back of the building in case the suspects tried to escape. The remaining six policemen began their climb to the second floor. The two men out front advanced slowly using their shields to protect their own heads and the group's from potential shots fired from the upper floors. The narrow staircase meant the soldiers were forced to move up in single file. It was more dangerous to do it this way, however. If they were attacked, only the leading policeman could fight back. The Commander signaled them to move faster. The dilapidated staircase creaked.

The group was now on the second floor, opposite the front door of the empty apartment. They listened. No noise. The captain pointed to one of his men and made a V with his right hand which he placed in front of his eyes, then indicated the stairs down. The other answered with a right thumb in the air. He had to watch the stairs and the landing to prevent any aggressors making their way up. Everything was understood without any words passing between them.

The leader made the signal for them to resume their advance. Everything was going according to plan, but they needed to stay focused; an attack was possible at any time. The difference between life and death was often a fraction of a second.

They arrived within sight of Yasmina Oufik's apartment, it was only six feet away from them. They slowed down to minimize the noise of their ascent. The two leading men positioned their shield so it covered the door in order to protect the rest of the troop from any gunfire coming from inside the apartment.

*
* *

When the flashlight he was carrying began to slip from his hand, Brigadier Philippe, who was following the two leading police officers, then made the huge mistake of trying to catch it. It was too late; it was already out of reach. The object tumbled down the floors, bouncing on the steps and clanging against metal stair rail, making a deafening noise. The soldier turned around and watched hypnotized as the light beam disappeared into the stairway. As he moved, the battering ram he was holding pounded against the wall, making an almighty sound to add to the cacophony. The flashlight eventually smacked against the wall at the bottom of the stairs and another loud noise filled the stairwell. The silence that followed lasted a few seconds, during which everyone remained absolutely frozen.

Four heads turned at the same time toward their commander. They'd lost the element of surprise and with two men in front of the apartment and the rest on the stairs, they were poorly positioned in case of an attack. The chief made a quick decision. It was one that he considered to be the best course of action considering the circumstances. He closed his fist and lowered his arm. The assault was ready to commence. The two policemen carrying the shield moved swiftly to the side so that Philippe could take the ram and break down the entrance. The two other members of the assault section, the commander and one of his men, had their automatic weapons ready to fire. They positioned themselves on either side of the door. As soon as it was open, they would throw in a stun grenade. These powerful devices had the capacity to create panic during an explosion; a catatonia that lasted for several seconds.

Philippe grabbed the light-alloy ram with both hands and, with a sweeping gesture, launched it in a rapid arc toward the apartment door.

*
* *

Pauline and the owner of the building were sitting in the back of one of the brigade vehicles, a Ford Transit van that had been refitted so it could transport a dozen policemen. Dalmont had an air of calmness about him that contrasted with all of the activity that was going on outside. The RAID team had arrived with large amounts of emergency and logistical supplies, so even though most of the vehicles were unmarked, they wouldn't go unnoticed for very long.

"Monsieur Dalmont," Pauline asked, "do you know the tenants of your third floor apartment?"

"Oh I see what's going on here now!" he responded quickly, a little surprised. "Why do you ask?"

"We think that one or more of your tenants may be linked to yesterday's bombing in Paris and we're looking for anything that may help us in our investigation."

"The terrorist attack? Yeah. I heard about it on the radio. My TV has been out for a week. Do you know how long it took them to arrive with help? Unbelievable! I even took an extension on the guarantee. The guy on the phone..."

"Monsieur Dalmont!" Pauline interrupted, "I need you to tell me about Yasmina Oufik. Can you do that for me?"

"Yasmina? No problem. Yeah, she's adorable. She lived here for three years. We got along pretty well, actually."

"She left?"

"Yes, she left the apartment to her brother Driss about three months ago."

"Where'd she go?"

"Someplace south, I think, around Montpellier. She found some new job. She's doing telemarketing. Making calls and that kind of stuff. You know the ones who call you as soon as you're sat down and they just want to sell you some windows or kitchens or whatever? I'm sure she's good at it though, she's nice enough."

"I'm sure she is", replied Pauline smiling. The old man turned out to be a very friendly one, too. "Continue, please!"

"Well, really, she was pretty tired of it all, you know? Tired of Paris, the suburbs, her past in the city that she couldn't shake off. She wanted to start a new life I guess."

"So, who lives there now?" Pauline inquired.

"When Yasmina moved out, she asked me if it was ok for her brother Driss to take the place. You know at my age looking for tenants is real tough and seeing as the second floor was empty, I said it was fine because it made my life easier."

"So have you gotten to know Driss at all?"

"Yeah, but he's a pretty shy kid. Nothing at all like Yasmina. He lives there with other young folks, but they're pretty quiet too. I never really see them. Hello, goodbye... same thing, always. Yasmina told me that he'd made some mistakes and he needed someplace to stay while he looked for a job. He pays me cash and that suits me just fine."

Dalmont seemed to think for a moment and added:

"Once, I had trouble with one of the other young guys, Malik. He kept putting his garbage on the floor and it kinda annoyed me. So I told him and he got real angry. Driss stepped in to calm him down, but the guy was mad. That was the only time."

"I understand" said Pauline, reassuringly. "Do you happen to know if Yasmina had a car?"

"Yeah, she left that to Driss, too. She said that taking it with her would cost more to take it all the way down south. I mean, if it ever would have gotten her there! It's an old car. Red one, I think."

"You were speaking about a... Malik?"

"Yeah, he's one of three people living there. I don't know anything about him. Not much of a talker."

"Thank you for your help. Oh, just one last thing, then we'll leave you in peace. Did you ever notice anything... weird about these young people?"

"Not really. They're pretty quiet."

"I'll come and see you again soon, Monsieur Dalmont. I'll have some more questions to ask you and I'll need to take a look at the apartment. Is that ok with you?"

"It'd be my pleasure. I don't often get pretty young women coming around here, you know" said the old man, his eyes shining with mischief.

Pauline smiled as she left the vehicle, before she was once again confronted with the reality of what was happening outside.

*
* *

The first volley of automatic weapons fired from the inside the apartment exploded in the night just as the battering ram hammered into the front door. Brigadier Philippe was directly in the line of fire. The shots were fired from the ground upwards. The bullets struck him in the legs before piercing his bullet-proof vest and exploding his helmet. He collapsed.

The two policemen behind him immediately opened fire and sprayed bullets trying to guess where the shooter, or shooters, were hiding. The one closest to the entrance threw a grenade. The explosion vaporized the windows. Smoke was everywhere, making it impossible to see anything. "Man down!" the captain shouted into his radio, before silence descended over the hellish scene. The staircase was pitch black.

Moments later, the smoke began to clear from the apartment, disappearing through the broken windows. A reddish light from the smoke that remained hovered throughout the room, meaning that visibility was somewhat distorted. Through the haze, a man lying on his back could be seen with an automatic weapon by his side. Everything inside the apartment was motionless.

The commander's radio was constantly streaming messages. Emergency services back at mission base were taking care of the officer's injuries. An officer bent down to take Philippe's pulse but quickly realized that it was already too late.

A voice broke the silence: "Moussa Zalif, come in! We got two fugitives fleeing from behind the building, we're going to intercept them!"

At the entrance, the policeman carrying the shield scanned the apartment with his torch. After a few minutes he could make out the walls and distinguish the shape of the main room. Just in front of the sofa there was a television on top of a low table that had been destroyed in the blast. A large, unglazed window flapped about in the strong wind that was blowing in gusts. Further to his right, an open passage gave access to what looked like a small kitchen.

"I've got a visual of a closed door to the left," he said into his radio.

"Wait for the order! Keep yourself protected behind the shield. Don't do anything without the order! The situation is messy enough already!"

"Got it!"

"It seems like there's no one in the apartment!"

"Is someone bringing the thermal camera? We need it now, not tomorrow!"

"It's coming," the voice in the radio replied.

Three minutes later, a technician brought a roll of wire ten meters long that was about as thick as a pen, at the end of which was a device that looked something like an iPad.

"Go ahead, get the camera under that door!" the policeman ordered, gun ready to fire.

The technician unrolled the cable, which quickly reached the closed door. The thin camera slid underneath so they could see the inside of the room. The thermal image immediately confirmed that there was nobody there. Switching to night vision allowed them to assess the scene.

A double bed, a closet with curtains, one side of which was closed. On the floor they could see a prayer rug. Dotted around were few bags and some clothes piled onto a chair.

"Nothing here!" declared the policeman into the radio. "It's empty!"

"Let's go," the commander replied.

They entered the apartment, securing their position. There was nothing in the main room or the kitchenette. Carefully opening the door to the bedroom, they confirmed it too was empty. Under the bed, a single mattress.

One of the officers pushed the curtain of the closet to the side and discovered a hidden board at the bottom. He tried to see if it would move. The board slid open easily, surprising the policeman.

"Holy shit. They made an escape tunnel! It's big enough to fit a person through!"

The beam of his flashlight lit up the construction site next to the apartment block. Scaffolding ran along the outer wall which meant the suspects could get away unnoticed.

*
* *

Arnaud and Moussa had positioned themselves at the end of Rue Heurtault, not far from the palisade surrounding the construction site next to Dalmont's apartments. They waited for the brigade to come back down.

"Gonna be another late shift!" said Arnaud, lighting up a cigarette.

"Right. You counting your hours now huh?"

"No! It's just... I'll just be happy when all this is done. What I'd give for a night in my own bed... and if I'm not alone, even better!"

"Dream on, Romeo. You think she'd wait for you? Anyway, you'll get home and crash like the rest of us!"

"No way! I..."

Shots of an automatic weapon rang out from the building. Arnaud and Moussa only hesitated a split second before rushing toward the the gunfire.

"Man down!" the radio in Moussa's hand spat out.

"Shit no!" Arnaud shouted, incredulously.

"Come on, faster! They might need us."

As they sprinted the fifty meters that separated them from the yard, a sound of metal grabbed their attention. It came from scaffolding on the outside wall of the building where the shots were coming from.

The area was badly lit but the two policemen were able to make out movement on the first floor. They took a few steps back and crossed the street so they could get a better view. They were unsure of what they were seeing at first, but soon realized that one or more people were trying to escape.

"What do we do?" Arnaud asked.

"We try to get in and neutralize them!"

Moussa grabbed his radio, pressed the button to talk and in a voice a little louder than he would have liked, shouted: "Moussa Zalif. Come in! We've got two fugitives behind the construction site. We're going to try and stop them."

The two policemen rushed to the entrance of the site. It was closed; a heavy padlock locked the gate shut. "Never mind," thought Arnaud. He jumped and grabbed the top of the gate, climbing it with ease. Moussa followed closely behind. After a little balancing act, the two policemen jumped down to the ground.

Moussa spoke into the radio again: "We're on the site! We're going to continue to pursue the fugitives." He clipped the radio to his belt and grabbed his gun. They pushed the door carefully and entered the construction area. The dim light of the night meant it was barely possible to discern contours or shapes. It was difficult to find one's bearings without knowing the place. They stopped to see if they could hear which direction the fugitives were taking. They didn't know if any of them were armed, so they proceeded with caution. One man down was already too many.

The noise came from the other side of the site, toward the bottom end. On their left was the scaffolding where the fugitives had appeared. In front of them was an enormous hole containing iron bars that had been planted into the ground. Casting shadows like frozen soldiers, they waited to hold the foundations of the new building. To the right was construction machinery. They headed forward slowly, always on the lookout. The fugitives were trying to cross the site to the reach the street at the other end.

"They're heading to the back! Block their way and lock down the neighborhood!" Moussa said into the radio.

"Copy that! I'm sending men now," the commander responded.

Arnaud and Moussa moved past the enormous machines. The silhouettes of the rusty-metal hydraulic monsters resembled silent guards. The ground was flat as they passed the line of construction cabins. One of them was lit by a grid lamp, allowing them to pick up the pace a little.

The end of the site was close.

As they approached, they could see two men climbing the fence. They weren't far, but there was maybe just enough time for the fugitives to jump down to the other side and flee.

"Stop right there or I'll shoot!" Arnaud shouted.

The two police officers, both out of breath, had no choice but to fire or continue the pursuit, otherwise it would almost certainly be too late. The two fugitives kept on moving as fast as they could. The first was at the top of the palisade. Moussa kept moving toward them.

"Stop! Right now!" Arnaud shouted. His orders were ignored again.

He fired. The fugitive out in front jumped and fell to the other side, disappearing from sight. It was impossible for Arnaud to know if he hit him. The shot seemed to give wings to the second man, however, who began to climb faster.

Moussa arrived at the fence just as the man was reaching to grab onto the top of the fence to pull himself over. Moussa took hold of the fugitive's right foot and pulled it back with all of his might. With a kick of his free leg, the fugitive struck Moussa on the side of his face, forcing him to the ground. The officer sat with his nose bleeding and one sneaker in his hand as the man jumped over the fence and disappeared into the night.

"Fuck! Fuck this fucking shit!" screamed Moussa, getting back to his feet.

Arnaud arrived and put away his weapon before helping Lieutenant Zalif to get up.

"You ok? Nothing broken?"

"I'm fine!" replied Moussa, visibly annoyed about what had happened

"We did our best, man! What else could we have done? They knew their way around and planned their escape before the attack."

"I had one of them."

"You're bleeding!"

"It's just a scratch."

"Yeah well you're bleeding pretty bad, you should put something on it to cover it. Hope they didn't break your nose!"

"I don't think so. It doesn't hurt too bad," Moussa replied, touching his sore face.

"Hand me the radio," Arnaud requested.

Moussa took the radio from his belt and gave it to Arnaud, while using a tissue to stem the blood.

"Lieutenant Lescure here. The two fugitives managed to escape from the back of the site. I repeat, the two fugitives managed to get out of the control zone!" Arnaud shouted into the radio, letting out all of his frustration.

"We can hear you, Lieutenant, no need to yell! I sent some men as soon as we heard from you. Hopefully they'll manage to catch them."

"Sorry Commander!"

"We'll keep you informed."

Arnaud and Moussa started to make their way back to the operation's base when they heard some bad news over the radio.

"The two fugitives have managed to escape. There was no sign of them when our men arrived."

"OK" replied the commander. "Continue to search the area. I'll ask the police for backup."

Pauline was at the base with Julie, Kader, Yvan and Clara when Moussa and Arnaud appeared, both looking thoroughly miserable. Moussa was still holding the tissue to his nose.

"We've been listening to what happened over the radio", said Pauline.

"I'm sorry, Commander! We gave it all we had but those assholes had their escape planned."

"You're injured, Lieutenant Zalif?" asked Pauline.

"No, it's nothing, Commander, I got kicked in the nose and it's bleeding, but I'm fine!"

"It's bleeding a lot. Go to see the paramedics so they can take a look at you!"

The ambulance carrying the policeman with the gunshot wound left the crime scene with its siren blaring. As it pulled away, the forensics team was arriving to perform their usual initial searches for fingerprints, weapons, explosives, that type of thing.

Anything that could help the investigation move forward. After all the action, it was time for data collection and analysis to begin.

Pauline had a brief conversation with the RAID commander. He was clearly devastated at the way the intervention had turned out. The death of Brigadier Philippe was more than enough to make sure of that.

It was at around midnight that Pauline ordered her team to go home: "We'll reconvene in the morning. 8am at Levallois, brigade."

*
* *

Pauline was running. She could hear the blood beating in her temples and feel the pain in her stomach. She counted her breaths and steps. A trickle of sweat ran down her back. Her shirt stuck to her skin. The feeling of being in control of her body felt good. "Another thirty minutes and I'll have done my eight miles", she said to herself. "One, two, one, two, one, two." The precise rhythm of her strides in the almost deserted early morning streets was relaxing. She entered the park and began the climb the small hill, at the top of which she'd stop to do some relaxation exercises before jogging home.

She'd slept badly. A recurring dream had woken her up earlier in the morning with a feeling that her stomach had been tied in knots. In the dream, Pauline would always be in a wedding dress. She'd be in the middle of a clearing that was lit by a blinding sun and it would be filled with people whose faces she couldn't quite discern. Her white dress would become heavier as she moved forward. She would hurry toward the crowd, knowing that a celebration was taking place just at the end of the path in front of her. As she'd get closer, the ghostly figures would disappear. She wanted to scream and call out for Laurent, but no sound would come out of her mouth. She'd struggle to continue onward, but her feet would no longer carry her. Right at that moment, the sun would disappear and she would wake up, heart beating, unable to go back to sleep. She'd kept having this dream her ever since the death of her husband, Laurent. It was extremely painful every time, and she had it far too often.

Pauline went home and took a hot shower. She brushed her hair and put on a little make-up. She took out some jeans and a white blouse from her closet, a blue belt and matching sneakers. A quick glance in the mirror and already she was feeling better. "I have to be 100%," she thought. "We've got to find those bastards."

She arrived at the office at 6.30 am.

*
* *

Wednesday May 3rd, 8 am – CTB headquarters

Commander Rougier's team reported to the investigation room on the second floor.

Pauline gave a summary of the current situation:

"Our team has identified the members of the cell responsible for the attack on May 1st. First up we have our kamikaze, Oualid Massourd," she said as she placed his photo on the meeting room table. "We also know that the terrorist killed in yesterday's disastrous search is Karim Kerbouche. A French national of Algerian origin, he was close to Massourd. His profile is available in your file," Pauline added, distributing folders to each member of the team. It contained all of the necessary papers for the meeting.

"Did you manage to sleep, boss?" Clara asked.

"Almost, Clara."

"I'll continue…" said Pauline. "There were five sets of fingerprints in the apartment. We can count Yasmina Oufik out as she's currently in the south of France. I sent a message to our colleagues there so they could question her, but we'll get her in, too, anyway. We found traces of Massourd and Driss Oufik. Both managed to escape. We also found traces of Karim Kerbouche." She placed three photos on the whiteboard, marking their names. "His fingerprints were found in a folder containing ID cards. There's one more individual that we still haven't been able to identify."

"So," Yvan concluded, "the two guys who ran away were Driss Oufik and the unknown individual?"

"Exactly, replied Pauline. Except that the owner of the building, Mr. Dalmont, said that the unidentified person is called Malik, and he's going to give us a facial composite later this morning. As soon as we have it we'll send the photos of our two fugitives to the press, to Interpol and everyone else in between. We need to find them! I've asked so we can set up a toll free number for people to give information. We're going to have a lot of calls to study."

"Do we have the whole team though?" asked Moussa, whose damaged nose was beginning to turn a slightly darker shade of blue. Do we know for sure that there's no one else on the run?"

"If there are any other members in the cell they didn't meet in Yasmina's apartment," answered Pauline. "Although we're not sure of anything at this stage, my feeling is that we've identified the whole team. We'll know more in due time about the links between individuals and what their respective roles were."

"Chief, what do we do now that we have the names?" asked Yvan.

"We continue to dig for information. Look for any links and try to understand how they were able to carry out this attack. Yvan and Moussa, you check out what you can on Massourd. Julie and Arnaud concentrate on Oufik. Kader and Clara, see what you can get on Karim Kerbouche. We'll meet at 4 pm here to compare notes. Find out the schools they went to, their friends, families, where they've lived. We need to find something that will help make sense of this mess!"

Pauline ended the meeting. She had an appointment with her own boss to deliver his daily update. He was also under pressure; the minister's office was on his back. They'd made good progress considering it had only been two days, but they were still yet to capture at least one of the cell members alive. Right now, their priority was to determine who had bankrolled the attack.

The facial composites of Malik and Driss Oufik were distributed to the press, Interpol and the European Anti-Terrorist Division at around noon. It was now a matter of waiting. The images would be shown on all of the main channels' one o'clock news shows and looped continuously from then on. The toll-free number would start taking calls at the same time. The problem was that, more often than not, they'd be from some crazed Tom, Dick or Harry who felt lonely and wanted to waste some police time for a few minutes with their theories on what happened.

Pauline suggested that the entire team go to lunch together at Gino's, the pizzeria on the corner of the block. They'd have some time to relax a little before the calls began to come through. She used the opportunity to tell the team in what order they'd be taking the calls.

She received the complete list of items seized during the search in the early afternoon. There was nothing conclusive. So far they had the automatic weapon that Karim Kerbouche had used to shoot the policeman along with five magazines and a Glock 19 with two boxes of 9mm bullets. There was also a set of keys for Yasmina Oufik's Golf, two disposable phones and a few passports. They would all need to be examined. It seemed that due to the surprise nature of the police raid, the cell members hadn't had the time to pack their IDs. Various items of clothing and a set of keys to the apartment were among the other items retrieved. There was nothing particularly revelatory, and significantly, no document that could help them in their investigation into the planning of the attack.

A team eventually found the Golf in one of the surrounding streets. There was nothing inside the vehicle nor in the trunk. Forensics meticulously scoured the apartment and the car for fingerprints, but they found nothing. Pauline couldn't understand how there were no personal items in the apartment whatsoever; usually there would be at least something. It was unlikely, if not impossible. There must be some cash or other weapons, not to mention the materials used to make the belt of explosives. She was convinced there was a safe somewhere, although at this stage there was nothing to suggest just where this safe might be, if indeed it existed.

* * *

Hundreds of people called the toll-free number to give information about the two fugitives that the police were searching the country for.

"OK, I'm sick of this" Clara declared, raising her hands in the air to stretch out some of the numbness in her body. "That makes four hours and still no call has given us anything."

"Same for me," Kader agreed, "but look, we don't have a choice. If anyone did see something, we'll find out soon enough."

"Yeah but come on," Clara insisted, "I had one guy who thought the terrorist had just come from a secret meeting with the President and that the whole thing is a huge conspiracy. Give me a break!"

"Oh really? Well I had some old lady who thought they were stealing all of the cats from her neighborhood."

"It's pretty annoying to study for five years after high school for...this!"

"At least you can put it on your CV" quipped Kader, a little smile at the corner of his mouth.

"I'm going to get coffee. You want one?" Clara offered.

"Yes, thank you. It's four thirty, we've still got, like, an hour and a half."

The phone rang once again and Kader grabbed the receiver.

"Lieutenant Kader Jaoui!"

"Is it you who's looking for the two guys?" A female voice enquired.

"Yes ma'am! Do you have anything that you can tell us?"

"Well, it depends."

"What does it depend on? If you have something to tell us, please do it now. These two men are extremely dangerous."

"Will they know who told you?" the anxious voice enquired.

"Could you tell me your name ma'am? Where are you calling from? I can see that this is a private number."

"I don't know what to do..."

"Tell me.... fuck! She hung up," said Kader, rolling back his chair and slapping his leg in disappointment.

Clara came back with the two coffees.

"I just got a really weird call. Some woman who said she knew something but was worried about telling us. She hung up before she said anything else."

"It doesn't really help us much, but it could mean the fugitives are still in France."

Commander Rougier entered the office suddenly. "We got something!" she pronounced. Kader and Clara, who were sat at their phones, raised their heads and looked at their commander, waiting to hear what she had learned. Arnaud and Julie, who were studying Driss Oufik's file in the next room, could see through the window that separated the offices.

"I've just got confirmation from Interpol. They've identified our unknown terrorist. His name is Malik Aertens!"

Pauline gave the team the lowdown on Aertens' background. He was of Tunisian origin, domiciled in Belgium and he was a pretty big fish, according to his record. He'd been accused of participating in a jewelry robbery in Brussels, however the Belgian police had been unable to prove his involvement so wasn't able to convict him. The police had reason to believe that the theft was carried out in order to finance the purchase of weapons for an attack within the country. Listed as dangerous, Aertens was known to be in contact with various terrorist groups.

"The product of a well-honed system," Kader replied.

"Wait 'til you hear this! He was arrested for carrying false papers after a routine check. The Italians were then able to link his fingerprints to a crime scene. Another robbery, this time a luxury fur store. He was radicalized in prison."

"Same story every time! They begin as a small-time criminal, then get a one-way ticket to terrorism after a little time in prison. We have to stop creating this problem for ourselves," said Kader, exhausted.

"The Belgian police think he's one of the people funding the Islamic State group, meaning he'd be bankrolling terrorists all across Europe. During their investigation into the massacre at the Jewish Museum in Brussels and the involvement of Mehdi Nemmouche, the Belgian police came across some information that shows that Malik Aertens was in Brussels the day before the attack. A dangerous guy, but one that could help us get back on the trail of terrorist financing. We need to catch him alive, and we need to do it now!"

Arnaud and Julie had since joined the group and were listening to Pauline.

"Are we going to replace the facial composite for a real photo then?" asked Clara.

"I'll speak to the communications team and ask them to get that done," replied Pauline.

"In any case, it doesn't change anything about where we're going with the investigation, replied Arnaud. We'll cross check Aertens' and Oufik's files and see if we find anything."

The hotline phone rang again. A hidden number. Kader raised his arm to get everyone's attention and tell them to quieten down. It was 4.48 pm.

"Lieutenant Kader Jaoui."

"It's me again," said the same female voice that Kader recognized immediately.

"Thank you for calling back," Kader reassured the lady as he tried to make sure he wouldn't lose her for a second time.

Silence.

"Ma'am, are you there?"

"Yes, yes. Listen, the fugitives that you're looking for... they live at my place." She seemed like she was about to lose control of herself.

"Are you sure, ma'am?"

"Yes, no... yes I'm sure. If they find out that that I'm the one who called the police... will they hurt me? They're dangerous. You said it yourself."

Her voice was trembling with fear.

"Stay calm, miss. Everything will be ok. They won't know anything. I just need your address."

"You're sure I'm fine? I'm alone. My husband is at work."

"Please just stay calm ma'am. We'll protect you but first I need your address."

"I live in Paris. Oh my God!"

They could hear voices approaching in the background, speaking what sounded like Arabic. Then they heard screams and the sound of someone being beaten. Then the telephone cut out. End of call.

"Hello? Hello?", Kader shouted. "Fuck! It cut out!"

Everyone in the office held their breath. The call had just raised the voltage by a notch.

"Commander, this woman knows where those two bastards are hiding! They stopped her before she could tell me anything more!"

"You got nothing at all?" asked Pauline.

"Actually, yes. They're in Paris."

"Get someone to trace the call immediately! Sometimes it's possible to locate private numbers."

"I'm on it."

"Calls are recorded, so get them to analyze the whole conversation. Maybe we can find something that'll put us on the right track."

"Got it."

"Kader. Pass the message to the entire team. Daily brief on the second floor, tonight, 6 o'clock."

Kader contacted the Head of Forensics, Pascal Le Cam, to ask if he could help them urgently.

The meeting at 6:30 pm didn't really reveal anything new. The investigation was at a standstill. They hadn't managed to locate the fugitives and Pauline knew that those above her were expecting to see some results soon. They'd identified four members of the May 1st bombing, two of whom were dead, but they still had no one to show to the journalists, and the public wanted someone behind bars. The people needed vengeance; someone of flesh-and-blood needed to pay to help alleviate the fear and frustration they all felt. The team needed to make progress, fast.

They went through the files, looking for dates and places, trying to find a link and make sure they hadn't missed any vital information. They got nothing. Tired eyes and other signs of demotivation began to appear. Pauline, being the good manager that she was, picked up on the feeling and sent everyone home at 8:30 pm. At least one evening with the family, she told herself. They all need it.

Pauline left the office to go home. She also needed a break but didn't want to be alone in her apartment where she still felt Laurent's presence. His absence still hurt her and she felt that the void was slowly taking her memories. How long before she wouldn't be able to remember all the things they did together? Those little things that make each couple unique? Like a tape onto which our memories have been recorded, slowly but surely being worn away and taking precious moments with it. From the beginning, from the very first time they met, until nothing more would remain, nothing but emptiness, after that terrible phone call nearly two years ago.

She put her keys into the small bowl which sat on top of the cabinet at the entrance to her apartment. There was also a Gaudi-style salamander bowl that she'd brought back from a trip to Barcelona a few years earlier. She kissed her index and middle fingers and touched Laurent's picture, attached to the mirror on the wall. It was a daily ritual that allowed her to maintain a semblance of intimacy with her husband.

She ate a quick meal, took a shower and went to bed immediately. She knew that her bad dream would come back again that evening to haunt her. She needed to recover her strength.

*
* *

Thursday May 4th, 7.30 am - CTB, northwestern suburbs of Paris

Pauline was dressed in martial arts gear and stood on the tatami mat in the Brigade's gym. She trained at least twice a week. She needed to stay in shape.

The coach had assigned Lieutenant Kowalski to be her partner. Pauline and Kowalski hated each other. Kowalski was the kind of cop who'd watched too many action movies and confused investigation with rodeo. They'd already had problems between them, especially during a complicated case six months earlier. Pauline and her team had done all of the work digging up information from files, before Kowalski decided to play special agent, compromising the entire investigation by performing a spectacular but extremely risky arrest that was totally against Pauline's idea of the spirit of cooperation. A guy who considered that being in a team served only as a way to get himself ahead.

"Hey Rougier, ready to get fucked up?"

"Don't be a dick Kowalski. Did you bring your balls with you this time? Seems like there's still nothing there."

"Still pissed then that I closed the investigation without getting your permission first?"

"Who knows? Why don't you ask your team what they think? They're still trying to find out where their boss is, or if they even have one."

"Rougier, just because you're a woman doesn't mean I won't put you on the ground."

"Give it your best shot Kowalski, I dare you! I'll fuck you up. I always carry a set of balls in my handbag for assholes like you!"

"We'll see Rougier, we'll see…"

Standing at 6ft with 180lbs of almost pure muscle, Kowalski towered over Pauline, who at just over 5ft had to stay on her guard. Lieutenant Kowalski had a reputation for being very physical during training sessions. After their small exchange of pleasantries, Kowalski was now quite upset.

They donned themselves with the necessary protection, gave a nod of acknowledgment and readied themselves for battle. Kowalski immediately attacked Pauline with a left hook. He'd raised his shoulder before unleashing which gave Pauline a clue about his intentions. Pauline noticed the tiny movement and ducked to dodge his flying fist. With her 125lbs, she was fast and had often surprised her opponents with her agility in combat. She remained on her guard. With the weight difference, if she took a hit or Kowalski caught her, she knew she'd be out.

Pauline punched Kowalski, who was a little too close to her after being carried forward by his failed left hook. She hit him precisely between the sternum and throat, the only place that was not protected by the thorax. Kowalski sensed the attack coming and took a step back to absorb it. He knew that she had deliberately tried to hurt him.

Pauline was sweating. The tension of the last few days and the fury after losing Laurent was coming to the surface. She wanted to explode, to leave this poor bastard on the ground. She needed to release the anger that had been building up inside of her.

Kowalski launched a sweeping kick to the face. Pauline jumped to avoid being hit and backed away, landing with both of her feet parallel, one meter from Kowalski. She moved toward him to get back into the fight. Pauline had seen the attack coming. She raised her right foot and launched a Mae Geri, a frontal kick, moving backward at the same time in order to transfer all the power from her leg into the move. Kowalski got hit. Pauline used the opportunity to follow up with a Ushiro Geri, a reverse kick that smacked Kowalski square in the face. He took two steps back, staggering as he tried to regain his senses. She'd shaken him.

He looked at Pauline, surprised, then his features began to betray the fury that was bubbling inside of him.

The two opponents nodded to each other again. Pauline was ready to take the inevitable assault. Kowalski's eyes said everything. He was going to give give everything back, with change. "Bring it on," thought Pauline.

He unleashed two punches that Pauline managed to parry. Her arms were hurting; he'd hit her hard. She'd have bruises tomorrow.

The policeman continued his attack with a knee kick that Pauline almost managed to avoid by raising her leg. She took a nasty shot in the shin. She retaliated with a double Tsuki, one of which landed. Kowalski and Pauline were both short of breath. Kowalski took the initiative again and landed a punch to the face. Pauline didn't the see the attack coming until it was too late, taking it on the back of her head just above her ear. She saw black and fell to her knees, both hands on the ground. That one had hurt, badly. She opened her eyes. Her loss of consciousness had lasted only a fraction of a second. Blood was pounding through her temples; her head was filled with a violence she could barely control.

The other fights in the dojo had finished. The police officers who had come to train were all watching Pauline and Kowalski. She could feel more than she could see Kowalski, who was now leaning over her. He wanted to see close up what he had done to her. Pauline got to her feet as quickly as she could, tucking her head into her shoulders as she rose. Her skull violently struck Kowalski in his ribcage. He was raised upward by the impact, moving in an almost-beautiful arc shape. For a second, he seemed like he was levitating, then he collapsed to the floor. Even with protection, he'd taken a serious blow. Breathless, he was holding his chest trying to breathe, but was having difficulty.

Pauline got up, bowed, and left the room. She was soaked. Her keikogi was stuck to her skin, her heart beating at 170 bpm. The automatic doors opened. As Pauline entered the airlock, she heard Kowalski's voice behind her:

"You're fucking crazy, Rougier!"

"Fuck you, Kowalski!"

The last image that the officers in the dojo saw was of Pauline, arm in the air, giving Kowalski the finger. Applause rang out behind her. She couldn't help but smile.

Chaos Theory

By 8.30 am, the whole team was already hard at work. Pascal Le Cam from forensics had called and according to him they shouldn't expect much. The recorded phone conversation from the day before hadn't given them anything of real interest in terms of the investigation but corroborated totally with Kader's feeling. The lady who had called was in a state of heightened stress, and, according to the psychologist, was on the verge of having a panic attack. Her anxiety was palpable.

He confirmed to them that the call could not be traced. If it had been made from a smartphone it would have been possible, but in this case it was from an old mobile with no GPS capacities. So they could hope for nothing on that side, either.

Things were flat lining.

The news channels had been continually broadcasting images of the terrorists since six o'clock in the morning. One channel had found an old video of Malik Aertens entering a court in Milan and had it playing it repeat, along with with the hotline phone number scrolling along the bottom of the screen.

Pauline's team took turns answering calls, but as always they were becoming more and more infrequent over time. They all hoped that the mysterious woman would contact them again, but the call at 4.48 pm the previous day remained the last that they heard from her.

Arnaud received a message in the middle of the morning. He wasn't able to reply immediately because he was with Rougier and Julie studying the dossier of Driss Oufik in more detail. His phone was on silent mode as it always was when he was with the boss.

He only noticed the three missed calls and voice message at around midday, just before going to lunch.

"Hel…Hello lieu…te…nant Lescure, it's Nathan from…from the Opera…tional Center of Video surveillance… Can you ca…ca…call me b-back please? We saw each other…w-when you ca-came t…t…to look for Dr… Driss …Oufik and Ou-Oualid Ma…Massourd. Do y-you rememb-ber ?"

"Nathan!" Arnaud knew who it was. Of course, he remembered the young autistic engineer, who was now having trouble getting his words out as he called from the Paris CCTV operations center.

"What does he want to tell me?" He wondered. "Maybe he's got some new information concerning the investigation. It's probably not essential, since we've already identified our guys. Should I call him before or after lunch…? I'm sure it will be fine to wait until after."

Arnaud contacted Nathan when he eventually returned from lunch at 2 pm.

"Paris CCTV operations center," the woman's voice said in a way that let you know that you were bothering her.

"Hello, it's Arnaud Lescure here, from the Counter Terrorist Brigade."

"Hello Lieutenant," the now-attentive voice responded.

"I'd like to talk to Nathan, please"

"Nathan who, Lieutenant? There's more than 150 people here!"

"Nathan I-don't-know-what, the one who works for Jacques Radier."

"Nathan I-don't-know-what? Do you really work for the police?"

"Look, I got a whole lot of things to do, so pass me to Jacques Radier, right now!"

"Whoa! Calm yourself there! I'm connecting you now. Have a nice day, Lieutenant."

Arnaud heard a few beeps down the line before finally hearing Radier's voice.

"Lieutenant?"

"Hello Jacques, how's it going?"

"Good good, to what do I owe the honor?"

"I'm trying to get hold of Nathan, but I've just realized I only know his first name."

"He's called Nathan Fray. I'll connect you to him now!"

"Got it, thank you."

There were a few seconds of elevator-like music before Nathan's voice could be heard again.

"Nathan Fray. Who's th-this?"

"Nathan, hello, it's lieutenant Arnaud Lescure from the CTB here. You called me but I was busy. I'm so sorry. What can I do for you?"

"Well Lieu...tenant, it's me, I think, who's going to b-be able...to d-do some-thing...for you!"

"You have some information?"

"M... more than th-that. I f-found the two guys that you're looking f-for!"

Arnaud began to become short of breath.

"You mean that you know where they are?!"

"Yes!"

"Are you sure, Nathan?"

"Yes!"

"I'm coming! I'll be there in... 20 minutes max."

"I'll be he-here!"

Arnaud rushed to find Pauline and tell her the news. She ordered him to immediately go and find out what the young engineer uncovered.

The ride took only seventeen minutes thanks to the sirens. Arnaud was certain that what Nathan had found was going to be crucial. He wasn't exactly sure how, but he somehow thought that the answer to the entire investigation was going to be found in Nathan Fray's office.

The elevator opened and Arnaud walked out onto the floor, a large open space that gathered together all of the agents who controlled the cameras. Radier saw Arnaud and came over to greet him. They went to see Nathan who was eagerly scrolling through images, handling his keyboard and joystick with incredible dexterity.

"Hi Nathan!" said Arnaud, offering his hand.

"Lieutenant! Glad to see you," Nathan replied with a big smile, dressed in a bright yellow jumper and creased pants. He ignored the outstretched hand.

"I'm sorry I didn't call you back sooner. My boss hates when meetings are interrupted by phones ringing. She thinks it's disrespectful to others."

"No problem."

Nathan wasn't stuttering anymore, only pausing on certain words. "Maybe the phone makes the stutter seem worse," Arnaud thought. "That explains why I didn't notice it the first time we met. I already knew he didn't like physical contact, so trying to shake his hand that wasn't very smart of me."

"Nathan, you've got something to tell me, or show me?"

"Yes Lieutenant. Actually, I wrote some facial recognition software based on some samples. It followed a curve model…"

"Ok, I believe you!"

"So yeah, I applied linear regression mathematics, compiled existing pieces of code that I found on the Internet and then improved them with a few tweaks of my own. I've been working on it for over a year. It can recognize people in the dark or when it only has a view from the side.

"Incredible! So you've installed the new program on here?"

"Yeah, well, I've just done a few tests. When you published the images of your two guys, I ran them through, but no luck. Then at

6 am this morning, I saw the video that's on the news channels where we see Malik Aertens in court, and I tried again. I got a few screen grabs and started my search, first in Aubervilliers..."

"And...?" asked Arnaud.

"Well, I found this. Look!"

Nathan typed a few commands and opened up a short video. There was a man that could clearly be identified as Malik Aertens coming out of a side street in Paris.

"Well, shit me!" Arnaud exclaimed.

"Not bad, huh?" said Nathan.

"What do you mean, not bad? It's unbelievable Nathan. Unbelievable! Do you have the address of this place?"

"Of course," replied Nathan, handing Arnaud a Post-it note.

"Do you have any more video?"

"I got quite a few actually, now that I know where he's hiding." He showed them some more footage. Aertens was with another man, who was without any doubt Driss Oufik.

"Keep them under surveillance while I send my guys. Any kind of movement and you tell me, ok?"

"Of course lieutenant. You can count on me."

Arnaud turned to Jacques Radier.

"You got a hell of a guy there with Nathan," Arnaud said.

"I know! He's ours, hands off!"

"Absolutely. I'm going to head back to the Brigade," said Arnaud turning on his heels heading for the elevators.

"It was a pleasure, Lieutenant," said Radier as Arnaud disappeared.

Arnaud opened the door of the surveillance building and hurried to his vehicle. He dialed the fixed-line number of Commander Rougier's office. "Damn! Answering machine. It's ok, I'll leave a message," he reasoned.

"Commander! It's Arnaud. We've got the address of Oufik and Aertens. Nathan is the man. They're at the corner of Rue Duperré and Place Pigalle."

Arnaud hung up and immediately called Pauline's cell phone.

*
* *

The phone rang in the office where the man was working in absolute silence. He was looking through his notes and imagining what the world might look like after the BLACKSTONE project had taken place. A fundamental shift in the balance of power on the planet?

He didn't have time to continue with his daydream, but it was only a matter of time, he thought to himself.

"I'm listening," said the voice.

"I just spoke to the cop. He told us they've found our two guys."

"They have the address?"

"Yes sir!"

"Excellent! Do what needs to be done. We can't have them being caught alive. And bring me the documents."

"What do I do about him?"

"How much did we say?"

"Ten grand!"

"Then give him the ten thousand! He's earned it," he said, as he hung up the phone.

He couldn't hide his smile. He'd always been fascinated by the greed of others. How easily they could be persuaded to betray the people or things close to them. Some causes could justify this type of act, but to do it just for money? It seemed so... short term. Lacking in vision. If only they knew how small acts of treachery could serve something that was bigger than themselves, they'd be more than a little surprised.

4. THE ARREST

Pauline's team was in place. She'd insisted on being there this time, on the frontline. After a strong exchange of words with her boss, he finally agreed to it being a traditional arrest. There'd be no RAID team, no big guys wearing assault gear. They'd hide, observe the habits of the fugitives and plan what action they'd take as and when necessary. It must be well-executed to minimize risk. Now that they've been identified and were under constant surveillance, Pauline knew that she had the advantage.

Her plan was simple but effective. At least she hoped it would be. The two terrorists were in a building that formed the corner between Rue Duperré and Place Pigalle in the 18th arrondissement of Paris. There were two entrance points. One was for the bar that occupied the first floor of the building, and the other gave access to the apartments above. One way in, one way out. They didn't know which floor the two men were hiding on, whether they had accomplices, or if the inhabitants of the apartment had now in fact become hostages.

It was impossible to form a perimeter around the busy neighborhood without getting themselves noticed. They decided to monitor Rue Duperré instead by positioning a car with two police officers at either end of the street. Pauline placed Yvan and Moussa in a vehicle at the corner of Rue Fromentin, while Julie and Arnaud pretended to hang out near the fountain. Kader and Clara, stationed at the corner of Rue Duperré and Place Pigalle, were ready to intervene at any moment.

At 4 pm Pauline entered the organic food store opposite the building that was under surveillance. She flashed her police badge and asked to speak to the manager. She explained that she had some suspects within her grasp in the building opposite. The owner was a man in his fifties and fortunately he was prepared to do anything he could to help the police. He told her that his store also had a floor above them and that the windows faced directly onto the building in question. It would be better for her than being in the shop itself, where customers coming in and out might make keeping watch a little difficult.

After climbing a small wooden staircase, Pauline reached the second floor. The organic store used it as a storehouse, so Pauline had to squeeze between large boxes and bags filled with other, smaller boxes in order to enter the room. It was in a poor state but was going to be redone to rent out to tenants according to the owner. The curtains that covered the tall old windows were dirty and damaged, but was an excellent location from which to observe.

They'd been waiting for around three hours. By 7 pm, they still had nothing. Nathan hadn't called, so he too had nothing new to offer them. The last few images taken from the camera hidden in the corner of the pharmacy in the square showed the two men entering the building without ever coming out. They must still be inside. The team just needed to be patient.

"Station one, do you receive me Stations two, three and four?" Pauline asked into her radio.

"Station two receiving, nothing here," Yvan responded.

"Station three receiving, we got nothing either. It's really quiet," Julie added.

"Station four. Same. We'd love a bit of action. This boredom is killing me!" Kader complained.

"Don't worry. Something's gonna happen before tonight, I'm sure about that, Pauline replied.

She was trying to see what was happening in the apartments opposite her hideout. It was a sunny day in May and the heat was baking the streets of Paris. The inhabitants opened their windows to let in the sweet perfumes of springtime, while Pauline was just hoping that this view would enable her to discover which floor the fugitives were hiding on.

After a few more minutes of diligent observation, Pauline began to lose patience.

She decided to leave the hideout and go check out the building. By taking a look at the mailboxes, perhaps she could identify the tenants and get some kind of lead to the terrorists. She let her teammates know what she was planning to do.

Pauline went down the stairs and left the shop. In front of her, on the opposite sidewalk, the entrance to the building was open.

Pauline made her way across and entered a low-ceilinged corridor that hadn't seen a lick of paint in years. It had been brown at some point. The floor was covered with broken cement tiles and the walls were lined with lead piping dating back to just after World War 2.

The diffused lighting, filtered by the dust encrusted in the sconces, gave only a rough idea of the place's layout. When her eyes got used to the dim environment, she was able to make out a series of metal mailboxes. Most of them were open, partially broken, full of flyers and had not been used in a long, long time. That's one reason the postal service is so bad, Pauline thought. She had her work cut out for her, finding a name among this mess.

She continued to explore, silently crossing a poorly lit passage. Just front of her there was a glass door that gave access to a small paved courtyard that was enclosed by a wall of cement. At the bottom of the wall were a few forgotten flower-boxes that now contained only a few dried weeds. In one corner there was a pile of dog mess and some old newspapers. To her right was an old staircase.

She began to turn around and make her way back out. She passed the metal opening and the row of antique mailboxes. At that moment her radio started to spit out inaudible messages.

Shots rang out just as Pauline came out of the building. They were the type of shots that would most likely come from an automatic weapon. She could hear loud, desperate shouting before another round of shots, followed by silence. It was impossible to say for sure where they'd come from. Pauline decided to turn around and go up the stairs.

"Commander, do you receive me?" someone asked. "We heard gunshots."

"Rougier here. Yes, I receive you. I'm heading upstairs. I confirm: shots fired."

Pauline ran to cross the hallway.

"Wait for backup, Commander!"

"I'm going to position myself at the bottom of the stairs!"

Pauline went through the door on the landing and hid under the stairwell to wait for her men, whom she was expecting imminently. As she waited, she heard some noises coming from what she guessed was the third floor, but she couldn't be certain. That's when she heard the footsteps of someone hurrying down the stairs.

When the footsteps got close enough, Pauline took out her handgun and shouted.

"Stop, police!"

The broken lighting meant that she wasn't able to see to whom she was giving the order, but it seemed that he was a short man of stocky build. Surprised by the unexpected voice, the assailant stopped sharply. Pauline had just enough time to throw herself into her hiding place under the stairs before shots were fired. She heard the bullets whistle past her head before hitting the walls.

The attacker turned back and started to make his way up the stairs. Pauline weighed up her options before deciding to wait for backup. He couldn't go far: the stairs were the only access point to the other floors.

Kader and Clara arrived on foot having run toward Pauline only a few seconds after the first shots were fired.

"Are you OK, Commander?" asked Clara.

"Yeah he missed me. But he wasn't afraid to start shooting," Pauline replied while taking hold of her radio.

"Station one here. Station four is with me. Station three, come into the building and wait inside the entrance by the stairs to block any chance of escape. Station two, when you arrive, stay outside and make sure they can't exit the building! Stop anyone who tries to get out. Same goes for anyone trying to leave the bar. No one gets out. Understood?"

"Understood for both teams, Commander".

"Is it one of the fugitives?" Asked Clara.

"I have no idea," Pauline replied. Who knows who we're dealing with, but what we do know is he's dangerous. Shoot first, ask questions later, OK?"

"Got it Commander!" Kader nodded his head to confirm.

"OK, said Pauline. We'll go up securing our position along the way. I'll take the lead."

The noise had died down. The man had backtracked and was now hiding somewhere. "Either he's in the apartment where the shots were fired from or he's hiding somewhere on the stairs, waiting for us," thought Pauline.

"The inhabitants must be terrified," Pauline worried as she mounted the first step, pistol in hand and all her senses fully alert. She placed her foot on the first floor landing. There were two doors, one opposite and one to the left. The one opposite opened easily. Pauline lifted her weapon instinctively and found a small aged lady hiding.

"Go home ma'am," whispered Pauline. "You can't stay here, it's too dangerous."

"He's upstairs on the third floor! I just saw him go up," the old lady replied, surprisingly calm.

"Which entrance?" asked Pauline.

"The door opposite, replied the septuagenarian.

"Thank you. Go home, lock your doors and find somewhere safe to hide, ma'am."

The little old lady disappeared as Pauline pondered how difficult it was going to be to get into the third floor apartment. She leaned back as far as she could against the railing as she tried to see the front door. She could only see walls.

They continued their perilous climb as quietly as possible. After three more steps, Pauline could see the two doors of the apartments on the upper floor through the railing. The one that was in front of them was open. She pointed her gun toward the door, expecting to see the attacker try to escape at any moment.

"Kader," Pauline said quietly, "go up and I'll cover you. When you reach the middle of the stairs, stop and secure your position. Clara, when Kader is in place, you replace me and I'll make my way up to the third floor."

Kader went halfway up the stairs. When he was in position, he crouched with his back to the wall, gun in hand. Pauline went up a few steps, leaving her place to Clara, who had her gun pointed at the door. Pauline headed slowly to the door, eventually finding herself facing head-on.

Just as Pauline reached the top of the stairs, a man came out of the apartment. He had his arms raised in the air and his t-shirt was smeared with blood. Pauline knew immediately that it was Driss Oufik, and that he was in a lot of trouble.

"Stop!" Pauline ordered. "Face down! On the ground! Now!"

The man followed the order, although with some difficulty. He was in a state of shock.

"Kader, come and cuff him! I'm going into the apartment."

Chaos Theory

With Oufik cuffed, Pauline pushed the door open. The gunfire started once more downstairs. A wave of automatic gunshots, followed quickly by two more individual shots. Amid all of the noise, Pauline recognized they were the sounds of police weapons.

"Station three here" said Julie over the radio, we've just seen a man jump into the square behind the building. As soon as he saw Arnaud he started firing! He's been hit. He's bleeding a lot!"

"We're sending backup," Pauline responded.

She turned to her two colleagues:

"Clara, go quickly. Me and Kader will take care of things here."

Clara left immediately. She hurtled down the stairs toward the ground floor as quickly as she possibly could.

As soon as she pushed the door, Pauline could feel that something hellish had taken place in the apartment.

There was a dead body in the entrance. He'd taken a hail of gunfire that had completely shredded his abdomen and chest. There was blood all over the walls. The man lay in a sticky bright red pool, indicating that it was still warm. In the main room, an unidentified person was lying on the floor in an awkward position. The power of the bullets had thrown him onto the coffee table which had given way under his weight. The television had been knocked over and was now resting on top of his head. There were bullet holes all over his body and the walls. The man was holding a pistol in his hand. Pauline knew without needing to check that he was dead. To his right there was a closet. It was empty. She went on in silence. An open door led to a small room with a double bed upon which a woman was lying lifeless, coldly executed judging by the single bullet that had exploded the right half of her skull. She was handcuffed to the radiator. Again, blood covered the bed and walls.

There was no trace of the killer.

—87—

In the hallway leading to the kitchen was a small open window. Pauline cautiously moved forward. She leaned over and discovered that the window looked directly over the courtyard. The shooter must have escaped this way. There was enough piping and pieces of lead in the wall for someone in good shape to climb down.

It was nearing the end of the afternoon so the courtyard was in shade, encircled by buildings on each side, the dim light concealing the ground and the opposite wall from being completely visible. She could hardly see the flower boxes she'd noticed there earlier.

A movement in the far-left corner caught her attention. A slight reflection in the dark, enclosed garden. Something was moving and climbing one of the walls.

She fired but missed. The shade enabled the target to move quickly; he was now at the top of the wall. Pauline wanted to fire a second time but the open angle made the shot dangerous. Pauline didn't know what was on the other side. She couldn't risk worsening the crisis any further. The man managed to jump over and make his escape.

"Shit!" Pauline shouted.

"Boss," a voice in the radio shouted.

"Yes Clara?"

"We're with Arnaud. It doesn't seem too serious. He was lucky!"

"Ask him if he thinks it's a good day to play the lottery!"

"You know what I mean, boss. He's bleeding but conscious. He got hit just above his vest. In the shoulder. It's not pretty, but he'll live."

"The emergency services are on their way!" Hearing Moussa's voice was a relief for everyone.

"There's nothing for them here," said Pauline. The apartment had been secured. "I have three dead bodies."

"I'm coming down with the suspect," said Kader. "Yvan, can you help me when I get down?"

"I'll wait for you downstairs, Kader."

"The operation is over," declared Commander Rougier.

*
* *

First interview with Driss Oufik

Kader and Julie ushered the suspect into the interrogation room at the CTB headquarters outside of Paris. After a quick check it was confirmed that it was indeed Driss Oufik that they were dealing with.

"Stay there!" said Julie, attaching one of Driss' hands to the table with the handcuffs.

The three-by-five-meter room was lit by a harsh light and smelled strongly of sweat. There was a one-way mirror on the wall opposite the defendant. Hundreds of suspects had been grilled here since the last coat of paint had been applied; traces of dirt stained the floor. Rings of coffee mug stains marked the table; the furniture and chairs were made of plastic to prevent them from being used as improvised weapons. Driss had been held there for two hours. It was always better to let the suspects simmer for a while before cooking them completely. Without being given any news, they tended to imagine the worst. It was a good way to condition them.

"I'm going in," said Pauline. "I'm sure he'll hate being interviewed by a woman."

"Make him talk commander. We need to know who was behind the May 1st attack."

Pauline was watching the suspect through the one-way mirror. He seemed ready to fight, sitting up straight like an arrow in his chair. After his arrest he had remained totally disconnected from the world around him. He'd not put up any fight during his transfer to the CTB and the police were beginning to wonder the reasons for what would be considered unusual behavior for someone in his position. After an hour in the interrogation room, he seemed to 'reconnect', as if he'd woken up. Little by little, he came back into the real world. He demanded a cup of coffee and became aggressive with the officers watching him, squirming violently in his chair. Pauline had been reading his file in her office. It was all too predictable. Twenty-two years old, born in one of the poorer suburbs of Paris. He was a failure at school and had had a few misdemeanors here and there. His criminal record was relatively clean before he became radicalized and left for Syria. He'd met up with troops in Aleppo. An international search warrant was filed by the United States against him for the murder of American soldiers in 2014. He'd then somehow managed to clandestinely make his way back into the country.

"Driss Oufik?" asked Pauline as she pushed open the interrogation room door. She received no response.

"Commander Rougier of the Counter Terrorist Brigade."

No reaction.

"Driss Oufik, as of this moment, at 9 pm, May 7th, you're in police custody."

Pauline was well experienced when it came to tough interrogations. She sat quietly and let the heavy silence weigh on the room around them. Nobody liked being confronted with emptiness, especially when they were the ones under pressure. One can often often get a reaction just by waiting and saying nothing. But on this occasion, it didn't seem to be working. The suspect gave nothing away.

"Here's how I see it," Pauline said after two minutes. "Here's a loser who couldn't make it on home soil, so he went to Syria to become a hero. But he came back to his shitty ghetto after doing the square root of fuck all."

Still no reaction, just an empty look into space.

"Fuck me, I bet they loved you over there. Hundred bucks says you can't even speak Arabic!"

Driss seemed lost in his thoughts, as if he were somewhere else entirely.

"Yep. You're too scared to even talk to me, am I right?" asked Pauline.

The prisoner sat back up in his chair before leaning forward as if he were ready to fight. His threatening gaze turned toward Pauline as he began to yank convulsively on his handcuffs that attached him to the table.

"Fuck you all. I chose to become part of the jihad and I'm a warrior! I've killed infidels and I'm proud of it!"

"Yep, a real-life superhero. Sure. A superhero that didn't die in battle and who came back home to hide."

"We're not hiding! We came back to take revenge for our brothers who died in Raqqa, Mosul and Aleppo! For every Muslim who has died we will kill ten French rats!"

"And cops too? You killed cops, motherfucker?!"

"No! But I would fuck you like the bitch that you are if I had the chance."

"You're not a warrior, Driss. You're just another poor bastard who had a shit life in his shitty ghetto and not much else. No job, a joke of a sex life, so you thought you'd go there and make something of your life, am I right?"

"Shut up, filthy bitch! You know nothing."

"Actually I do. I really do! They gave you a weapon over there and you could choose the women you wanted. I bet you went to Madâfa, the supermarket where you get women instead of groceries. The one in Raqqa. Maybe you even got yourself a Yézidis sex slave, the ones who are only good to fuck! Jesus Driss, is that the the pure life you were looking for? That's your new world?"

"We fought for an ideal!" Driss was now shouting, expressing the rage that he had inside of him. We killed the infidels and the caliphate will create a more fair and dignified world, far from the decadence of your fucking West."

"Understood, Driss. So it was a real battle! So you massacred, pillaged, raped, and then what? That's the big project for Islam? Where's the respect? Respecting others, but let's not forget self respect, too!"

Pauline noticed he was beginning to display some nervous tics. Driss was blinking his eyes uncontrollably. His fingers were tapping on the table while his feet seemingly weren't able to find a permanent position either. "He's feeling the pressure," thought Pauline.

"Go to hell!"

"Driss, you have no idea of the kind of shit you're in! Here's what's going to happen: for some reason we're kind of nice to you 'revenants' when you come back from your little vacations. Don't ask me why. If it was up to me, I'd send you straight back to Syria. You wanted to leave, so we let you leave. Everyone's happy! But you're fucked Driss, because you can't blame the folly of youth and beg for forgiveness. You came back here onto French soil and decided to carry out a terrorist attack."

"I've got nothing to say to you. I prefer dead cops."

"Right. So you want to kill a cop, you fucking asshole?"

Pauline took out her weapon.

"How about I shoot you right now? You want to show how brave you are? Now's your big moment you goddamned martyr fuckhead! Don't be scared. Tell me to do it and I'll do it! It's right now motherfucker! Do it!"

Kader and Julie were watching the clash through the one-way mirror.

"Commander, I think maybe you should get some air," said Kader, touching the visibly-shaken Pauline on the shoulder then taking her by the arm, encouraging her out of the room.

"You ok, Commander?" asked Julie.

"Yeah, yeah, I'm fine thanks. You're right, some air would do me good."

The suspect had gone back into his inner-world. Staring into the abyss. Driss once again sat straight-backed, shoulders rigid, looking at nothing. Would he ever reveal his true self? How far had this man gone in his journey toward an ideal that the only way to express it was through violence and terror? He dressed his violence with a veil of politics and religion, but in the end, weren't they simply just looking at a killer? Kader pondered all of these questions. Driss remained somewhere far, far away.

Pauline left the interrogation room with her colleagues. Drops of sweat were forming on her brow. Her heart was beating like a bass drum. She had been a hair's breath away from shooting the suspect. She needed to get a hold of herself.

Murdered police officers was something that Pauline could simply not even hear of. The loss of Laurent, who had died while serving, was still too recent; the wounds were too deep. She was beginning to behave irrationally and she knew it. She couldn't help it, but she knew she couldn't go on like that.

"Feeling better, Commander?" asked Julie.

"I'm fine but I feel like he kind of made me lose control there. I just need to breathe a little, that's all. What do you think about him?" Pauline asked her two lieutenants.

"I'm confused," said Julie. "It's like he's not even there and suddenly he gets really aggressive, even dangerous. We've got ninety-six hours to make him talk and we'll need to use every minute of it. You think he's on anything? Coke? Might explain his 'on off' behavior."

"Seems to me like he's not the guy battling for peace as he would have us think," Pauline added. "He seems weak, even. I'm going to call Doctor Leroy to get a psych's opinion on him. He's either playing with us or there's something wrong with him."

"Shall we keep grilling him?" Kader asked.

"It's OK, we'll stop for tonight," said Pauline. It's too late now to make any real progress. We'll get back on it tomorrow morning. I'm exhausted. Meet back here at 8 am."

Pauline went home. She couldn't even eat. She went to bed and fell into what would be an uncomfortable sleep.

* *
*

Friday May 5th – CTB headquarters

The radio alarm clock showed 6:20 as Pauline opened her eyes. She could feel the blood pumping in the sides of her skull as she lifted her head. A dull, throbbing pain radiated from her brain and she had the sensation that a needle was being slowing plunged into her right eyeball. The waves of suffering were coming and going at the exact same rate as her thoughts. She couldn't work in this state. She decided to take a powerful painkiller and go back to sleep for a few minutes.

6:50. She'd managed to sleep a little more and felt a little better. Just a little, but better nonetheless. Sitting at the end of her bed she tried to summon the strength to get to her feet.

As her first foot touched the floor a wave of nausea washed over her. She ran to the toilet and vomited immediately. She flushed, took another pill with a glass of water and forced herself to eat a light breakfast.

The hot shower did her some good. She let the water wash over the top of her head. The heat dilated her blood vessels and the increased flow helped reduce the pain.

At 7.30 am she left for CTB HQ. She fished around in the key bowl, grabbed her keys and kissed Laurent's photo, just as she did every day.

Pauline had organized a meeting at 8am with Doctor Leroy at the CTB. As she scanned her emails at her desk, a familiar voice greeted her.

"Commander Rougier! What a pleasure to see you."

"Hey Doc, you seem to be fine spirits!" Pauline said as she looked up to see the psychiatrist's friendly face. "You want a coffee? It's disgusting but that's all we got. Don't worry, I'm paying! With the headache I've got, I think a coffee would do me some good."

"If you insist!" Leroy replied with a smile.

Doctor Alexandre Leroy was often at the CTB. After a successful career as a psychiatrist and clinical psychologist, he had been working for the police force as a consultant for a few years now. Around sixty years old, this affable man had already been of great service to Pauline, studying the psychological profiles of suspects for her. She knew she could count on his judgment when it came to Driss Oufik.

Pauline and Leroy entered the cafeteria. She saw Kowalski sitting in a corner of the refectory with a young female operator, who had the dubious privilege of being the recipient of his most beaming smile. Pauline briefly caught eyes with him. You didn't need to be a genius to figure out that nothing was ever going to happen between those two. After a little small talk with some other colleagues, she grabbed a tray and placed a small plate upon it.

"The usual?" she asked Leroy. "Black coffee and pain aux raisins?"

"You know me better than my daughter," Leroy joked.

There was an element of regret in the way he had said that, thought Pauline. She ordered a strong espresso. She'd always liked strong coffee.

They found a table in a quiet area so they could talk. Leroy looked at Pauline and thought for a moment before speaking.

"How's it going, Pauline?"

"It's going, Doc."

"Hmm. It'll be two years soon, right?" he asked.

"Yes. Two years already. October 2nd!"

"How are you dealing with the shock?"

"It's not easy but I know I have to move on."

"I heard about your great victory in the dojo the other day. I heard it was like a street brawl. Out of control. You want to tell me about that?"

"I'll tell you that you spend too much time with Kowalski, Doc."

"Are you angry?"

"I guess!"

"Well I think it's pretty certain that you are. Do you have any idea why you might be angry?"

"It's my fault Doc, not his. It's not his fault." Pauline's voice was almost inaudible.

"Yes, but yesterday there was the whole thing in the interrogation room. It can be normal to become angry when a loved one is taken from us. But if that becomes a daily problem, you need to find help. It's essential if you want to build yourself up again."

"I'll think about it. Do you know anyone that could help me? Maybe it'd be a good idea."

"I'll talk to some of my contacts. I'll find you someone that can really help."

"Thank you, Doctor."

They drank their coffees in silence for a while, before Pauline asked:

"So, have you seen Driss Oufik?" The bitterness of her coffee made her grimace. "Are we faced with a violent fighter who's on the edge, or is he faking it?"

The psychiatrist, having seen the first interrogation of Driss Oufik, gathered himself for a moment before speaking, opting for a neutral tone of voice that marked a change from the personal conversation he'd just had.

"My diagnosis is that your suspect is suffering from Post-Traumatic Stress Disorder, without doubt linked to the time he spent in Syria and the death of his mentor, Oualid Massourd."

"So, what do you recommend?"

"I think that if you keep pushing him, he'll continue to alternate between silence and violence. Each time he loses control, he's actually reliving some moment from the past which he hasn't yet faced up to. Any hostile act toward him pushes him further into this state of morbid anxiety. It's as if he's reliving the trauma again and again."

"Tell me more. I'd really like to understand what we're dealing with here," Pauline added.

"Ok sure! It's important, especially if you plan on interviewing him again and want to establish some kind of dialogue."

Dr. Leroy began to give Pauline a detailed explanation of her suspect's condition so she'd be able to better understand his fragile emotional state.

"Post Traumatic Stress," Leroy continued, "is a change in the psychic system. Those suffering from it are liable to commit suicide or engage in serious anti-social behavior. That's what we have on our hands with this subject who has become obsessed with creating a 'better world'."

"Does he know that he's sick?"

"Yes and no," Leroy replied. "To give you a visual idea of what I'm talking about, imagine the psyche as a sphere, surrounded by a membrane protecting it from external attacks. A kind of firewall. Inside the sphere are our mental representations connected by tiny wires. Within this network, low amounts of positive energy circulate. It's a simplified version of our 'thinking apparatus'."

"Ok, I'm with you so far."

"When we experience trauma," continued Leroy, "for example when we think we're going to die and we're faced with the very real reality of death, this representation penetrates its way into our psyche, going through our firewall bringing with it such amounts of energy that it can destabilize us, even going so far as to destroying our mental capacities."

"So, in your opinion, he's experienced a severe traumatic shock?"

"Absolutely," the clinician replied, nodding his head. "I'll be straight with you. He's anxious and could become delusional. Each time you put him in a situation of extreme tension, his brain will replay the violent image he has embedded within his 'thinking apparatus' and he will relive his traumatic experience as if it were happening again. You will see him gesticulate, shout, and probably just be silent, mostly. He'll act as if he's disconnected from real life."

"So then how do I get through to him? We absolutely have to make him talk."

"Listen. Make sure he knows that you're empathetic. You see Pauline, the brain, this incredible machine, learned way before our politicians did how to disconnect. Make him trust you. What's truly surprising is that he needs it and it's more than possible that he'll confess everything to you if he feels that you're not a threat to him personally."

"Easier said than done! We're not exactly best buddies…"

"I know, but you're dealing with a sick person here! You'll have to be patient."

"Thank you, Doctor. We'll try a different approach and be a little easier on him."

Pauline went back to her desk. She'd had two missed calls while she was gone. She immediately recognized the number of Pascal Le Cam, who answered immediately when she called back. It appeared that the head of forensics had some news for her.

"Hi Pascal, It's Commander Rougier."

"Hello Pauline. Thanks for getting back to me so quickly. I've just finished my preliminary report on the apartment in place de la

Pigalle. Would you like me to come by and show it to you? There's still some work to do, but I can give you the summary and explain the most important findings."

"I'll be right there!"

Pauline went down to the basement where Pascal Le Cam and his team carried out their work. She crossed the open space where the technical team worked before knocking on his door.

Le Cam's deep voice boomed:

"Come in!" He looked slightly unwell and his two-day beard indicated that he'd worked through at least part of the previous night.

"Hello again Pauline. Nobody can say that working with you is boring! My team have been going at it all night. They're still at the apartment, its like a slaughterhouse in there!"

"Thank you Pascal. I know that everyone's been trying to use your services recently. I hope this is going to help us crack the case."

"There's still a lot to do. With crime scenes in Aubervilliers and Place Pigalle, we're gonna be busy until Sunday. Follow me!"

The office of the CTB's Head of Forensics was in his own image: impeccably neat and tidy. Not even one file was out of place. There was a blue organizer laying open next to his computer.

"Sit down and let me explain to you what's really going on here, according to our findings. It's better if I explain because not everything can be written."

He put on his glasses and began to scan the document.

"Well! To summarize, we have every reason to believe that all of these people were murdered."

"What makes you think that?"

"The entry point is intact so what may have happened is this: a guy knocks on the door. They open it and before even saying hello, the visitor shoots him right there on the spot, from below, firing upwards, exploding his thorax and abdomen. We still haven't been able to formally identify the occupants of the apartment."

Le Cam acted out the scene as he explained it to Pauline, moving his hand from down low and moving up, indicating what the shooter had done. He put down his report and continued with his summary as he looked at Pauline.

"Another man, Malik Aertens as it happens, who was in the main room at the time, rushed to the door. Considering the amount of time that it took him, he must have already had his gun in his hand. He peeks through the slightly-opened door and the intruder, obviously not in a very chatty mood, inflicts the same treatment on him. We think he used a Bullpup assault rifle. 7.62mm cases were found all over the apartment. Anyway, the shot was so powerful that Malik was thrown backward, crushing the living room coffee table and ending up with a television set on his head."

"So it wasn't a friendly visit," Pauline concluded sarcastically.

"It would seem not. But that's not everything. The footsteps show that this vile visitor decided to leave before coming back to the apartment later."

"He went back after I stopped him on the stairs."

"You got it. Once he was back in the apartment, he made his way to the room behind the living room, where he found a woman chained to a radiator. The bruises on her wrists indicate that she'd been there a while. He didn't even blink before executing her with a single shot to the head. There's a level of perverse self-control that just creeps you out. That's when he made his escape through the window leading onto the courtyard, before climbing over the wall."

"The guy's had training," Pauline added.

"Training? I'd say more than that. He's either a soldier or a professional killer of some other kind. We're not talking about a beginner."

"As he's climbing down from the window he spots Arnaud and Julie who are on the ground floor. He sees them through the glass door that looks out onto the courtyard."

"That's right. When he reaches the bottom they're right there. He doesn't think twice before he starts shooting, all the while running toward the wall where he will try and make his escape."

"I'm in the apartment at this point," Pauline adds, "I look out the window and see the suspect trying to jump. I fire and miss him."

"Right. He jumps over the wall and that's the end of that chapter. He's a specialist. I can assure you that this was a professional execution."

"We still need to figure out how Driss Oufik managed to get out of this shit show completely unscathed."

"That one's for you to figure out Pauline."

The office fell into silence. Le Cam and Pauline were both picturing the scene and trying to imagine what might have happened in the aftermath. The head of forensics gathered his thoughts, looked at Pauline and added:

"Follow me, I'll show you the evidence we got. We're still analyzing some of it but you're free to take a look."

There was a pile of plastic bags on a table at the entrance to the lab that contained everything they had seized from the apartment in Place Pigalle. Pauline studied their contents, one after the other. Nothing in particular seemed to be of any real interest. There was a gun that they needed to run a license check on, a few phones, one of which looked like an antique, and some wallets. There was also a handbag, several sets of keys, one with two keys held by a ribbon and some mundane key rings. Pauline looked through the transparent bag and read 'Reelax' on one of the keys. It must have been the name of the manufacturer.

"Where did you find the keychain with the ribbon?" asked Pauline

"Ah that one! It was around the neck of Malik Aertens."

"Strange!" She thought. "Pascal, have you taken prints from these keys?"

"Yes. Only Aertens' are on there."

"Did you try them in the apartment?"

"Yes. They open nothing. I mean, not the front door or any locked cupboards."

"Can I take them with me?"

"Sure. But I'll need to have them signed out."

"No problem."

"Wanna see the stiffs?"

"I'll give it a miss. It's been a rough morning, I don't think I could take seeing any of your colleagues right now."

Le Cam opened a door. On the autopsy tables were three dead bodies, covered with white sheets.

"Thanks Pascal, but I'll read your reports in detail later!"

Pauline walked toward the elevators. There were a few questions that needed answering which seemed vital to moving forward with the investigation, for the May 1st attack and the massacre of Place Pigalle.

Firstly, why send in a professional killer to take out people that could potentially launch another violent attack on your behalf? It doesn't seem like their usual way of doing things. In general, they either blow themselves up or hide away somewhere. Killing them didn't seem to fit into this pattern. Maybe it's because they knew something that was imperative to keep away from the police.

Secondly, how did the killer find Driss Oufik and Aertens so quickly? They were obviously in hiding. The police had managed to locate them thanks to Nathan's facial recognition program. But how could someone else have done it?

Thirdly, why did Aertens carry a bunch of keys around his neck? They must have been so important that he couldn't take any risk being apart from them, let alone losing them. But what did they unlock?

"The further we get with this case, the less clear things become," thought Pauline.

Part of the job of working for the police involves doing paperwork. A lot of paperwork. She had a meeting with the boss at 4 pm, which wouldn't leave her a lot of time to write the reports on yesterday's operation. She also needed to pay Arnaud a visit in hospital. She decided that seeing her colleague was the priority. The reports could wait a little while.

All hospitals are the same. From the moment she arrived in the parking lot, she began to feel unwell. The smell, the people that pass you with anxious-looking faces. The impossible maze of corridors and departments. People whispering because they're afraid to disturb the patients, but in reality they only add to the heavy atmosphere of the place. The noise of the machines; high-pitched beeps which beat the rhythms for the musical scores of the lives that were being played out in these dark corridors. Pauline mustered up some courage and entered.

"Commander Rougier. I'm here to see Lieutenant Arnaud Lescure. He was admitted yesterday afternoon."

"Ah yes, the bullet wound. That one?" The nurse at reception asked while checking the register.

"You have to check?" Pauline asked, surprised.

"My shift just started."

"I'm sorry…"

"Room five." The head of the department read out Arnaud's file from the computer. "He came back from the recovery room at 10.45 pm last night. He slept well. You can go see him, but not for too long, he needs to rest. The operation went well. He got lucky. His shoulder will recover."

"Thank you!"

Pauline pushed open the door and saw Arnaud sleeping. There were wires and tubes everywhere measuring his heart rate and blood pressure, another one draining waste. A drip administered antibiotics intravenously. All of it was enough to give Pauline the chills. She hated this sterile environment with a passion. "I should have brought something" she said to herself. Arnaud opened his eyes.

"Oh. Hi Arnaud, how's it going?"

"Slowly, Commander! It's going slowly. It hurts like hell."

"What kind of pain meds they got you on?"

"I'm not sure but I'm taking them by the fistful. If I take any more I won't be able to talk."

"Glad to see you've kept your sense of humor."

"The operation went well, I'll be able to come back soon."

"Take your time, Arnaud. You'll need to be at 100% before you get back in the field."

"I know... how's the investigation going?"

"I've just been with forensics. We agree that the guy who got you must have been a pro who's been highly trained. You think you could recognize him?"

"I didn't get a good look at him, Commander. He was facing away from the light, too. I don't think I can help you. But you saw him too, right?

"Yes and no. He came hurtling down the stairs. I stood up, took out my weapon and told him to not move any further. He fired and then left. I hardly even got a glance!"

"Lucky we're police officers, you know what I mean?"

"You got that right!"

"Tell me something. When you called me to say that you had the address where our two fugitives were hiding, did you leave a message, or did you call my phone directly?"

Arnaud rubbed his eyebrows. He was thinking about the question.

"First, I called your office and left a message. When I didn't get and answer, I tried to call your cell directly."

"You're sure?"

"Totally sure. Why?"

"No reason. I'm just checking. Look, get some rest. They told me I could only stay for a few minutes. Do you need anything?"

"Don't worry, they're taking good care of me and I've had a couple of visits. Thanks anyway, Commander. You can go ahead. Get this case closed! I'd love to know who the bastard behind this attack is. You still haven't found him?"

"Still nothing. And that's also strange."

Pauline left the hospital feeling a little relieved. She was breathing rapidly as she got outside, finally letting out a big exhale. Every time she was there it was hard. She got into her car and began to think. She was certain she hadn't received the message from Arnaud on the internal messaging system that supposedly gave her the location in Pigalle.

*
* *

Saturday May 6th - CTB

Pauline was interviewing again. Driss Oufik was still alternating between violence, stubborn silences, and periods where he decided he would talk. Pauline was beginning to better understand the links between Massourd, Aertens, Oufik and Kerbouche, the foursome responsible for the attacks on May 4th.

They had the leader in Oualid Massourd, exalted and absolutely convinced by his 'Cause'. They had Driss, follower of Massourd, upon whom he was extremely dependent. Then there was Kerbouche, a revenant who had served with Massourd in Aleppo. He had not been shy when it came to using his weapon during the assault by the RAID team.

Driss described Malik Aertens as someone who was harder to read. He was always on the telephone talking to other people, as if he were connected to people in higher places within the organization. He was the one who had the money; he always had cash on him, he paid the rent and was the person who had been the contact for the arms delivery. Naturally violent, he'd frequently clash with Kerbouche, whom he judged to be impudent, as well as with Driss. But Oualid Massourd had made it clear that messing with Driss meant messing with him… and no one wanted to have any problems with Oualid.

Although they were beginning to get a better understanding of the relationships between the four men, they still had no idea about the organization itself. Who was giving the orders? Who decided upon the objectives? It seemed like the investigation was getting nowhere.

Pauline began thinking again about the bunch of keys that Malik Aertens had around his neck and wondered how she could find out what they were for.

*
* *

Monday, May 8th, 11 am – CTB

Pauline and Driss Oufik had seen each other every day for hours at a time for almost three days now. More often than not, Driss was willing to talk. Pauline learned a lot about his past and the living conditions of those who served the Islamic State. From time to time, however, he'd close up and there was nothing she could do to break his silence. They'd increased the strength of his meds in order to calm him further and make him less susceptible to the panic attacks he'd been suffering.

Now that she was done with the confrontational approach, Pauline decided to try the softer method of questioning that psychologist Alexandre Leroy had recommended. She would now listen rather than accuse. She was getting to know Driss a little better, and although his actions were unforgiveable, she found that she had a certain empathy with this young twenty-two-year-old. Since Driss has been on the meds, he'd been much calmer and his violent episodes were rare.

"Hello Driss!"

"Hello Commander."

"Where did we leave things yesterday?" asked Pauline.

"We were talking about Yasmina."

"Ah yeah, that's right. The fact that you got along well."

"Absolutely. Yasmina and I were close. My mother worked evenings, and in the mornings, she'd do little jobs here and there. Cleaning offices, stuff like that."

"So Yasmina looked after you. She was like, what? Three years older than you?"

"Yeah, but actually I hung out with Oualid more. He was really into my sister. So he was always at our place."

"And what about her?"

"She couldn't have cared less. Didn't even notice him!" Driss replied, laughing.

"How'd he take that?"

"He was really pissed. It's kind of that which made him flip."

"What do you mean by that?"

"Oualid was pretty much known as a tough guy around the city. He was respected, but when people found out that Yasmina had knocked him back, he became more violent. You know, he wanted to be respected!"

"So what did you do when he was like that?"

"Thing is, Oualid was like my brother. He was five years older than me. I followed him around everywhere. I was a kid, but I knew I could count on Oualid. No one could touch me!"

Driss' eyes were a little teary.

"He protected you."

"Yeah. And I wasn't exactly the biggest kid around, so when he was there, if anyone gave me shit, Oualid would deal with them."

"You helped him out?"

"Yeah... he was dealing a little back then. I was still at school. I was fourteen years old, him nineteen. I did little jobs for him, deliveries, stuff like that."

"And?"

"Shit, that guy earned a lot of money! He got himself a big car to impress Yasmina, bought her gifts. My mom knew that he liked her..."

Driss stopped. Wiped his eyes.

"Could I get a cup of tea, Commander?"

"I think we can do that for you Driss. But then let's get back to business afterwards, OK?"

"OK. I'd like to be done with all that. I know I'm going straight to jail, but I don't care. I got no place else to go."

They brought in the tea. He took his time to drink it, blowing more than was strictly necessary to cool it down.

"You know, Oualid got two years for trafficking drugs."

"I do. I saw on his record.".

"Yeah! Well, the whole thing is that he was never the same once he got out."

"You mean he got radicalized in prison?"

"Exactly. He went to the mosque all the time, prayed and everything. He was never the same."

"What about you? How'd you end up in Syria?"

"I followed Oualid. He'd always been there for me, and he told me it would be good for us, that we could be fighters, kings over there. Fuck! What bullshit. Complete fucking bullshit!"

"Why'd you say that? Things didn't go as planned?"

"We ended up in Turkey in a unit with almost only French Muslims. The heads of the Islamic State treated us like dogs. We could hardly speak Arabic and understood pretty much nothing.

They gave us shitty missions to do, super dangerous. They didn't give a damn about us. Oualid was on the front lines in Aleppo."

"What about you?"

"I was a fucking prison guard. I was never at the front, except a bit at the beginning, but when things really began to get heavy I couldn't … I left to find somewhere better. It was hell on Earth there."

Driss seemed like he wanted to say something but changed his mind.

"You want to say something? Go ahead. We're listening."

"Well, it's like for the attack. I was just the driver. I just drove Oualid, that's all. We lived at Yasmina's place, but she left because she'd had enough of the whole goddamned thing, the suburbs and all. She wasn't exactly impressed with Oualid doing time or us going to Syria, either."

Driss lowered his head and stared at the floor. He was visibly shaken.

"When did you come back?"

"Six months ago. We both came back through Turkey. When we got back to Paris, I hid out at my mom's place in the suburbs. Oualid just disappeared. Then, two months ago, he contacted me. Said he needed someone to help him. I went to see him. He was with Malik. So that's how it happened."

"So, you just show up and decide to join in?"

"What did I have to lose?"

"What happened next?"

"On the morning of May 1st, Oualid asked me to take him to the center of Paris. Before leaving, he told me that he was my brother and that he loved me. He was in a trance. He showed me his belt full of explosives. He said he would shout the name of Allah."

"So what did you do?"

"Nothing. Fucking nothing!" Tears ran down Driss' cheeks.

"You couldn't have done anything anyway, Driss."

"I don't know. I should have tried. But I pussied out. Again."

"What happened next?"

"After that? I dropped him off near the Pont de Sully bridge. You know the rest."

"Thank you, Driss. I want to know who backed the killing of your brother. You know who was behind this attack?"

"I just know that I drove Malik into a parking lot just outside the city once. A guy arrived with a Mercedes. He gave Malik a bag and then they chatted for a while in his car."

"Then what?"

"Well, the guy left and we went home. That's all I know."

"Did you ask Malik who it was?"

"Yes. He told me, 'just drive and only worry about things that concern you' So I left it there."

"Would you be able to recognize him?"

"I think so!"

"You think so or you're sure?"

"I'm sure."

*
* *

In the early afternoon, Pauline went back to Dalmont's place, the building in Aubervilliers where the terrorists had been hiding out. She wanted to take a look around Yasmina Oufik's apartment again. The four terrorists had been there for months, so even though forensics had been unable to find anything that could help them, she wanted to make sure that no stone was left unturned.

She parked in front of the building at the corner of the building site, pushed the door that was already open and rang the doorbell to Mr. Dalmont's apartment. The old man opened and smiled as soon as he saw his visitor.

"Commander Rougier! Now there's a nice surprise!"

"Hello Mr. Dalmont. I told you I'd come to see how you were doing, so here I am, keeping that promise. Maybe I should have called ahead?"

"Not at all. You see how old I am, I'm never out! Come in! Come in! Can I get you a coffee?"

"I'd love one!"

"Please, sit down, I'll just be a few minutes."

Pauline leaned back in the worn out sofa and sank into the moldy old cushions. The interior of his place smelled stale. Odors from the kitchen stagnated in the room. The TV had been repaired because it sat enthroned once again upon its furniture, surrounded by photo frames. Pauline looked at the photos and discovered a young Dalmont, about thirty years old, with a woman. They were obviously on vacation. With a full head of hair, he had a broad smile as he held the young, slim-waisted blonde woman around her shoulders. He was a handsome man, Pauline thought. She picked up another portrait, this one of a young man in his twenties who looked a lot like Dalmont. His son maybe? Her host returned from the kitchen and Pauline quickly put the photo frame back, feeling guilty.

"All that's left are the photos," Dalmont smiled, holding two mugs of coffee.

"Thank you" Pauline replied, taking one of them. "Your wife and son?"

"That's right Commander! Both of them taken too soon. My wife died ten years ago, my son followed her two years later. Car accident."

"I'm sorry. I'm so sorry."

"The most important thing is to keep them by my side and keep going, but not let it take over my life."

"Have you been able to do that?"

"Some days I can… most days. I know that Madeleine, my wife, she's here with me. She guides me and supports me. That's just how it is, Commander."

"You can call me Pauline."

"OK. Pauline. I'm Étienne. So, what about you? I can see there's some sadness in your eyes, or am I wrong?"

"No, you're right. I also lost someone close to me."

Pauline drank some of her coffee. It was strong and very bitter. She had tears in her eyes. She ran her hand through her hair and cleared her throat.

"It's nice."

"I like strong coffee. But I don't think that you came here to talk about my family?"

"No. How are the repairs going in the place?"

"I've had a lot of experts come around, sizing things up. It's tough. No one wants to take responsibility for the damage. Everyone's passing the buck and now they want the state to pay the costs. It's going to take time, and that's just what I don't have, Pauline."

"But you want to rent them out again, right?"

"I decided to sell. I reached an agreement with the company that's developing the site over there. They're going to do a whole new building. I guess that's progress. When they started the works two years ago, they made me an offer, but back then I wasn't ready to sell. Now, with everything that's happened, I think it's the right time!"

"You've had this place for a long time?"

"My wife inherited it. But like I said, you got to keep going. You have to make a decision and not let those who have passed control your life."

They finished their coffee and Pauline took out the keys that Malik Aertens had been wearing. She showed them to Dalmont.

"Have you seen these keys before? We found them on Malik Aertens. Nobody knows what they're for."

Dalmont looked keenly at them. He got up and came back with box full of keys that he handed to Pauline.

"These are all of the keys to this building. You want to check if it matches any of them?"

"Yes, thank you."

Pauline checked the keys one after the other. Nothing was like the one Aertens had.

"Étienne. I'd like to take a look at the apartment. Would you come with me?"

"Go ahead. You know the way. I'm waiting for some builders who are arriving this afternoon. They should be here any minute now."

Pauline thanked Dalmont and made her way up the stairs to check one last time that they hadn't missed anything. She cut the seals and the door creaked open. The doorframe that had been broken by the police ram's blow had not been replaced, yet the doors somehow stayed on its hinges. Pauline entered the apartment. Traces of the struggle were still visible: tiles shattered during the explosion of the grenade; bullet holes in the walls; a smoke-burned parquet from the smoke grenade. Pauline tried Aertens' keys in the lock. They wouldn't go in. She went to the closet and found another lock. No keys matched. She looked around. It was time to face up to it: nothing on this key ring opened anything in the apartment. She left and headed downstairs feeling discouraged. Étienne Dalmont was talking to two men in white overalls.

"I'm going to say goodbye now, Étienne. I'll come back another time. Let me know how it goes with the repairs and the sale!"

"Will do! And remember: keep them close, but it's not them who decide. We're the ones at the wheel!"

"I got it, don't worry!" replied Pauline, smiling.

"OK, I'll let you go. These gentlemen are here to do the tiling on the third floor. I've got some masons coming to fix the hole in the closet later, and to top it all off the door on the second floor won't open! It's a pain, I'm telling you."

"Good luck."

Pauling got into her car and headed for CTB. She was no closer to understanding what the keys could be for. She drove a further 200 meters before the answer suddenly came to her. She braked suddenly, made a U-turn and, arriving once again from where she started, parked haphazardly in front of the building. She ran to the door. Étienne Dalmont was discussing animatedly with the workers.

"Étienne, would you mind if I just took a look at something again?"

"Pauline, you're back?" Dalmont responded, surprised. "Of course, of course!"

Pauline leaped up the stairs, taking four at a time. When she got to the second floor, she took out the 'Reelax' key and placed it into the lock.

It began to turn, then she heard a 'click' as the latch was released. Pauline pushed lightly as the door started to creak open. Her heart began to beat faster. She was right. Aertens had been using the empty apartment to hide things from the others. No need to go too far; why not simply use a place nearby? He knew that Dalmont, a reclusive old man, never went there. And in any case, if Dalmont had somehow realized that his key no longer worked in the lock, he'd have to call a locksmith, giving Aertens time to hide whatever was inside. It was the simplest and most discreet solution.

Pauline went into the apartment. It was identical in shape to the one on the third floor and equally as antiquated. She put on a pair of surgeon's gloves before entering so she wouldn't contaminate the scene. There was dust all over the floor with traces of footsteps; no doubt those of Aertens. Pauline set about scouring the place from top to bottom. If Aertens had been here, it meant he had something to hide.

She found nothing in the living room. She went into the kitchen a looked inside the cupboards. Nothing. In the bedroom there were two sliding doors. On one side there was a wardrobe, on the other a box. She opened it and found a gym bag inside. It was closed with a padlock. She took the second key out of her pocket and slid it easily into the lock. The padlock clicked open and Pauline opened the zipper.

It was like a terrorism starter pack. Pauline found a dozen passports from various countries, some never used. There were credit cards, handguns and a large amount of cash. Pauline counted the bundles quickly; at least €30,000. Her attention was caught by a small notebook at the bottom of the bag.

Flicking through the pages, she saw column after column of indecipherable notes and numbers. Entire columns of just names and figures. Malik was supposedly the man financing the organization. Had Pauline just stumbled upon the group's accounts? If that were indeed the case, then it's no wonder that a few people didn't want Malik to talk, she thought to herself.

She found a loose piece of paper folded up within the notebook. A name: ZURICH INVESTMENT & SECURITIES BANK – together with records of a few transfers. Each of them for hundreds of thousands of Euros.

"What's a Swiss bank doing being mixed up in this mess?" Pauline wondered.

*
* *

Monday, May 8th, 5 pm – CTB

Pauline returned to the CTB and went to see Pascal in forensics. She placed the bag in front of him and emptied the contents. It would be all need to be analyzed before being sent to the evidence room.

The antiterrorism judge had asked for Driss Oufik to be released in order to formally charge him with "Organized Assassination and Terrorism Association" and begin his interrogation. Pauline and her team had completed their investigation. They hadn't been able to find out the identity of the attack's backer. Driss was going to help them to make a portrait of this man. It was a start.

The killer from Place Pigalle was still at large and forensics were testing the bullets they'd found following the murders, taken from the victims' bodies. The results brought nothing new to light. The gun wasn't registered. They'd probably never find him.

They had identified the two bodies from the apartment on Rue Duperré. Driss had confirmed that it was a couple with whom Malik Aertens had stayed in the past, before he'd got involved in terrorism. The dead woman was the one who had called the toll free number. Malik caught her by surprise while she was on the phone to the police. He hit her, gagged her and tied her to the radiator. Her husband was being watched by Malik at the time.

The killer had burst into the apartment and shot everyone. Driss Oufik was in the bathroom at that time. The noise and violence of the fighting shook him physically. He fell to the ground and lay face down, disconnected, just as he had done during his arrest and the first interrogations. He was in an intense post-traumatic shock. When he began to come out of the trance, he left the bathroom, stumbled into the pool of blood at the entrance and left the apartment. It was at this moment that he came face to face with Pauline, who proceeded to arrest and handcuff him.

Pauline went to fetch Driss. She took him to the lobby of CTB while they waited for the police who would escort him to prison.

"Sit down, Driss. You're out of my hands now. You'll be examined and spend the night in prison."

"I spent a lot of time in prison in Iraq. I was a guard back then, but honestly, I think I was as much of prisoner as the guys I was guarding."

"Stay here. This won't take long. I just have to sign the transfer papers and we're done."

Driss sat staring at the television in the lobby of the CTB. The news channels were looping through the brave events of the RAID team assault, and the unfortunate death of one of its members. Videos showed the building on Rue Duperré and the arrest of Driss Oufik, an alleged terrorist linked to the May 1st bombing. There were pictures of the four terrorists inset, embedded permanently onscreen.

The channels would then switch to their usual schedules, with one broadcasting a report on the new exhibition which would be inaugurated the next day at the Institute of the Arab World in Paris. Young Islamic-inspired designers, photographers and sculptors were presented, competing for the Mohamed Abdul Latif Jameel Prize, sponsored by an eponymous Saudi businessman who promoted artistic production throughout the Arab world.

The Saudi ambassador and his entourage would be there to open the exhibition.

Driss was watching now from the corner of his eye. When the camera zoomed in on the officials he froze.

"That's him!" Driss exclaimed. "The guy that me and Malik met with, that's him, right there!" Driss pointed to the images of the dignitaries arriving at the exhibition.

"Who? The ambassador?" Pauline asked, incredulously.

"No, the guy next to him. That's him. I'm sure of it!"

Pauline sensed that the terrorist investigation that she was involved in ran a lot deeper than she had imagined. No rush. She had no idea who this man was, but she knew she'd find out quickly and would not like the answer.

* *
*

Driss had just left, escorted by the officers in charge of his transfer. Pauline felt like a weight had been lifted off her shoulders. Before closing the investigation, she had one last problem to solve. She wanted to find answers to a question that had kept perplexing her. Why didn't she get the message that Arnaud left her on her office phone after he'd been to see Nathan? Arnaud confirmed that without any doubt he had called her office fixed line phone before calling her cell. He left a message detailing the address where Driss Oufik and Malik Aertens were hiding. Yet she had never received it. It wasn't there. Pauline knew one thing was for sure: messages, like emails and many other things, do not magically disappear.

The answer, that she had just seen a glimpse of, wasn't pleasant, but she wanted to know for sure.

She took the elevator to go to the office of Charly Dumont, chief of information technology at CTB. She had a look through the glass door and saw him completely absorbed in his screen, ensuring that all of the computers used by the police at the Brigade were functioning as they should be. No small task. Pauline knocked.

"Come in!"

Charly's office looked like some kind of secondhand electronics store, full of used printers and old telephones. There were hard drives, wires, circuit boards, and everything else you'd need to build a homemade PC lying all around him. He was an energetic man in his thirties, and had a reputation for his hacking skills and problem solving. If something was broken and needing fixing, ask Charly and you can consider it done.

"Hello Charly, I see you're getting better! Now we can open the door to your office without causing a landslide of computer parts."

"Yeah, I've really got into systematic storage recently" said Dumont, laughing.

"I can see that! There's even a piece of carpet, just there! Look!" replied Pauline, pointing to a half-square meter of floor that wasn't covered with a carcass of electronic waste.

"To what do I owe the the privilege of having Commander Rougier come to my office? A computer issue? The network? A lost cable?"

"No, none of the above. I need your help, but first of all you have to swear to me that everything I'm about to ask you will stay between us."

Charly Dumont closed his laptop and looked at Pauline insistently.

"You know me well Pauline, and you know that you can trust me."

"I know, and that's why I came to see you."

"So, what's the problem?"

"Can you find a voicemail message from my landline that was mistakenly erased?"

"Of course, easy! Do you know exactly when it was recorded?"

"Yes, Thursday, May 4th, between 2 and 3 pm."

"OK, give me five minutes!"

Dumont opened his laptop and connected to the voicemail application. He tapped various numbers and letters for two minutes.

"Well, I think I found what you are looking for. I... wait, wait... five messages between 2 pm and 3 pm on Thursday, May 4th. Not bad huh?"

"Can we listen to them?"

"Of course."

Charly clicked on the first message. Pauline listened intently. "No," she said. Charly clicked on the second. The third was the one she was looking for.

"Message three, at 14:42," said the electronic voice. Then, Arnaud: "Commander, Arnaud here. I have the address where Oufik and Aertens are hiding. Nathan is the man. They are at the corner of Rue Duperré and Place Pigalle."

"End of message three."

"Thank you, that's it."

"Can you tell me what time it was erased?"

"Yeah, no problem. At 3.10 pm"

"Now, I need you to research the use of security cards within CTB. Is it possible to do that for me too?"

"That and lots of other things, Commander," Charly said, winking at her.

"Let's start with the badges, OK?"

"Whatever you want!"

"So, find me all the security cards registered in the system that were used between 2.30 pm and 3.10 pm. I'm looking for those who used one to open the door of the north wing on the 4th, where my office is."

"Looking for who could have entered during this time slot?"

"Exactly. I'm looking for a card that would have been used to get in and out within a very short time, say, ten to twenty minutes. If we find nothing, we can expand the search."

"OK, I'm on it."

"I'll give you the numbers of all of the ID's so you can sort through them... so if we focus on those who came in and out there is... in fact only one badge. Number 249367."

"And who's hiding behind this number?"

"Well, it's... Lieutenant Marek Kowalski."

"Kowalski!"

Pauline was surprise but had expected something like that. She was going to keep this to herself for the time being.

"Thank you, Charly. You've been great as always."

"At your service Commander. If there's anything else I can do for you, just let me know!"

"Remember what I told you. This stays between us!"

"My lips are sealed!"

*
* *

Chaos Theory

5. THE MEETING

Thursday, May 9th

President Lavalette's car stopped in front of the new Federal Chancellery in Berlin, an ultra-modern, U-shaped steel concrete building with a transparent façade.

The entire 130,000 square-feet culminated 120 feet above the ground. The Chancellery is the largest administrative building in the world; eight times the size of the White House in Washington. The main part of the building houses six floors. On the ground floor is the state guest reception room, 'Le Foyer', where he was being awaited. The Chancellor had her apartments on the 8th floor while the government used the floor just below.

After admiring the building for a minute or two, Lavalette thought about how it was a very German construction in its design. Few frills, austerity on display. It was far from the Palaces and the splendor of buildings at the disposal of French politicians. The imposing ensemble of this construction symbolized Germany's position in Europe and in the world.

His car stopped in the middle of the central courtyard. He was quickly escorted into the Chancellery, followed by Henri du Plessis.

To his great surprise, he was taken to a meeting room where there were four desks, with some tea and coffee to one side. He realized that they had not come for mutual congratulations; this was going to be a serious meeting.

Chancellor Konrad arrived at 1 pm precisely. Punctuality was something taught at a young age in this country. She was followed by a man in a dark suit. He was carrying a few files, along with a transparent smile. He shook the president's hand.

"Heidrich Füller, Economic Advisor, pleased to meet you, Mr. President."

The Chancellor signaled for them to sit, and she began to talk.

"Monsieur Lavalette, let me first congratulate you on your recent election victory and extend to you the support of Germany. The reason I wanted to meet you so soon was to enable us to align our economic positions. I am aware that you will name your government very soon and give, through Mr. Du Plessis, the general policy speech that will give direction to your term in office. It was essential that I explain the position of Germany before you speak. Global balances are fragile, and recent changes in the United Kingdom and the United States are challenging those balances."

"Madam Chancellor, I am listening. You know that I am a fervent defender of European project and I hope that together we will be able to build a common future for our two countries!"

"I'll explain the nature of our concerns," said the Chancellor. The European economic situation is worrying. Europe, even though it may be unloved by its own people, remains a stable anchor for its members. Less Europe would mean for most countries, including France, economic and monetary stagnation."

Paul felt that the Chancellor was about to start talking about a major issue. Otherwise, what is the point of bringing him here now? Why did she seem so tense?

She looked at Lavalette, before beginning again.

"The election of the new president at the head of the United States has significantly changed the economic field, accelerating, among other things, the redistribution of capital. Since coming to power, the Federal Reserve has already raised its interest rates twice, capturing huge financial flows. The value of investments in the US is now much greater than those in Europe.

"This I know," Lavalette asserted, "however…"

"Please allow me to finish Mr. President, if you would. You will have plenty of time to respond when I have finished. As I was saying, the American president has launched a massive $1 trillion infrastructure renewal program. Nobody thought he would do it, and everyone was wrong. This historic program to upgrade US infrastructure has immediate implications for us. Among other things, it pushed the Fed to raise its rates by two points in order to attract the necessary capital and in turn forced the European Central Bank to raise our own by one percent... That alone is costing us dearly."

"If I understand your reasoning correctly, the recent rate hike by the ECB is a direct reaction to the Americans' decision to borrow a trillion dollars from the financial markets, via the issuance of public debt?"

"Unfortunately, that seems to be the case! If the Americans put debt on the markets at a better rate than ours, they'll have more success than us when it comes to selling it. It's the law of supply and demand, isn't that the case?"

"Indeed" responded Lavalette.

"In the end it means that we have to raise our rates in order to remain competitive."

The President, who wasn't a trained economist, understood the reasoning of the Chancellor, but he wasn't sure where this was all going.

Chancellor Konrad turned to her advisor to invite him to talk.

"Could you continue please, Herr Füller?"

"Certainly, Chancellor. The implementation of the US policy to raise interest rates is causing inflation on the repayments of sovereign debt. Clearly, investors have the choice and they prefer to buy US debt. However, countries that use the Euro, France in particular, don't simply turn their backs because long-term debt elsewhere costs next to nothing. They have continued to borrow at negative rates until today. But that balance is broken - how can France's economy survive if interest rates rise by two, three or even more points again? It would mean finding ten billion more per year for every one percent increase! And that's just to fill the hole."

The Chancellor interrupted Füller and began to talk again:

"Mr. President, what we're trying to tell you is actually very simple. The time of low interest rates is about to end in favor of inflation for which we cannot predict the trajectory. France will not be able to support its debt if it doesn't introduce a series of difficult reforms, immediately. With a GDP of two trillion and a 100% percent debt level, a rise in interest rates of two or three per cent would be an utter disaster."

"We are very aware of this!" Lavalette responded. "That's why my manifesto included a plan to inject €40-50 billion into the French economy in order to give our competitiveness a serious boost."

The President was beginning to understand what was happening. Germany sensed that the Euro train was entering the red zone and that a derailment of the financial system was possible. It would affect everyone in a similar way to the subprime crisis, except worse.

"We believe that if investors decide that European countries can no longer repay their debts, a financial earthquake is on the cards, one that would be much worse than the subprime crisis. It's a time bomb that could explode. A bomb like that would destroy the Eurozone, taking everyone's savings along with it. We could witness a chain reaction of bankruptcy for financial institutions. Imagine a bankrupt France that would then bring down Germany in its wake, followed by all of the other member states. We'd have another crisis like in 1929. The cause of the Great Depression was, first and foremost, the loss of confidence in the system and the end of credit."

"I think you're going a little far, Chancellor, we're not there yet! Debt can be renegotiated, can't it?"

"Even if the mother of all debt renegotiations were to happen in order to avoid the worst, such as allowing staggered repayments or a moratorium on interest, the loss of confidence in the markets would still be catastrophic. Such a collapse would propel European stock markets to historic lows, making our companies worthless, unless they were nationalized. But again, with what money could we do that?"

"I understand. But what do you want us to do?"

"Mr. President, I think that the recovery measures in your program are good, but they would at best stabilize the situation. In no case will they be able to withstand the incoming wave. I fear that we must take braver measures than this! France must not back down. The stability of Europe and the world is at stake."

"It's exactly what I said during my campaign. Reduce the deficit and get the economic machine back on track. I think we're aligned on this issue?"

"Unfortunately, what I'm asking you goes way beyond that! You must present to your compatriots a balanced budget for the five years of your term in office."

"But that's absolutely impossible. It's..."

"It's not impossible! But I concede, it will be painful."

"I can't agree to this!"

"This time, I believe, there is no alternative, Monsieur Lavalette. France is in an unprecedented situation. It's a situation that requires a balanced budget beginning this year. That's a reduction in your spending of €100 billion per year, starting immediately!"

"But that's madness!" Lavalette stormed, "do you realize the political implications? It's impossible! I'd have to reduce the number of workers in the public system, cut health spending, social benefits, unemployment payments and raise the retirement age to sixty-five or even sixty-seven. I understand your reticence but surely there are other alternatives? What will happen if, in two years, the rates are at four or five percent, and we haven't anticipated the wall the we'd undoubtedly hit? We'd be in an even worse situation!"

"I agree, but we need to take the time to reflect. You can never have good politics and good economics at the same time. Anyone who has ever tried to make the two align has always failed! I ask you to think carefully," Konrad insisted, "the implications are serious. France, like everywhere else, has lost its sovereignty by taking on such debt! You can not refuse to pay the price! Our majority shareholders are Qatari and US pension funds. By accepting their capital, we've all lost some of our sovereignty. If you refuse, Germany would have no choice but to isolate you on the public scene by officially issuing a communiqué expressing doubts about the solidity of France... Can you imagine the immediate impact? Here is the text that would be used in case we do not leave this room with an agreement."

She handed her proposal to Lavalette, who read it attentively. It was clearly a distancing of Germany from France. "Unbelievable!" he thought. "How did we get here?"

"Mr. President," continued the Chancellor, "in the unlikely event that we had to publicly assert our differences, the position you are proposing to take would have several effects. The first; that of considerably weakening the euro against the dollar and other currencies. That would be good for Germany because, as you know, we are predominantly an exporting country. A weak Euro is good for our foreign trade. The second immediate benefit for us would be to disrupt your monthly issuing of bonds, making those from Germany all the more attractive. Finally, this would significantly reduce France's credit rating, which would propel your interest rates to stratospheric levels."

"It would be a catastrophe!"

"I know. It's highly likely that you'd be forced to put in place measures that are just as tough as the ones I've just described to you. Unfortunately, I don't think you have many options... I urge you to think about this with a clear head. I sincerely hope you'll be able to reach a decision about these pressing questions."

The Chancellor turned to her advisor.

"Herr Füller, please show President Lavalette the forecasts that we have made. He can have a look at them in detail on his return to Paris."

Lavalette looked at Henri, then at the Chancellor.

"I think we've covered everything, Madam Chancellor. I need to discuss this all with Mr. Du Plessis. Will you accompany me to the press conference?"

They made their way to the conference room, marching down long, austere corridors. A few pieces of furniture here and there tried to give the place a minimalist look. Everything just seemed to make the situation feel even heavier still.

They entered the press room.

A loud clamoring crowd awaited them. The press pit was completely filled with journalists. The reporters were talking to each other, as well as ducking, dodging and elbowing one another to try and get to the front. Each of them wanted the best view for photos, or better, to ask the heads of state their question if given the opportunity. The cameramen took their final requests from the editorialists.

Lavalette looked around to get a feeling of the place. It was a large open space on the ground floor. The ceiling was twenty feet high. The polished concrete floor reflected the bright light from large bay windows at the southern end of the room. The west wall, in front of which podiums had been arranged where the two politicians would talk from, was raw concrete. In this month of May, the brightness of the room was in stark contrast to President Lavalette's rather morose feelings. On the east side of this huge open space was the Chancellor's Gallery, which proudly displayed painted portraits of successive heads of the German state.

The French and German flags had been placed on either side of the podiums, while a long European Union banner crowned the end of the room.

Lavalette couldn't help but think that these flags, symbols of the togetherness of a people, were losing their power. The dependence of most countries on the diktats of finance would end up eradicating even the very notion of their identity, whether the people liked it or not.

President Lavalette settled in behind his podium, with the tricolor to his left. The Chancellor did the same on the other side, flanked by the colors of Germany. She began.

"President Lavalette and I had the pleasure of discussing in a very informal way our respective positions on the key issues of the European economy and the cooperation between our two countries for a stronger Europe. It was a first preparatory meeting for an official visit that we will arrange as soon as the President has taken up office. I will cordially invite him and his finance minister to return to Berlin so that together we can define a common economic program aimed at consolidating the position of our two countries in the European Union. Mr. President?"

"Thank you, Madame Chancellor. Indeed, as the newly elected President, it is important for me to meet the Chancellor in order to begin establishing a relationship. The bilateral links between Berlin and Paris remain an essential axis of stability for the European Union. This difficult economic period within a global context, in a world that is losing its bearings, requires our two countries to collaborate and bring our points of view even closer together. It is in this spirit that we have begun our first dialogue.

He had just taken political doublespeak to a whole new level.

The Chancellor thanked the media but refused to take any questions. A loud rumble echoed throughout the newsroom, reporters bemoaning that the conference had lasted less than ten minutes, was one-way and had no real content. What was the new

French President's manifesto? What would the two countries be doing to re-launch their bilateral relations that were now at a low?

They took their leave. Giving away anymore at this stage in the debate would only have made things worse. It was better to be careful and keep things short.

Lavalette and the Chancellor exchanged a warm handshake in front of the podiums. The main doors behind them opened. Lavalette and Henri du Plessis walked down the same austere corridors that had lead them to the stage, before making their way to the courtyard of the chancellery. They left rather hastily, getting into the car that would immediately take them to the airport.

As soon as they had closed the doors, the car started amid what was a heavy silence. They were both in shock after what had just happened.

After a few minutes, Lavalette exploded.

"Damn it! We're in an impossible situation. I know the Chancellor is right. If we do nothing and the rates shoot up, we'll be bankrupt. You realize that if tomorrow one of the rating agencies decides that France can't meet its obligations, the Euro would plummet, hard. Our own economy would do the same. The end of something we have all taken for granted: making the people believe that we still have the means to maintain their standard of living."

"I know," answered Henri, "but do have we a choice? I understand her position. She's trying to stop us from sinking. None of the other politicians before us have done anything, so she's forcing things, hoping to get the system back on track before one big, final derailment."

"She's digging in hard with these negotiations, that's for sure! Yet they have debt and they know that by making the people poorer they will only bring about dangerous politics. By making the people go hungry, Henri, only one thing can happen, and that's chaos. Look at what's happening in the US! By bowing down to Wall Street, they've found themselves with rife unemployment among the white population who feel abandoned by the elite and who are completely rejecting globalization!"

"At least their president is trying to make them competitive again!"

"You really think that the future of the United States lies in reopening the coal mines to give people work? Of course it doesn't!"

"I know that too, Paul," replied Du Plessis, who was preparing himself to weather a verbal storm.

"It's not like we haven't had a few serious warnings over the past few years! Don't you think it should have awakened the political consciences of the European heads of state?"

"I agree with you. The people of Europe no longer want the Europe that we're offering them. Nor do they want the globalization or the financialization of the world around them. But what else do we have to offer them?"

"And do you think that the answer is to push extreme reforms and justify them by saying we need a stable Europe? No one will buy it, especially seeing as our policies are already so far to the left. We can't go about breaking our entire social model!"

"Of course not, but how much longer can it stay like it is? Public finances are disappearing, we have six million unemployed, and benefits can no longer cope. Let's not even talk about retirement!"

"But politics is about making measured, calculated decisions!" Lavalette retorted, now enraged. "Yes, reforms are needed, but this is going too far!"

"And what if we did have more time? Isn't it time to stop avoiding these big questions? We're paying for the fact that our predecessors did just that, time and time again. Not just in France, but all nations and political colors across Europe! They've put us in a corner, and now the Chancellor doesn't want these painful decisions to be made by the French. She thinks we're incapable."

"Look, we have one week to decide what we're going to do. You understand that this must remain between us?"

"Of course."

"I'm counting on you. Try to get meetings with the UK and the Italians. If we have to announce bad news, let's find out first what's happening with our neighbors. That will help to cover the tracks, as it were. We don't want anyone questioning our change of perspective just after a visit to Berlin, right?"

"I'll take care of it, Paul."

*
* *

The Chancellor and Füller left the press room and took the elevator to the seventh floor where their offices, and those of the other government ministers, were located.

"Thank you for your help, Herr Füller. I think they got the message. I think that from the face of President Lavalette he knew we weren't in the mood to negotiate."

"Yes, we were quite persuasive indeed."

They went their separate ways. Füller closed his door and sat at his desk. After making sure that nobody could come and bother him, he opened his drawer and took out the telephone that was hidden beneath some files. He tapped in a number that couldn't be traced. The recipient picked up immediately.

"Allo!" the voice on the other end answered. "I was waiting for your call."

"It's done!" declared the Chancellor's advisor.

"Good," said the voice. "I'll let our friends know."

Füller hung up. He had accomplished his mission.

*
* *

Thursday, May 11th

The President elect was working in the office of his Paris home, waiting for the arrival of his future Prime Minister so they could take stock after the difficult meeting in Berlin. He hadn't slept well for the past few days. Not only that, he'd also been working flat out trying to form his government and giving interviews to the media. The international press had requested meetings so he could provide them with more detail about his manifesto. Various heads of state had called him, including a few minutes on the phone with the American President who had invited him to visit White House by the end of the year.

The bell rang and Paul got up to welcome his guest:

"Hello Henri!"

"Bonjour Paul..." There was an awkward silence. "Can I still call you Paul? Don't we have to be a little bit more solemn in our relations now? After all, you are the new President-in-waiting for one of the world's biggest powers. Even though we've know each other for years, your status creates a sort of distance between us, don't you think?"

"We'll see how it goes. The inauguration ceremony isn't long now. We still have some time."

"Thanks," Du Plessis replied, a little embarrassed.

"You know that we are two sides of the same coin. There cannot be any space between us. Especially after what happened in Berlin. Any separation is a weakness, and right now we need to be strong. Very strong."

"It seems from what you're saying that you've made a decision?"

"Not yet, but I've thought about it a lot, obviously. I'm still in shock from the election. It was so close. What will happen next time? If we let things get worse then it's us who will be blamed. It would be as if we handed over power to the far right."

Henri nodded his head. "In doing what we think is right, we can cause a political chain reaction that will bring about exactly what we're trying to avoid."

"Social breakdown will cause a rise in the political extremes and nothing can be done about that. We'll generate discontent, and movements on the street will be inevitable. The streets, Henri! That's the only thing that counts. If we can't explain and convince them of the reasons behind our policies, we're certain to fail. I believe that if we can get past the most difficult phase, we'll regain ground. If businesses become more competitive, employment rises again, well, then we can start to have hope again! The thing that keeps all of this going is hope. The hope of a better life."

"Are we going to be the ones who give this new hope to our nation, Paul?"

"I believe we are!"

Silence. The two men, who both knew how to put up a political fight, began to look out over the abyss they had to cross.

Paul began to think deeply to himself: "Expressing this type of political idea and having it accepted by your own party and followers is hard enough. Many have avoided it, not because it didn't fit with their ideology, but because they compromised or because it was bad for their career. Going through with this could end up destroying you. But you must think of the greater good."

The President raised his head and looked at Henri with a new passion in his eyes. They were illuminated with positivity.

"The question is: are we ready to implement what it takes to bring about this vision? It would be an enormous blow not only for our party but for the country as a whole. We'll be criticized and rejected. The level of struggle that we impose upon the people by doing this will be mirrored by the violence on the streets. But this time we cannot compromise! We cannot back down Henri!"

"We need to share this vision with the other members of the party."

"That's the last thing we want! We need to do this gently and not put all of our cards on the table at once. If we start negotiating, we'll end up with a compromise. One that has no real substance."

"We can wait some time!" the prime minister insisted, "Konrad is bluffing! Harming France would be like harming themselves. Our futures are linked."

"It's too risky. I've studied the figures and projections. I think she's right. I don't think she's lying, it's quite clear. She is correctly convinced that by avoiding sacrifices today, we are putting our futures on the line."

"But even Brussels is saying we need to end austerity and breathe some air into the national budgets. The technocrats are also beginning to worry about the rising xenophobia and the feeling of a growing distance between the member states."

"They're always going against the grain. It's demagoguery! We're going to announce that we'll balance the accounts. We're going to do it, Henri. We're going to save what we can from this system of ours. Political courage is not very fashionable nowadays, but it will be the hallmark of our term.

*
* *

6. TAREK LAID

Tarek Laid looked at himself in the mirror and was satisfied with what he saw. He wore an impeccably-ironed shirt in pristine white, a dark suit and perfectly-waxed black leather moccasins. Now forty years old, this sociologist, philosopher and recognized theoretician of the Quran had climbed the steps of the political pyramid. As an imam and preacher, Tarek was an essential figure of the Muslim community in Paris as well as throughout the rest of France. A doctor's son, he was born in Egypt and had come to France at the age of fifteen. It had now been one year since he became the rector for the Grande Mosquée de Paris. He was currently preparing himself for an appointment that he knew was of extreme importance.

A man of rather frail constitution, Laid sported a small chinstrap beard and round, golden-framed glasses that gave him the air of a teacher or an intellectual, and that suited him just perfectly. His friendly smile and measured manners could quickly put you at ease and make you feel comfortable beginning a conversation with him. He also had an innate talent for preaching. His ability to handle words made him an excellent speaker.

His interphone buzzed, letting him know that his car had arrived. He answered the phone to confirm that he was on his way, then he checked himself one last time in the mirror. He left his apartment, pressed the button and waited for the elevator that would take him downstairs.

The driver that was waiting greeted Tarek politely and opened the door to the Mercedes S Class.

Standing at 5"9, this large-shouldered man with a neck as thick as a bull's, a short-cut beard and skin that was brown from the desert sun mustn't only drive luxury cars for a living, Tarek thought to himself.

The light traffic meant they arrived quickly at the prestigious address on Rue Marbeuf. It was here, near the Avenue Georges V in a very exclusive part of Paris, that the hotel of Fouad Al-Naviq was located.

Fouad Al-Naviq, a Saudi businessman, was from one of the richest families in the Kingdom. His father was one of the close collaborators of Ibn Saoud, who founded the Kingdom of Saudi Arabia in 1933. In 1945, aboard the USS Quincy, his father was present during a meeting between President Roosevelt and Ibn Saud that took place just one week after the Yalta agreement. It was here that the United States declared itself as a protector of Saudi Arabia, promising to defend them against any exploitation of their oil wealth.

The company that would eventually become ARAMCO (Arabian Oil Company) was thus founded. In 1972, retaliating against US support for Israel during the Yom Kippur War, the Saudi government nationalized ARAMCO. The Al-Naviq family, still being close to the reigning monarchy, was granted a small stake in the company. Little did they know then that 50 years later they'd be sat on a fortune worth over $200 billion.

Producing over ten million barrels per day, ARAMCO is by far the world's largest oil producer, twice the size of Russia's Rosneft.

Its value is estimated to be $3.4 trillion, the equivalent of the total value of the ten largest companies in the world. The Kingdom of Saudi Arabia could buy, in cash: Apple, Microsoft, Exxon Mobile, Facebook, General Electric, Amazon, Wells Fargo, AT&T, Nestlé and Procter & Gamble by privatizing ARAMCO, all while maintaining control of their capital, which is around $400 billion.

Tarek Laid wondered what the businessman wanted from him. Why had he asked that they meet, considering they didn't know each other at all?

The hotel owned by the Al-Naviq family was quite simply breathtaking. The incredibly high ceiling of the vestibule, the walls that displayed paintings by Impressionist masters; all was magnificent. Old parquet floors and Murano chandeliers imposed a more baroque style that gave the ensemble a harmonious balance between traditionalism and modernity.

Tarek was immediately escorted to the private reception room of Fouad Al-Naviq. His host, sitting at a desk with oak legs topped with leather and Sicilian alabaster, stood up to greet him. The walls on either side of the entrance were lined with mauve-pink silk, interspersed with Venetian mirrors. They helped to highlight the library behind the desk. A chair of precious wood in shades of orange and upholstered with rare, ancient rug gave the whole space a touch of refinement and elegance.

"As-Salam-u-Alaikum wa rahmatullahi wa barakatuh (1), Fouad Al-Naviq!" said Tarek Laid, respectfully greeting his host as he entered the room.

"As-Salam-u-Alaikum wa rahmatullahi wa barakatuh, Tarek Laid, and welcome to my private room," a smiling Fouad Al-Naviq replied.

"Thank you for the invitation!"

— (¹) May the peace, mercy and blessings of Allah be with you.

The two men's first introductions were done using an articulate and literary form of Arabic, and Tarek soon understood that his interlocutor was more than just a businessman.

"Please, take a seat. I've taken the liberty of ordering some tea for us to enjoy while we speak," said Al-Naviq.

"Excellent!"

Fouad was well into his fifties and seriously overweight. He was dressed in a Gamis, a long traditional white robe. His head was girded by a black Agal, a kind of double hoop that embellished the outfit. His deep look of obvious intelligence cut through his baby face that was framed by a short, chinstrap beard.

They discussed various subjects for just under an hour, trying to discern each other's respective personalities, all while sipping on some traditional mint tea. Tarek happily let himself be carried along in the conversation thanks to his unlimited patience. Fouad would ask the questions that had brought him to arrange this meeting in the first place in good time. Arabic culture is bursting with wisdom, and time is infinite. Al-Naviq's servant served the tea as the two conversed. Finally, the businessman looked at Tarek intensely before starting to speak again. It was time to move on to more serious matters.

"Tarek Laid, I've followed your career for a long time. Your sermons and publications have attracted our attention," Fouad began. Spicy aromas from the mint tea surrounded them.

"Thank you, Fouad Al-Naviq, I'm honored."

"You have brought subjects that are controversial to people's attention. The place of religion in society and being tolerant to those that are not our own! There have been many animated discussions within our community."

"Do you have any questions that you'd like to ask me in particular?"

"Absolutely. I'd like to talk about your vision of Islam in our society, as you discussed in your last book."

"Yes, it's a vast subject which I've often talked about."

"Indeed. Your thinking, your ability to re-read and redefine the boundaries of an integrated Islam suitable for this time, seem to me to be essential."

"Unfortunately, this evolutionary view is not shared by the few who are radicalized."

"That is correct, however I think we need to enlarge this vision and bring it to all of the Muslims living in France!"

"I completely agree with you," Laid responded. "Bringing religious practice back into a secular society can only be beneficial to its expression."

"So why do we not begin with such a project? What is stopping us from bringing our Muslim brothers together?"

"Our community is fragmented. The youth are desperate, attracted by radicalization and endorsing an unthinking fundamentalism, while another population of Muslims has to suffer it."

"And so don't we need something, a project, that will bring everyone together and give it all some sort of sense?"

"What do you mean?"

"I think it's time to create a political force, the blueprint of a societal project. It would be something that could attract those at the periphery of society and bring them together, into the center of a common project."

"A political force? But on what basis?" asked Laid, surprised by the suggestion.

"Yes, a political force! A shared expression of a militant Islam that would give those who want to engage a platform to make their voices heard" said Fouad Al-Naviq, now very animated.

"And you thought of me?"

"Yes. I want you to take up the role! That you bring the fight for us!"

"You're offering me a future in politics?" Laid asked, totally taken aback. His tea was getting cold in front of him, but by this point he couldn't even see the mug in front of him, so engrossed was he in the discussion.

"Yes Tarek, I believe in your political destiny and I'm convinced that you're the only person capable of fulfilling this important role of unifying the Muslim population here."

Fouad was drawing up on the spot a project that would launch Tarek Laid right to the forefront of the political scene in France. But was he ready to carry a project of this magnitude on his shoulders? With what means? And when?

"I... I'm very honored by your proposal, but how can we develop and launch such a project? We would need huge support, massive financial contributions and a solid political program!"

"I'll give you all of the financial means you would need! I suggest that you start a political party to unite Muslims, all Muslims, and write a new page in the history of Islam in this country!"

"But we have to make a real plan! Develop a manifesto!"

"The manifesto is already there, and in any case, you're going to bring much more to people than this. You're going to bring them hope!"

They were interrupted. Someone was knocking at the door of Fouad Al-Naviq's private office.

"Come in!" Fouad instructed, in the type of voice that one could hear was used to giving orders.

Tarek's driver entered the room. He was carrying a message; a folded piece of paper on an exquisitely decorated tray. Fouad read the note.

"Tarek, I'd like to introduce you to Khalid Alzadi. Khalid is one of my closest collaborators. In your new role as leader, you two are going to need to be very good friends!"

"Indeed," replied Tarek, "a new political force that represents Islam is going to stir up quite a fuss in political circles."

"Fuss is such a weak word! Uproar is far more appropriate. Khalid will be your driver and he'll take you anywhere you need to go. He will be your security."

"I don't think I'll be needing a bodyguard!" replied Tarek, smiling.

"Believe me, he is indispensable to you. The more popular you become the more you will need him. You need to be aware that the media backlash against you is going to be severe in the coming weeks. Khalid will simply make sure that you are able to get on with your work without any distractions... and I'm afraid that this is not negotiable!" he added in a friendly manner.

"Well, in that case, I don't see that I have any other choice!"

"Excellent. Unfortunately, I have run out of time, I'm delighted that you have accepted this difficult challenge. I know that what we are doing for our brothers is the right thing. We will see each other again soon."

The two men said their goodbyes. Tarek was quickly escorted to the lobby. Fouad and Khalid remained in the room alone for a few seconds.

"Khalid, don't let him out of your sight. I'm counting on you!"

"Don't worry, sir. I will be his shadow."

*
* *

Tarek's arrival at the studio of a primetime television news program came not long after their meeting, throwing him quickly into the limelight. A brief handshake with the presenter who welcomed him before being shuffled into makeup. The studio team was bustling around him, trying to get the lighting just right.

Everything was like a well-oiled machine, everyone knowing exactly what they should be doing.

"The big day has come!" Tarek thought to himself. Television scared him. Any mistake was quickly jumped upon in the world of the media. He needed to be good. He needed to be better than good. His job was to convince Muslims to come out of the apathy into which the extremists had forced them. Allah would be with him. He was sure of this.

A member of the team came to get him. It was time. He got up onto the stage just out of shot. The camera was fixed on the face of the presenter which was displayed in close-up on the control screen of the studio table. They sat Tarek down. The technician silently gave him hand signals: three, two, one…

"Today we have with us Mr. Tarek Laid," the presenter announced to the camera. Turning toward Tarek, who was now smiling and relaxed, he continued:

"Tarek Laid, good afternoon. Now, you're a well-known intellectual in the Muslim community. You have an impeccable academic record and you are the grand rector at the Mosquée de Paris. You've published many works which deal with the interpretation of the Quran and now you're launching a new political party in France, a Muslim party that's called the FMP."

"That's correct. I thank you for inviting me."

"It's a pleasure to have you," the journalist replied. "You're relatively unknown by the general public, but I'm sure that this political party is going to enable you to get a lot more media exposure."

Tarek Laid was now feeling completely comfortable. It was the first time that he'd had the opportunity to speak on television at a time when there was sure to be a large audience watching. It was important to get his point across. He smiled. With his all of his experience as an Imam and his natural ability to articulate his ideas, he continued:

"The Muslim community in France has nowhere where they can express themselves. With six million Muslims in our country, it has become imperative that there be a way for them to have their voices heard, to express their political opinions."

"Of course, you understand that by launching a political party, you're going to be creating some waves, especially following the attacks of last month?"

"It's important not to get the two things confused," responded Tarek, "Muslims deplore these attacks and reject totally the barbarism of these acts. I am speaking for them. The vast majority of Muslims simply want to be considered only as regular citizens. These are the people that deserve a voice that can represent them."

"Tarek Laid, you have taken the side of the Muslim brotherhood concerning the wars in Iraq and Syria, could you explain to us in more detail your thinking regarding these subjects?"

"France has lost the battle in the Iraqi-Syrian territories. The country of so many of Les Lumières, of so much enlightened thinking, of Rousseau and Descartes… that very country refused to enter into a dialogue with these countries at the table. The result of this 'empty-chair politics' is that it left a gaping hole for Russia to come in and take the lead."

"But wasn't that due to a lack of potential interlocutors to engage in such a dialogue?"

"That's the whole problem! The spectrum of alliances on the ground ranged from the Muslim Brotherhood, who are the most moderate faction, to the Salafists who are the most radical. It's impossible to promote the ideology and universality of Western thought in an environment where it cannot be heard!"

"Tarek Laid, do you think that it's acceptable that countries from the West, and France in particular, are working on reconstructing these countries with these radical factions?"

"Again you are changing what I said. What I am saying, in essence, is that it is impossible to do it like this. I let politics decide the conduct of France, but without representation, the voice of France will not be heard! As President Lavalette has said, when you are invited to a friend's house, it is right to behave like he does while in his house. It seems to me that it works both ways. Why would you want Muslims to follow the French way, with France imposing its ideology on Muslim soil? It doesn't work like that!"

"What are the conditions like for the women there? Do you believe they should try to be integrated more into society, or are you staunchly multiculturalist? It's questions like this about society that I'm sure form the very heart of your movement?"

"That's right. It's about an evolution in society that we're going to have to accept sooner or later. Yes, Muslims have a different idea about the kind of conditions they want for the society in which they live, and yes these Muslims are French, born in France. We cannot ignore them any longer. My goal is to bring together all of the men and women who want to end the stigmatization surrounding Islam and Muslims. We will work together to construct a project that will bring about a society where everyone is included, all French people. We will build a society in which everybody can live together, in peace."

"And that's why you've chosen the slogan 'A hope for tomorrow'?"

Tarek Laid became energized upon hearing the words. Now was the time to start the machine that was going to help to propel him to the very forefront of the political scene in France. He needed to be convincing. He looked directly into the camera and began to talk.

"Yes indeed, 'A hope for tomorrow' is about all Muslims. Young people from poor areas who, with no prospects, no job, and many of whom with no practical training, want things to change. We need to become a serious political force in order to get through to the people in French society who are ignoring these millions of citizens. The French Muslim Party must position itself as an alternative to radicalization, which has become the default option for those who see no other choice except for war."

"That's for sure. Could you give us some idea regarding the timing for the launch of your party?"

"Of course! I'll be embarking on a tour of Muslim areas, concentrating much of my time in the poor city suburbs, ones that have been deemed to warrant being called be a risk and today I'd like to invite anyone who would like to be a part of this movement to join me for a meeting at the end of September in Paris."

"Tarek Laid, thank you very much!"

"Perfect," thought Tarek. The interview went exactly as he would have liked. "I hope the message got through to people. There's no going back now." The nervous tension disappeared as the studio floor team wrapped the show. The presenter approached Tarek with his hand extended to say goodbye, and added:

"You've got your work cut out for you. I don't think that all French people are going to be too happy to see this project get off the ground! Come back at the end of September, after you've had your meeting, and take us through how your tour went, OK?"

"Is that an invitation?"

"It certainly is."

"I'll be there!"

Tarek said his goodbyes to the members of the editorial team and left the stage. His new friend Khalid Alzadi was awaiting him there.

*
* *

Some successes take time to build. They may even take a lifetime. It is patience, the cement of action and time, that gives these great projects longevity and the people that drive them the strength to resist the temptation to abandon them.

For Tarek Laid, success happened immediately. It came like lightning. From the very moment he launched his party, the blogosphere and online fascist groups were sent into a frenzy. They did not let up against what they considered to be a major attack on the sovereignty of France. These people believed that Islam and Muslims were responsible for all of the ills within the country.

On Twitter, the hashtag #TAREKLAID broke records in terms of mentions, likes and retweets, even though Tarek preferred not to be central to the debate.

There were a fair few hashtags used to insult him too, of course. Some of the more popular ones included #LaidDownTarek, #TarekLied, and the very creative #FMPFuckingMuslimPricks. They were tweeted, retweeted and posted on thousands of walls. The interview was viewed millions of times in the few days following his appearance on TV. If the old adage that there's no such thing as bad publicity were true, his notoriety had come on leaps and bounds.

Tarek did everything he promised he would: visiting communities in the suburbs, going to towns and villages delivering his vision and asking for support. Following the heavy media backlash, a wave of Muslim support flooded in, not only from individuals but also mosques getting behind the movement and wanting to be involved. Although Islam lacked a clergy in the strict sense, and consequently occasionally had difficulty organizing themselves en masse, the imams and various 'spiritual guides' of the country made efforts to convince their followers to get behind Tarek Laid fully and support his cause, their cause, all the way. A few of them did believe that some of his views were too relaxed and even somewhat overly progressive, but this unique opportunity to give the Muslim community a voice on a national scale was too strong to ignore. The FMP saw its number of members skyrocket.

While all of this was happening, there was a violent and deplorable counter-movement brewing. It began with simple anti-FMP demonstrations during the public appearances of Laid, and evolved into a large-scale organized protest movement.

During a speech in Nanterre in the west of Paris on June 4th, gangs armed with baseball bats and iron bars caused mayhem, storming into the city center where the gathering was taking place. The number of injured Muslims who had come to listen to Tarek speak was countless.

On June 25th in Trappes, a commune to the north of Paris known to be a center of Islamic fundamentalism, the FMP were expecting a crowd of no less than fifteen thousand people, and security had been ramped-up accordingly. The armed forces covered the place. The meeting was to be held at the leisure park near the city center. The start of Tarek Laid's public event was planned for 2 pm, but from the middle of the morning, enthusiastic activists set up camp, bringing with them their barbecues with which they'd cook up traditional merguez sausages to share around. It was a beautiful spring day with entire families coming out to cheer on their new political leader, soak in the atmosphere and enjoy a little picnic for good measure.

At 12.30 pm, gangs dressed in black hoodies & baseball caps and armed with iron bars began to file in toward the sports center from four directions. The area upon which it was located was extremely difficult to secure due to its sheer size. The aggressors cut through the wire fence surrounding it and even approached the grounds by coming through the forest. They swept through the picnic areas attacking men, women and children while chanting racist remarks and shouting "Death to the FMP!"

The police officers who had gathered at the main points of entry were completely caught off guard. The time it took them to travel the distance to where the aggressors had gained entry meant that by the time they got there it was already too late. The assailants had planned their attack down to the last detail, making sure that it was as rapid as it was efficient and leaving absolutely nothing to chance. They had come and gone within minutes. What was supposed to be a day full of joy and celebration had turned into a living nightmare.

Injured people, cars with broken windows and windshields, overturned barbecues and fires filled the scene. There was wailing and there were tears. That's how this day ended up.

Unfortunately, the worst was yet to come. Having secured the sports center building, and after calling for backup and patrols to secure the perimeter, the police found two bodies by the side of the lake. The bodies looked like they had taken serious beatings, judging by the marks on their skin. It seemed like they had died from heavy blows. Two youths from the northwestern suburbs of Paris had been ruthlessly and brutally murdered.

That same evening, many of the young Muslims from the same suburb as the two victims headed into Paris to exact their revenge. The police did everything they could to contain them. Tarek Laid meanwhile was appearing as a guest on the 8 pm news show. He used the opportunity to urge the Muslim community not to fall into the trap of hatred and to refrain from escalating the violence. With some difficulty, the tense climate of the last few hours was somewhat calmed. Everyone was still on edge, but the worst had been avoided, at least for now.

Khalid Alzadi, the chauffer and general right-hand-man imposed upon Laid by his patron and sponsor Fouad Al-Naviq, was watching the leader of the FMP talking on television. Khalid had been working for Fouad for many years and held an admiration for the Saudi businessman that knew no limits. His own family had worked for the hyper-rich Al-Naviq family for generations and had always been well treated. Khalid enlisted in the Saudi army when he was twenty years old and held the role of field officer. He'd served in numerous theatres of war and so was well versed in combat situations. He was untouchable at bareknuckle fighting but could also handle handguns and knives with superlative expertise. Al-Naviq had hired him to undertake missions which would not generally have been categorized as official. A few of them meant dealing with undesirables. He was ready to give his life to serve his mentor.

However, he didn't feel even remotely the same about Tarek Laid. In fact, he took him for a traitor. To listen to him explaining to French Muslims how they should simply abide by the laws of this country, while watching their brothers thousands of miles away being killed, was totally and utterly unacceptable to him. To let their daughters go to school dressed as whores and to say that it was ok to miss prayers was simply inconceivable. Even worse, it was admitting that the laws of this country were above those of the Prophet. This man was dangerous.

But if Fouad Al-Naviq was behind all of this, then there must have been some greater reason and so he would do nothing to contradict his master. If it were up to him however... it would suffice to say that he hated Laid.

After his appearance on television was over, Tarek Laid shook a few hands and walked toward Khalid.

"Another long day done," he sighed.

"I can see you're tired, sir!" replied Khalid, smiling.

"I'm exhausted, Khalid. Shall we go?"

"Come out of the main door in five minutes, I'll bring the car around."

"Thank you, Khalid, you're truly a great help to me."

"It's nothing, Sir," Khalid replied, as he left to get his vehicle.

*
* *

July 17th, Paris - Lavalette / Tarek Laid

"Mr. Tarek Laid!"

The voice of the butler echoed in the antechamber of the presidential office.

"Come in!" Paul Lavalette replied.

Tarek Laid was shown into the Holiest of Holies, the place where the President met with very important guests and close collaborators to hold confidential meetings. Like everyone, he had seen images of the presidential office many times, but the majesty of the place, as well as the weight of history, gave the room a very particular solemnity. Lavalette smiled at Tarek, stood up to greet him and offered him a warm handshake. There were a number of files piled upon the presidential desk. "He cleared some space in his agenda to see me," Tarek thought to himself. "No doubt he's got a few things he wants to talk to me about!"

"Please, take a seat Mr. Laid," the President said, offering him one of the two armchairs arranged on either side of a coffee table decorated with a bouquet of flowers. "I'm delighted to meet you. We haven't yet had the opportunity to talk, but I think the time has come for us to discuss a little about the future."

"Indeed, Mr. President."

"Judging by your recent media appearances, you've succeeded where many before you have failed by bringing together and unifying the thoughts of your community. It's for this reason that you are to be considered a serious political force and therefore having a dialogue with you is absolutely necessary."

"Here we go!" thought Tarek. This was without doubt the first time in the history of France that the head of state was reaching out to the Muslim community in the hope of finding some sort of agreement. It was politically motivated of course, but it would be an agreement nonetheless. It remained to be seen just what the boundaries of this dialogue would be.

"The recent FMP meetings have been an undeniable success. Fifteen thousand supporters came to see you in Trappes. Soon you'll be able to fill the national stadium! I sincerely condemn the violence you suffered from the members of the outrageous radical right. I fear that you've caused a new type of vocation to appear: political hooliganism!" The two men laughed, before Paul began talking again, this time in a serious manner:

"You are aware that the last election was traumatic for this country. We were very close to seeing the Front National in power."

"Yes, Mr. President. That's one of the reasons I decided to found the FMP and to offer 'A hope for tomorrow' as a response to what could have become catastrophic for French Muslims."

"I think that this country needs you! You are putting up a barrier against the extreme, and that is why we must move forward together."

"Do you have an idea of how us working together might look?"

"Yes, but before discussing it in more detail, could you explain a little bit more about how you see your party developing, and its position in the national political spectrum?"

"With six million Muslims in this country, it seems reasonable to estimate that around three or four million will vote at the next election. All of them will be holding the FMP manifesto in their hands. But this is only the first step. There is such a thirst for expression that I envisage an unprecedented mobilization of the Muslim community."

"So, if I'm to understand this correctly, you see the FMP as a party of power, not as a political force that wants to see French society move forwards and evolve?"

"Absolutely! The proportion of Muslims in certain communities means that we will be able to gain power there as soon as we have the next local elections. Many of these places are around the outskirts of Paris, while of course Marseille and many other towns and cities in the South will support us. And let's not forget those places in the North."

"Right," said Lavalette. "In that case, you'll have to solve the problem of Islam being incompatible with the laws of the Republic!"

"Muslims could have a future with the republicans if something is proposed to them in which their identity is protected."

"So your vision is in fact to change our society! But will we be able to accept, and do we even want these changes?"

"The way I see it, Mr. President, is that sooner or later our communities are all going to have to make some kind of effort to ensure that we are able to live peacefully together. We need to determine what components are required for the Muslims of this country to have a 'positive social identity'. This will form the foundation of a new and unified society."

"Maybe that's exactly the type of work we should be doing in common, rather than going down the route of having another revolution!"

"But that's exactly what the whole world is experiencing! A revolution! In the Middle East of course, but also on the doorstep on Europe. We've already seen anarchy, communism and fascism have their time."

"But communism, just like fascism, was defeated, unless I've missed something?"

"It was. They were. But the Islamist revolution is based on a unique truth. The law of God."

"That makes it more legitimate?"

"Which in any case makes things far more difficult to change, without a doubt."

"Mr. Laid, in the event of a political victory in the suburbs for your movement at the next local elections, how are you going to manage the upswing in radicalism?"

"Mr. President, I'm a man who believes in progress. We need to learn to walk before we can run. It will take some trial and error, involving a few mistakes along the way, before we can advance. We are creating a progressive Islam in the heart of our cities. That is our aim."

"What we don't want to happen is that even more people become marginalized. People who have already been affected by the rupture of the republicans."

"I am aware of this Mr. President. Believe me, I am aware."

There was a silent pause. A palpable sign of the ideological gap that separated them. Between this right-wing man of sixty and this young Arab intellectual, the differences, even civilized ones, remained alive. Would they be able to build a common project together?

The two politicians agreed to meet again in September to start working on a schedule. The President wanted to take charge of things. The trauma of the past election was still fresh in his mind. Tarek Laid left the Palais de l'Elysée discreetly, the Head of State not wishing at this stage to appear publicly with the sulphurous FMP. Tarek found Khalid Alzadi and got into his car. He began to go over in his head what had just been discussed during the meeting with Lavalette.

Firstly, the President wanted the FMP to become a political force; he was not in any way opposed to it. This probably solved the President's immediate problem with the Front National. By bringing a new population to the polling stations, he was mathematically weakening the nationalist party. There would be more voters in total, therefore fewer percentage votes for the FN. It was also going to siphon votes from the Left to the National Front. It was all going to be of benefit to Lavalette. The coming elections would be contested mainly between the traditional right and the extreme right, and so again he would receive another batch of additional votes. Not only that, but by working to find new solutions for Muslim integration in France, he hoped to position himself as the unifying candidate that he hadn't managed to do in the previous election. "This man is clever," thought Tarek Laid. "But I am, too. My political destiny is taking shape and if our meeting in September is a success, I'll be sure I'm ready for any opening in parliament." The planets were aligning, and Tarek felt he was only at the very beginning of his ascent.

He still had to solve one fundamental problem: that of his conscience. He knew deep down that Islam, as many of its followers saw it, was a religion which by its nature was above the laws of the republic. Tarek was fighting to convince himself of the merits of his fight. The ancestral anchoring of belief, as well as certain practices, could not be dictated by the Civil Code. There was a gaping gap that he had to fill.

*
* *

Saturday September 23rd – Meeting

Tarek Laid was feeling good. He'd come a long way since the formation of the FMP. The incredible success had caught him off guard, however, as had the media response. He imagined that after the launch there would be a gentle rise in popularity as they approached the elections. There hadn't been many people at the first few meetings, but the acts of violence against them had galvanized the community, bringing in large numbers of Muslims who saw a way to show their unity in Tarek and the FMP. As he had mentioned to President Lavalette, he'd succeeded in creating a positive social identity. The press and the TV stations didn't report on it, but they could no longer deny it. The evidence was there that there was a latent demand for representation from the Muslim community in France.

The Stade de France, the country's national stadium, had been preparing to host the FMP for several days. This meeting would be the high point of the party's launch. They'd already had one million membership registrations. The mosques had relayed the message and the inscriptions had skyrocketed. So much so that Tarek could claim now to be leader of the number one party in France.

The death threats and incessant insults on Twitter and other blogs had not changed his mindset or his commitment. "They wouldn't go so far as to kill me anyway. They don't want a martyr on their hands!"

His campaign had been peppered with scuffles and clashes. Although his meetings were now all largely secure, incidents like at Nanterre or Trappes were still possible. They had to remain vigilant. The radicals on the right wanted to scare his supporters. This ridiculous approach would not stop people from believing in a future, but it helped to associate the FMP with anger and violence, things that Tarek wanted to avoid at all costs.

At 11:00 am, Laid went onstage for the sound test. His speech was scheduled for 2 pm. He'd chosen to hold the event early in the afternoon so that everyone could still return home by public transport. Many of his supporters didn't have a driving license, let alone the means to buy a car. The Muslim community was not the richest in the country.

By noon, clashes between Muslims, thugs, skinheads and other radicals had already begun outside of the stadium. The Muslims had clearly decided that they would go blow for blow with their attackers. The shops were closed on Saturday, and the police had requested that all shutters be closed. Despite this request, shop windows were broken and many people were once again wounded.

Gangs armed with clubs, bats and knuckle dusters blended into the crowds as they left the train station before the police could intervene, dispersing immediately. It meant that making arrests was almost impossible. The police still somehow miraculously kept control of the situation.

The event was held amid high tension, yet the crowds kept on coming. They had hoped that twenty-five thousand people would show up. It was going to be far more than that.

Tarek Laid made his way onto the stage at 2 pm sharp. He was greeted with an ovation. He found it immensely difficult to remain calm and manage the wave of emotions that were almost overwhelming him. This impatient, ambitious man who was so close to his community savored the moment. He waited for several seconds that seemed like minutes, before taking the floor.

He knew his subject by heart. He began by thanking all those who had made the trip, then Allah who had given him strength. Then, as he did during his sermons using his cleverly poised and warm voice, he articulated his political project.

He spoke continuously for almost an hour and a half. He alternated between French and Arabic. The people before him were Muslim, so it was necessary to identify with them, but also to express oneself using a vocabulary that was comprehensible to all. Many of his supporters were young and from the suburbs and their Arabic was often not particularly advanced. It was another sign of the instability of this poorly integrated group that considered themselves neither French nor Arab. They had been unable to understand the subtleties of French culture and found nothing within it that they could identify with, or hold on to, as theirs.

He ended his speech by urging all FMP members to come together for the next election. Meanwhile, he would be handing the President a document that contained the fifty resolutions for 'A hope for tomorrow', which would bring communities together and build the foundations of a united France.

During Tarek's speech, his chauffeur Khalid Alzadi had received a call on his second phone. It was a prepaid device that he always carried with him. It was a private number.

"Yes?" asked Khalid.

"The time has come," said the voice that Khalid recognized immediately.

"Today?"

"Yes."

"Inshallah!" replied Khalid.

They hung up.

Tarek came down from the stage. He was exhausted. He spoke for a good while with the event organizers and other personalities backstage, thanking everyone for their hard work and telling them that it was thanks to them that this day had been, without any doubt, an incredible success.

Khalid Alzadi helped Tarek Laid into the Mercedes and closed the door. He got into the driver's seat and fastened his seatbelt.

"Take me home Khalid! I've got no meetings for now and I'd really like to go and get a little rest."

"OK sir," replied Khalid, looking at his watch. It was already 5 pm.

The Mercedes left the stadium's VIP parking lot. Tarek couldn't stop thinking about his meeting with President Lavalette on July 17th and wondered what the president was thinking now. It was he who had joked about filling the Stade de France. "He didn't think that I would actually be able do it," thought Tarek. They'd been driving for fifteen minutes and were now coasting alongside the banks of the Seine.

"Sir, do you have your seatbelt on?"

"Of course, Khalid. As always. Why do you ask?"

"I think we're being followed. The two cars behind have been with us since we left the stadium."

Tarek turned around and saw two black vans following them closely. He wasn't scared. He was sure that, no matter what their objective was, they would be unable to do anything to him. He was now so visible and implicated in the political scene that he was effectively untouchable. If he were to disappear, it would cause more problems than good for the likes of the groups who had hurled abuse at him on the Internet or who had caused mayhem at his events. Creating a martyr would only serve to accelerate what was already in progress. They knew very well that killing the messenger wouldn't kill the message. Tarek Laid was simply the spokesperson for the millions of people he represented.

One of the vehicles suddenly accelerated past them, while the other positioned itself to their left, just as they were beginning to cross the bridge. There was virtually no traffic on the road, which was a little unusual for a Saturday. The van that was now in front of them braked suddenly, forcing Khalid to stop violently in the middle of the bridge.

Tarek's heart was pounding. Two men armed with metal bars got out of the van in front and headed toward the Mercedes. Two more men then appeared from the side door of the second van.

The four hooded assailants approached with an aggressive determination. Tarek was now beginning to get scared. They had the sidewalk blocked and any attempt at escaping would be impossible. Trying to run would be suicide; they had him covered from both sides.

Khalid leaned forward and in a flash had removed the handgun that was in his glove box. The stocky, powerful man opened the driver's side door and his sheer speed of movement surprised everyone, including Tarek. He understood very quickly why the Saudi businessman kept Khalid so close to him. This man was a soldier. A very highly trained soldier.

The two attackers who came out of the van on the driver's side had no idea what was happening to them when Khalid attacked.

They thought they would have the element of surprise on their side, and that fear would give them the edge over Tarek and his driver. But the soldier they were up against had served in enough operations to know that it was the aggressor who always conceded the advantage.

Khalid was face to face with the first two assailants. He unleashed a roundhouse kick and floored the first one with ease. His gun was still in his right hand. The second lifted his arm to strike Khalid with the metal bar.

As all of this was happening, the two men that had exited the van in front were making their way toward the fight. They hesitated. Do they go directly and get Tarek, which is the objective of their mission, or go and help out their two colleagues who seemed to be having a serious struggle?

They chose to give their two associates a hand.

As the second attacker was about to strike with the metal bar, Khalid pointed his weapon at him and fired once. The light in the hooded man's eyes disappeared. The last emotions displayed in them were surprise and fear. He fell, dead before he hit the floor.

The other attacker on the ground tried to get to his feet but was struggling due to the immense pain. Khalid had burst his spleen. He couldn't continue and was trying to get back to the van. He fled without even acknowledging his colleagues.

When Khalid's gunshot rang out, the two men walking toward the action paused. They looked at each other and the confusion in their eyes betrayed the fear inside them. Khalid turned his attention to them. One more second passed.

After their hesitation, the two assailants decided that the only option was to take the fight to Khalid. Each one lifted their iron bars simultaneously and ran in the direction of the soldier.

The whole time that this was going on, Tarek was sat in the Mercedes trying to figure out what he should do. He was completely out of his depth. Getting out to fight would achieve nothing. It was also too dangerous to try and escape. He decided he would leave his bodyguard to take care of the present situation, then he would take care of what they should do next.

The two hooded men attacked Khalid at the same time. There was little gap between their van and the car, so they couldn't engage in combat from the front. One of them went to the side while the other remained facing the Mercedes. Khalid skillfully evaded the charge of the first man. He turned his body in order to dodge the blow and readied himself to fight the attacker, who was now on his left side. It wasn't going to be easy; this one seemed more highly trained than the rest of the gang. The attacker kicked him, surprising Khalid. He dropped his gun, letting it fall to the ground.

"Not as confident now without your gun are you, motherfucker? You're going to die, bitch!" the man shouted after he landed the kick.

Khalid smiled. He took the knife that he always had hidden strapped to his right ankle. He took two paces back and composed himself.

"Allah is on my side!" he responded.

"Let's see how Allah is going to save your ass now, prick!"

"Let's fucking do it!" the second shouted.

They attacked together, both with their iron bars raised, shouting as if it would give them strength or courage. The first one swung for Khalid. Once again, the soldier managed to avoid the shot, and the assailant stumbled forwards, carried forward by the weight of his weapon and the momentum of his attack. Khalid cut his throat as he passed. It was a move he'd performed many times before. The cries turned into gargles, the blood splattered onto the Mercedes. He fell to the ground, holding his neck with two impotent hands.

The last remaining fighter heard the van behind him begin to accelerate. He realized that the man who had just hit the ground had ordered the driver to leave in the seconds before his demise. He ran toward the vehicle as it drove away, banging on the side of the doors. The van sped off and left him alone in the middle of the road.

In the meantime, Khalid had picked up his handgun. The man turned back toward the Saudi. He'd just seen his best chance of escape leave him for dead. He froze as he saw Khalid holding his gun once again, watching him, full of hatred.

"Please! Have mercy!" the man said, falling to his knees.

"Why should I?" Khalid replied coldly.

The shot echoed. The unarmed assailant seemed to transform into a marionette without strings and crumpled to the ground in slow motion.

Tarek couldn't believe what he was witnessing. How could Khalid execute a man like this? It was obvious that the man was surrendering. It was inconceivable that someone could do such a thing. He opened the door of the car and got out onto road. He ran in the vague direction the Saudi, feeling a dull rage mounting inside of him. Khalid was meanwhile picking up the metal bars.

"No, but, what .... this is...just disgusting!" Tarek shouted as he reached his driver. "How can you execute someone who is giving himself up to you?"

"These dogs deserve only death."

"But this is murder! Do you even realize that you've just murdered someone? In cold blood!"

Khalid smiled. "That's not a good sign," thought Tarek. "How could anyone who had just done that smile?" It was all becoming surreal. Moments ago he was in front of thousands of people trying to convey a message of peace and solidarity, yet now here he is, in the middle of the road with three dead bodies and a smiling sociopathic murderer. Khalid walked toward him. In his eyes was all of the hatred that the Saudi had from the first moment he met this proud preacher who didn't respect the teachings of the Prophet.

Tarek understood that he too was about to die.

"Allah Akbar!" said Khalid Alzadi as he slammed the bar into Tarek's skull.

His head exploded on impact. His last thought was that "we are always betrayed by our own." The black descended upon him, the abyss was now his kingdom.

When he returned to the car, the soldier Khalid Alzadi took out the prepaid phone upon which he had received the orders during Tarek Laid's speech and dialed a private number.

The recipient answered after the first ring.

"It's done," said Alzadi, calmly.

"Excellent!" replied the voice.

"In fact, we had a little help. We were attacked on our way back from the stadium. Laid's murder will go down as being done by activists. The radical right, no doubt."

"As always, Allah is with us! Call the police immediately!"

"Yes sir."

Alzadi took out his official phone and called the police. His other phone was thrown over the bridge and would end up at the bottom of the Seine.

*
* *

"Hello!" the dry sounding voice of Paul Lavalette answered.

The President was working at his desk in the Palais de l'Élysée at the end of this Sunday afternoon. He was concentrating as he read a memo from Bercy that contained the unemployment statistics for September. They were bad. Really bad.

"Mr. President, it's the Prime Minister's residence. I'm putting you through to the Prime Minister."

"Paul?" the worried voice of Henri du Plessis asked.

"Good evening Henri, what's going on?" responded the president, who had understood from his friend's tone of voice that all was not well.

"I've just been speaking with the Interior Ministry. I've got some bad news."

"Is it serious?"

"Tarek Laid has been assassinated."

The news was met with silence, that after a few seconds Lavalette became the one to break.

"When?"

"Let me see. It's 6.30 pm… it's been about an hour, maybe less."

Silence again. The President was thinking.

"Do you have any details?"

"Nothing yet, Paul. From the very first pieces of evidence they've managed to obtain, it seems that Laid and his driver were attacked while driving along the river on their way back from the Stade de France."

"Do we know who did it? Do we have any leads?"

"Well, it would appear that the chauffeur gave it everything in trying to defend his client. From what we know at this moment, there were six attackers and he managed to kill three of them. Three others escaped. The investigators took prints from the scene and found records. The attackers seemed to be members of the far-right movement, Résistance Républicaine."

"Idiots!" The President couldn't hold in his anger.

"I called to let you know, but also so we could decide upon a plan of action. It's going to cause a major reaction when this is announced. You know very well how popular Tarek Laid was."

"I know. I also liked him a lot. We saw each other a few weeks ago and we'd decided that we would work together on the problem of integrating these young people. He was an honest man, engaged in something he believed in. He wasn't like one of these wind-vane politicians, facing in whichever direction the wind was blowing."

"The Interior is concerned that the already palpable tension after the attacks during the FMP demonstrations will result in a rise in intercommunal violence. They think that the people in the suburbs will set fire to anything and everything."

"When will it be made official?"

"In the 8 o'clock news…"

"Good God, that doesn't leave us much time to get ourselves organized!"

"The Interior Minister will need to speak tonight at 8 pm," said Lavalette. "Call the speech writers. We need to use clear language that indicates our outrage and confirms all the police are working on it. Maybe we should keep the possible perpetrators to ourselves, for the moment at least, don't you think?"

"I agree, Paul. I'll contact the Minister and let you know if we have any more news."

"Henri?"

"Yes Paul?"

"We need to meet with representatives from the French Council of Muslim Worship tomorrow. Can you organize the meeting as soon as possible? Everyone is going to want to have his say on this one. We need keep control of the situation as much as possible. This is going to blow up like nothing else in the media."

"I know Paul… I have a call, it's the Interior. I'll leave you for now, but I'll keep you updated as soon as anything happens."

The leading story of every 8 o'clock news show covered 'The Tarek Laid Affair'. There were images of Laid giving his speech on the stage of the Stade de France in front of a dense and attentive crowd. They reviewed the sudden and astonishing success of the party launched by this "new kind" of politician. Hundreds of images showing these thousands of Muslims, mostly of a young age, who regarded Tarek Laid as a prophet; as the one who would make things change; the one to rebalance the scales that had never tilted in their favor.

As expected, there was an endless parade of indignant commentators, some sincere, others not so much. Real friends and fake friends, people who were truly close to Tarek Laid and those who just wanted to pretend they were. President Lavalette shuddered as he watched on his television.

He realized how blind and insensitive they were to what was happening before their eyes. His keen sense of politics told him that all these young people would take this loss as an affront. Paul Lavalette, alone in the presidential lounge on this Saturday, September 23rd, felt that a black veil now covered the country.

*
* *

Sunday, September 24th – Paris

The phone was ringing as Pauline Rougier, Commander of the Counter Terrorist Brigade, opened the door to her office. She quickly tried to remove her handbag which promptly fell to the floor.

"Shit!" she said as she picked the phone up.

"I'm sorry?"

"No! Err, Commander Rougier speaking!"

"Pauline? Hi. It's Delmas, from the criminal brigade police."

"Delmas?" Pauline asked, a little surprised. "Ah bonjour François!"

"How are you, Pauline?"

"I'm great. It's been a long time!"

"Almost three years."

"Already?"

"Yep... the network was dismantled in 2014."

Pauline knew François Delmas well, having worked with him on numerous occasions while she was still in drug enforcement. He was a man of about fifty years of age. He was a good professional, well liked by his teams. They'd previously combined their forces to combat a group of smugglers who were funding terrorists. After a year of hard work, they managed to bring down the members of a large trafficking network, making a record seizure of cannabis in the process. Pauline joined the CTB partly thanks to the result of this high-profile case.

"What can I do for you François?"

"I'm in charge of the Tarek Laid case."

"And what a case it is!"

"Yeah. I can't even begin to tell you the amount of political pressure that comes as baggage. You saw how they reacted in the streets. I need to nail this one, fast."

"So what do you need from me?"

"I've just read your report about the May 1st attacks."

"And what did you find?"

"We've just completed a search of Tarek Laid's home and I came across a number of confidential documents that he had locked away in his safe."

"What type of documents?"

"Financial. He apparently had a lot of investors who had an interest in his political career. He'd received many millions of Euros via a Swiss bank account."

"A Swiss bank?" asked Pauline.

"Yes, and that's why I'm calling you. He received vast sums of money via the Zurich Investments & Securities Bank, the same one that's associated with the attacks on May 1st. There are also some financial movements involving a company called Millenium Dust."

"OK?"

"Have you heard of Millenium Dust, Pauline?"

"Never, why?"

"Well, it's a little complicated to explain by telephone," said Delmas, "so we're going to need to meet as soon as possible. A Swiss man, named Thomas Delvaux, contacted me this morning and told me a story that's a little, let's say, unbelievable. But whaddya know? Zurich Investments and Securities and Millenium Dust got mentioned. I'm meeting him in a café at 11 am near HQ. He said he wants to be discreet."

"Zurich Investments and Millenium? Things are getting pretty big here."

"Right! So seeing as we worked together in 2014 and I could really do with some help on this, I was just hoping that you might be able to back me up for this meeting with Delvaux. Maybe he'll have something that could be good for both of our cases."

"You think these two companies could be linked to the attacks?"

"Really, I don't know at all. Tarek Laid often had meetings at an address in Courbevoie, just outside the city. It is the same address that Millenium is registered at. It's enough to get me curious. Will you come with me? We're meeting at Soleil d'Or, near my office."

"I'll be there François, thank you for letting me know."

Pauline couldn't figure out what the relationship between a dead terrorist and a rising-star politician might have been. Nor the roles that a Swiss bank and an investment firm might have played in a terrorist attack. What she did know, however, was that there was enough evidence to suggest it could be related. And that did not bode well.

*
* *

Part two:

Anti Game

7. JACK CAMPBELL

Monday, September 18th – New York

Jack Campbell had been an economics journalist at the New York Times since 2005.

His daily coverage of the subprime crisis had given him his moment of glory. Thanks to him, readers were able to follow the story of the collapse of Lehman Brothers as live witnesses. He described the disasters that befell the derivatives market every day in a column that had become famous in Manhattan. As the offices of Wall Street emptied a little more day after day, he would interview the dazed employees. These people who had now, as one, been plunged into their own poverty, left their offices with incredulous looks on their faces, escorted by security guards, holding in their arms a box that contained their office knick-knacks: family photos, degree certifications, employee of the month awards, and so on. They were a pathetic image of the world of luxury and vanity that never found its limit. An evanescent Tower of Babel.

Jack loved to hammer home the point that simply cutting the debt into smaller pieces didn't make it go away. Smaller shareholders and modest households were the hardest hit. When they found themselves with $2.2 trillion of debt to be repaid on the evening of September 15th, 2008, most were completely ruined. The crisis had meant five million people were forced to give up their homes.

Now forty-three years old, Jack would have liked a job that gave him the kind of lifestyle that let him enter retirement age serenely. That didn't happen; journalism wasn't exactly relaxing work. He spent most of his time behind a desk writing articles that weren't even published. Deadlines were a daily stress trigger.

Standing at six feet five with brown wiry hair and an athletic build, this giant of a man could easily be described as attractive. The gray hair around his temples only added to his allure.

Jack had grown up in an apartment in downtown San Francisco before attaining a master's degree in economics and mathematics at Stanford University. He'd entered into journalism after graduating in order to try and make a good living, but he stayed in for the love of it. His first job in the early 2000s was to gather all kinds of information for journalists at the San Francisco Chronicle. Within two years, he became the go-to source for all of the editorial staff, dishing out facts and figures that hacks would include in their all-too insipid articles that were only legitimized by the quality of the information provided by Jack. If you wanted to know how many cops there were per capita, which businesses were the cleanest in California, or how many single-parent families there were in San Francisco, you just had to ask Jack.

His enthusiasm helped him to meet Jenny, another newspaper employee. They'd gotten together after only a few months and enjoyed a passion that united them for two memorable years. Their daughter Hailey, a cheerful baby, was born in the summer of 2000. She was six months old when it happened.

Jack didn't see the truck, even though he was driving slowly. He wouldn't have been able to avoid it anyway, he'd cut him off at full speed. There was no way that he could have known that the truck, with its drunk driver at the wheel, would have been there at that moment. It was a one in one hundred thousand chance. The impact on the right side of the vehicle was extremely violent. The paramedics told him over and over again that it wasn't his fault it and that he was lucky to be alive. How can you be lucky though when you've just lost your child?

Their marriage had been in crisis. Jenny couldn't cope with it all. They'd separated, and the entire story ended abruptly in January, 2001.

At first, he thought he'd be able to manage by himself, that he'd be able to put everything behind him and carry on alone. That's when he started drinking. At the beginning it was just from time to time, to forget and to take away the pain. Then it became a habit. Without really knowing how, he became an alcoholic and spent many years battling it with the help of Alcoholics Anonymous on Broadway, which he visited two evening per week. He'd been sober for six months. Not exactly something to write home about, but it was a start.

He walked into the editorial room at 8 am like he did every morning with his Starbucks coffee cup in his hand. Every morning without fail he'd get his double latte.

He took off his jacket and as he was putting down his briefcase his phone began to ring.

"Jack."

"Morning Jack, how's it going?"

Jack knew the voice on the other end immediately. It was that of Thomas Delvaux.

"Thomas! Good to hear from you! It's been a long time!"

Thomas Delvaux and Jack had been friends since meeting during a press conference at CERN (Centre européen de recherche Nucléaire). Located on the Franco-Swiss border, it is one of the biggest and most prestigious scientific laboratories in the world. The research center had invited journalists from all over the world to attend the conference, and Jack had had to fill in for one of his colleagues who hadn't been able to attend. He didn't understand too much when it came to nuclear physics, but seeing as he was the only journalist on the team who had even the slightest scientific education, he was asked to go and see what he could get.

And so he met Thomas Delvaux, a Franco-Swiss mathematician. After having abandoned research ten years ago,

Delvaux had founded FraNex, a company specializing in the development of high-performance algorithms that enabled the analysis of high-frequency financial transactions. A partner with all major banking institutions throughout the world, Delvaux had made a name for himself in the financial community and his company was now worth many, many millions of Swiss francs.

"I hope you're well! I haven't heard very much from you! How's it going on your side of the Atlantic? Your new president hasn't banned you from spending dollars overseas yet, has he? Still thinks he doesn't need anyone and that Uncle Sam can get along by himself?"

Jack, amused by Thomas' banter, replied:

"Hi Thomas. No, we're still a part of the world and he hasn't built a wall on the Mexico border, and as far as I can see we still get Chinese imports. At least, we do for now! Anyway, I'm pretty sure you aren't calling me to talk about our president. And you know for sure that I'm a Republican!"

"Of course! I know you're one of those awful colonizing, speculating Republicans! I bet you're even a member of the Tea Party, right?"

"Ha. Ha. Ha." Jack emphasized each syllable. "This is coming from a Swiss guy, from the country where the national sport is money laundering?"

"Alright Jack… that's enough joking around. I'm calling to see if you'll do me, and maybe even yourself, a favor."

"Go on... I'm all ears!"

"You recall that I'm a specialist in high frequency trading?"

"Of course. Automated trading, stuff like that?"

"Yep, that's basically what it is. You know that these trades are the lifeblood of the financial markets?"

"Absolutely! And seeing as there are millions of them done each day, we leave it to robots."

"You got it. If you were to buy shares in a raw material, or in fact whatever, you'd do it via the local exchange. But did you know that seventy percent of the transactions in your country are done between private parties directly? They don't go through the national stock exchange and they're managed by computers located in private server centers, and all this is called the Dark Pool?"

"It didn't realize that it was that significant," said Jack, surprised by Delvaux's revelations about the financial system. "But what does that change about the financial world?"

"It's here where the system is opaque. For the most part it's hedge funds that are doing the trading, generally speculatively, buying and selling for hundreds of billions each day on behalf of people who clearly wish to remain anonymous!"

"So, if I understand correctly, trades are done which are outside the control of the national system. But we knew that already, so where's the story?"

"Alright, alright! I'm getting to that. Have you ever heard of the Guerilla or Sniper algorithms from Credit Suisse or Goldman Sachs?"

"Never."

"They're computer programs used by banks to manipulate the financial markets."

"Manipulate?"

"Yes, manipulate, Jack. When an order is made to buy or sell, it leaves a trace. It's a visible order."

"I see."

"So if you have the technology available that's able to recognize these transactions, and if you can get yourself into the mix just before they're executed, even if they're just tiny, tiny gains, if you do it thousands of times a second you can imagine how it accumulates into colossal amounts of money."

"I think I get it. Someone is selling a share at $10. But its rate is fluctuating between $9.98 and $10.02. So when I see a demand for a sale at $10, I buy at $9.99 and sell it at $10 immediately? Getting $0.01 profit per share. Is that right?"

"Exactly. It's like a form of tax. A tax taken by the banks for share transactions. Gone are the days when crooks came and stole from your safe. These days you take just a tiny little bit, but from the entire world. All. The. Time. No one really notices, and it's virtually undetectable."

"No one is doing anything about this?" asked the journalist.

"We have the Securities Exchange Commission, the stock market police over there in the US. It takes them months though to analyze only three seconds of trades, making their efforts to exert any type of control pretty pathetic."

"But tell me, Thomas, why aren't the major share buyers up in arms about this? The giant hedge funds? Surely they're losing a lot of money through all this?"

"You're asking the right questions. That's a sensitive subject right there. Imagine, you're a hedge fund manager. You're in control of billions of dollars, and they ask you to be part of something that takes from others. What do you do? You know that you can't stop the system from existing, so you try to benefit from it. You develop your own algorithm with the help of specialists, or you use the one made by the bank which you believe is more effective."

"Eat or be eaten huh? At the very least just don't let your piece of the pie get taken by someone else!"

"You understand that given the size of the fraud involved, which to some extent is legal, they've got firewalls and other types of protection in place."

"They've got a way to defend themselves?"

"Pretty much! To get rid of competition, their computers inundate the system with fake orders. A kind of background noise, if you like, that hides the real transactions."

"Ok, so I get the basics of what's going on here, but where are you going with this?"

"I'm getting to that! My company is specialized in analyzing the traces of these high-frequency financial transactions and my own savoir faire is being able to find out where the real ones among the millions of others are being issued from. Thanks to my algorithm, I can find out who, what and how much. This is the service I provide to banks."

"Right! Now I understand how you were able to get that beautiful house on Lake Zurich!"

"It's true that I am one of the links in this giant chain... but I've noticed something happening that is so intriguing I had to give you this call. I've only analyzed the last twelve months.

Because of how many transactions there are, I was only able to look that far back, but there's nothing to suggest that this wasn't all going on before then."

"What was happening? You're talking like a politician…and that's not a good thing these days."

"Forgive me. I found that there's a company, a totally unknown fund that I can't find any trace of and for the last twelve months they've been buying shares in incredible quantities for various sums, without ever selling! I've done some research and asked specialists involved with speculating funds, but no one has any information on them. They've never even heard of them."

"What's the name of this fund?"

"Millenium Dust."

"How much are we talking?"

"Right now, about one hundred billion dollars."

"Wait. One hundred billion dollars? No. You said million, right?"

"Billion, Jack."

"Jesus, Thomas! That's huge! So you can simply hide a hundred billion dollars and no one is any the wiser?"

"Perhaps you know this already, but there are around two hundred and eighty billion orders each day on the stock exchanges. Now that seventy percent are going through Dark Pool… yeah it's a lot of money but it's completely possible."

"Incredible!" Jack couldn't believe what he was hearing.

"In this exact case, the shares are always bought in thousands of different transactions which are then abandoned. They're smart enough to hide what they're really up to by creating fake orders. That's how they've managed to stay invisible, until I stumbled upon what was going on by chance."

"And here I was thinking that since the crisis in 2008 they'd decided to make things a little more transparent! I mean, what do you think about all this?"

"When you realize that the largest hedge fund in the world is worth around a hundred billion dollars and that the top ten are about four hundred billion in total, it's very worrying."

"What do you think they're trying to achieve?"

"I've got no idea, but if I was trying to hide massive amounts of money that would sit quietly until I was ready to unleash it onto the markets, that's how I'd do it!"

"Like for some kind of hostile takeover or something?"

"Yeah but these guys could even launch a hostile attack on an entire country! They've got enough money to have a seriously destabilizing effect on any nation's stock market."

"It's making me shudder," replied Jack.

"I was thinking that seeing as it's not too far from where you are, you might want to go and check it out? Perhaps with your journalistic senses you might be able to figure out what they're up to hiding a one hundred-billion-dollar fund though micro transactions. What do you think?"

"Let's say that you've got me curious. Where do I find these people?"

"Take a wild guess. They're on Wall Street. I'll send you the address that I found."

"Thank you. I'm gonna check this out and get back to you right away."

Jack hung up. Just as he was getting up, Gerry Small appeared at his office's door.

"Hey Jack, how you doing?"

"Gerry! I'm doing great!"

Jack was being wary because normally when Gerry appeared at your door, some bad news was about to follow. The news was always accompanied by a smile which varied according to how serious it was. Right now, Gerry was grinning from ear to ear.

"What can I do for you, Gerry?"

"Could you come to my office so we can talk?"

"Give me a few minutes."

Gerry Small had been in his late 60s for a little while now. As one of the editors at the paper, he was in charge of around fifty journalists on this floor, including Jack. Gerry Small was a little peculiar. He was an authoritarian with virtually no nose for the most interesting stories and he still thought that the typewriter was the best way to write. He had no redaction skills, but was always quick to make judgments about the work of others. He'd been lucky enough to meet one of the paper's shareholders many years ago and had been in the job ever since just off the back of that. He'd held the same position for thirty years without ever showing any sign of improvement and had never been promoted. Hated by almost all of the journalists, Small never liked Jack Campbell, who never looked to him for help and didn't give two hoots about what Small thought about him. Having Gerry Small at the center of your work life was professional suicide, he thought. So far Jack had managed to stay out of Gerry's way. He knew that a meeting in Gerry's office though meant his morning was going to be wasted, and he'd probably be sent on a one-way trip to report on the color of NASDAQ's new carpet.

He felt his phone vibrate. It was a message from Delvaux: "25, Broad Street – Good luck, Thomas."

He decided to leave the newsroom to visit the Millenium Dust & Associates fund. Broad Street was only twenty minutes away by taxi. He'd also be able to walk a little and appreciate the city; a city that during September moved to a particularly gentle and sweet rhythm that reflected the end of an Indian summer.

*
* *

Millenium Dust

Coming out of the New York Times building on 8th Avenue, Jack felt the beauty of this day that seemed to be inviting New Yorkers to enjoy the pleasure of being outdoors for just a little longer. Soon it would be autumn, then winter would return and with it torrential rain and snowstorms which always made life a little more difficult for the inhabitants of the Big Apple.

Jack had settled between Tribeca and Little Italy on Broom Street in Lower Manhattan. He lived in a typically New York apartment on the fifth floor of an old building. It was a decent size, separated into four rooms with metal beams, vintage rugs and red-brick walls. His living room was decorated in a modern style and bathed in light thanks to the large bay windows. There were a few pieces of furniture and sofas with beige throws that helped to give the place a cozy atmosphere.

He liked to spend time in his home office, where stacks of files sat next to unopened mail and cups of coffee that left black circles on the wood. Jack had many qualities, but he hadn't inherited his mother's gift for storage and order. He bought the apartment in 2012 using royalties he'd received for his writing. At the end of 2008 he'd published a compilation of work that described the day-to-day unfolding of the events that had changed the world. It received very favorable reviews at the time of its release. The price of real estate in Manhattan meant that he'd had to use all of the royalties and his savings to make the purchase.

Jack hailed a taxi, which took no time at all. One of the many great things about New York.

"25 Broad Street."

Twenty minutes later, Jack arrived at the address Thomas had given him for Millenium Dust. The traffic had been noticeably light on this September morning. He paid the driver, adding a little tip as he waited for his receipt. You always needed a receipt when dealing with Gerry Small. He looked at the building located at 25 Broad Street. A large bronze plaque on the outside wall to the left of the entrance proudly displayed the name of the company: Millenium Dust.

He went through the revolving door and saw a huge reception desk made of light wood. In front of him were two elevators framed by the various logos of the companies that were present in the thirty-floor building. The company was on the twentieth. At least the view must be nice, Jack mused.

He stood in front of the reception. Two large security guards who didn't look like they were there to joke around looked at him in the kind of way that made you think that unless you were in an emergency and they were on your side, you would've been better off staying at home. They wore gray flannel pants and black blazers that were so shiny you could see your reflection in them.

"Gentlemen, my name's Jack Campbell, I work for the Times," he said as he presented them with his card. "I'd like to meet with one of the managers here at Millenium Dust."

The two men turned their heads and continued to talk between themselves behind their reception desk. Zero reaction. Jack wondered whether it was because they were deaf, or they just didn't like the look of him.

"Maybe you didn't understand me?" Jack said, giving them his best smile.

One of the men, who seemed to be in possession of the larger of the two brains, deigned to turn his head. He opened his eyes and raised his eyebrows in surprise. There was no chance of winning the Oscar for Best Actor, Jack thought, still smiling. His experience told him that good humor generated generally positive reactions. Even if in this case, he was not sure what might happen.

"Do you have an appointment?" the security guard asked.

"Not exactly. I'm doing a story for the Times on hedge funds and I'd love to get the input of the communications director at Millenium Dust. I'm going around doing interviews at all the investment firms before I begin to write."

A few seconds went by as the information was slowly filtered into the brain, where it then needed to be processed and understood. Nothing... The guard then picked up the telephone and spoke for a few seconds to someone who was obviously asking the guard a lot of questions.

"Campbell, right?"

"That's what it says on my card!" replied Jack as he placed his card on the reception desk.

"From the New York Times, huh?" the guard asked as he scratched his chin.

He went back to the questions and answers game on the telephone. Eventually he hung up and told Jack that someone would be with him shortly.

"Thank you!" replied Jack.

They took his photo using the webcam on the desk and gave him a visitor's badge. After a few minutes, a 'ping' indicated that the elevator had arrived at their floor. A man of Mediterranean origin in his thirties got out of the elevator and began to approach them. He was wearing a cheap, almost-clean suit and a two-day beard.

"Mr. Campbell? Hi, I'm Ralik!" the man said as he shook Jack's hand. "You've come to meet the heads of Millenium Dust?"

"Nice to meet you, Mr. Ralik. Yes, exactly. I'm writing an article for the Times, and I'd like to include a few words on the funds you represent, if I may."

"I see. Follow me. I'm worried you're going to be a little disappointed, though!"

Ralik pushed the number twenty in the elevator and they began to ascend. A few seconds later the doors opened.

"After you!" Ralik used his electronic pass to open the door to the office just opposite the elevator. He invited Jack to enter.

The offices were tiny. The entrance gave access to two doors. To the right was what seemed like what must be Ralik's office. The other gave access to a mini kitchen.

"It's not much, but please, let's go in and sit down. I'll go first."

"This is Millenium Dust?" Jack asked.

"Like I told you, sorry! I manage the company's mail, I answer the phone when it rings, and to be honest that's pretty much it. There's not much to keep me busy! A little over three months ago we had this entire floor rented out, but they liquefied everything and now all that's left is this little office."

"Have you been here a long time?"

"I replied to a part time job advertisement. Said they paid twenty dollars an hour, a little less than two months ago now. It was the temp agency 'Executive Staffing' that got me the interview. Obviously they gave me the job. I do two and a half days a week. I tend to do afternoons because I live outside the city. Subway's quieter in the afternoon."

"What do you know about them, Mr. Ralik?"

"Not a lot really! I'm their mailman. When I get a letter, I fax it to them. That's all I can tell you."

"That's crazy," said Jack. "No one to give you any crap, basically the perfect job!"

"Yeah, except it's almost over. The temp agency called me last week. The office will close at the end of September and I'll be out of work."

"Do you have anyone I can get in touch with? I still need to do this article."

"Sorry, I don't."

"Well alright. Thank you for your help, Mr. Ralik." Jack knew that he wasn't going to get anything else out of this guy.

"No problem. Wish I could have helped you more but I know nothing about this company." No website, no phone calls. I hope they're not into any illegal things?"

"I don't think so. You've got nothing to worry about. So you really don't have anything to give me, someone who I could talk to?"

"Nothing! Except maybe…"

"Yes?" enquired Jack enthusiastically.

"There is one guy, the same guy every time, who sometimes calls here. He's got an accent."

"What kind of accent?"

"German maybe? I mean, I'm no expert."

"Does he ask for something in particular?"

"No, that's all I can tell you. The number where I fax important mail is a 203. That's all I can tell you."

"Thank you, Mr. Ralik."

After the repeated "that's all I can tell you", Jack began to wonder if it was really the case. The guy seemed calm. No eye movements that would suggest he was lying. Just simply not involved. Can you be involved when you're paid twenty bucks an hour?

"Would it be too much to ask for the fax number?"

"Yeah. I ain't paid much, but you know how it is."

"Got it! Well, all's left me to say is thank you for the info. Here's my card, and if you hear of anything that could help me get in touch with anyone from Millenium, you know. Let me know."

"I'll come with you to the elevator."

Jack made his way back to the entrance, the reception room where he gave his security pass to the two guards, who were so engrossed in their discussion they didn't even glance at him.

The sun was shining and warming the city's streets. Jack took a few steps and found himself in front of the New York Stock Exchange. In 1929, it was here that the poor people left behind by the crisis came together every day by the thousands. It was also here that the police had charged a harmless crowd. A harmless crowd that scared them. Several workers were killed, bewildered fathers waiting for something, anything, to happen. The NY Stock Exchange was no more than an empty building. The time when stockbrokers screamed and bustled around trash cans was over. Today, the financial system was managed by machines and the financial industry surrounded itself with an opaque smoke through which nothing filtered. What remained were hedge funds containing dizzying amounts of money that were manipulated each second of every day, and a tiny rented office with one guy who forwarded faxes.

Jack was trying to summarize the conversation he'd just had with Mr. Ralik. He claimed that he knew nothing and saw no one. So, first question: what was he there for? He'd mentioned that a guy with an accent, maybe German, had called several times. He needed to find out who that was and if there was a connection with Millenium Dust. Finally, he transferred the documents to a number with the prefix 203: Connecticut. The last piece of information: the place would close at the end of September meaning his only contact would then be the Executive Staffing temp agency.

Jack looked at his watch. 11 am. That meant 5 pm in Zurich. He typed the number of Thomas Delvaux into his phone. It rang once, twice, a third time and then voicemail.

"Thomas, it's me. I went to the address you gave me for Millenium Dust. I got nothing we can really use, but I do have information to send you. Call me as soon as possible. Bye."

Jack decided that he would use his network to find out more about the company. His experience as a journalist told him that they had their finger on something. They would need to dig further because there was almost certainly something below the surface. When large sums of money like this were involved, one would expect some kind of storefront, maybe financial analysts, portfolio managers, and a real, physical office. But there was almost nothing. "Mysterious," he thought, "it's all very mysterious."

His phone rang. He thought it must be Thomas. He looked and saw it was a number from the paper. Gerry. "I'll call him back. Later."

*
* *

Thomas Delvaux hung up the phone. He'd just given Jack the info about Millenium Dust, and he couldn't help thinking that these people were hiding something much bigger than just fraud. After weeks of constant surveillance, he decided to track their financial transactions. His goal was to identify the trades initiated by Millenium in order to find the bank or the stock exchange working in parallel that dealt with its orders.

In order to succeed, he needed to intercept the trades at the exact moment that they were executed within the system. It was a difficult task and neither his calculators nor his algorithm were good enough to do it. But through months of dedicated hard work he'd modified and improved his software.

His idea was simple: since it was impossible to identify the order at the precise moment that it was issued, he'd have to wait for it instead. To lay a sort of trap that would capture the order when it arrived on one of the banking network's computers. FraNex, Delvaux's company, had agreements with almost all of the banks to help them improve their competitiveness. He assured them that with his software, their stock market orders would be executed as quickly as possible and at the best price, giving them the best position when performing financial transactions. Naturally they used his system. That meant his computer program was present on almost every bank's computer in the world.

With the new version of his software, as soon as any transaction were initiated by Millenium Dust, it would be captured by the receiving bank's computer and sent to FraNex. That would give him plenty of time to dissect the order: the issuing bank, bank account and the amount. He'd then have at his disposal all of the information necessary to study it more closely.

Like a silent snake, this new update of his algorithm would be lurking at the heart of the web, on the lookout for its prey, ready. He'd baptized it Black Mamba, a venomous snake that struck like lightning. So fast its prey didn't see it coming.

He launched the compiler in order to integrate the changes into the source code. The genius of his idea lay in the agreements he already had with other financial institutions. His program was already present on the computers of his clients, they wouldn't notice anything. At least, that's what he hoped.

The compilation was in progress. A few seconds later, the console of his computer displayed a message: 'Compilation completed'. The new version was ready.

Once the update was finished, all of the banks using his application would be unknowingly working for him and his investigation into Millenium Dust.

He looked through the glass partition of his office. His associates were busy with their tasks; no one was interested in what he was doing. The source code could be changed without anyone noticing. He didn't know what he was getting into and didn't want his employees to be involved in anything. Installing a program that would be run by most banks without their knowledge was illegal, and if anything bad were to happen, Delvaux would be in serious trouble.

One last command and Black Mamba was online. Hundreds of servers would receive the notification that a new version was available. Within two hours, all of the banking world's computers would synchronize and download the application. They'd then hunt the Web in search of Millenium Dust. He just had to wait for them to crawl into the lair of his virtual snake.

He hoped it would all be done as quickly as possible.

*
* *

Jack thought that he had a little time to spare, so he decided to pay a courteous visit to Executive Staffing, the temp agency through which Ralik had found his job. A quick Google search informed him that it was on 7th, just opposite Penn Station. It was conveniently on the way to the office.

Jack lifted his arm and a taxi stopped almost immediately. "New York is the only city in the world where there are almost as many taxis as inhabitants," Jack thought to himself, "and that's not counting Uber." It goes without saying that there is simply no need to own a car in New York, especially when one considers the price of parking, which costs the average monthly salary of someone living just outside the city.

"Penn Station!" Jack instructed as he opened the door.

The driver started the counter. Commercials for the hottest new restaurants and bars in town played in a loop on the screen behind the passenger seat. After a few minutes Jack recognized Penn Station.

"You can leave me here, in front of the Pennsylvania!" A valet opened the door. Jack paid for the ride and, of course, remembered to get a receipt.

Next to the hotel was the front of Executive Staffing, to the left of it was Joe's Pizza. From what Jack could see, there was nothing too executive about the place at all.

Jack opened the door and met eyes with the hostess. The furniture and the carpet were worn. Everything about the place indicated that this was a second-rate agency. At twenty dollars an hour, Ralik probably had one of the highest paying Executive

Staffing assignments in New York. On each side of a colorless wall, coffee pots of undoubtedly bad coffee sat on filthy tables. In the background were the managers' offices, where, to the right-hand side, one could make out the noise of conversation. In front of the hostess sat a computer screen and a switchboard. Behind her, low cupboards upon which were piled up loose files, mail and unopened junk mail.

Jack approached, smiling. Her nametag read "Linda". Caught somewhere between two ages, she was a good forty with blond hair and large breasts. A red blouse that plunged fairly low brought out some bulges at the waist and seemed to push out the breasts from her black bra, which was doing its best to hold them in, and more or less succeeding. Her nails were painted, glittered and French manicured.

"Yes?" She said, looking him up and down.

"Hello, err, Linda? I'm Jack Campbell from the New York Times!"

"You looking for work?" It was obvious Jack was her type of guy.

"Very possibly! Jack looked around him, and feigned surprise. "With offices like this I guess you're looking only for CEOs! Maybe a startup director? I want stock options thrown in too!"

"You're right, honey," the secretary giggled. "Only the very best positions here. You saw the sign? Executives only!"

"Linda, my dear, beautiful Linda, could you do me a little favor?"

"That depends," she said with a little wink.

The office door behind her opened and a bald man in a tattered suit walked out.

"God damn it Linda, I've asked you three times to bring me the Farling file!"

"Coming, Mr. Wright! I was a little busy, I'm sorry!"

She grabbed a blue folder on the desk behind her and stood up to take it to Wright with a walk that would have earned her a place at the Miss Arkansas final. She sat back down and looked at Jack inquisitively.

"A favor?" she said playfully.

"Let's say that if I could find any info about a company that employs someone that goes by the name of 'Ralik', a company called Millenium Dust, on Broad Street for example, I'd be very happy."

"And how would I know anything about this Millenium thing?"

"Millenium Dust, Linda! You'd know it because it's you who got the job for Mr. Ralik there."

"And why would I do that?" she said leaning forward, forcing her breasts to reveal just that little bit more of their shape.

"Because if someone did me this little favor, maybe I'd be grateful enough to ask them out for a drink after they get off work."

"Well it would be the right thing to do."

"Except of course, I would be needing this piece of information rather quickly."

"If I were you, I'd suggest meeting at the Pennsylvania bar and you might get lucky."

"It's a deal." Jack winked and got a smile in return.

Wright poked his head out of his office. He looked at Jack and Linda.

"May I help you?" he asked, staring at the journalist.

"Unfortunately, I don't think so. Apparently Google already has a CEO. Real shame! I'll come back another time."

"5.30 sharp." Jack whispered to Linda who was already counting down to the end of the day. He went to the exit and stepped out onto the avenue.

It was already noon. Jack had a fifteen-minute walk to get to the newsroom. A little exercise wouldn't do any him any harm at all. He bought a pastrami sandwich from one of the street vendors that you can find all over Manhattan. Sandwiches, hot dogs and pretzels were a must for busy locals and curious tourists who wanted an authentic taste of the New York lifestyle.

He checked his phone. Two missed calls. Both from Gerry.

*
* *

He'd barely even stepped into the newsroom when he bumped into Gerry.

"Everything ok, Jack? I must've called you fifteen times this morning."

"I'm sorry Gerry! I went downtown to talk with some hedge fund managers. I was thinking of doing an article on some of the investment strategies of these financial giants."

"He wants us to do a big story on the probable change in fiscal policy for the President's new term. Wants to see what it'll mean for the retirement and savings of Americans."

"I'll think about it!"

"You'd better think quick. It's the first Tuesday of the month so editorial is meeting today at three. I don't want to end up looking like a jackass in there with nothing to show so get your brain in gear and come up with something. Fast!"

Classic Gerry. "He should just hurry up, retire and play some golf," Jack thought. The meeting should only last a couple of hours, tops, meaning he was still good for his rendez-vous with Linda at the Pennsylvania. Hopefully she'd have something for him.

Perhaps the fact that the editor-in-chief wanted a story wasn't such a bad thing at all, Jack thought. He could suggest the story about Millenium Dust; it was about investment funds, after all. If he did it in the right way, he could link the government's policy to the deficit and its effect on the average American. Weren't these funds holding nearly all of the pension money of the United States' citizens, anyway?

After he'd returned to his desk, Jack decided to call an old friend of his: Inspector Harry Rozberg, NYPD. They'd met in 2008. In the aftermath of the fall of Lehman Brothers in the December of that year, Harry Rozberg was entrusted with an investigation into the ransacking of windows and offices on Wall Street. It was never mentioned, but a few days after December

15th, anger had followed the state of collective shock and groups had formed. Anti-globalist radicals who were violent and determined. Many financial institutions, bank branches and insurers were attacked. The NYPD investigated these small groups and Harry was in charge. Jack had written an article on the whole affair, discussing the collateral damage from the collapse of the system. Their friendship had survived the years with each of them helping the other one out from time to time and grabbing the occasional after-work beer.

The phone rang once before Harry picked up:

"Harry? It's Jack. From the Times!"

"Hey Jack, how's it going?" a cheerful voice replied.

"I'm pretty good! Not too snowed under with work?"

"Of course I am! That's what keeps me going here, I know I'll never have nothing to do. The bad guys keep coming and we have to get 'em with less and less money."

"Trying to keep up with your own reputation? Always complaining!"

"Come on! At least I don't have some cushy job in an office writing articles for some prize-winning asshole wondering if there's even a future for this god forsaken world!"

"Don't forget that the reason this world is still holding on is thanks to people like me. We make some kind of sense of this mess and give it to those who don't have so much."

"Why would you even do that, Jack?"

"We do the same job, you and me," replied the journalist, "we help the people sleep at night."

"We hide them from the ugliness that surrounds them. We paint the sky blue so everything appears like it's ok."

"Actually Harry, I need you to help me make this world a little better by finding me a phone number. Think you can do it?"

"You know I can't do that. I'd need a warrant, there'd be tons of paperwork, I'd probably need a reason of course and then a judge would have to give it the go-ahead. What do you need it for?"

"Look, I'm onto something. I can't tell you any more because I'm not even sure that I'm right. But I need to find out more about what's going on."

"So, let me get this straight: I can't know and I just have to trust you?"

"Not right now, but as soon as I find anything, you'll be the first to know, I swear."

"Alright. I'll see what I can do. But this is between us, nothing official."

"Thanks Harry. OK, so I need to know who the company Millenium Dust is faxing documents to. They send them over almost every day."

"By fax? Ha! I thought since the Internet those things were all packed away in the basement. Except for us of course! I think the NYPD is still the world leader in using fax machines. They only replaced the word processors a few weeks ago."

"I hear you! That's something else I've kind of always wondered about. Can you check it out for me? They're at 25 Broad Street."

"Ok Jack! But remember, this is not official business."

"I got it. You have my word!"

"I'll call you if I find anything."

It was already three o'clock. Jack hurried to the thirty fifth floor where the editorial meeting was taking place. The regular meeting was held on the first Tuesday of each month in the editor-in-chief's office. The editors, like Gerry, were all expected to attend so they could discuss and plan the articles that were to be written. In addition to the stories that followed the news, they also defined those which dealt with deeper questions that required more time and often meticulous inquiry. Editors were asked to submit topics which were then presented to the editorial board and selected, or not, by a vote.

Jack had been invited this month because, as Gerry had mentioned, the editor-in-chief wanted to give him a specific assignment. Jack decided that he'd explain a little about what he'd found on Millenium Dust and see if he could get permission to follow up on the story.

The large meeting room boasted a breathtaking view over New York and the Hudson River to the west. In the distance, one could see tiny boats crowded with tourists crossing the bay. The wind was picking up, with clouds hovering over the buildings forming a tormented and changing sky. The sun, which was losing its intensity as the months of the year rolled by, was beginning its decline, covering the river and the opposite bank with an orange light. Silver reflections danced on the Hudson, decorating the scene with autumnal, end-of-season tones. "The best is yet to come," Jack tried to convince himself.

The meeting began on time. The busy editors, as usual, sat around the table with laptops open in front of them. Some of them were unable to tear themselves away from the news for even a minute, glancing regularly at the huge screen at the end of the room with CNN on loop. Eyes fixed on the finger that was always on the pulse. Even without sound, this continuous flow of information gave one the feeling of being part of what was going on. A few other journalists had been invited. Twenty people were ready to define the content of the Times for the next thirty days.

The editor began by giving them the basic outline of the current economic situation before proposing working themes for the the following month's articles.

After an hour of lively discussion, the topics agreed upon by the committee were endorsed and distributed among the various newsrooms.

"Check it out!" One of the journalists pointed at the screen, with a puzzled look on his face. "Can someone turn it up please?"

Everyone was now watching the television. A CNN reporter sat in front of an Eiffel Tower background was showing what had been happening at the Stade de France.

"Tarek Laid, a man who has become a rising star on the French political scene since the launch of his FMP movement, is busy preparing for his big rally on Sunday at the Stade de France. About twenty to twenty-five thousand people are expected to attend, a turnout that would send a strong message and is likely to signal a major change in the political landscape of the country.

Laid is equally emulated in Belgium and Germany, meaning similar parties could emerge in these countries too very soon. Is this about integration or is it merely a demonstration of differences? Will the Muslims of France impose themselves as a political force here? CNN will be here all week making sure you miss nothing in the lead up to this historic meeting. We'll be interviewing various political leaders to comment on this trending news story, so make sure you stay tuned. Angel LaRue in Paris, reporting for CNN."

The editor cut the sound, looked at the team sat around the table and began to speak.

"We need to cover this meeting. I want a feature article on Tarek Laid and his political impact on French society. We've seen a lot of violence going on due to this meeting in Paris. We need to explain to our readers what's happening in France, in Europe, and the impact of these profound transformations that are linked to communitarianism."

"It's because of the Jews and immigrants all that!" exclaimed Gerry Small. "Always the same thing! They fuck everything. The suburbs of France are on fire, guess who did that? Immigrants! We got the Latinos causing shit. Apparently it's society's fault though, and they got nothing to do with it. Bullshit! Get 'em all out and things'll be back to normal in no time, I'm tellin' ya!"

The rest of the room looked at Gerry, dumbfounded. "What an asshole," Jack thought. Gerry Small is a certified idiot. It was known that he voted Republican, but he'd gone too far now. Way too far. Unfortunately, Gerry had not been ambiguous in expressing his feelings. At all. Not to mention that approximately half the people in the room were Jewish or writers that had roots abroad, like most Americans for that matter. Election after election, the dark side of American society resurfaced, the filters imposed by political correctness temporarily discarded. For many rural Americans, foreigners were either rapists or drug traffickers. Probably both. Like a varnish that was beginning to crack, xenophobia and homophobia, yesterday relegated to the bench of this single-minded society, resurfaced with force. The Ku Klux Klan was back, and there were accusations of revanchist Americans denouncing their ex-friends on Twitter. Messages such as: "I hope you are not going to deport Henriqué, who lives in such and such a place," giving the floor number and "bottom left, door code 24849." Pitiful. "How long before the burning cars and automatic shots in churches, mosques or synagogues," Jack wondered.

"Shut the fuck up, Gerry," said one of the editors. "You're talking out of your ass."

"Oh really? You know that getting rid of Muslims and immigrants is the best way to protect ourselves."

The editor-in-chief told Gerry to be quiet with a nervous gesture. A heavy and embarrassed silence hung over the room. After a few seconds, the discussions resumed in half-tones. One wondered what Gerry was doing there, and many thought that retirement would probably be a good idea.

Jack spoke and proposed to study the predicted effects of the government's policy on pension funds. He specified that an investment fund, without giving the name, had caught his attention and that he would focus on it first. He had the advantage of being able to say part of the truth without revealing his whole story, which was still very thin. After all, lying by omission was journalism 101.

His proposal was accepted. "Good work," thought Jack, who was now free to go ahead and continue his investigation.

"5 pm. I'll need to be quick," said Jack, "if I'm going to meet Linda at the Pennsylvania."

*
* *

Jack already knew that it was a bad idea as he pushed open the door to the Pennsylvania Hotel. It was the first time he'd been in a bar since he'd started the AA meetings, and simply the atmosphere of the place, with its dense crowd and after work excitement, was enough to summon all of his demons. His stomach contracted and he felt a pain in his abdomen. The sleeping monsters in the hollow of his belly began to waken from their slumber.

He started to turn around in order to leave, but Linda arrived at the very moment, grabbing him by the arm and offering a warm smile.

"Linda! I wasn't sure if you'd come."

"A promise is a promise!" she replied, still smiling broadly.

"Let's find somewhere to sit!"

Like all Manhattan bars, the Pennsylvania bar had found the formula for success and stuck to it. The large black bar made of imitation wood was encrusted with white and blue lights. Lined up against it were purple faux-leather stools upon which one came to rest after work to grab a drink before going home. Bartenders who seemed to be in ten places at the same time juggled bottles and filled cocktail glasses which they filled with crushed ice and topped with paper umbrellas. Behind the bar was a huge, illuminated mirror upon which translucent shelves displayed whiskeys from all over the world. Everything was set to a soundtrack of loud, bass-heavy house music.

Jack couldn't take his eyes off the bottles that seemed to be calling his name. He suddenly became aware of the heat inside the bar and the sweat that was making his shirt stick to his body.

The other thing that all Manhattan bars also have in common is the noise. One has to shout simply to be heard. Two people got up from the bar and left their stools free, so Jack and Linda settled into their places.

"Linda, what would you like to drink?" Jack shouted, rather than asked.

"Glass of Chardonnay!"

Jack gestured to the barman who leaned in to take their order. "A glass of Chardonnay and… and a whisky". He knew it was wrong, that he shouldn't, but the monsters had been awakened and he couldn't prevent them from inflicting their torture upon him. They'd been cooped up for too long now, and it time for them to take revenge. There was no getting out of this.

They found a table and put their glasses down. Jack could feel the beads of sweat on his forehead beginning to drip down his temples. He was shivering, staring at the golden-colored liquid which he could dive into and find relief for his distressed soul and explore the depths of his loneliness. He was terrified.

"Are you ok? You don't seem too well!" Linda said, worried.

"Err. Yeah, I'm fine!" He responded in a voice he didn't even recognize.

"Here. I brought you what I could find on Millenium Dust."

Linda handed a thin file to Jack.

"There's not much there, you know. It's just an address, that's all."

"Excuse me Linda, I'll just be a minute."

Jack rushed to the restrooms. He ran down the stairs. He only just managed to close the door before vomiting. Once the spasms had finished he wiped his mouth and sat on the toilet to gather his thoughts. He was cold and shivering still. The monsters been put back to sleep again, for now. Looking at himself in the mirror as he washed his hands and face, he saw a man with a worn face and dark eyes. He decided he would go upstairs and continue to fight and conquer his demons.

"I'm really sorry, I have to go. I'm sick. I was fine just earlier but I think I have a fever. Please, forgive me. We can do this another time. I'll call you, we can get a drink sometime in the next few days."

"You really don't seem too good. It's a shame..."

Jack swiftly took his jacket and gestured to Linda as he left. The wind had picked up and the coolness of the evening did him some good. He grabbed his phone and dialed an emergency number.

"John Kirby!"

"John, it's Jack from AA."

"Jack, what's going on? You seem a little stressed. You ok, buddy?"

"No I'm really, really not good. I'm about to crack. I need your help."

John Kirby was Jack's sponsor at Alcoholics Anonymous. A former drinker, John knew very well the kind of challenges faced by people trying to give up drink. It had been a long time since he'd spoken to Jack. At the beginning, Jack called him every day. Although there were highs and lows, Jack seemed to be getting better, and even though his sponsor had told him to be careful and never let his guard down, today Jack had had a moment of weakness.

"When can I see you? I'm really not good."

"Come over right now Jack. Right now! Get in a taxi and come to my place."

"Thank you." They were the only words Jack could muster.

He hailed a taxi and gave the address of his sponsor.

8. STORX

Tuesday, September 19th – New York

Jack opened one eye. Light filled the apartment. He was at home and feeling better. The moment of distress had past, his sponsor had helped him to keep his head above water. He knew he'd been close to drowning. "Not this time," Jack thought to himself. He got up and took his meds to help with the alcohol withdrawal. He was going to hold on today, just like he would tomorrow and every other day. All of this had to stop.

After a shower, Jack leaned back in his office chair. He noticed the beige folder on his Mac. It contained the information that Linda had given to him last night. He looked at it with interest.

Inside the folder he found a copy of the contract signed between Executing Staffing and Ralik, Millenium Dust's address and Linda's cell phone number. The company was located in Woodbridge, near New Haven, Connecticut, a stone's throw from Yale University on Ansonia Road.

It's less than a two-hour train ride on the Acela Express, Jack thought. The Acela Express was the East Coast's high-speed train service. He decided he would go there to discover for himself what this secretive company looked like. He knew he'd have problems getting this past Gerry Small, so he called the editor of the newspaper directly to let him know that he was going to visit the pension fund to avoid any problems with Small. He left a message with the editor's assistant. Jack booked a return trip on the Internet and hired a rental car.

Jack arrived at Penn Station at 9.45 am. His train left New York at 10.03 am and arrived in New Haven at 11.35 am. If all went well, he would be at Woodbridge by noon. He'd have plenty of time to poke around and learn more about Millenium Dust before returning in the evening.

His telephone began to vibrate in his pocket. Private number. Jack answered it anyway.

"Jack Campbell!"

"Hi Jack. Hope I'm not bothering you? It's Harry Rozberg!"

"Hey Harry. No, you're never bothering me! You're calling me from a private number?"

"Yeah, I'm calling you regarding our unofficial business, remember?"

"Of course I remember. It was only yesterday; I know that Alzeimer's creeps up on you but come on!"

"Ok, are you sitting down? You're gonna see why I'm calling you from a hidden number."

"I'm not sat down. Should I be?"

"Maybe. I was checking out some stuff on Millenium Dust and I ended up getting a call from the FBI."

"Oh shit! What happened?"

"Well, I don't really know what you're getting yourself into here Jack, but you're not the only one with your eye on these guys."

"After we spoke, I contacted someone I know at Verizon. I gave him Millenium's address in New York so he could give me a list of numbers they've called, faxes too. Look, what I did is illegal, you know that. Keep it quiet and I'll let you know when I need a little favor too, ok?"

"No problem! What's the use of a cop and a journalist being friends if we can't help each other out from time to time?"

"There's an address in Connecticut on the list he gave me. I looked into the company a little more and found there's a link to the Cayman Islands. Nothing too surprising there, but it somehow set off an alert at the FBI. I got a call straight away from a special agent asking me what I was doing. I told him I'd had some problems with a guy who worked with them on Broad Street this morning.

"So what are you thinking, Harry?"

"I got nothing else!" the policeman answered.

"Do you have an address?"

"Yeah. It's in Woodbridge, Connecticut."

"Thanks bud. I'd got that from somewhere else already. Are there any other numbers or faxes that I should check out?"

"Not really. Everything else seems legit."

"Why are they using a fax machine? Why not email? Would be easier."

"That's not really true, Jack. I've done a little research and faxes are a lot harder to trace. Emails go through servers and leave a record everywhere. On your computer, on the computer of the person you've sent it to, and anywhere else it had to pass through in between. Even your service provider has access. Faxes can disappear. Once you've sent it, as long as no one's tapping your line, it's gone."

"I see. As a cop what does it tell you that the FBI call you like that?"

"I have no fucking clue, but if I were you I'd get out of this one sharp and move on to something else."

"OK, thank you Harry. You can leave all this but I need to carry on searching! If I find anything significant I'll pass it on to you."

"I thought as much, but I just wanted to warn you anyway."

There was a silence before the policeman asked in a worried tone:

"Jack?"

"Yes?"

"Just be careful."

"Don't worry, I'll be fine!"

Rozberg had already hung up.

The journey there was quite relaxing. "This high-speed train really is a good thing," he thought. "I get why Europeans like traveling this way." He'd taken a first class ticket and he was entitled to a good meal. He arrived precisely at the scheduled time. He picked up his rental car at 11.35 am from the station and by 11.55 he was driving his Toyota Prius.

His vehicle's GPS told him it was eleven miles or twenty-six minutes to Ansonia Road in Woodbridge, going via Whalley Avenue and then Fountain Street before taking Main Street toward the north west and Ansiona Road.

Jack put the radio on. Phil Collins was trying to reassure the world by singing "It's another day for you and me in paradise." "Funny thing, paradise," thought Jack, mentally going over what had happened the night before, during which he'd nearly hit bottom again. He refocused his attention on the road.

Connecticut was beautiful at this time of year. As soon as Jack came out of the urban area of New Haven, he found himself on a wooded road. Halfway between New York and Boston, the trees were shimmering with their autumnal colors, and in Connecticut, as in all of New England, the Indian summer would soon bow out to let the cold settle in early. He skirted past a vast lake upon which sailboats were taking part in a regatta. All proudly had their sails and spinnakers up displaying the colors of Yale.

He drove alongside the Woodbridge Country Club and its golf course. Everywhere, signs pointed to different parts of Yale University, this factory of champions and pride of the United States. With over eleven thousand graduate students and eight and a half thousand undergraduates, the university is one of the largest in the country. Each student pays $53,500 a year, making Yale the most expensive university in the US but also one of the most popular. It has educated no less than four former presidents: Gerald Ford, Bill Clinton, George Bush and George W, as well as two almost-presidents: John Kerry and Hillary Clinton.

The GPS let Jack know that he was about to reach his destination. Jack applied the brakes gently. The entrance told him he was entering a zone of offices. He turned and followed a road through the middle of some woods. There were large rocks laid on either side, apparently to give the scene a wild look, accentuating at the same time the opulence of the companies that were present on the site. Biotech companies on the one side, computer research companies on the other. This was a road that ran between some large companies involved in serious activities. The proximity to the university was probably not a coincidence.

Jack stopped when the GPS indicated that he had reached his destination. Hidden behind a row of old trees just in front of him was a large, brand new building. There was no ostentatious signage. He put his hazard lights on and left the main road to head down the hundred or so meters of perfectly-paved driveway. They didn't skimp on safety, Jack thought to himself. The immense single-story building in all white had an entirely glazed facade composed of metal arches and natural stone. Due to its size there could easily have been several hundred people working there, although there were very few cars in the parking lot. The Prius stopped in front of a security gate that was being watched over by a guard.

The guard, wearing a petrol-blue uniform and a suspicious look on his face, came out of his aquarium. He leaned over to Jack through the car's open window:

"What can I do for you?" asked the guard.

"I'd like to meet the director of this site."

"Do you have an appointment?"

"Not exactly."

"And you are…?"

"Jack Campbell, from the New York Times," Jack replied, showing his card.

"Please wait a moment, Mr. Campbell. I'll let them know you're here."

The security cameras didn't stop pointing at Jack for one second, continuously taking photos and videos of him. The guard ensured that all entries and exits were secure before picking up the phone. Jack could see that the guard was having a rather animated conversation. The Cerberus was waving his hands around inside the booth and his awkward body language suggested that he was uncomfortable. After what seemed like an endless back and forth, the gate finally opened. Jack started his car's ignition and began to move past the checkpoint. The guard pointed in the direction of the visitor parking lot adjacent to the building, just a stone's throw away from the main entrance.

Jack parked his Toyota next to a top-of-the-range Audi Q7, whose parking space was marked 'CEO'.

"Now there's something you don't see too often these days," Jack thought as he walked up to the automatic door that opened silently upon his arrival.

A young female switchboard operator was sat behind a modern reception desk in the entrance hall. The walls alternated between wood laminate and white paint, while the floor was made of slate. Soft lighting emanating from within the wall panels gave the whole place a rather cold ambiance. Two large black leather sofas arranged at an angle and a coffee table were the only furnishings in the vast room.

"Mr. Campbell?"

"Yes," Jack replied, giving his most friendly smile. He held out his business card.

"Please, take a seat! Mr. Storx, our CEO, will come to get you shortly," the hostess instructed more than offered as she showed Jack to one of the sofas.

After a little while, a man in his forties with a crew-cut hairstyle and dressed in a dark suit appeared from Jack's left, walking purposefully toward him. He wouldn't have looked out of place at a reunion dinner for ex-soldiers.

"Storx!" he declared, giving Jack a vigorous handshake.

"Campbell!" Jack responded, wondering if he'd get all of his fingers back in one piece.

"Hello Mr. Campbell. Please, follow me!"

Jack followed his host through an invisible door hidden in the wall panels, into what Jack guessed must have been his office. It was a very spacious room. Large windows and mahogany furniture gave an almost raw light to this monastic space. An abstract painting and a photo of a group of people in uniform were the only decorations; the rest was all white-painted walls and a tobacco-colored carpet. In terms of furniture, there was a round, frosted glass meeting table around which were four armchairs. Although it was comfortable, the whole thing just felt like it was a little cold, and calculatedly so.

"Please, take a seat! Can I get you some coffee? Some water?" Storx offered while picking up his phone and showing Jack to the meeting table.

"Some water would be great," replied Jack.

"Two bottles of water, please," Storx ordered before hanging up.

A young woman appeared almost immediately with the two bottles. She placed them on the table.

Storx looked at Jack carefully. He seemed to be probing his every thought with his almost transparent blue eyes, which made Jack nervous. Storx did not look like a CEO.

"Mr. Campbell," Storx finally said, "what can Millenium Dust do for you? And more importantly, what gives us the honor of having a journalist from the New York Times visit us here in New Haven?"

"Well, I'm doing an article about hedge funds and I'm interested in your company. I'm looking for information about your investment strategies and your clients, among other things. Anything you could tell me that would interest our readers."

"OK, I see," said Storx. "Unfortunately, we're a fairly discreet company and I'm sorry to tell you that this type of information is confidential."

"No problem, I understand. Could you at least tell me what the purpose of the company is? Its goals, how it's organized, for example?"

"All I can tell you is that we represent private interests. We buy and sell financial products. We have a very rich and carefully selected clientele."

"Do you have specific investment techniques, or do you work with banks who do this on your behalf?"

"We've developed our own trading algorithms. Our services make use of very advanced technology to execute financial transactions." Storx compulsively clenched his jaw muscles.

"Got it," replied Jack. "And why did you decide to close your offices in New York to be here, in this rather secluded location in Woodbridge?" Jack began to wonder if he was making Storx nervous.

"The development of our software is finished and the day-to-day management of our clients can easily be done outside the hustle and bustle of the city. It's more expensive there too, of course. Our offices in New York will close definitively at the end of September. But how did you find us, Mr. Campbell? We did not advertise our move." Storx stared at Jack intensely.

"Being a journalist allows me to get hold of certain information that ordinary mortals don't have access to," Jack said, forcing himself to smile and grabbing a bottle of water to make himself feel more comfortable.

"Mr. Campbell, it's a long way to come from New York without having an appointment don't you think? You took quite a risk."

"I had to do an interview with one of the professors at Yale. This was on my way," Jack lied.

"Oh, of course. I see. Which professor is that? I know a lot of people at Yale!" Storx's eyes seemed to pierce directly into the center of Jack's soul.

"You know, us journalists, we're also pretty discreet when it comes to our work. How many people are employed here? You've got the financial analysts, what about fund managers?" Jack asked, trying to change the subject.

"Unfortunately, I can't tell you any more. Again, we don't like to give away this type of information about our enterprise."

Storx knew that Jack had lied. He was no stranger to this type of interrogation, but this journalist lacked the type of training necessary to fool him. He stood up to leave.

The interview was obviously over. Jack would not be able to get anything else from this man. It was no use hanging around any longer.

"Right, Mr. Campbell, I hope of been at least of some help and have given you some of the information you needed about Millenium Dust."

"You have, thank you so much!"

Jack took his leave and soon found himself back behind the wheel of his Toyota. As he was leaving, he wondered who this military-like man really was. What made a financial trading company move out here to New Haven, and why such a big building for so few employees?

It was 1.30 pm. Jack decided he'd head to the center of Woodbridge and find something to eat.

*
* *

Storx watched as Jack left and walked toward the visitors' parking lot. As soon as his car was out of sight and hidden by the trees at the end of the building, Storx opened a drawer and grabbed his phone. He had to let the hierarchy know what was happening. He dialed a foreign number:

"Yes?" a man with a German accent answered.

"It's Storx. I'm not calling too late?"

"No, go ahead. I'm listening."

"I've just had a journalist from the New York Times here. Jack Campbell. He was asking questions about Millenium."

"A journalist? That's worrying. What was he looking for exactly?"

"He said he was writing an article about investment funds and that he was interested in the company's strategy."

"And you believed him?"

"Of course I didn't. He would never have come all the way from New York just for that. He told me that he had an interview with one of the professors at the university, but there was no way I was buying that. He answered too quickly when I asked. His eyes gave him away, anyway."

"Has he found anything?"

"I don't think so. At least he didn't say anything that made me think he had. He wanted to know why we were out here, how many worked here, things like that."

"Nothing else?"

"No. I only agreed to meet him so I could hear what he wanted. I preferred to do that, rather than just send him away."

"You did the right thing! Give me his details: phone number, address... anything you got. We'll check him out on our side."

"Ok. I'll send you a copy of his business card."

"Will we be ready for the big day, Storx?"

"Yes sir! We'll be operational within two or three days. We're ahead of schedule."

"Excellent. The BLACKSTONE project will soon be underway, as planned."

Storx hung up the phone. He still had a few problems that needed solving, but he didn't want to worry his interlocutor. These people don't have time to waste, after all.

*
* *

Woodbridge was the quintessential quiet American town, with a main street running through the center that was lined by shops and restaurants. There was the small convenience store that sold alcohol and cigarettes, also doubling as a pharmacy. Then there was the bike store, the book shop and the place selling smartphones that shared its student client base with the hip organic food store and gym. The parking lot was almost empty as the busy inhabitants walked up and down main street on this early afternoon.

Jack found what he was looking for. A bar-diner that sold hamburgers and also did takeaway. He opened the door and saw the imitation leather seats separated by dull, wood-veneer tables that would have been better off on the scrap heap. The old-school hi-fi was playing music that seemed to have hypnotized the only two customers who were sat at the bar, lost in their whisky.

The owner didn't appear to have noticed him walk in, or was just letting it be known that he would not be waiting after him. Jack looked around and in a surprised voice said:

"I don't have a reservation. Can you fit me in? Looks kinda full!"

"Don't know, I'll see what's available," replied the owner. "Ah yeah, you can take table five!"

"Which one's that?" asked Jack.

"Whichever one you want it to be!"

Jack squeezed into the booth that was closest to him. It had a view of the road. He picked up the menu that was smeared in grease, stuck between the serviette dispenser and the salt and pepper stand. After a quick scan he'd made his choice.

"Hamburger. Double cheese and peppers."

"Drink?"

"Coke! Better just stick to a Coke for now," Jack replied.

His pulse had rocketed within the space of a second. He took some deep breaths to regain his composure. The events of the previous evening at the Pennsylvania came flooding back to him. He could feel a panic attack coming on and the cramps at the bottom of his stomach reminded him of what he was missing out on. He breathed in and out, slowly and mindfully, his hands gripping the menu tightly. Eventually his heart rate began to get back to a normal rhythm and the attack began to subside. He closed his eyes for a moment before reopening them to find the man still standing there, eyes firmly fixed upon him. It seemed like he knew what was happening. He nodded his head a smiled at Jack, before declaring:

"I'm on the Coke too! Been years now. Not easy when you're a god damned barman, I can tell ya!"

"Been six months on the wagon," said Jack, "nearly fell off just yesterday!" Jack was surprised at how good it felt just to talk about it.

"Hamburger for table five!" the owner shouted to the chef, winking at Jack.

"Thank you."

"No problem. You come to take a look at the university?"

"No," Jack replied, I came to visit a company out in Woodbridge over on Ansonia in the business park.

"Which company?"

"They work in investments. Millenium Dust."

The owner nodded his head toward one of the customers at the bar.

"Allan over there, his company did their electricity. Did their CCTV cameras, too. Hey Allan! It was you who worked over there at Millenium this summer, right?"

"Yeah, worked on the site with George in July and August. Was weird, huh, George?"

"Sure was!" the second whisky enthusiast, George, confirmed with a nod.

"Weird?" Jack probed.

"Well yeah. I mean, they told us they were stockbrokers, you know, like, finance, but the system they had us put in there... wow. They wanted a lot of power," Allan explained.

"What did they need it for?" Jack enquired.

"No idea. They didn't let us stick around long enough to find out. Seems like they're all a little paranoid over there, huh George?" George nodded again.

"What do you think's going on?" asked Jack.

"We saw a load of trucks arriving carrying a bunch of computers and cabinets to put disks and electronic cards. They got enough power there to fire up a nuclear reactor. Ah yeah... we also installed an AC system that could keep a fallout shelter cool, too. Ain't that right George?"

"Woo yeah!" replied George, this time placing his glass on the counter as he nodded his head.

"It kinda surprised me that there weren't so many cars in the parking lot," the journalist continued.

"Wouldn't be surprised if I were you. There's hardly no offices there. Most of the building is basically an enormous server center anyway!"

"Thanks, guys. Can I get you a drink?" Jack concluded.

"You havin' one?" asked Allan.

"No, I can't. Doctor's orders. Just Coke for me..."

Allan and George looked at each other and gave a pout that expressed their deepest sympathy. "Poor bastard," the two barflies seemed to be thinking.

"Double cheese with peppers!" The owner came out of the kitchen holding a plate.

Jack inhaled his meal and didn't regret for a minute stumbling into this little burger joint. And he was beginning to learn a little more about Millenium Dust.

Jack looked at his watch. Three o'clock. If he hurried, he could get a train and be in New York for six. He thought about Thomas Delvaux and decided that he would call him in the morning. It was 9 pm in Zurich; Thomas would be with his family. Jack started the electric car and headed for New Haven train station.

*
* *

Thomas Delvaux was having a sumptuous evening. The weather had become a little cooler recently, so they'd dined inside the house. The barbecue, upon which they'd cooked perch fillets fished from the lake, was still smoking outside. The glowing embers in the hot ashes could still be heard crackling. The bottle of white wine was almost empty. Thomas' wife, Hanna, was putting their two little girls to bed.

The days were getting shorter as the end of September approached, and the early evening light covered the landscape with a monochrome filter. Delvaux's house overlooked the lake which was always a beautiful spectacle, no matter the season. The lights of the city were reflected upon its silent waters, trapped by the vapors rising from the calm surface of the rippling waves.

Thomas enjoyed watching the autumnal colors that had begun to appear during the daytime. His home was fifteen hundred feet high on one of the hillsides of the northwest shore, overlooking this body of water that covered the horizon as far as the eye could see. In the distance were the alpine peaks. In the wintertime, when snow would hide the tops of the mountains, the landscape would give one a sensation of total wellbing, a feeling that only snowy expanses could do.

After setting up his company, FraNex, Thomas Delvaux definitively left teaching around ten years ago to devote himself to programming, the job that had made him his fortune. Around one hundred million Swiss francs, give or take five or ten million, depending on the fluctuations of the markets.

Delvaux was in his fifties. A mathematical genius, he'd spent far too much time in front of blackboards in classrooms trying to solve the mysteries of the infinitely small and discover the secret of atoms. He'd never been very athletic, and now that his academic career was over, he'd transferred all of his energy into creating an algorithm that could analyze financial transactions in real time, a revolution he'd started ten years ago. At around the same time, he married Hanna, five years his junior, whom he had met at FraNex. They quickly had two children, Lola and Rebecca.

Hanna came out of the girls' bedroom and sat down next to Thomas.

"The children are asleep."

"Thank you Hanna," Thomas responded. "I'm going back to the office to work a little more."

"Again? You already stayed late last night. You have a new project you're working on?"

"Something like that. Thanks to my software, I've discovered a company that's trading stocks in a way that makes them almost invisible, and I'd just like to know a little more about them."

"Ok if you think it's worth it, I'll leave you to work. But you don't know what you're missing," Hanna replied, choosing her words carefully to ensure they contained as much innuendo as possible.

"It's just for tonight, I promise!"

"Don't go to bed too late. You're not twenty years old anymore, in case you forgot!"

"I won't forget my love. I'm reminded every morning."

Hanna kissed Thomas and went to watch TV. Thomas grabbed his jacket and car keys. It only took him a few minutes to get to his office. He worked most of the night, trying to improve his electronic capturing tool, also checking that his software had been updated on all the computers of the banks with whom FraNex had a contract. That meant most banking systems in the world. Everything seemed to be in order, although he had yet to capture any of Millenium Dust's transactions.

When Delvaux left the headquarters of his company at three o'clock in the morning, the electronic snake 'Black Mamba' was lurking in cyberspace, hunting its prey. He turned off the lights and the offices were plunged into darkness. Only the cursor of a computer was flashing, a sign that his program was running.

Thomas activated the security system and went home. An hour later, the computer beeped and flickered into life. Data began to scroll down the screen that had been on standby. A battle was commencing at the heart of the Internet.

Millenium Dust had launched some trade operations and they'd immediately been picked up by one of the computers in the network. Delvaux's virtual snake silently uncoiled to catch its prey. Black Mamba issued thousands of orders in response to the requests to delay the transactions; just enough time for his program to identify the shipment address, copy the order and locate the bank hiding behind all of these operations.

Thousands of lines of data continued to stream down the screen. It was all information that Thomas Delvaux would need to dissect. What he would discover within these lines of information would confirm his suspicions that Millenium Dust was indeed extremely dangerous.

*
* *

Anti Game

9. THE BLACKSTONE PROJECT

Wednesday September 20th – New York

Jack jumped when the alarm clock sounded. His heart was pounding. "Six-thirty," he said to himself, opening his eyes. He'd taken a sleeping pill and the loud alarm had shocked him out of a deep, artificial sleep. As often happens after a difficult crisis, he'd resorted to medicinal help in order to help him drift off. He listened to the sounds of the city. New York had its own music that comforted him; inimitable and instantly recognizable. Car horns of busy taxis, sirens from the police station at the crossroads between Broom Street and Broadway. All those reassuring noises that made him love this city.

Jack mustered up the courage to put one foot out of bed. Last night had been calm. He'd not felt any compulsive need to drink and he had the impression that he was regaining control. The day before, he'd called John Kirby, his sponsor at Alcoholics Anonymous, to let him know that everything was fine. John was his lifeline when he sank, and knew better than anyone what to say and what to do when Jack was at the bottom of the hole. He too had been there many times. No one stops drinking at the first attempt. Weaning is a long journey, and every period of abstinence is a victory. It would take a lot more to win this war. Jack was perfectly aware of that.

He switched on the TV to to catch up on the latest business news on Bloomberg. He listened with a distracted ear to a report on Shuito Pharmaceuticals:

"There was a new Flash Crash on the Tokyo Stock Exchange yesterday afternoon at 1 pm, local time. Shuito Pharmaceuticals suffered heavy losses, with its share price tumbling almost fifty percent. The crash occurred suddenly after a massive sale of the pharmaceutical laboratory's shares. The crash was amplified as trading firms' robots triggered mass sales as a response to the company's abrupt price change. Over three hundred million dollars was wiped from Shuito's value in less than eight minutes, without the giant making any statement about its financial health. The CEO of Shuito has blamed speculators and denies that such a phenomenon could have occurred without some sort of targeted intervention. An investigation by the Japan Exchange Regulation self-regulatory body is in progress. I'm Lena Voslberg, reporting for Bloomberg in Tokyo."

He made himself a quick sandwich, took a shower and then grabbed his cellphone… only to find that he'd forgotten to charge it. He'd do it when he arrived at the Times' headquarters. Jack went outside and jumped in a taxi to 8th Avenue. After buying his usual café latté at Starbucks, he took the elevator. The doors were barely open when he heard a recognizable voice. The noise came from the office of Gerry Small who was violently scolding a young freelancer. Jack knew that he'd not be able to avoid him. He decided to nip in the bud any chance that his editor might make his day difficult. He rushed into Gerry's office with a determined air about him:

"Hey Gerry!"

"Mr. Campbell, I thought you'd disappeared! No news, didn't reply to my messages and your office looked very sad and empty!"

"You didn't get the chief's message?" the journalist asked, faking guilt.

"What message?"

"I'm doing some work for him. I have to follow the trail of a pension fund. These guys might be crooked. You realize what that means? If we discover that these people are squandering the money of our retirees, it's a bomb that's going to explode, Gerry!"

"I didn't hear anything about that."

"Really? Take it up with him, I got work to do!"

With that, he quickly left the impeccably tidy office of a Gerry Small who had been caught unprepared. "Good!" Jack said to himself, "now my story just needs to hold up long enough for him to leave me alone today."

Jack plugged his smartphone in and switched it on. He had three new messages.

First message: "Hello Jack, it's Linda. Linda Miller from Executive Staffing. Just wanted to know how you are? Hope things are better. I was kinda worried after the bar thing. Hope it's nothing serious? Call me!"

Jack felt guilty that he hadn't spoken to Linda. He made a mental note to get in touch with her soon. He saved the messaged and moved on to the next one.

Second message: "Jack, it's Thomas! Call me, it's urgent!" Delvaux's worried voice boomed.

Third message: "Jack, it's Thomas again! Call me when you get this message!"

Jack knew that Thomas had found something important. He dialed his number hesitantly. Delvaux answered immediately.

"Jack! God, you took your time!"

"Sorry Thomas, my battery died. I've just plugged it in now, at the office."

"I don't know if you found anything new on Millenium, but I got something this morning that I wanted to talk to you about. I'm not sure what I should do."

"Go on, I'm listening."

"I basically set up a watchdog for Millenium Dust on the Internet. I was waiting for them to make any kind of financial transaction so I could use it to find out more about them and their DNA."

"Did it work?"

"You could say that! You ever heard of Shuito Pharmaceuticals?"

"Kind of, this morning. The Japanese company that was targeted by speculators who managed to get hold of quite a lot of their capital? That was Millenium?"

"Exactly. Their idea is simple. They buy a part of the capital in a discreet way over a long period of time. That way they remain invisible and hide their identity, nobody notices anything. Then suddenly, they sell large blocks of shares, which causes the share price to tumble. Other investors, seeing the value fall, follow suit. When a sufficient volume is reached, the robots running software that scrutinizes stock prices detect that the stock has fallen sharply. They all join in the game at the same time and we see the company's shares descend into hell in just a few minutes. And for the ones that orchestrated the whole thing, all they have to do is buy back the shares at their lowest point by ensuring that they buy back at a slower rate than they are being sold so the price doesn't go back up. And voila! Most of their transactions are done on the Dark Pool, the parallel stock market, or the gray market as it's known. The transactions are over-the-counter, so it doesn't go through official stock exchanges and leaves no trace. Amazing, right?"

"Is it legal?" Jack asked.

"No, they're manipulating the market. The tool they're using for this entire operation is extremely finely calibrated. Everything is tuned down to the last millimeter. I think their computer program is ahead of any other bank's. It's possible that they've developed an entirely new type of algorithm! If that's the case, they can do almost anything they want, since all transactions are automated. For Shuito, it's earned them nearly two hundred million dollars in cash!"

"Jesus! Just like that!"

"Yeah, but that's not all. I think that was just a test. I have a feeling they're planning something much bigger. Think what could happen if they did that on an even bigger scale."

"But that would require enormous amounts of capital."

"Don't forget what I told you a few days ago. I've identified almost one hundred billion dollars-worth of transactions by Millenium, and we still don't know if that's all they've got in their reserves."

"Unbelievable! And they're able to mobilize this amount of money whenever they want?"

"Yep. And when they do, it's gonna make a hell of a noise in the world of finance, I can tell you."

"Can they cause an entire market to fail?"

"It's possible, Jack!"

Delvaux's voice was getting lower, a sure sign that he was worried and that he couldn't hide it. A few seconds of silence passed between the men. Each of them was trying to comprehend the level of threat that Millenium Dust posed. Delvaux scratched his throat before talking again.

"By analyzing their transactions, I've discovered the bank behind it all. Zurich Investments & Securities Bank. Here in Zurich we call them ZIS. They're just on the other side of the lake. Sometimes I can even see their offices from my place!"

"In a way, that makes things a little easier."

"So what do we do?" Delvaux asked.

"I'll tell you what I found, then we can decide?"

"OK!"

"To put it briefly, I heard that Millenium's New York office is going to close in September. They've moved all their operations to New Haven, in the countryside. I've no idea why, but that's what they've done. I asked to meet the director there, some guy in his forties. He was like a real mercenary. Seemed more of a soldier than a finance person."

"New Haven?" Delvaux interrupted.

"Yeah, near Yale."

"I know. I went there a few times when I was teaching. You got any idea why they'd want to be there?"

"Not a clue."

"All the universities in the US have fiber-optic connections, so their communications networks are among the most powerful in the country. With the research labs on their campus they need it. That's why they're there, Jack! They might be in the middle of nowhere, but they're on one of the fastest networks in the United States."

"I had no idea! But wait. I randomly met the two guys that said they did all the electrics at their offices. They told me that the whole building is basically a server center, housing tons of computers, with as much power as a nuclear power station, to use their words."

"That kind of fits with the whole computer fraud idea, right?"

"Well it seems to be more and more likely that that's what we're dealing with," said Jack. "The last thing I found won't do much to reassure you either: the FBI are watching them. The legal setup of Millenium is in the Cayman Islands, very difficult to trace. It's all been done so that finding out who's really behind all this is next to impossible, unless the FBI decide to investigate thoroughly. But we're not there yet."

"So what do we do, Jack?"

"I think we're really onto something big here, Thomas. Before anything else, I'm still a journalist, right? So I can't let this go. We need at least a name so we can start to ask questions. We can see where we go from there."

"We have one. Marco Ziegler! He's a Swiss guy who's the director for Zurich Investments & Securities, here in Zurich!"

"I think I'll book a flight to Zurich then. We can interview this Marco Ziegler together. I'll call him right now to set up the meeting. Good for you?"

"Yes Jack! Let's find out what's hiding behind Millenium and ZIS."

"I'll let you know as soon as I've cleared it all with the editor."

Jack Campbell had always had the journalist's instinct. He made a name for himself after the 2008 crisis by publishing a book that, like a logbook, retraced the events of the weeks that followed the fall of Lehman Brothers. Rather than taking the usual angle of why it all happened, he decided to tell how it was from the inside, in memory of those people, those victims, who had been crushed by the system.

And he knew, like the wolf that puts his nose to the wind, that danger was approaching.

Anti Game

***

The private jet was cruising at almost 800 km/h. It took about an hour and thirty minutes to fly from Berlin to Zurich. The flight was comfortable with clear weather and no turbulence. Heidrich Füller, Chancellor Konrad's strategic advisor on economic affairs, was enjoying a Gin & Tonic while waiting to land. He looked at his watch: two o'clock. His appointment with Marco Ziegler, the CEO of ZIS, was scheduled for five.

Heidrich Füller was a puny little man. He was thirty-six years old with sparse brown hair and a long face riddled with acne scars. His deep, tense look made him look much older than his age. He wasn't very inclined to physical activity; he had always shone through his formidable intelligence. This German academic, trained in economics, was of rare intellectual acuteness. He was first noticed within the Deutsche Bank when he recommended that the bank sell their entire US housing portfolio and invest the money in gold instead, just at the end of June 2008. Everyone thought he was crazy. At the time, gold was seen as being little more valuable than reinforced concrete. After September 15th, when Lehman Brothers collapsed and the market tanked, the housing assets became worthless. The report that Füller had written was visionary in every way and highlighted the risk that he had sensed on the other side of the Atlantic. This document had landed on the Chancellor's desk and earned him the job offer that he had gladly accepted.

He believed that Germany was in danger, and that incompetent hands were maneuvering this drunk ship that represented his homeland toward treacherous reefs. This great danger was the European Union, within which the great Germany was going to be dissolved. He could not stand it anymore. Why should they be the ones to pay for all of the other countries in the European Union? They had made sacrifices for ten years and all that to fatten profiteers who were unable to make reforms? No, something had to be done!

When the members of BLACKSTONE approached him, he knew immediately that it was the best solution. The cards needed to be reshuffled. Germany needed to pull out of the EU and the Euro, and as violent a blow as possible needed to be inflicted upon the hegemonic, protectionist and completely egocentric America that essentially ruled the world. The introduction of customs duties on German cars made in Mexico and on all Chinese products, the construction of the wall with Mexico, the abandonment of NATO, closer ties with Putin; all conflicts of interest and nepotism. A huge alarm should have sounded all over the world to denounce the excesses of a drifting United States, and yet everywhere a resigned silence reigned.

The BLACKSTONE project would give a true shock to this status quo. It would cause a reorganization that compromised the global supremacy of the US and redefine the contours of a dying Europe.

They had invested millions of dollars, but in the end, the results had far surpassed their expectations. The latest test on Shuito Pharmaceuticals was proof of that. By creating just a few tiny cracks upon the surface, they'd managed to decimate the value of the company in just a few seconds and take control of the high-potential biotech company. And they'd made two-hundred million dollars in the process. It was Füller who had conceived of the software program, this new-generation of artificial intelligence, thanks to the money of the members of Millenium Dust. Software that was capable of manipulating any stock market in the world. The Shuito test was the latest of ten that they had performed over the last few years.

They were ready.

Their program calculated the precise percentage of a company's capital needed to take control of it. Artificial intelligence knew exactly how to put shares onto the market to create conditions that would be enough of a call for value holders to sell them. All that remained was to train robots that responded to market stimuli in a predictive way. If they had the exact thresholds for each bank that triggered the automated sales, and if they could accurately predict how each one would react, they would become the master of the game.

One thing needs to be clear: no financial transaction is done manually anymore. Everything, absolutely everything, is managed automatically by robots. They're plugged into the stock exchanges, counting orders, evaluating risks and calculating thresholds. But they are machines. They have weaknesses. If someone can figure out how they work and know how they react, there would be no limit to how the financial markets could be manipulated.

This new weapon had been created.

"It's your Captain speaking. We are approaching Zurich and should land in less than ten minutes. Thank you for fastening your seatbelts, we hope you had a pleasant flight."

The hostess leaned over Heidrich Füller who was visibly absorbed by his computer screen.

"Mr. Füller, we're about to land at Zurich airport, can I clear some of these things away for you?"

"Of course! I'm sorry!"

"No problem, please fasten your seatbelt for landing. I hope you had a nice flight."

"Yes, yes, very nice indeed actually," Füller replied, smiling.

The Falcon 7X began its approach. It was 3.35 pm in Zurich and the mild weather at the end of September offered a breathtaking view over the city. A few minutes before landing from the north east, they flew over Lake Constance. The buildings appeared soon after and then, in the distance, the city bordered by Lake Zurich's emerald waters.

The jet landed smoothly and stopped in front of the hangar reserved for private planes. Füller picked up his belongings and went down the footbridge, at the bottom of which the Mercedes was waiting to take him directly to the headquarters of ZIS. Even with a journey of about twenty minutes, he'd be perfectly on time for the video conference at 5 pm. Customs and passport control were only a formality because he was a member of the Chancellor's government, even though this time he was traveling for personal reasons.

The headquarters of ZIS was located right on the banks of the lake. The three-story square building proudly displayed its Art Nouveau heritage and the large bay windows let a stunning bright light into the room next to reception. The one hundred-year-old bank managed the fortunes of some very privileged clients. Marco Ziegler, the sporty forty-year-old CEO, immaculately dressed in an impeccably tailored three-piece suit, was waiting with some trepidation for the arrival of Heidrich Füller. BLACKSTONE members did not have a reputation for being easy people.

The Mercedes parked safely and the driver opened the door for Füller, who without a glance made his way toward the bank's headquarters. He climbed the three steps of stairs and planted himself in front of the awaiting Ziegler. The CEO squeezed Füller's soft hand before leading him into the videoconferencing room. "Did you have a nice journey, Heidrich?" asked Ziegler, making small talk.

"As nice as it could be, thank you. Is everything ready for the conference?"

"Yes. We still have a few minutes before it starts. Would you like a coffee? Some water?"

"A coffee would be good."

They entered a private elevator that exclusively served Marco Ziegler's office and its adjoining meeting room, equipped with the videoconferencing system. They entered and Füller chose a seat in front of the large wall-mounted screen.

"I'm going to prepare for the call. If you could arrange for my coffee to be brought to me."

"I'll have that done right away."

The conference began at 5 pm sharp. Füller had some good news and he wanted to share it with his sponsors. Marco Ziegler sat next to him, arranging a series of files on the table in front of him.

The musical alert announced the first connection request. Füller pressed the button to accept.

Dimitri Volkov appeared onscreen.

Next, it was Yuchun Lio.

Finally, Fouad Al-Naviq.

"Good day everyone, and a good evening to you, Yuchun. It is midnight in Beijing, if I'm not mistaken?" Füller began.

"It is indeed," replied Lio, a little delayed due to the satellite link.

"Good evening from Moscow," the inimitable voice of Dimitri Volkov announced.

"Greetings from Paris," Al-Naviq added, from the private room of his hotel.

"We're all here," said Füller, "so I propose we get this meeting started. This will without doubt be one of the last times we meet before launching project BLACKSTONE, as now we are reaching the end of our preparations."

"Rrreally?" enquired Volkov, rolling the 'r'.

"I believe so, but here I will let Marco Ziegler talk so he can give you a more concise summary of the situation."

"Thank you, Heidrich," replied Ziegler. "Indeed, gentlemen, our centers in Paris, London and New Haven are operational. The last one on the list was Connecticut, but having spoken to Storx on the phone earlier, I can confirm that everything is ready. We can start the operation at any time. At the end of the day tomorrow I will go to the United States to handle this directly, although I have full confidence in Storx. A former officer cannot lie. I will then go to our premises in Paris, via London, to perform the same inspections. I need to remind Storx tomorrow morning to give me a final update on the progress of the project in New Haven."

"Good!" Füller started again. "Without doubt you'll all have followed closely what happened in Tokyo regarding Shuito Pharmaceuticals. Once again the test played out exactly as we predicted. The technology that we have developed is performing perfectly."

"Indeed, it was a great success. I congratulate you," added Yuchun Lio.

"Thank you, Mr. Lio. In other news, I can also confirm that the Chancellor and I have met with most of the European politicians. Thanks to my advice, she gave a very firm speech to all the leaders, who are now under pressure to push through some very painful reforms. As we planned, this will result in rising discontent and therefore political extremes, and will help us to maintain a Eurosceptic climate."

"Mr. Füller, gentlemen, if you'll allow me," Fouad Al-Naviq demanded.

"Please, go ahead!" Heidrich Füller obliged.

"Thank you. I'd like to announce that we will be able to launch BLACKSTONE within the next few days. The exact date will be September 25th."

"How are you so certain of this?" Dimitri Volkov questioned.

"For the moment I'm not able to share that information, but the September 23rd will be the moment when the countdown begins."

"The 23rd?" Yuchun Lio added.

"Exactly. In order to begin the project, we need an initial act, a spark, something that will then start a chain reaction of events that all result favorably for us, isn't that right?"

"Yes, it must be said that this is precisely what we are trying to bring about," Füller responded.

"Well that's exactly what will be happening here on the 23rd! Here, in Paris!" Fouad Al-Naviq concluded.

"What is that, Mr. Al-Naviq?" asked Dimitri.

"I propose that we vote for the fuse to be lit for BLACKSTONE on the 25th of September, if the events that I imagine will occur on the twenty-third should indeed come to fruition."

"Gentlemen?" said Füller.

"Fouad, are you absolutely sure?" Volkov pressed.

"I assure you that there won't be a better opportunity."

"In that case, on the condition that we vote on the morning of the 24th, once Fouad has confirmed, I'm OK for this date," said Volkov.

"Me too," Yuchun Lio added.

"Same for me," Füller said to complete the circle.

"Gentlemen, do we have any other questions to address today?"

"I need to warn you that a journalist from the New York Times called me this morning," Ziegler declared, "he asked to see me. He asked me about Millenium Dust and ZIS. He wants to ask me some questions. He wants to do an article about fund managers."

"Did you know about this, Herr Füller?" Al-Naviq asked.

"Absolutely not!" replied an eager Füller.

"I don't think he knows much," said Ziegler, "but I'll meet him in order to find out more. Does everyone agree?"

"Mr. Ziegler?" Dimitri Volkov asked. "If this man becomes a problem, I trust you'll do what's necessary?"

"Don't worry," replied Ziegler. "If I suspect something's not right, I'll be sure to let all of you know, but it really is highly unlikely."

"Good," declared Füller, "that's everything. Thank you all for your presence and we'll speak again on the 24th at the latest."

The speaker system beeped as the callers logged off. A heavy silence descended upon the meeting room. Füller and Ziegler looked at each other incredulously.

"Here we go Marco! The dice have been thrown! After all of these months of work, all of these years. We're finally there!" Heidrich Füller was excited. He jumped out of his seat in one swift movement. This man, who was normally so quiet, was now moving about with sweeping gestures. Füller had never called Ziegler by his first name.

"Now we just have to wait for the big day! Four days, as of tomorrow!" replied the banker.

"Many things can happen in four days, Ziegler." Füller calmed himself and made sure to put the distance between himself and the CEO of Zurich Investments & Securities firmly back in place.

*
* *

Dimitri Volkov, the Russian billionaire, picked up his remote control and switched off the screen in front of him. He was happy with the progress the BLACKSTONE project was making. The wealthy oligarch owned part of the Rosneft company which produced Russian oil. A former member of the KGB and a close ally of the Russian president, he made the decision to join the project after the United States and the EU imposed unacceptable sanctions against his country. In 2014, the whole world was united against Greater Russia. Now they would discover what it was like to be deprived of resources. He'd invested a large part of his own fortune and capital that had come from secret sources into the BLACKSTONE project. His associates were not exactly the most wholesome of people, but they were very rich. The return on their investment now needed to be enough for all of them. But for him, the goal was different: to weaken Russia's enemy states and to permanently shift the balance of power in the world.

Yuchun Lio got up from his desk after ending the encrypted satellite link to the conference. One can never be too careful. The Chinese businessman was not well known to the public. He had come from a small village and had grown up in poverty. He looked out of the window of his office that was at the very top of his tower. All he saw was gray; a gray, invisible sky clouded by the smoke from factories that the wind carried in intermittent waves; the gray of the polluted world that surrounded him.

The property and telecommunications magnate, who was in fact the real brains behind the Minister of the Economy, smiled. "What a journey," he thought, from the farmlands of Sichuan where he grew up nearly a thousand miles from Chengdu, the capital of this western Chinese province.

He'd been noticed by a teacher in his village for his incredible intelligence and sent to a government school. Once he'd graduated, he joined the Governor's office. From there, he had made various investments in real estate, then in the country's mobile communications network. His fortune was colossal.

Many of his assets were not in China. He had learned to be prudent from an early age as a cadet of the Communist Party. To succeed, one had to be invisible and indispensable. The BLACKSTONE project would allow him to become one of the richest men on the planet. For Yuchun Lio, money was a most noble motive.

Fouad Al-Naviq logged off and closed his laptop. Sat on his armchair made of precious wood, he was thinking of the best way to detonate his bomb. He loved to make important decisions here, in his Parisian salon, in which venetian mirrors reflected warm light, filtered by the walls lined with pink and mauve silk.

He'd created the current media darling. Before meeting Fouad, Tarek Laid was known only by a small community of practicing Muslims close to the Mosquée de Paris. But Fouad had made him an A-lister. He'd catapulted him into the spotlight, right into the center of the political scene. He had turned him into the future incarnate for the Muslims of France.

Fouad knew that one could lose everything: riches, possessions; all of those futile and derisory things that bonded us in an illusory link to a society that continually pushed us to consume more and more.

But men, no matter what their origin or their belief could never go without the essential thing that satisfied the heart and gave meaning to everything else: hope.

Fouad Al-Naviq was preparing to make Tarek Laid disappear, and along with him this new hope. By doing this, he knew he was throwing a grenade into the social sphere of the country, and that the explosion would cause absolute chaos. This shock would be the detonator of the BLACKSTONE project.

Fouad was part of a group of people that wished for the Caliphate to be fully established in Europe. He wanted the total destabilization of the Western world. He was the one who had orchestrated the May 1st bombing so the Front National would be elected. With him came the beginning of the battle. He knew that social cohesion in France, already severely tested by previous attacks, had been eroded, spread now into a fine dust, a symptom of the premature wear of the wheels of a broken democracy. He was about to deliver the knockout punch. The assassination of Tarek Laid would be the banderilla planted in the neck of France to bring it to its knees.

*
* *

The vibrations of the 747 gently rocked the passengers. After the bustle of boarding, coupled with the palpable excitement of those who didn't travel very often, calm reigned in the cabin. The meal service was over and Jack Campbell, a sleeping mask on his eyes, was having some rest.

Things were suddenly moving a lot faster.

As soon as his conversation with Thomas Delvaux ended that very morning, Jack had rushed into the chief editor's office with military precision, narrowly avoiding the assistant who was blocking the way. No one was supposed to see him without an appointment and without being announced. Jack had everything he needed to give a summary of the situation to his boss; just enough to describe the activities of Millenium Dust and Zurich Investments & Securities bank. The editor signed a blank check for his trip to Zurich.

Jack then called Marco Ziegler to arrange an interview for the next day, which, a little unusually, Ziegler had accepted immediately. It was as if he had been expecting such a visit.

He had just enough time to tie up all of his loose ends in New York, book a flight on Swiss Airlines, find a hotel in Zurich and tell Gerry Small that he'd be out of office for the rest of the week. And that he was already at home packing his suitcase.

His plane would take off from JFK International Airport at 6.50 pm and arrive in Zurich the following morning at 7.55 am. He would use the journey to prepare for his interview with Ziegler.

10. MARCO ZIEGLER

Thursday, September 21st – Zurich

Jack's arrival in Zurich was greeted by rain. The weather had begun to turn, and the next few days were forecast to be both cold and humid. Thomas Delvaux was waiting for Jack in front of gate number five of Terminal 2.

He was a little surprised by the airport, which made him think more of a local airfield than the economic capital of Switzerland. There were just two rather small terminals and only a few passengers. Everything seemed very calm, including the border police checks, which only took a few minutes.

After retrieving his suitcase, he headed for the exit. Once he passed through the security checks and exited the gate, he saw a smiling Thomas Delvaux waiting for him. It had been seven years since they last saw each other. Sporting jeans, a crumpled linen shirt and a blue jacket, Thomas had not changed a bit. A little rounder perhaps and less hair without doubt, but he was the same. Casual and always wearing a smile on his lips. Thomas Delvaux embodied the positive attitude.

They exchanged a warm handshake.

"Nice trip, Yankee?"

"Yes sir! A few bruises here and there. Unfortunately, not all of us work for for rich and generous banks! First Class passengers get all of the best treatment."

"For €5,000 one way, that's the least they could do for them, right?"

"You're right. Journalism ain't what it used to be, though."

"Hope you brought some sweaters and a warm jacket, apparently the next few days are going to be arctic."

"I'll be fine, I got what I need!"

"When are you leaving, by the way?"

"I'd planned to go back Monday or Tuesday. I've taken the weekend so I can have a look around the city."

"Ok great. Welcome to Zurich Jack, it's wonderful to see you again!"

"Thanks Thomas. It's great to see you too."

"What time's the meeting with Ziegler again?"

"Eleven o'clock. That gives me enough time to go back to my hotel, grab a shower, and put on my best suit."

"It's right next to ZIS, probably five minutes walk. Come on, let's go," said Delvaux.

Queues of traffic on the highway as far as the eye could see confirmed that driving around Zurich was a nightmare. The A1 was completely backed up with cars. Heavy rain fell continuously and the thermometer in Thomas Delvaux's SUV indicated an outside temperature of fifty-four degrees. "Not enough for heatstroke," thought Jack. Autumn was fast approaching.

The two men began to talk about their respective lives since they had last seen each other and reestablish their friendship. It's not possible to recount seven years of life in just a few minutes, but the friendly and lively discussion allowed them at least to fill in a few blanks here and there. The twelve-mile journey to the hotel took them forty-five minutes. Jack looked at his watch. It was already 9.30 am.

"I think the best thing to do is for you to park up, I'll check in and take a quick shower, then we can meet at the bar for a coffee and prepare for our meeting with Ziegler. Sounds ok?"

"Perfect. Like I said, we're not far."

"I'll see you at the bar in half an hour!"

*
* *

Confrontation

Jack and Thomas climbed the three steps to the entrance of ZIS. The door opened immediately and they were greeted by an obsequious receptionist in a light blue suit and yellow silk scarf emblazoned with Hermes, hidden behind an old desk.

"How may I help you, gentlemen?"

"We have a meeting with Marco Ziegler," Thomas replied.

"Jack Campbell from the New York Times," said Jack, offering his card to the receptionist.

"Ah yes, here we are. 11.00 am, is that right?"

"Exactly."

"Mr. Ziegler will see you shortly, gentlemen," replied the receptionist as she showed them into the waiting room.

The room, with its walls covered with royal blue fabric and marquetry furniture dating from the Belle Époque, offered a perfectly clear view overlooking the lake. The gray sky and incessant rain gave a gloomy appearance to the expanse of water, flickering with black reflections, upon which a gentle swell formed from the persistent autumnal wind.

They knocked gently and the door opened. A young woman posing as Marco Ziegler's assistant invited them to follow her. They took a private elevator. The pretty blonde assistant was also dressed in blue uniform and yellow scarf. She pressed the button for the first floor. "They must have clients here whose millions are as numerous as their age," Jack thought. "No way that they can use stairs, even for one floor."

A quiet beep let them know that they had arrived. Jack and Thomas left the elevator and followed behind the assistant, who then knocked on an invisible door, completely hidden in the wooden walls.

"Please," she indicated for them to enter the room once the ZIS CEO had confirmed he was ready.

Jack and Thomas walked into an office the size of Jack's apartment. Old floors, stucco, modern furniture and Murano crystal lighting in the style of the Belle Époque. It was stunning, especially with the paintings, which weren't copies.

Ziegler got up from his desk to welcome them, full of smiles.

"Mr. Ziegler, thank you for taking the time to see us!" Jack began, offering his card.

"Don't thank me, Mr. Campbell, your call piqued my curiosity."

"Delvaux!" Thomas introduced himself, greeting his host.

"Please, take a seat, gentlemen! I don't have much time. Do you think we can get through all of your questions in, say, thirty minutes?"

"We'll be as quick as possible," Jack replied, taking out his Dictaphone. "Do you mind if I record the conversation?"

"Of course, please go ahead."

"Thank you!" Jack pressed record and looked at Ziegler.

"Mr. Ziegler, could you please introduce yourself and tell us about the activities of your bank?"

"Our establishment is a reference in its field. We have existed since 1896, you know. Our activities are mainly focused on fund management."

"I see. Thank you. Who are your clients? Are they private? Or institutions?"

"We have a client base that is composed of almost uniquely private investors."

"So if I understand correctly, you look after the holdings of private clients and advise them on investment funds?"

"That's right, yes, and we trade their portfolios daily. We also reserve the right to promote financial products that we fund through our own investments. In fact, I am presenting at a conference tomorrow morning on alternative investment strategies for the end of this year. I invite you to come and listen."

"Thank you for the invitation, Mr. Ziegler. So if I'm following correctly, you speculate on the markets to increase your returns?"

"Something like that! We're also an investment bank. We have strong equity capital. We're very active in mergers and acquisitions."

"So, a part of your business is to make partnerships with large banking networks to buy and sell their financial products to your customers?"

"Precisely."

"In that case, could you explain to us your relationship with the company Millenium Dust?"

"I don't know what you're talking about, Mr. Campbell. Millenium Dust? No, I don't know it."

"So, no relationship, not even business, with Millenium Dust?"

"We have no relationship with this business that I know of."

"But if you did have one, you would know about it? Am I correct in saying this?"

"Certainly! Nothing happens here without a decision from me first."

"Do you have any knowledge of, or have you had any knowledge of your bank's activities in relation to Shuito Pharmaceuticals?"

"Absolutely not! Why do you ask?"

"I'm afraid I can't answer that. As you can imagine, I am subject to the right of journalistic confidentiality and I must protect my sources. But I must insist: you confirm that you have no knowledge of ZIS investments in Shuito Pharmaceuticals?"

"I confirm, Mr. Campbell!"

"Ok, thank you Mr. Ziegler. For your information, this biotech company has been the victim of recent stock market attacks, and we believe that one or many financial institutions are implicated in this attack."

"I have nothing more to add regarding this subject, but surely you don't believe that my company would have anything to do with such an attack?"

"No, or course not!" Jack replied, his two hands raised in front of him.

"This would obviously constitute a violation of our code of conduct," the CEO felt obliged to add.

"Thank you, Mr. Ziegler, I have no further questions!" Jack declared after a few seconds, switching off his Dictaphone.

"Good. I will see you out," replied the banker in a tone which was lacking in any of its initial friendliness.

Ziegler pressed a button on his desk and the door opened as if by magic, letting the pretty receptionist back in to escort them all the way to the exit.

The CEO of ZIS wasn't smiling anymore. He had no idea how these two men were aware of the existence of Millenium. Storx confirmed that Campbell had come to question him, which was already a cause for concern, but Shuito... he couldn't keep this to himself. He had to warn Füller. He would know what to do.

The rain continued to fall heavier and heavier, and a strong wind from the lake was pounding the front of the buildings in raging gusts. Jack and Thomas were holding their jackets close to them to keep the cold from getting in.

"That didn't get us very far!" Thomas lamented. "He straight up just denied everything!"

"Of course it got us somewhere! That was just a bit of fishing; laying the bait. You saw his reaction when I mentioned Shuito? He wanted to know what we'd discovered about Millenium. But when we started to talk about Shuito his jaw almost hit the floor. It's just bait Thomas... trust me, we'll get a reaction."

"You're sure?"

"Totally. Now they're going to want to know exactly what we know, how we know it, and, especially, who else knows! Don't you just love fishing, Thomas? Don't you? It won't be long before they bite. Then we just reel 'em in!"

"Easy!" said Delvaux. "But a little dangerous, maybe?"

"I don't think so. They can't get rid of a top journalist and a talented developer just like that. One hunk, the other a little bald, but still."

"I hadn't noticed that you were losing your hair," quipped Thomas, his smile showing all of his teeth.

"Well in any case, I think it would be a good thing for you to go to his conference tomorrow to see what that's about. What do you think?"

"Sure, but first we need to go and see Luca."

"Who's Luca?" asked Jack.

"Someone I know through work, he's an IT expert and a good friend. I'd even say that he's an ally."

"You can't tell me any more than that?"

"You'll see. Let's just say that it's someone who could really be a help to us."

*
* *

Delvaux's 4x4 got back on the road, and despite the howling wind and rain that whipped the windshield, they drove for a good hour at a pretty decent pace. Once out of the city, they left the highway and started to climb the ridges of the massif that surrounded the lake. They were coasting along a road that overlooked this vast expanse of water, which took on disturbing colors in shades of gray. There were large broken clouds hanging on the side of the mountain, disappearing in the wind. The whole scene gave the landscape the appearance of a black and white photo.

"Almost there!" declared Thomas.

"Even in this weather it's beautiful," said Jack, who couldn't take his eyes away from the view.

"It's the type of landscape that has some personality, you know? Sometimes welcoming, other times a little cantankerous.

That's why the people here wouldn't leave for all of the gold in the world."

"I hope you didn't just bring me here to admire the view?"

"No, don't worry. We're here!"

Delvaux slowed down, turned off the road and went into a courtyard of what looked like an old but perfectly restored alpine farm. The entire building formed a 'U', with the main house in the center. The 4x4 stopped, and the front door of the house opened. Two large dogs ran towards the car. Luca Hanser, behind them, hurried to the open door for Delvaux.

"Come in, hurry!" Hanser said loudly, his voice almost completely drowned out by the wind.

"Thank you!" replied Thomas, "This weather!" Delvaux kept his arms tightly around his body to keep his jacket from blowing open, one hand holding the collar.

"You've brought a visitor?" asked Luca.

"Yes. I'll explain."

The group ran toward the open door which was blowing in the wind. In the few seconds it took to fight the gusts of wind to reach the house, everyone had received a good soaking. Luca Hanser disappeared for a few seconds before returning with some towels so they could dry themselves off. This lanky guy in his thirties with long hair that covered his eyes, an old t-shirt and ripped jeans, looked something like a child who was visiting for the weekend. It was difficult to believe that he was in fact the owner of this farm lost in the middle of the valleys of Switzerland. "Coffee?" Hanser offered.

"Wouldn't say no!" the two visitors responded in harmony.

Jack was impressed by Luca's home, decorated in the manner of a traditional alpine farm. This type of rectangular wooden building, with its low roof that prevented snow from accumulating, was dotted all around the Swiss valleys. This one had been tastefully transformed into a modern house. Enlarged windows to let the light through, open walls covered with old wood and rough stone. They'd installed a huge bay window that gave a direct view onto the lake. In one corner, was a sleek fireplace that added a contemporary character to the main room.

The temperature outside had fallen to just below ten degrees. A warm welcome radiated from the lit fireplace.

Luca took three mugs from the cupboard and placed them under the Jura coffee machine. It started to grind the beans and noise filled the room.

"Strong or very strong?" Luca asked, turning toward his guests.

"Strong!" the visitors responded simultaneously.

"Luca, this is Jack Campbell, a journalist at the New York Times," Delvaux began.

"A journalist, huh?" Luca replied, a little nervously.

"Don't worry, Luca, he's a friend. You can trust him."

Hanser put the three steaming mugs on a tray and invited his guests to sit down. Jack was unsure of what was happening; Luca was being somewhat defensive. Jack decided to take a backseat in the proceedings.

"Just so everyone's clear about who's who, I'll do the introductions," said Thomas, picking up his mug.

Luca and Jack looked at each other and nodded.

"Jack, this is Luca Hanser. Luca is a computer expert whom I've often worked with. He helped me to develop my high frequency trading algorithm. It's partly thanks to him that I'm able to scan in real-time the financial world and find out who is buying what, for whom, who's putting out false orders to cover their tracks and so on."

"OK!" Jack replied.

"Wait, wait! You remember how I listened to the networks so I could trace Millenium's activities?" Delvaux asked, deliberately placing an emphasis on 'listened'.

"Of course, that's how you were able to find out about ZIS," Jack confirmed.

"Exactly! In order to do that, I needed some help in modifying my software. Guess who it was who gave me that bit of help?"

"Luca?"

"Right again! We've known each other for a few years, and as well as his work as an IT consultant, Luca also helps with cases that are, let's say, unofficial."

"I see."

Delvaux turned toward Hanser:

"Luca, this is Jack Campbell. Jack's an old friend of mine. We met while I was still at university, which tells you everything. You can trust him as you trust me. We're investigating Millenium Dust and ZIS together."

"OK," Luca responded.

"Good, the introductions are over. Now to what brings us here."

"Tell me!" Hanser urged, looking insistently at Thomas Delvaux.

"I believe that Millenium's plan is to take control of certain companies. Shuito Pharmaceuticals is a good example, but something tells me that they're going to let that one go. Imagine if they attacked bigger capitalizations. I'm sure they've designed a super-powerful software tool, and soon they're going to use it on a large scale. I don't know when or where, but we have to be ready."

"With you so far."

"Our options are limited. We can't go to the police. We got nothing except some elements that were obtained illegally. So we're alone."

"What do you propose we do?" asked Jack.

"I'm getting to that. If Luca were to have connections with, let's say... other individuals that were able to help us. With their help, we too could write a tool that could be a sort of firewall against Millenium Dust."

"Don't even think about it, Thomas," Luca interjected, "it's too much work!"

"I know, that's why I had this idea." Delvaux removed a hard disk from his jacket.

"What's that?" Jack enquired curiously.

"This is part of my life!" replied Thomas. "On this disk is Black Mamba. It's the name of the virtual snake I created because it lurks in cyberspace, and when it sees the type of transaction that I'm looking for, boom! He captures it."

"Black Mamba!" exclaimed Luca.

"Yeah, well, marketing isn't exactly my forte. It's better if I just stick to what I'm good at, right? But the content is there. If we have enough developers working on it, with Black Mamba as the starting point, we could write some software that would allow us to pre-empt any type of attack by Millenium."

Jack and Luca looked at each other. They began to understand what Thomas Delvaux had in mind. If indeed Millenium had a virtual weapon of mass destruction that could attack the financial system and nobody knew about it, with the time it would take to get the story out and o build a case, it would definitely be too late. The idea of building a firewall, a kind of defensive mechanism in case of an attack, would be an effective countermeasure. Plus, they didn't really have any other options.

"What do you think?" Delvaux asked, turning to Luca.

"Maybe it's not such a bad idea!" replied the IT expert. "The thing would be to position ourselves between the initial order and the computers that process the buying and selling information, then filter what happens. If it's Millennium, we can stop it or at least slow it down. Given that their technology is without doubt an incredibly smart automaton that scrutinizes stock prices, if they are disorganized, it could be enough to cause their attempt to fail. Very tempting, Thomas!"

"So, you're in?" Delvaux, eyebrows raised, looked in Luca Hanser's direction.

"Woah there! Slowly… I'd have to talk to my people who I work on the web with and then make a decision. But you know, these guys are more about causing havoc on the Internet and generally being a nuisance to corporations… they're not so much into defending them!"

"Yeah but this would be a casus belli… a war to prevent a war. If we do nothing at all to stop them, we could all wake up one fine morning with a very ugly hangover! We don't know who is behind Millenium, but it's possible that they have some seriously bad intentions!"

"Listen, Thomas, I can't answer you now, but I promise I'll speak to the group."

"That's all I was hoping for. I'm going to leave you with the crown jewels. Please take good care of it, OK?" Delvaux said, handing Luca the disk drive containing Black Mamba.

"Thanks, Thomas. Your exotic virtual pet is safe with me!"

"I just have one last question."

"Go ahead."

"I need a cube. You don't have one here, do you?"

"Follow me!"

Luca opened the door and walked to the building next to the main house, followed by his two guests. They were fighting against the wind, their heads bowed and their eyes narrowed to protect themselves from the rain that was lashing their faces. The weather didn't seem to want to let up. All three of them entered a large room that was still under construction.

"I haven't been able to finish all the interior renovations yet. When I bought the farm, it was falling into ruin. Welcome to my lair!"

The space must have been the barn. The room boasted an impressive high ceiling and had been completely redone. The plasterboard was still unpainted, but the whole setting was more than comfortable for an office.

Jack couldn't believe his eyes. In front of him was a huge worktop covered with computers and screens that were displaying data in real time. Obviously, Luca was connected, hanging on the breath of the world's stock exchanges. A library containing technical books and open books, alongside a soldering iron and electronic tools, placed between two computer carcasses during assembly or disassembly.

"I think it's in the other room. Wait a second, I'll just be a minute."

"What does Luca actually do?" Jack asked in a lowered voice.

"He's a developer but he also does some hacking... I thought you had gotten that?"

"He's got the gear, I can see that!"

"He's well known on the Internet. But no one in town knows his name."

"Except you?"

"Except me…"

Luca came back holding a box. It was a black cube, about six inches on each side.

"Here you go. You know how it works, right?"

"Sure. Thank you, Luca!"

After a few words of farewell, Jack and Thomas shook hands with Luca and headed back to Zurich. Jack was beginning to feel the fatigue that had accumulated during the trip and after this long day. He needed a good night's sleep. His demons were being strangely calm. A change of scenery and a break in his usual routine was doing him rather well.

Thomas and Jack had planned to go to Ziegler's conference on investment strategies. They needed the CEO of ZIS to see them in order to put a little more pressure on him. When you go fishing, you have to wiggle the bait if you want something to bite. Thomas would pick Jack up the next day at 9 o'clock.

*
* *

Anti Game

11. PIRACY

Friday September 22 – Zurich

Thomas Delvaux parked his 4x4 in front of the hotel at 9 am sharp. Jack was sat at a table blowing on a hot cup of coffee, with a plate of scrambled eggs and bacon in front of him. Thomas joined him and ordered a coffee while they waited until it was time to go to the conference. The historic center of Zurich was not very big, and the hotel where the event would take place was not far.

Jack looked out the bar window. The weather had barely improved. The wind was dying down but the rain continued to blur the surface of the lake.

They arrived at the conference venue at 9.30 am. It was a very old hotel in Zurich. Delvaux was carrying a backpack that Jack guessed contained Luca's magic cube.

They followed the signs that directed guests to the conference and made their way to the first floor. Everything was supposed to begin 10.30 am, so no other guests had arrived yet. Only the staff who were working the event were there placing name badges of the registrants on the tables ready for the first arrivals, who they expected to be there for around 10.

Delvaux gestured to Jack for them to go back down the stairs where they took a seat in the chic hotel bar.

"Jack?"

"Yeah?"

"You know that we're not here to listen to Ziegler sell his strategies to indecisive investors?"

"Yes, I know. But what are you planning to do?"

"We're going to tap his phone."

"Tap his phone!" Jack repeated, whispering.

"Exactly!"

"You can do that?"

"You know, I've been listening to networks and working in computer espionage for years. It's all been legal of course, but it's espionage nonetheless. So you can imagine I've picked up a few things along the way."

"Working with a certain Luca, for example?"

"For example. But that was a long time ago now. Here's how we're going to do it: we'll both go upstairs. We have Ziegler's number on his business card. When he arrives, I'll start up the device. It's really quite simple, how it works. It's a mini computer that can set up a local Wi-Fi network that scans all of the phones here within a thirty-meter radius. As soon as it recognizes Ziegler's, it will pair with it. The network will look exactly like the hotel's, so it should be totally undetectable. Once that's done, I'll come back down to the bar and do what needs to be done."

"As easy as that?"

"Almost! I'm missing out a few of the details, but yes, in principle it's extremely easy to gain access to someone's phone."

"Won't you need his code to unlock it?"

"Most codes are made up of four digits. Six, maximum. That's easy to get through once I'm connected."

"What if his Wi-Fi isn't switched on?"

"That would make things a little more difficult, but it's still possible to do. If that happens, I'll turn the device into an antenna. Basically, I position myself between the operator's signal, which will be somewhere on the street, and Ziegler's phone. That way it thinks that I am the antenna. You know that phones connect and reconnect to the network multiple times a minute in order to ensure the signal quality is good. So as soon as the phone sends a signal to the antenna to test the network, I get hold of it and put myself in between the two. He won't notice a thing. You'd have to look very closely to notice anyone interfering."

"Then what?" asked Jack, a little perturbed that it was that easy to tap into someone's phone.

"Then I'll make him think that he needs to reconnect and ask him to re-enter his PIN to unlock his phone. Then, bingo!! I can do what I want."

"Unbelievable!"

"Yep. The worst thing is that most high-level people work in organizations that make sure their offices are something like a digital safe. They invest millions of dollars to be certain that their networks aren't interconnected so they can't be hacked and no data gets leaked. Like for example when we were at ZIS yesterday, I ran a check and sure enough: no Wi-Fi. They had blockers to make sure no info can get out. It's water tight."

"But…!"

"But. As soon as they leave their offices, they walk around with the key to all of this information hanging around their neck, with a scrolling sign on their forehead with the message: "come and get me". It's pathetic. You know that the secret service from your country had to erase the information on the BlackBerry that Obama carried around with him. Don't even get me started on Hillary's emails!"

"Maybe his phone is encrypted?"

"That is a possibility. If so, we're screwed. But what can I say? I don't think for a second that it will be. The problem with secured smartphones is that you can't do anything with them. You use loads of apps on your iPhone. Snapchat, WhatsApp, email, Internet browser, Microsoft Office, and so on…"

"Yeah, like everyone does."

"Sure. That's why no one encrypts their telephone, it's just too heavy. You wouldn't be able to use even standard apps. On the contrary, everyone wants to be connected."

"Agreed."

"And I bet you he has an iPhone," Delvaux concluded, sure of himself.

"OK, I'm going upstairs. I think the first guests are here. Join me as soon as you see Ziegler?"

"Let's do this."

It was 10.10 am. Jack went up the stairs and was greeted by a young man who asked him for his name. His name wasn't on the list. They gave him a name badge in exchange for some ID.

With a glass of orange juice in his hand he awaited the arrival of Ziegler. The first guests were settling into their places in the conference room.

When the CEO of ZIS made his entrance, Jack hid behind a group of visitors who were discussing the good performance of the markets. Thomas Delvaux, a backpack carelessly resting on his shoulder, magically appeared next to him.

Ziegler saw Jack approaching him with his hand extended for a handshake, and his smile immediately disappeared.

"Hello Mr. Ziegler! It's good to see you again. As you can see, I followed your advice and I can't wait to hear some of your investment recommendations for the coming year."

"Welcome," Ziegler responded scornfully, before disappearing.

Thomas placed his backpack on one of the tables next to the entrance door that Ziegler had just walked through and acted like he was absorbed in looking for something important.

After a few minutes he looked at Jack, smiling. He nodded and made his way back down the stairs.

At the same time, Marco Ziegler was busy walking around shaking the hands of people who approached him. Suddenly he stopped, his phone vibrating in his pocket. He answered it briefly, hung up and then, by force of habit, turned it off as he always did before giving a talk.

During those few seconds, Jack was able to see that Marco Ziegler did indeed have an iPhone, exactly as Thomas said he would.

Downstairs in the bar, Thomas Delvaux had just managed to connect to Ziegler's phone. He hadn't taken the time to switch off the Wi-Fi. In just a few seconds the connection was set up. Everything was going as planned. He launched the program that would find the phone's password, when suddenly he lost the signal. Thomas launched the search again. Ziegler's number had disappeared from the scanner. His phone was off.

On the first floor the conference had begun. Jack did a quick headcount. Fifty people. All of these financiers had come to listen to the vision of the private bank's CEO. After a flattering introduction from the organizer, Marco Ziegler, all smiles, began his presentation. Nothing very revolutionary, Jack thought, as he went through his PowerPoint presentation.

Forty minutes later, after some light applause, the presentation was over and everyone was invited to stay for a drink.

A member of staff walked up to Ziegler, who leaned sideways as the hotel manager whispered something into his ear. He then nervously took out his phone from his pocket, inspected the screen and typed in a number. He had a brief conversation before hanging up, visibly upset. He seemed to be looking for something as he typed on the keyboard. After a few moments he placed the phone back in his pocket.

Jack was watching all of this unfold in the room opposite him. He didn't know what to think. He saw Thomas mingle into the crowd, backpack on his shoulders, before repeating what he had tried to do before the conference. He placed his bag once again on a table near the corridor, rummaged around as if he were searching for something inside, and then disappeared.

Jack was talking to a few of the guests. Too young, too finance and too full of themselves, he thought to himself. After around twenty minutes, he decided to go and find Thomas at the bar.

Delvaux seemed to be very busy with something. He was typing frantically into a tablet that was connected to the cube. Lines of data continuously streamed down the screen. Thomas took out a USB stick and plugged it into the tablet. He looked at Jack and instructed him to sit down. They didn't have much time.

Once the USB as connected, Delvaux typed in a command. '1% complete' the blue progress bar on the table indicated as it crept right. '10%', '20%', then '50%'. Suddenly it stopped. Thomas rubbed his eyebrows. A few seconds later, the bar began moving again and the data grab continued. Within less that a minute the bar was at 100%, then disappeared.

"There you go Jack, it's done!" Delvaux seemed relieved.

"We should get out of here," urged Campbell.

"Wait. There's just one more little thing I need to do."

"OK, but hurry!"

He took another USB key from his bag and plugged it into the tablet that was still connected to the cube by Bluetooth. After he'd entered a few more commands, a message appeared on screen: 'Upload in progress'. The hourglass icon turned a few times before a new message appeared: 'Upload successful'.

"Boom! Take that!" Delvaux couldn't help but let out a little victory cry.

"You're really done this time?"

"I'm ready. Let's go!"

Delvaux left a ten Swiss-franc note on the table, packed up his things, and they left the hotel together.

*
* *

They drove along peacefully in the 4x4. The rain had stopped and the wind had lost its morning vigor. The freshness of this early autumn seemed to have settled in Switzerland for the long run. Jack contemplated the center of Zurich where old buildings with Alemannic accents alternated with recent buildings. Jack felt no attraction to this quiet city and its endless gray façades, where dull inhabitants all walked with their head down. He was missing New York. Its craziness, its perpetual movement and especially its incomparable music scene.

"So?" asked Jack.

"Mission accomplished!" replied a euphoric Delvaux. "I copied his whole phone. Emails, documents, his diary, his messages, I even got access to his playlists if that floats your boat. What do you say about that, Jack?"

"I don't know what happened, but he switched off his phone before the presentation. I mean, what else should we have expected! Then, when one of the hotel employees came up to him afterwards, he put it back on. That was kind of lucky, don't you think?"

"You think?" asked Delvaux, smiling ecstatically.

"It was you!"

"You got me."

"How did you get that to happen?!"

"After the conference had finished, I called the hotel pretending to be a ZIS employee and asked for Ziegler to get in touch with his office asap because there was an important message waiting for him."

"That's why he made the call, to check if they had this message for him!"

"Yep! And that's how I managed to connect to his phone."

"I still can't believe it. It's so... stupid of him not to secure his data better."

"Always the same thing. They're all sinful in their pride. Think it only happens to other people. You've heard about that before, right?"

"We're going to your place?"

"Yeah, I don't really feel like going to the office, and, you know, I'd like you to meet Hanna!"

"Will your kids be there too?"

"No, they'll be at school now. You'll see them tonight, if you'd like to have dinner with us. If you want!"

"That would be great, I'd love to. In the meantime, can we take a look at what's on that USB?"

"That's exactly what we're going to do. I hope it's going to clear a lot of things up for us."

"By the way, Thomas?"

"Yeah?"

"What's on the second USB?"

"Oh that one? Nothing really important! The real question we need to ask is what's on Ziegler's phone?"

"And what do you think the answer is?"

"Probably a virus!" replied an enigmatic Thomas.

They stopped in front of Delvaux's house looking out over the lake. Once the car was parked, Jack made his way down to take in the magnificent view. While the still-low sky perhaps didn't give the landscape its true depth, the view of the two undulating banks with their winding paths of asphalt intertwining between the buildings was captivating.

Hanna's car wasn't there; they were alone. They went in and Thomas led Jack into his office. The rectangular room had a large bay window that took up almost an entire wall. The view of the lake was breathtaking. An iMac sat atop a glass surface on Wenge-wood furniture, adding to the room's overall feeling of soothing cleanliness.

Thomas switched on his computer and plugged in the USB, which gave a little beep as he did so, confirming that it was connected. Thomas launched the FraNex app and within a few seconds some more icons had appeared on the screen. The entire digital life of Marco Ziegler was there, right in front of them: emails, SMS, his calendar, contacts and everything in between.

"Where do we start?" Thomas asked.

"Check his most recent mail. Then we'll get into his calendar on contact list."

"Let's do it!"

They spent much of the afternoon trying to make sense of the email exchanges of the bank's CEO.

*
* *

Marco Ziegler was in the car on his way to the airport, watching the landscape roll by. He'd left the conference not long after it had ended and his flight to the United States was scheduled to take off in less than one hour. Upon his arrival he was met by Storx who took him directly to their New Haven offices for one final inspection. The acceleration of the launch of the BLACKSTONE project required that all the centers be ready for the 24th. On his way back he would make stops in London and Paris for final checks. A little bit of pressure never hurt anyone, he thought. Everything had to be operational on D-day.

He still needed to deal with the two interferers. The American journalist and his shadow represented a real danger to the project. He couldn't be sure what they knew, but the mere fact of being able to connect Millenium, ZIS and Shuito, was more than enough to cause serious concern.

Thinking back to his discussion with Füller still gave him the cold sweats. When Campbell and Delvaux had left his office, he contacted the Chancellor's adviser immediately, who had been very clear. It was necessary to get rid of these two troublemakers as soon as possible. "Definitively," he specified.

Ziegler was no altar boy, and he knew that when it came to business, things weren't always done by the rules. But killing was not his job. It was not part of the contract. Füller didn't seem to care much for small details such as this, however, leaving Ziegler no choice but to do the dirty work.

He'd contacted his chief of security, an ex secret services agent, and it was he who was going to fix the problem. For added security, Ziegler asked that this be done when he was on the plane. If things went wrong, he could always prove he wasn't there on the day of the accident. He wanted to put as much distance as possible between him and the problem. It was not cowardice but prudence, he tried to convince himself.

*
* *

Jack and Thomas were piecing together the chronology of events using Ziegler's emails. They didn't have all of the answers yet, but already it was clear that Ziegler and Storx were in frequent contact, and that Millenium was the armed wing of ZIS that bought and sold shares on the financial markets on their behalf.

They'd also discovered that Millenium had offices not only in New Haven, but also in Paris and London. If it could be extrapolated that these offices were computer centers, one might begin to wonder why they needed them in three different countries. They saw from the very latest email exchanges that Ziegler was putting pressure on the three operational centers' directors, reminding them of the sensitive nature of their activity and that security was an absolute priority. There was almost a threatening air about his messages, of repercussions should any information happen to slip out under their watch.

They came across an email containing requests for approvals for expenses. It was close to fifty million dollars. After reading through the conversations they deduced that it was for the centers' IT equipment. Jack thought back to with his conversation in the Woodbridge hamburger restaurant. If indeed they had built offices that had access to extraordinary power, it is to be expected that they also had a lot of equipment that required it. The question was: why?

There was something else that had grabbed their attention: in many of the emails, a project called BLACKSTONE was continuously being mentioned without any explanation as to exactly what it was. They cross-checked the information and concluded that a videoconference had taken place two days earlier between the members of this BLACKSTONE project.

Oddly, his phone contained very few contacts. "Ziegler is not completely stupid," Jack thought. "He knows the numbers of important people by heart. He doesn't want to leave any traces."

There were many emails concerning the management of the bank, ZIS' clients, financial arbitrations, and so on. Daily business. Nothing that needed to have the fine-tooth comb treatment.

Ziegler must have set up his phone so messages didn't remain on it for very long before being deleted. There was nothing older than ten days on it.

"Good!" said Thomas Delvaux, rolling back on his chair and folding his arms.

"What's good?" Jack responded, a little surprised.

"I think I'm beginning to understand. I'm having to use my imagination, but I think I'm starting to get what's going on here."

"Lucky you. I'm completely lost!"

"Let me explain a little. Firstly, there's this company, Millenium Dust, that buys and sells shares on the financial markets but stays in the shadows so that it remains anonymous. I stumbled upon this company, because after all, my job is to scrutinize the markets. With me so far?"

"Yep!"

"So, the other thing that got me curious is that over the last twelve months, Millenium has bought over one hundred billion dollars-worth of shares Jack! One hundred billion dollars. Can you even imagine how much that is?"

"Yeah, especially when you consider the grand total traded on the markets each day is two-hundred eighty billion, that's a lot of influence on the markets."

"Exactly. And that's precisely what they want."

"How so?"

"Added to the fact that Millenium Dust even exists, we have ZIS setting up super-powerful operations centers, and we also know that they're at the very epicenter of a secret project called BLACKSTONE. Then you take into account what happened with the manipulation of Shuito Pharmaceuticals' shares, and what conclusion do you reach, Jack?"

"No idea."

"I think we come to the conclusion that these people have a weapon of massive market manipulation. They have the technological competence, as we saw with Shuito, they have the capital and they're currently finishing up the construction of multi-million-dollar computer platforms."

"Jesus! You think they're about to unleash something?"

"That's what I'm worried about. I think this damn BLACKSTONE project is what I've just described to you. It's the name they've given to their plan for market manipulation on a global scale."

"Let's say that you're right, what exactly are we looking at? How dangerous could this be?"

"It depends who's behind all this! If they're objective is to make money, we're going to see a massive sell-off."

"Or...?"

"Or... they could completely destabilize the global markets. Even worse than that, they could target specific businesses, taking over the entire capital of... I don't know... sensitive companies, like nuclear or biotech firms or research centers. Anything is possible, Jack, that's the problem!"

"Enough to send shivers down your spine... what do we do? We can't be sure about any of this, it's just speculation!"

"That's true, but I don't think it's very far from what's really going here. There are still some things that don't add up, but when you put together what we do know, it spells very bad news. Bad news that we can't share with many people at all."

"When do you think they'll do it?"

"It could happen at any time! I think they'll need some big event to set it all off, though. Some kind of happening that will signal the charge. If we can somehow find out what that event is that will put the spark to the powder, we'll know then!"

"Any ideas?"

"Nothing. Not yet, anyway."

Delvaux, whose unrelenting good mood seemed to be unalterable, was beginning to look tired. The wrinkles on his forehead and his frowning eyebrows indicated that he was worried. After inspecting Ziegler's cell phone, he'd called Luca Hanser and spent an hour on the phone with the hacker. He said nothing about the content of his discussion, but his absent air and closed expression did not bode well.

Once Jack got back to his hotel, he started to write down what had happened. Just as in 2008 during the subprime debacle, he was keeping a journal about their investigation and noting each discovery day by day. Should any big, explosive event indeed happen, he'd have something on which to base this almost unbelievable story on, and let the world know how it all came to be.

It was Friday and Delvaux's wife had called. She was going to spend the night at her parents' with the kids. Jack and Thomas decided they'd go and have dinner at a restaurant just on the outskirts of Zurich. Thomas arranged to pick Jack up at 6.30 pm. Dinner is eaten quite early in Switzerland and that suited Jack just fine, especially seeing as he always suffered terrible jetlag.

*
* *

Anti Game

12. INTIMIDATION

Delvaux's 4x4 was waiting for Jack in front of the hotel right on time. "Swiss punctuality is not just a myth," Jack remarked as he climbed into the vehicle. He just had time to put on his belt before they were on their way. Neither of them noticed the white Ford Transit that had been following them for several minutes.

Thomas' restaurant was located about twenty miles from the city center in Wyssenbach. They skirted the west bank of the lake via the A3 south to the Richterswil exit, and then took the D8 to the two Michelin-starred restaurant where Thomas had made a reservation.

The road narrowed as the urban setting gave way to a landscape of fields and forests. The radio played classical music. There was almost no traffic now, allowing Thomas and Jack to relax, each one lost in their own more or less dark thoughts.

The shock was violent.

A white van had hit the rear of the 4x4, which skidded on the narrow road. Thomas's sudden swerve sent them toward the verge at the side. The automatic assistance took over and the vehicle was able to recover. The two surprised men understood only too late that it was not an accident, but a deliberate maneuver to get them off the tarmac.

Delvaux looked in the rearview mirror by reflex and braked as Jack turned to see who had tried to bump them. He realized after a few moments that their pursuers were trying to overtake them on the left and was about to hit them hard on the side.

The quick speed of the aggressors in changing their tactic meant there wasn't enough time to avoid the maneuver. The impact this time was even more brutal than the first hit, sending them into the ditch. Delvaux wasn't able to straighten his wheels and the 4x4 was being pushed little by little towards the trees. Another car was approaching them from the opposite direction, causing the attacking driver to apply a little more gas and take the place of Jack and Thomas in order to avoid the oncoming vehicle.

Due to the power of the side impact, the 4x4 was now off-balance. The car began to rise into the air as the left wheels lost contact with the road.

The Ford Transit narrowly avoided the driver coming from the opposite direction, who passed them sounding his horn.

The passengers in the 4x4 saw the trees spinning. The sky was slipping beneath them and for a fraction of a second that seemed to last an eternity, they were weightless. Then, as if someone had just reconnected them to reality, they felt the shock just as the roof of the car violently hit the ground. Their circular motion was stopped as they collided with a tree. The windows exploded under the power of shock. Thomas felt intense shooting pain in his arm the moment they hit. The airbags inflated upon impact, and within a millisecond a dull bang sounded in the cockpit. They were now slipping on the wet soil from the rains that had fallen over the past few days. Jack lost consciousness. He was bleeding profusely from the nose.

Eventually the 4x4 stopped moving. After the shock, the sound of screeching metal and the explosion of windows, there was silence.

They remained thus, upside down, suspended only by their seatbelts. Thomas looked at Jack. The journalist was lifeless and covered in blood that was dripping from from his hair.

"Jack?" Thomas called. No answer. He realized that his left arm was not responding.

"Jack, can you hear me?" Thomas repeated, a little louder. Still no reaction. He could see that his passenger breathing slightly.

"Shit, shit, shit!" Thomas cursed.

His head was spinning. Shock and adrenaline, no doubt. A veil began to blur his eyes. He felt tired. His last thought was that they were both alive. Then he was caught in the void, the light disappeared and the black covered everything.

The car that narrowly avoided the Ford Transit stopped a few meters after the accident. With his hazard lights activated, the passenger went out to observe the horror of the accident he had just witnessed. He approached the 4x4 to try to save the occupants of the vehicle while the driver called for help. A cell phone kept ringing in the crashed vehicle.

*
* *

Hanna had just left another message on Delvaux's voicemail after he failed once again to pick up. She was beginning to get worried. Usually, Thomas picked up on the first ring. She was having dinner with the kids at her parents' house when the security company called her. FraNex's alarm, connected to Thomas's phone, had sounded, but they couldn't get in contact with him. She was second in the list of people to call in case a problem such as this should arise. As soon as she had this information, she ran into the office.

The scene was surreal. The flames rising high into the sky could be seen from hundreds of yards away. The police had stopped traffic from entering the area where Thomas's company was located. They evacuated the site and put security at the entrances. She introduced herself as the manager of FraNex and was allowed to park.

The offices were in flames. At this point, there wasn't much left of the company. The fire had devoured the building and the roof had collapsed. The firefighters, who had been hard at work for an hour, had managed to prevent fire spreading to the other companies on the opposite side of the car park, but they couldn't do anything to save FraNex. The flames had consumed everything and the hoses had sprayed many cubic meters of liquid onto the building containing computers, printers, and other mostly electronic equipment that would not be able to withstand the wet conditions. To put it simply, this conjunction of fire and water meant that FraNex no longer existed.

Hanna gazed at the distressing spectacle with tears in her eyes. Her cell phone rang. She looked at the number and immediately felt a little better. She swallowed her tears. It was Thomas.

"Thomas?"

"Madam Delvaux," replied the stranger's voice at the other end of the line.

"Who's speaking?" Hanna asked, surprised.

"Hmm!" The voice sounded a little concerned now. "I'm calling you from the University Hospital of Zurich, Madame. Your husband and a passenger traveling with him were involved in a road accident approximately one hour ago. Please be assured Madam that their lives are not in danger. We'd be grateful if you could come by the hospital as soon as you possibly can."

Hanna burst into tears. She was crying so much that it blurred her horrible view. Too much repressed anxiety, too much emotion. She tried to contain herself. She grabbed a tissue and dabbed her eyes. Her mascara was running down her cheeks, but she didn't care. "Thomas at the hospital?" she thought.

"Madam, are you still there?" the voice insisted.

"Yes, sorry!" Hanna found the strength to articulate. "I'll be there as soon as I can. Sir?"

"Excuse me, I should have introduced myself. Brigadier Trudeau of the cantonal road police. We were notified of your husband's accident and we made sure he was taken to the hospital. He's in good hands. Meet me at the reception as soon as possible and ask to talk to me."

"How is my husband? How did it happen? It's serious?" The questions flickered in Hanna's mouth.

"He's fine, ma'am ... considering the situation. His days aren't numbered. He's being looked after by the on-site emergency team. Don't worry too much. Come here as soon as possible and I'll give you all the details."

"I'll be there as soon as possible!"

She hung up. What was happening? An accident, the company in flames. She felt that all this couldn't be a coincidence, a sentiment that filled her with dread.

Mrs. Delvaux went to the fire department and explained to the chief that she had to leave. In any case, they could do little more and the fire was visibly extinguished. The police would have to make the usual tests before anyone could even enter the site to save whomever and whatever may still be there. Of course, between some charred computers and Thomas, she knew where her priority was. She called her parents to tell them that she wouldn't be home for a while, but gave no more detail than that. It would be useless to scare them, too. She asked her mother to put the children to bed and kiss them goodnight for her. Ten minutes after the police call, Hanna was on her way to the hospital.

Emergencies have the particularity of making anyone outside the medical profession nervous. The patients, surrounded by sophisticated machines that beep every minute, slept for the most part. At regular intervals one could hear tensiometers inflating and alarms sounding far away, triggering nurses' arrival in blue and pink pajamas.

When Thomas opened an eye, the first thing he saw was the white ceiling and the light strip above him. A harsh light that made him close his eyes with some pain. He reopened them carefully to see the monitor in front of him displaying his vital data. He wanted to move his right hand and felt the catheter connected to a pipe, which was spinning towards a pole containing a pocket of colorless liquid. His bandaged left arm was causing him terrible pain.

The moment of surprise passed, he remembered Jack bleeding in the car before he'd lost consciousness. A nurse leaned over him.

"How are you feeling, Mr. Delvaux?"

"Good," Thomas answered softly, his throat was dry and talking was difficult.

"Excellent! Do you know where you are?" asked the nurse.

"In the hospital, I guess."

"Can you tell me what day it is today?"

"Uh... Friday, September 22nd?" a hesitant Thomas managed to articulate.

"Good! Everything seems to be in order. You were lucky if I understood correctly. It was a serious accident. You could well have stayed there."

"There were two of us in the 4x4, how's the other passenger?"

"He's fine. We've already taken him back to his room. He was bleeding profusely from the nose, but that's all. In any case, he'll have some beautiful bruising."

"My arm hurts!"

"Not surprising. The good news is that you have nothing broken. Your humerus dislocated at the clavicle at the moment of impact. It's bad, but there is nothing you can do. No plaster. Just patience and painkillers. That's all."

"I'll be like this for a long time?"

"I'd say at least a month. I'll call the doctor. He'll listen to you and if everything is in order you can go back to your room."

"Can I have some water please?"

"Not for the moment. As soon as you're up there you'll be given something to drink."

"Thank you!"

"You're welcome. I'll send the doctor right away."

Five minutes later, a guy in a white coat who seemed important asked him a few questions, then signed a document before hanging it on the bars in front of his bed. A nurse transported him through endless corridors. He found himself in a room as sad as a jail cell.

He sank into a restless sleep when someone knocked on his door. Hanna peeped her head through the door and smiled at him. She entered, accompanied by a policeman in uniform. She rushed in to kiss him.

"Thomas, I was so scared!" she said, taking his hand.

"I'm sorry, Hanna, it all happened so fast."

"I know, the brigadier told me," she said pointing to Trudeau, who was watching the scene in silence.

"How do you feel?" Tears began to roll down Hanna's worried face.

"Tired! It must be the shock. Don't cry, my love. All is well, everything is fine!"

"No, everything is not fine." Hanna, who had been crying silently now burst into tears, shaking with violent sobbing.

"It is, look!"

"No. FraNex burned down, Thomas. There's nothing left! Nothing!"

"What?"

"A fire broke out at around six thirty. I kept trying to call you but you didn't answer." She wiped her nose and tears. "I left you several messages."

"Burned down? Was it an accident?"

"Why?" asked the brigadier. "You think it could be arson?"

"No, no, of course not!" answered Delvaux, a little too quickly.

"Well then why would you ask that question?"

"No reason, I just wasn't even thinking," replied Delvaux, caught off guard.

"You weren't thinking, huh?" said Trudeau, displaying a dubious air.

"Is it badly damaged?"

Hanna nodded. Her eyes were red from tears and fatigue.

"Everything has been destroyed, Thomas, everything!"

Delvaux felt his belly tie up into knots. "FraNex has been destroyed! They tried to kill us and now they've reduced our chances at any kind of retaliation to zero," he thought.

"God fucking damn it," Delvaux whispered.

"Sorry?" Hanna asked.

"Nothing, I was talking to myself, Hanna. Where are the children?"

"At my parents'."

"Ok good. They'll be fine there."

"Mr. Delvaux, I'd like to ask you a few questions about the accident."

"I'm a little tired here!"

"It'll only take a few seconds. Witnesses have said that the white van deliberately attempted to force you off the road. Is this also your impression of the incident?"

"No, not at all. They were attempting to overtake us when a car coming from the opposite direction caused them to swerve into us, so I lost control. That's all."

"So, in your opinion, this was an accident?"

"Of course it was, what are you trying to suggest? They were a bit stupid to try the maneuver there, I'll give you that. But there was nothing more to it."

"OK, good. I'll come and take your full testimony tomorrow. I'll be back in the morning. Rest, Mr. Delvaux. You're going to need it. I'll leave you to spend some time with your wife"

"Thanks, Brigadier," answered Hanna.

The policeman left the room. Delvaux made a gesture for Hanna to approach.

"Hanna, please listen to me. You have to do exactly what I tell you, OK?"

"What's going on Thomas?" She was no longer speaking quietly.

"Ssh," Delvaux urged. He lowered his voice. "You have to go get some clean clothes for Jack and me. He's much taller than me and a lot thinner, too, so you'll have to just find what you can and bring them to me. Then take the kids to your sister's house!"

"Tonight?"

"Yes, tonight, and do it as soon as you can. We've uncovered a case of some serious financial fraud going on and it's given a big kick to the anthill to say the least. What you're seeing now is the result!"

"So, the accident was not an accident?"

"No, it was not an accident, and I'm afraid they'll come back for more. Jack and I have to get out of here, right now. I'll call you at your sister's house tomorrow. The priority is to get us some clothes. We need to get away from here as soon as we can."

"Where will you go?"

"Can you let Luca know what's happening?"

"Hanser?"

"Yes. Ask him to come get us. What time is it?"

"Eight thirty."

"He'd needs to be here by ten. Tell him to wait for us at the taxi stand."

"Okay, I'll call him when I leave. But you didn't answer me. Where will you go?"

"To the Miroir."

"The Miroir? Good idea! But how will you get there?"

"Don't worry, Luca will help us. He and his friends have already had to deal with emergencies."

"Are you sure?"

"Yes. Luca is used to living a little in the shadows, and for us, right now, a little bit of shadow would be welcome. We need to disappear."

"I understand. I'll go and be back as soon as possible, Thomas."

"Thank you. Hanna?"

"Yes?"

"I love you."

"I know, Thomas."

She left. The painkillers were beginning to take effect. Thomas felt like he was floating. "They must have used something pretty strong," he thought. The pain in his arm was gone. He tried to stay awake. He rang the nurse on duty. He was extremely thirsty.

It took about an hour for Hanna to make the round trip. She entered the room and discovered Delvaux deep asleep. He hadn't been able to fight the cumulative effects of the difficult day he'd just had and the drugs.

Hanna shook him gently. He opened his eyes; they were lost.

"Thomas, it's me! I brought you a bag with some spare clothes and your things to shave. I also got your passport and all the cash I could find."

"Thank you! Did you manage to get hold of Luca?"

"Yes. I explained the situation. He said he was leaving right away. He just needs to leave the farm and he'll be here not long after. Don't forget your things. What's left of them anyway. They put everything you were wearing in the closet. Take everything before you leave, okay?"

"What did you get for Jack?"

"He won't look as sharp as you! I just took what I thought might fit him, but I can't guarantee anything."

"You know where he is?"

"Yes, I just went to see him and told him that you were going to leave here in secret. He agreed. I'll bring him the bag with the things. Room 107, right down the hallway."

"You're an angel!"

"Yes, but, you know, I'm scared. You think they could hurt the kids?"

"I don't know, but we can't take any chances. Go with them and when things are a little clearer, I'll call you."

"I'll go and get them as soon as I leave and we'll disappear."

"Perfect Hanna. I'm so sorry!"

They kissed. Hanna left the room and took the change of clothes to Jack.

Thomas put one foot on the ground. His head was spinning. He needed to get used to being vertical again. He sat on his bed and started to get dressed. He stood up again. He was feeling better. He just needed to remove the catheter. He tore off the sticky tape that covered the tube and pulled gently. A drop of blood formed when the needle came out. He put the bandage back on to stop the bleeding.

*
* *

The two men, each wearing jeans, a black bomber and a red police armband on his right arm, entered the Zurich University Hospital. The first was tall, athletic and obviously the leader. He walked determinedly toward the reception desk. The second, bloated and balding, was used to playing second fiddle. He watched the door.

"Can you check the room numbers of two of your patients? Delvaux and a certain Campbell, please?" the black-eyed man asked peremptorily.

"The road accident victims?"

"Yes. They arrived at the end of the afternoon."

"There are no visitors allowed at this time, sir," the receptionist answered.

"That doesn't apply to us," the officer insisted, showing his armband and staring at the young woman with a look that said "you can trust me."

"My apologies!" She looked at her computer screen and scribbled the two room numbers on a Post-it note which she handed to the policeman. "Second floor," she said.

"Thank you," he replied before joining his colleague.

The two men made their way to the elevator, which beeped when the doors opened. "First floor," said the nasal voice through the speaker. The leader pressed the button for the second floor before the doors closed.

Hanna entered the reception foyer having taken the stairs just as the policemen's elevator began to ascend. She left the hospital.

"You see, I was right. All you got to do is wear an armband and be persuasive enough. You can get in almost anywhere," the leader boasted.

"What now?"

"Rooms ninety-six and one hundred seven," the tall, muscular man replied, looking at the Post-it.

"She could at least have asked to see some ID!" The side-kick seemed flabbergasted by the ease with which they had managed to gain entry.

"She should have. Obviously she didn't feel like it. Works out better for everyone like that. It would have created trouble..."

Silence reigned in the trauma department. Thomas left his room and headed down the hall. The nurses' office was on the other side of the building, so there was very little chance of him meeting anyone who might have asked what he was doing wandering the hallways. 104, 105, 106. He knocked on the door of Room 107.

"Come in!" He recognized Jack's distorted voice.

Jack was already dressed and ready to leave. His face, swollen with shock, was beginning to turn red. In a few days it would be black and before taking on a more purple hue. They'd put gauze in his nose; he must have been bleeding profusely.

"Are we going or are you staying here?" Thomas asked.

"I'm ready. You seem to be okay for someone who just ruined an expensive 4x4!"

"My left arm is pretty messed up, but other than that I'm all good. What about you?"

"I feel like I have been in a washing machine and my nose is making me feel sick. So, you know, on top of the world! How are you going to get us out of here?"

"Like everyone else. We'll take the service staircase."

"So you know where the secondary exits are?"

"I've been living in Zurich for quite a few years now. I've visited a few people in this place. You know I have a terrible sense of orientation, so I've lost myself a couple of times in these stairs and corridors. I know there's a service staircase that the people who work here use to avoid cluttering the elevator in the lobby."

"What'll we say if we bump into someone?"

"We don't say anything. If anyone asks, we'll say we got lost. Must happen all the time!"

"So, which way to we need to go?"

"Unless I'm mistaken, it's at the end of this corridor. Anyway, the hospital is a laid out in a 'U' shape, so we just need to go to the end of this one and if it is not there, it must be at the end of the other one."

The two policemen left the elevator. The signs on the wall indicated the directions for the rooms numbered eighty through eighty-nine, ninety through ninety-nine and one-hundred and up. The rooms ninety through ninety-nine were just ahead.

They walked silently towards room ninety-six. They arrived at Delvaux's door just as Jack and Thomas were entering the service staircase.

The chubby one took out his pistol and screwed on a silencer. He entered the room without knocking, gun in hand. The room was empty.

A quick look around allowed and they saw the used hospital pajamas thrown onto the bed, with the drip and catheter placed onto the small nightstand. The two fake policemen soon understood that Delvaux must have fled.

"Shit!" the little one cursed.

"He can't have gotten far."

"What do we do?"

"Let's check one hundred seven!"

Turning back around on themselves, they ran to Jack's room. Gone.

They rushed to the elevator that had already moved floors. To the stairs. They hurtled down the stairs taking four steps each time.

Jack and Thomas had just arrived at the ground floor. They needed to cross the entrance of the hospital that was being watched by the receptionist and they didn't want to be noticed. After a few moments, two men, with their police armbands on show, burst in front of the reception desk.

The taller of the two, visibly very angry, leaned in to the hostess. The young woman seemed to want to disappear behind her screen:

"The rooms are empty!" He shouted aggressively. "Did you see the two road accident victims leaving here?"

"No, gentlemen, no one has left, I can assure you."

"So where are they?" the fat one shouted.

"I don't know, but you shouldn't talk to me like that," said the employee, mustering all of her courage.

"Get me the trauma service on the phone. I want to talk to someone. Right now!" He hit the counter with the flat of his hand to punctuate his request.

"Stop screaming!" cried the young woman, clutching her ears with both hands.

The muscular man went around the reception, entered the small glass office and took out his weapon:

"Stay calm and take us to the people who can give us answers. Now!"

"You're not policemen!" murmured the terrified receptionist, her face now covered with tears.

"Shut up and take us to the Head of Department!"

The two men and the young woman disappeared towards the elevators. Jack and Thomas, still hiding behind the door leading into the lobby, looked at each other.

"Shouldn't we do something?" Jack asked.

"What do you want us to do?" answered Delvaux, "If we get involved we're dead!"

"We can not let this girl get hurt without doing anything!"

"Listen Jack. They're soon gonna find out that no one knows where we are and they'll stop. They're not going to kill all of the staff here! Plus, we don't have a weapon. And even if we did, I wouldn't have a clue how to use it."

"Let's get out of here and call the police?"

"I think that's the smartest thing to do!" Delvaux acquiesced.

They crossed the entrance to the hospital. The cold of the night hit them. Just as they got out, a vehicle parked next to the taxi station starting to flash them. Luca Hanser had answered the call of Thomas Delvaux. Seconds later, they were en route to the farm.

At 11 pm, the car entered the yard. They recounted to a stunned Luca the situation which they had plunged themselves into during the journey. He showed them to their rooms and they agreed they'd all catch up again the next morning. In any case, it was too late now to do anything and a good night's sleep was needed after the trying day they'd just been through.

Delvaux called the number of Hanna's sister and left the following message: "We're at the farm. We'll leave for the Miroir tomorrow morning."

Part Three:

Checkmate?

13. LE MIROIR

Saturday September 23

The landscape rolled past them at high speed. Luca was focused on the driving while the two other occupants dozed. Next to him, in the passenger seat, Delvaux was making a superhuman effort to keep his head up which was rolling back and forth with the movements of the road. So far, he had been unsuccessful.

Thomas and Luca's friendship had begun over ten years ago, just before the birth of FraNex, while Delvaux was developing the algorithms that he would use to listen to the financial markets. To test the initial results of his programs, he needed to connect to the banks' networks. No easy task. Luca, an inexperienced hacker, had rendered him his unorthodox services. This young man had quickly built a reputation and a name for himself within the hacker community. The competition between hackers is intense, and to be recognized in this underground network of geniuses, one needed to show an extraordinary level a skill. Which corresponded well to this tall boy with a frail figure. All he needed was a computer or any device with an Internet connection and he could get himself into any network or find out in just a few minutes your most secret information. If Luca Hanser wanted to make your digital life public, nothing could stop him doing it.

Luca's decision to work once again with Delvaux was an easy one, as soon as Thomas had told him about their attempted murder, the hospital scene and the FraNex fire. Together, they were going retaliate against these assassins. Ziegler and his data centers were now their targets. When the prey turns into a hunter and the latter chooses the field of confrontation, the outcome of the fight can turn in their favor. The hunt was going to be done in cyber space, and on this land, Luca Hanser was a master.

Jack, with his head resting against the back window, opened his eyes from time to time, a sign that he was awake, without uttering a word. All these events had happened one after the other far too quickly and it was high time to take stock. The pain in his nose had come back; the painkillers the hospital had administered him were no longer working. They'd have to refuel at the next pharmacy. Finding sleep when you've just survived an assassination attempt is not easy. The journalist was beginning to make this realization, in any case. He watched the road and the trees, the 4x4 coasting through the air and the silence, then the sound of crumpled metal, the broken windows and the endless screech of the car sliding on the ground. The spasms in his belly reminded him that he had not swallowed his anti-alcohol drugs for two days now. The sleeping demons were starting to wake up. The monsters were fidgeting, and he could feel their claws tickling his belly, ready to take their revenge. He began to panic, feeling the same symptoms as those in the New York bar a few days before. He breathed harder, he had to control himself.

The seven-hundred kilometer trip from Zurich to Paris wouldn't take too long. It was almost 9 am and they'd been driving for more than three hours now. There had been no border control, neither on the Swiss nor the French side. The road had been clear, although since they'd turned onto the A6 the traffic had gotten much heavier. The GPS of Luca's Volvo announced that they'd arrive in Paris for one o'clock.

Luca turned on his indicators so they could stop and take a break. They needed to refuel in any case. The car braked and the occupants, surprised by the change in engine speed, opened their eyes.

The 'Miroir', as Delvaux called it, referred to the company he'd acquired in Paris two years earlier. Its involvement in IT development, in addition to delivering financial algorithms to banks, consisted of analyzing transactions and markets. However, to produce the statistics and the studies which he resold at the price of gold, he had to store large quantities of information. Its server center was in Zurich at FraNex, but via a specialized connection he kept a duplicate of all the data on the Paris site for security. The function of the Miroir, besides helping him with developing, was to ensure that his activities could continue should any type of disaster occur. He hadn't foreseen that a cataclysm like the one he had just undergone could be intentional. But he was right to be careful. Not only had he lost none of his data or his business, but he and Luca would soon be able to get to work to stop these dangerous fools of Millenium Dust and BLACKSTONE.

Getting into Paris was always complicated, thought Thomas Delvaux. Luca was battling against the French drivers who seemed to think they were in some kind of video game. "We're not in Switzerland anymore," he thought, trying with difficulty to keep up with the other drivers on the road that encircled the city. Coasting in the middle lane, scooters were passing them on both sides.

"What am I supposed to do with these motorbikes blocking me from changing lanes?" asked Luca.

"Do what everyone else does. Put on your indicators, close your eyes, and you pray that they let you past," quipped Thomas Delvaux, amused by Luca's first experience of the Parisian péripherique.

"Doesn't seem very safe to me!"

"Well, you know I'm fifty-fifty, Luca: half French, half Swiss. So my Swiss side thinks "yeah, this is completely nuts", but the other thinks "meh, it's not that bad"!

"Yeah, well, me too. I'm also fifty-fifty," replied Luca. "Half Swiss from my father's side and half Swiss from my mother's side, and both of them agree it's absolutely ridiculous. Anyway, are we nearly there? I need to get ready to turn!"

"Come off at Porte Maillot. Then turn when you see the Hyatt Regency."

"So where's your office?"

"In La Défense Luca, like everyone else!"

"Is it far?"

"Fifteen minutes."

After having arrived at the premises of Delvaux's company, the two computer scientists sat opposite each other in the minimalist office and began to work under a silence that was only broken by the sound of typing on their keyboards. Night had fallen, and the weak halo of their lamp alone pierced the darkness. From his window Delvaux looked out across the deserted promenade of La Défense, illuminated by the innumerable lit buildings.

By the beginning of the afternoon, the two men were working at full speed on their project. Using the information that Delvaux's spy software Black Mamba had identified, they would go back and track Millenium's sale orders in order to hack into their computers. They wanted to get hold of a copy of their artificial intelligence program to understand properly how it works. There were many obstacles to achieving this. First, they needed to identify the source server. Luca was confident they could do this, however. He knew anything that passed through the Internet left some kind of trail, and he knew where and how to search for it. No, the most difficult task would be to circumvent Millenium's network security. Getting hold of the program once they'd broken in should be a breeze, at least in theory.

*
* *

Storx was waiting for Ziegler's flight to London to take off. Only then would he be able to breathe again. His work had just been put under the microscope and his boss seemed happy with what he'd seen. The US center of Millenium Dust was now officially operational. There was a little bit of fine tuning left to do, but the project BLACKSTONE could now be launched at any moment. Using resources from the other centers around the world they'd been able to perform simulations to test the outcomes. Everything had gone without a hitch. They'd checked input and output bandwidth, while any attempt to break into the system was confirmed to be impossible. The security barrier they had designed and deployed was impervious. Nobody could get into their network. Even if some hacking genius were able to get in, which was extremely unlikely, they'd be able to identify them within a few seconds and respond with a blazing attack of their own. Storx wasn't worried in the slightest; nobody would be able stop them once their project was up and running. In fact, he was eager to test their artificial intelligence. Now it was just a matter of waiting for Ziegler's green light to launch BLACKSTONE, then he'd be rich beyond his wildest dreams.

The plane left New Haven private airport at 8 pm local time. The engines roared with a hellish noise as they flew into the strong Connecticut winds on this autumn evening. Ziegler was smiling. Storx had managed to put a virtual nuclear warhead into operation on US territory. Their project had been to build operational centers in countries that were home to some of the biggest stock markets in the world: New York, London, and Paris. He'd originally insisted that instead of Paris they should set up in Germany, but Füller had refused. He was scared of having the finger point at him should anything go wrong. In any case, everything was now ready for launch. If Al-Naviq kept his promises, the big day would soon arrive.

He ordered a glass of champagne from the hostess and checked his messages. The smile he had been sporting, however, disappeared soon after. The situation concerning the journalist and the computer scientist had still not been resolved. It must have been 2 am in Switzerland. His hired idiots had achieved the incredible double-feat of first not finishing the job in the car accident, and then managing to lose their targets. Not to mention the untold mess they'd caused in the hospital. Now it was imperative that they find them and put an end to all of it. They knew too much. A police investigation had been ordered by the prosecution following the intrusion of the two fake policemen into the hospital. This in turn had crystallized the efforts of the investigators trying to find the two intruders, obviously posing a huge problem to the advancement of the BLACKSTONE project.

Checkmate?

His chief of security had recruited two fools and now they were dealing with a veritable crisis.

*
* *

Jack was curled up in bed, shaking. Although the temperature of his hotel room was warm and cozy, he felt like he was surrounded by an inescapable cold that was chilling him to his bones.

He fought hard, but this time he'd lost the battle. His months of struggle, his pride, his self-esteem; he'd just swallowed all of it in one thirsty gulp. After Luca and Thomas had left, he returned to his room alone. Once inside, the red light of the minibar had begun to taunt him. Like a demonic eye that would not leave him in peace, the possessed fridge had become encrusted in his mind. He closed his eyes and tried to think of something else. At first he rejected the idea, but the haunting glimmer of light eventually conquered him. He answered its devious call.

Once he'd devoured the entire contents of the minibar, he headed downstairs to the hotel bar and drank until the barman refused to serve him any more. Raising his voice in protest, he scared off the remaining tourists and businessmen, who chose not to stay and watch this sorry sight of an inebriated and aggressive alcoholic.

He was escorted by security back up to his room where he could sober up.

Jack wrapped himself up in the blankets without undressing. The ceiling was turning now and he was beginning to gag. He stood up. He swayed a little but managed to hang on to the bedstead. He stumbled forward. He convulsed, vomited on the ground and fell to his knees.

Checkmate?

* * *

Thomas had spent all of Sunday trying to come up with what he hoped would be a response to the BLACKSTONE project. Although he hadn't yet identified whom the targets would be, he still expected that an attack on one or more large companies would be launched at any time.

Luca was also making progress. By sifting through the data from the surprise attack on Shuito Pharmaceuticals, he'd managed to find the network addresses of the Millennium centers in Tokyo, London and Paris. There were always traces left on Internet servers. His main goal was to break into the Millenium network. Knowing their addresses would at least allow them to knock on their door. The Paris operational center was only a few miles away. In order to test their security, he'd stealthily approached their firewall as quietly as possible, trying not to be spotted. He still hadn't managed to find any hidden door. The simplest way would be a frontal attack, but he had every chance of being blocked, and he didn't have enough power in the Miroir to support such a strategy. If they spotted him, he could also become their target. He had to be smarter.

They were both tired and decided it was time to go back to the hotel for some dinner with Jack.

* * *

At 7.45 pm, breaking news on all of the TV channels announced the assassination of the leader of the FMP. The circumstances under which the assassination had taken place were unclear, with nobody giving much detail about what had happened. While it was known that a road 'accident' had taken place, everyone was quite convinced that Tarek Laid had been murdered.

The Minister of the Interior had been invited onto the set of the news shows to give details of the incident. He informed the public that Tarek Laid had lost his life while on his way home from the rally. There were four dead in all, but for the moment there was no further information regarding their identities. The politician was being cautious and refused to answer any questions, preferring instead to give the investigators time to draw the first conclusions. With a defeated air about him, he pointed out that the death of Tarek Laid was an immense loss for the Muslim community and that everything would be done to shed light on this odious assassination. Social networks ignited immediately. The identity of the murderers was clear to most Internet users. It was the far right, whose objective was to prevent a rise in power of Muslims in the country, in anticipation of upcoming elections. The hard right didn't want an organized community led by a charismatic leader who was anti-establishment.

The Front National gave a confused statement about the incident, declaring that the death of a political leader was unacceptable in France but never formally denouncing the death of the leader of the FMP. They played with words, and political doublespeak was de rigueur. The other political leaders that were interviewed at short notice didn't do much better, using the platform to denounce the drift toward the right in the country and not-so-subtly hidden suggestions that Lavalette was to blame. Others pointed out the poor state of the security policy within the country.

* *
* *

"Poor idiots," thought President Lavalette at the end of the news show, as he called his prime minister. For him, the response of politicians to this hammer blow against democracy was too soft, too narrow. In any case, the government's reaction was far from the expectations of all of those supporters who had ever come to hear Tarek Laid speak. In thirty years, almost no other political leader had aroused so much enthusiasm among the people. Something had to be done, a strong message needed to be sent to all Muslims. He felt that it was up to him to do it, and he needed to do it quickly. The reactions of the other politicians hadn't surprised him. None of them seemed to realize the possible social repercussions of the situation.

He dialed the phone number of the prime minister's residence. An assistant answered and transferred Paul to Henri du Plessis.

"Henri?"

"Yes, Paul!"

"What's going on?"

"I have no more information to give you. As I said, the three men who died were members of the 'Résistance Républicaine'. That doesn't leave much room for doubt about who's behind this, nor does it leave us searching for a motive."

"Has it been confirmed? We've got some tough guys who are proud that they've gotten rid of Laid?"

"No, that's the problem. Everyone from the little world of the reactionary right denies having anything to do with this attack."

"What are the RG saying?"[2]

"It's the same everywhere. No one has any info. The attack took everyone by surprise."

---

[2] The Direction central de Renseignements généraux, or RG, is the intelligence arm of the French police. It performs a similar function to the United States' FBI.

"OK. Keep trying to gather whatever you can from the ground. I'm worried about what might happen now. We can't let the situation get any worse. If the government becomes implicated in this, we could have riots in the suburbs."

"I don't think that's going to happen, Paul. For now, things are calm. I haven't seen anything that suggests things will go beyond what we're already seeing."

"Ask the Interior Minister to stay on the alert. I have a bad feeling about all this, and I'm rarely wrong, Henri. You know that."

"Do you want to raise the alert level?"

"I think it's the least we should do."

"I agree. The Interior has already sent orders to do so, but I'll check."

"Summon the Muslim leaders tomorrow morning for an emergency meeting. We need defuse this thing, Henri, and we must make sure that we remain irreproachable in every way. I'd prefer that we do more than we need to rather than not enough."

"I'll take care of it."

"I want to be updated every hour. This is extremely important."

"I'll make sure of it, Paul."

"Thank you!"

Lavalette hung up. An alarm had begun to go off somewhere in the President's head.

*
* *

The telephone at the police station in Les Mureaux had been ringing for several seconds. The officer at the reception, who had gone to get a coffee from the machine at the entrance, came running back, spilling some of the hot drink on his hand. It was only 11 pm and the evening had so far been calm. Apart from an arrest due to a fight between two motorists after an accident in the city center, nothing of note had happened.

He picked up the phone. The excited male voice at the other end shouted something but he wasn't able to understand what he'd said.

"Mureaux Police Station, could you speak a little more quietly sir, I can't understand anything of what you're telling me!"

"I'm calling you from the Three Gables neighborhood! There are five cars on fire and I see people trying to light more." The man was trying to keep himself calm.

"Five cars? Are you sure? How many people did you see?"

"Yes, yes, it's a whole gang! My car's out there, I'm going to try and get it!"

"Stay right where you are, sir. I'll warn my colleagues and send a patrol. Can you give me a specific address?"

The orderly noted the address and transmitted it by radio. No sooner had he put his his pen down than the phone was ringing again. He answered a little tentatively.

"Mureaux police station!"

"There's a gang in the city center destroying everything in their path! They're hitting cars with bats, attacking storefronts. They're throwing stones through the windows. It's unbelievable!"

"Give me the name of the street, sir!"

He hung up. The evening, which had begun slowly, was turning into a nightmare. Anxiously, he passed a new radio message to his colleagues, who were already heading into in town.

The phone rang again and he realized that this night was going to be one of those to remember. And not for good reasons.

He didn't have time to pick it up this time. The door of the police station exploded. A car had just smashed through the entrance. He protected himself by crouching behind the the reception desk. Looking over, he saw at least a dozen men approaching wearing jackets and hoods. One of them threw a Molotov cocktail into the reception and everything went up in flames. The officer hid behind the counter on his stomach. With no idea how to handle this type of situation, he decided the best thing was to stay there and lay low for the moment.

One of the attackers shouted: "This is for Tarek Laid!" They proceeded to systematically break all of the office windows and threw bombs all over the premises.

They disappeared as quickly as they'd arrived. It had only lasted two or three minutes.

The whole police station was on fire. The municipal agents, scurrying around, stunned by the attack that was as violent as it was quick, had not had time to react. There were no victims. The evacuation was done in relative calm. When the firemen arrived, there was nothing left of Les Mureaux police station.

*
* *

Lavalette had been awake since 3 am and hadn't put his cell phone down since. For hours on end he had call after call with his Police chiefs, who nervously tried to answer all of his questions, trying to find the words to give him a factual overview of the situation. They struggled to describe in detail the scenes of the urban wars that were happening all over the country. Lavalette had seen it all coming and now he was cursing himself for having been right. The situation was explosive, with several police stations set ablaze and city centers being systematically destroyed. The worst had been avoided when a police car was attacked in the northern neighborhoods of Asnières. Fortunately, the officers had managed to escape but the vehicle had been utterly destroyed. The aggressors were well organized and all claimed to be members of the FMP. The youth of France did not want to let the assassination of Tarek Laid go by without showing any kind of reaction. They let violence take over and were using it as a means to unite them. President Lavalette was thinking of ways he could respond that would restore calm and avoid a further escalation of the violence. It was going to be a long night.

*
* *

Checkmate?

14. PARIS

Sunday, September 24th

At 8:30 am, François Delmas was standing behind the chief of Police. An experienced policeman who had worked in the Paris Police headquarters for over ten years, he was the obvious choice when it came to the decision of to whom they should assign investigation, with the police prefect insisting that it be entrusted to a conscientious police officer who knew how to maneuver in politically polluted waters. It was undoubtedly going to be an explosive case. Delmas didn't like being under media fire, especially in this kind of volatile context. He'd come to the press conference at the express request of his boss, who himself was only acting on behalf of the minister. Given the media coverage of this assassination and the difficult night that had just traumatized the country, it was essential to relieve some pressure. One of the actions was to give the Muslim community a pledge of good faith.

The urgent press conference was about to start. Delmas, with an air of resignation, sat down on the chair that had been reserved for him, in front of the forest of microphones and cameras installed by the journalists who were now crowded into this tiny room, elbowing one another to get the best place for themselves.

Just to be sure, he grabbed the folded paper sign in front of him and had a quick look to confirm he was in the right place. He read the name of the minister. He smiled and exchanged it with the correct one.

The minister, the chief of the Police and the Prefect of Police of Paris took their respective places. Delmas found himself at the end of the table, a little removed from the other participants. He had been told nothing, but he knew that he wasn't a part of the important circle. The other three were the big shots here. There weren't four people sat at the table, but rather three plus one.

That suited him just fine. He was a man who was usually active on the ground and was neither used to nor interested in being in the limelight. This whole exercise only served one purpose anyway: to give the press the information they wanted them to have.

The minister stood up and walked to the podium. Delmas was going to be introduced as the investigator and would answer questions only if his boss asked him to. If necessary, he would refer to him occasionally, but Delmas would remain seated. The elected official asked for silence and the noise within the room gradually subsided. He scratched his throat, adjusted the microphone in front of him and began to address the crowd:

"Ladies and gentlemen of the press, I'd like to thank you all for being here. As you know, Tarek Laid, leader of the FMP, was assassinated yesterday at 6.30 pm on the banks of the Seine. His driver, Khalid Alzadi, defended himself and Mr. Laid during the attack, and although he was not able to save the life of Mr. Laid, three of the attackers were killed during the incident. Their identities will not be revealed to you here, but I am able to confirm that they were members of a far-right group."

The sound level rose a notch in the room and questions began to come in from all sides.

"Please, ladies and gentlemen! Silence please! The Prefect and the Chief of Police will answer your questions once I have finished this short introduction."

The silence diminished a little and the minister continued.

"The circumstances of this murder remain unclear and all of our staff are on the ground trying to shed some light on this case. The investigation has been entrusted to Lieutenant Delmas."

As he said his name, he held out his arm to present the lieutenant. Heads and cameras turned to Delmas, who suddenly felt very hot.

"It will be up to the police to find the answers to the questions posed by this assassination, an assassination for which no group has claimed responsibility for at this stage."

"Minister?" A journalist who was a little more enthusiastic than the others present took the opportunity to interrupt the politician during a very brief pause. "Why has no one claimed responsibility? If no one comes forward, is it possible that something else caused this?"

"I don't see what else it could possibly be!"

"Sir?"

The journalist was Jacques Prudot of the newspaper Free Republic, the publication that supported the ultra-conservative right. And he had just raised an essential point.

"Mr. Prudot, for the moment we have no evidence that could either affirm or invalidate any hypothesis."

"That may very well be, Monsieur le Ministre, but if a right-wing group are responsible for this attack, they would very much want that to be known, isn't that so?"

The minister decided not to answer. But this man had made his point, and made it well. The fact that no one had claimed the attack cast an additional shadow on the case. Neither the RG nor any informers had any more information. This raised a legitimate question.

"The government and I want to emphasize the importance of uncovering the truth about what has happened here. Tarek Laid represented more than just a political movement. His mission to bring together the various communities of Muslims in France was of inestimable importance. In this time of doubt, I ask all Muslims, and the youth in particular, to keep their calm. All police forces are engaged in finding out the truth. Violence is not the answer here. The rioting such as that which happened last night must stop! The police must be given time to carry out their investigation in a calm atmosphere. Thank you all."

The minister sat down again and started the question and answer session. After twenty minutes of a dialogue of the deaf, during which the journalists wanted more details and where the police responded with a laconic 'no comment', the press conference ended.

Prudot approached the investigator before going out.

"Delmas?" asked the reporter.

"Prudot! From the Free Republic, right?"

"Yes. I can tell you right now that none of this has got anything to do with us!"

"Us? Who is 'us', exactly?"

"Well, let's say the Republican and active right..."

"How can you be sure?"

"I know it, that's all. You can decide not to believe me, but I'm telling you that you'll need to look elsewhere to find who did it."

"You can't deny what happened at the scene though, surely? There were three dead, all members of the right."

"Of course not! But I'd heard it was supposed to be something more like intimidation, scare tactics. Not murder."

"Maybe things just got out of hand?"

"I can assure you that's not what happened."

"Well where exactly would you point the finger then?"

"I have no idea. But it's not us, that I know!"

"He turned and disappeared, swallowed up in the crowd of other journalists who were still present."

*
* *

Jack woke at around 7 am. Darkness enveloped his room. He had a terrible headache, a sad memory from the previous night. After a few minutes, the thud that beat in his temples and the pain that blurred his vision diminished. Sitting up in his bed he contemplated the mess he was surrounded by. Shame hugged his heart and he felt like crying. He got up to take a hot shower.

At 8:00 am, after cleaning the floor and changing his clothes, he turned on the television as he did every morning in New York.

Checkmate?

All the news channels were showing videos of what had happened last night. Cars on fire, downtowns demolished, police stations burned to the ground. It all resembled the riots in the cities of Charlotte or Los Angeles following police brutality against Trayvon Martin and Rodney King.

Jack changed channels to CNN Europe which was broadcasting the press conference. He couldn't understand what was being said directly, but the television journalist summarized the address. Jack suddenly had a revelation. Thomas had said that Millenium was ready to launch its attack. The only thing that was missing was a trigger event powerful enough to have a massive effect on stock prices. What if this case had that very effect? And if one were to take this argument even further, what was the probability that such a situation to could happen right now?

He had to talk to Thomas about it. They had arranged to meet for lunch in a few minutes. He decided to go downstairs, even though the thought of eating anything made him positively nauseous.

The receptionist stared at Jack as he arrived at the front desk. He must have been on duty last night, thought Jack, who tried to look innocent as he entered the breakfast room.

Luca and Thomas were sat down, looking as though they were having a deep discussion. Jack walked over to join them. A waiter soon approached to take his order. Jack opted for a black coffee. In any case, his stomach wouldn't allow him to drink anything else on this delicate morning.

"You look tired," Jack said.

"Obviously you haven't seen yourself!" replied Thomas.

"Yeah, I had a tough night."

"You missed us?"

"You could say that. If you'd been there I think the night would have turned out different."

"Do I detect a hint of regret?" Thomas asked.

"Not a hint. More like a ton."

"You want to talk about it?"

"Not really."

"We worked most of the night. Luca's convinced his friends to help us if we can get our hands on Millenium's software." Luca nodded, his hair covering his eyes.

"Give us a hand doing what?"

"Well, let's say that the collective he represents has voted. They agreed to help us write a program that could thwart Millenium and their artificial intelligence."

"That's great news! Have you made any progress?"

"This is where it gets complicated. For them to help us develop something, we'd need to break into the network in order to hack Millenium's code, but Luca's having a tough time getting through their security at the moment."

"Ouch! Even for experts like you? What's the plan B, then?"

"There isn't one. It's imperative that I manage to get through the security. If I need to stay awake for one week in order to do it, then that's what I'll do," snapped Luca.

"What if you can't do it?"

"I can. Quit breaking my balls!" Luca wasn't a fan of anyone who questioned his abilities.

"You know, Jack, Luca is employed by massive companies to test the quality of their firewalls. It's his specialty and he always manages to get through," Thomas replied, cooling the atmosphere a little.

"I never doubted it!"

The conversation was interrupted by the waiter who brought over Jack's piping hot coffee. Everyone dug into their breakfast, if only to move away from the subject. Talking about computer security and Millennium had the power to put the nerves on edge.

"Thomas, I had an idea while watching the news this morning," Jack said after a few minutes.

"That's all we've been talking about. Kind of kept us going through the night. The minister even gave a press conference to try to calm things down."

"What if all this is somehow linked to Millenium?" Jack asked.

"What do you mean?" asked Delvaux, taken aback.

"What I mean is that we believe some people with bad intentions are going to launch an attack on the Stock Exchanges, right?"

"Yes."

"And that to do this, they've built centers, one of which is here in Paris. With me so far?"

"We're with you Jack."

"And as if by chance, something's happened right here that's easily big enough to have an impact on the entire country."

"If it's true, and that's what's happening, it would be huge."

"Yes, but think about what we said after we hacked Ziegler's phone. We were saying that there needed to be a trigger that would upset the balances. Something that would serve as a starting point for this god damned BLACKSTONE project." Jack paused to give time for Luca and Thomas to take it all in.

"I don't know what to think," said Delvaux. "Maybe you're right. If things were to deteriorate here again, it could bring down the Paris Stock Exchange and with it the other European countries' exchanges, too. It's possible. I don't see the link, but it's something that is in the realms of possibility. You know, maybe there is something to this. I mean, there's nothing to stop them using this to launch the attack, whether they're behind it or not. We need to talk to someone. It's too big for us. What do you guys think?"

"I don't want to deal with the cops, or anyone else for that matter," Luca said, defensively. "I need to stay discreet. Actually, scratch that. I need to be invisible."

"I understand," Jack concluded. "Then what if we called the investigator who's looking into the murder? Couldn't we talk to them about Millenium and see what they think?"

*
* *

Checkmate?

Luca and Thomas were standing in front of the whiteboard in the office, conceptualizing the program that would allow them to enter Millenium's computer maze, when someone knocked on the door.

"Come in!" said Delvaux.

"There's a delivery for you, sir." His assistant approached and handed him a package the size of a whiteboard eraser.

"Thank you, Malik."

Thomas opened the box and smiled. He'd just been given his new iPhone and SIM card. He'd been using an old one since he'd escaped from the hospital, so he didn't have access to his usual apps or even his emails. He'd finally be able to reconnect with the world.

After putting the card into its slot, he switched on the phone that seemed to then beep with contentment. He connected his device to his iTunes account and a few seconds later his apps were being loaded. He also took the time to download some of his personal apps from the Cloud.

He restarted the device to allow it to update. After five minutes or so, the iPhone gave off a very particular alert. It sounded three times at different pitches. Delvaux rubbed his eyebrows, before a big smile filled his face.

"Luca, I think we just got lucky!"

*
* *

Ziegler was furious. He walked into the Paris offices of Millenium Dust like a tornado. His frustration obviously came from his team's inability to locate Campbell and the computer scientist. It was as if they they had simply disappeared into thin air. Not to mention that no one knew where the two henchmen were after the fiasco at the hospital. He needed to call Füller to let him know what was happening and he was sure that the news wasn't going to go down well.

Checkmate?

He stormed past reception without saying hello or even looking in the vague direction of anyone else, and entered the office that had been reserved for him and sat down at his workstation. At the very top of his agenda was calling the ZIS headquarters. After all, business waits for no man. If BLACKSTONE were to be launched tomorrow as planned, a number of positions in the bank's investment portfolio had to be adjusted in anticipation of future changes.

He connected to the office Wi-Fi network on his phone to get his messages and e-mails. In doing so, he didn't notice the virus installed by Delvaux start up. Once it was up and running, the Trojan took his passwords, available IP addresses and confidential settings, then sent them all to Thomas in absolute secrecy.

Ziegler took a deep breath, gathered up some courage and dialed Füller's number. Füller recognized the caller and immediately answered:

"Füller speaking. Hello Ziegler."

"Heidrich, how are you?"

"I am very well, thank you! Where are you calling me from?"

"I'm in Paris. I'm finishing my inspection tour of the centers."

"Very good. Everything is in order?"

"Absolutely, they're ready to begin as soon as the order is given."

"So Storx managed to be on time?"

"Yes, although the work started later than planned."

"Excellent! But Ziegler?"

"Yes?"

"I'm guessing that you didn't call me just for a little chat?"

"No, I thought that you'd like to be kept informed of our progress."

"Yes, I would. Thank you. But do hurry up, I have meetings with officials that are about to start and I mustn't keep them waiting. So, is there anything else? I sense that you're worried about something."

"In fact, yes there is... it's about those two guys who have been sniffing around."

"Do you have good news?"

"Not really. We couldn't find the journalist... or the computer scientist... they're still at large."

"I thought you were supposed to fix this problem yesterday?" Füller's voice had become stern.

"It was impossible to locate them. It's like they evaporated. Yet we have people everywhere."

"Is it incompetence or stupidity?"

"Whoa there! We're doing our best, but we can't wreak havoc in the process. We must find them quietly, without being spotted."

"And the two puppets at the hospital?"

"No better there, either. For now."

"We have a videoconference with the other BLACKSTONE members at 5 pm. I hope you have something better to tell them by that time, for your sake."

He hung up and Ziegler felt the sweat running down his back. He noticed that he was gripping his phone so hard that his knuckles were white.

After a few seconds of rest to relieve his stress, he called his security chief and put some pressure on him. After all, there was no reason that he alone should be the one to take the fall.

*
* *

The little icon on Thomas's smartphone was flashing, indicating that information had just been sent to him from Ziegler's phone. Thomas was absolutely delighted with himself for having taken the time to implement the virus when they hacked the device. With the new generation of virus developed by Luca, if you had access to someone's phone, you could retrieve any confidential information from the networks they were connected to. Including passwords. That would give you continuous access to all of their content. It was a giant window onto a courtyard with an unblemished mirror. See without being seen, the Holy Grail for any hacker.

"Luca, Ziegler's in Paris!" declared Delvaux, resurgent with energy. "Finally, we can take a look into their system. He's in Millenium's office right now. Thanks to your Trojan horse, I'll be able to get their Wi-Fi password. He just connected!"

"Perfect," Luca replied. "Give it to me so I can go on a little underwater hunt."

Luca, who was now animated by an unrelenting determination, got to his keyboard. He cracked the joints of his fingers in an unconscious sign of defiance. Just like a virtuoso artist at the beginning of a performance, he gathered his concentration before plunging into the labyrinth of Millenium's computer network.

After only a few minutes Luca had reached the front door of the security system. The cursor on his screen blinked for a few seconds, the time it took to start the connection procedure, before the following message was displayed: "Please enter the password".

Behind this screen were the secrets of an organization whose goal was to destabilize the world by attacking its Achilles heel: finance. The fragile balance of modern society was largely based on the tacit agreement of countries to safeguard assets. Changing this precarious stability would permanently alter the balance of power between countries. As the distribution of the planet's wealth is a zero-sum game, the losses of some, especially in our interdependent economies, were the gains of others.

Millenium Dust and its BLACKSTONE project represented a much greater danger than simply capturing wealth for the benefit of some unscrupulous speculators; it would shift the balance of power from rich and democratic countries to states with very questionable values. Neither Luca Hanser nor Thomas Delvaux could comprehend the extent of the danger posed by the BLACKSTONE project. This ignorance was in some way beneficial to them as it meant they wouldn't be paralyzed by the responsibility that was in their hands.

"Honey, I'm home!" exclaimed Luca.

"You're in?"

"Yeah. I logged in with Ziegler's password. They're using Linux servers. No problem, it's all good! I'm making my way through their system now."

"Still not been spotted?"

"No, so far so good. Bingo, I just found the network admin password. I'll create a ghost account so I can reconnect without going through Ziegler's user profile."

"Shit, that was quick!"

"No kidding! Now that we're in, everything should be a piece of cake! Ok, let's calm down a little. I'll reconnect with my new account to avoid losing our access point, just in case Ziegler decides to cut his Wi-Fi connection. Let's wait and see... and boom! I'm in!" Luca was ecstatic. He was in the system and could now take a walk around the secret Millennium Garden.

"So, what are you doing now?" asked Delvaux.

"I'm looking for their program, their AI, so I can download it. Then we'll be able to study it in our own time without having to worry about being caught. And while I'm there, I'll find out how they organize themselves. I'm sure there are plenty of things for us to learn."

"Don't get caught, huh?"

"No, don't worry. I'm connected via anonymous servers so they'd never be able to trace us. With my ghost account, it's basically impossible for them to find anything."

"I know, but still, let me be a little bit worried. We won't get a second chance at this."

Luca was completely absorbed in his task and didn't even hear what Delvaux had been saying to him. Data scrolled down screens in front of him which he studied with closely. Occasionally he would nod his head or scratching his temple, visibly stunned by what he was seeing. He connected a USB key and an external drive to his PC and started the data transfer.

Checkmate?

*
* *

"Hello, my name's Thomas Delvaux and I'd like to speak to Lieutenant Delmas."

Thomas had been battling now for ten minutes, but kept getting passed from one service to another. He was beginning to wonder if contacting the police was such a good idea in the end.

"What's the subject of the call?" quizzed the sad, flat voice of the police switchboard operator. They didn't seem particularly inclined to transfer Thomas's call.

"I have information about the Tarek Laïd case, ma'am, but if it's of no interest to you, I can just as well hang up."

"Whatever you want, sir!" She had no idea what he'd just said to her. She must have been the only person in the whole country who didn't watch the news.

"Listen, it's very important! Can you put me through, please?"

"I'm trying!" replied the laconic voice, then nothing. Thomas was about to hang up when a male voice answered at the other end.

"Lieutenant Delmas!"

Delmas mechanically closed the report he had been carefully studying. It was the file for the May 1st attack; the case being managed by Commander Rougier. The case was absorbing him. Not least because following their investigation, Rougier's team identified the sponsor as being the driver of Tarek Laid. A certain Khalid Alzadi.

More surprising still, the accountant of the Paris attack, Malik Aertens, had books of accounts in which Zurich Investments & Securities Bank was mentioned. The same establishment used by Tarek Laid to finance his campaign.

Delmas switched his focus to the phone call.

"Hello Lieutenant, Thomas Delvaux speaking."

—305—

"Mr. ....?"

"Delvaux!"

"Mr. Delvaux, what can I do for you?"

"I saw you on television during this morning's press conference. Are you in charge of the Tarek Laid case?"

"Yes, absolutely!"

"I think I have some information that could help you in your investigation, Lieutenant."

"Hmm... what kind of information?" the voice of Delmas suddenly showed a clear interest in this conversation.

"It's quite complicated... I'm not even sure if I'm right or not," Delvaux said.

"Please, go ahead. We'll decide together whether it matters or not!"

"No, no, I know it's important..."

"Well then I'm listening to you!"

"Lieutenant, have you heard of Millenium Dust, Zurich Investments & Securities Bank or BLACKSTONE?"

"It's possible, Mr. Delvaux." Adrenaline was now pouring into Delmas' nervous system. He was now paying absolute attention.

"I have good reason to believe that there's a link between the assassination of Mr. Laid and secret financial trading, the scope of which could be global," Thomas continued.

"And how did you come to be aware of these things connected with our investigation?" Delmas didn't want to say too much, but he needed to make Delvaux continue talking.

"I think we should meet if you want to know more. In all honesty, I think it would be better if we met today. It's a matter of urgency that you know what's happening here!"

"Can't you tell me anything more now?"

"Not by phone."

"Why not?"

"Well... me and a New York Times reporter are in the crosshairs of ZIS."

"Do you think you're in danger?"

"I don't think so Lieutenant. I know it! They tried to kill us in Zurich two days ago."

"Really? Can you come to the Police headquarters?"

"I'd prefer someplace more... discreet. In public."

"How about the Soleil d'Or café? At 11 o'clock? It's right next to my office."

"Let's do the Soleil d'Or."

"At 11 am, Mr. Delvaux?"

"At 11 am, Lieutenant! I'll be there with my friend."

Delmas hung up, feeling a little puzzled. If they could connect the assassination of a politician, hidden financial funds and the same bank being linked to the attack of May 1st, they'd have some questions to ask.

He picked up his phone and called Pauline Rougier. He trusted her and knew that she'd be involved in this case that was in some way linked to the May 1st attack. Maybe she'd be able to join him for the meeting with Delvaux.

*
* *

By 10 am, the situation in the country had become worrying. There had been several occurrences of automatic gunfire at mosques. A man had just been shot in Marseille. The perpetrator was a hard right activist. The assassination was immediately claimed by FMP activists. Similar movements were being reported in Belgium and Germany. Muslims were demonstrating, holding up placards bearing Tarek Laid's name as a show of support. The loss of the politician was raising questions that went beyond the borders of France. Police had been forced to intervene in Germany, and footage of violent clashes between police and protesters in Berlin was looping on the news channels.

Checkmate?

*
* *

Luca watched as the blue download progress bar on his screen crept towards completion. It had just gone past ten percent. He waited. Up to this point, everything was going well.

Meanwhile, in Millenium's Parisian office, Ziegler's phone sounded a notification indicating FaceTime request. It was from the security director. This was an unprecedented and somewhat surprising occurrence, but Ziegler accepted the call nonetheless. Perhaps the director had some important information that he needed to communicate to him.

"Herr Ziegler?" A stranger with a rounded, smiling face appeared on screen.

"Yes that's me. But who are you? Where is Daniel Hassler, my chief of security?"

"He's right here! Take a look!"

The cell phone's camera showed his henchman tied up on a rusty iron bed. The room looked like a squat, with crumbling walls and sheets of paper littering the ground, all lit by a single naked light bulb diffusing a nauseatingly unhealthy light. Daniel Hassler, formerly of the special forces, was gagged and his eyes were clearly filled with fear. His swollen face showed that he'd been beaten and was now bleeding heavily. His almost-closed right eye was starting to turn black.

"But who are you?" Ziegler asked.

"I thought it was you that ordered your henchmen to get rid of us?"

"Not at all, I don't even know who you are!"

"Oh!" The man turned to Hassler. "You see Daniel, your boss never ordered you to kill us! Are you sure, Herr Ziegler?" the man with the thick face and bald head insisted. He pointed the phone's camera toward his partner. He was a visibly tall and muscular guy. "What do you think?" he asked.

"No reason to doubt the word of the boss!" replied the big man who turned his attention to Hassler again. Ziegler could see the man had a gun in his hand. Stood next to the bed, he began to speak again.

"Listen Ziegler, this is what we do to guys who want to harm us!" As he spoke, he pointed his gun at the prisoner tied to the bed and fired a first shot. Hassler shook convulsively. A large hole opened in his chest. A second shot sounded with a few tenths of a second delay from the image. Half of the Zurich Investments & Securities Bank security director's face exploded, and a large blood stain appeared behind the bed, splashing upon the wall.

"My God!" Ziegler exclaimed involuntarily. He realized now that the two madmen were the henchmen who'd screwed up the job of killing the journalist and the computer scientist at the Zurich hospital.

"That's right, asshole! You tried to fuck us, huh? Now we're going to fuck you." The stranger stared into the camera. His expression of murderous fury gave Ziegler the chills.

The connection was interrupted. The heart of the ZIS CEO was beating wildly. Witnessing the live execution of his employee live and being threatened with death himself, none of this was in his job description. "The two guys completely botched the hospital job and now they want me," he thought. He had to calm down. Above all, he mustn't mention any of this to Füller, at least not yet. It would help no one to keep adding gasoline to the bonfire. "I'm not cut out for this. Not at all," he thought.

At least not in the field. He quickly gathered his thoughts again when an alarm sounded in the meeting room.

The employee at Millenium Dust responsible for the security of the computer network must have only been around 25 years-old. With short brown hair, he seemed to be a rather skinny fellow, but in fact was hiding a toned, muscular physique beneath his overly-baggy clothes. Those evenings and weekends spent in the gym had paid off.

The alarm had been blaring for several seconds, yet everyone was remained motionless even though they'd practiced this drill several times before. Everyone had been taught exactly what to do in case of a computer attack, and that was obviously what was happening right now. It's easy to keep cool head when it's only a practice and nothing is really at stake, but the cold reality of this situation had caused what seemed like a distortion in time and space. Everything was going slower, but certain simple tasks still needed to be performed to ensure an information leak was prevented. In a situation like this, the first thing to do is disconnect your computer from the network and turn it off. Then, you need to do the same with your phone and any other equipment that can connect to Wi-Fi. Next, leave your office and lock it. This is the standard procedure to prevent viruses spreading and stop information from being hacked due to the use of hardware with a network or Wi-Fi connection. It took several minutes, however, for the Millenium Dust employees to perform these small tasks.

The security officer, Henry Dwight, ran down the hall and rushed into the server room. His immediate priority was to find out where the alarm was coming from. By connecting to the main computer he was able to quickly scan the list of users connected to the network. There was an IP address that he didn't recognize. It was Ziegler. He disconnected it. If the boss wasn't happy, that's too bad; Dwight had an emergency to manage. He found nothing that could have triggered the alarm, which was still sounding at a stressful and deafening volume. He pressed a button in order to stop the noise that was preventing him from thinking clearly. A silence immediately fell upon the large machine room. For peace of mind, if nothing else, he sent a command to the Linux server to prevent any new connection to the network, except for himself.

Henry took a quick look at the list of active processes to identify who was trying to take data from the network. If no one had downloaded any information, he could contain the problem by disconnecting all of the company's hardware.

Port 901 displayed that there was a connection that had been made through a ghost process. "There you are!" Henry thought. He'd found the culprit, but he had to admit that whoever this hacker was, they were good. They weren't visible in the list of connected users and yet they were still able to downloading data undercover. A shiver ran through him when he saw that the connection had been active for fifteen minutes. He checked which files were being downloaded, suddenly becoming extremely flushed when he realized that it was BLACKSTONE, their Artificial Intelligence program. The good news was that the hacker was trying to steal source code that had already been encrypted. So even with the file, it would be impossible for them to read it. So far only twenty percent had been transferred; the AI program was huge. There was still a lot of time before the download would be complete.

He thought about disconnecting the intruder, but changed his mind and decided that he'd prefer not to lose him immediately. As long as he was online, Dwight kept some kind of contact with the hacker. First, he launched an application to regulate incoming and outgoing data flows from the server room. Then he reduced the speed of the hacker's connection, allowing them to continue to download the data, albeit so slowly that it almost amounted to cutting him off entirely, while at the same time giving Dwight the necessary time to identify the culprit.

On Luca's screen the download progress bar continued to move slowly. It had just past twenty percent and the gauge was indicating a download speed of 50 Mb/s, which was about right for a non-fiber connection. For several minutes however the progress seemed to have frozen. He looked at his screen closely and set up a speed test. The result didn't seem to make any sense. He did another test. Same result: the download speed had dropped to a few hundred kb/s.

Henry launched an application that could track all of the connections across the network. The first attempt revealed an address somewhere in the Czech Republic. He couldn't let this hacker drive him into some Kafkaesque nightmare, he thought. The address came from an Internet information hub. The hacker was probably using multiple servers to cover his tracks. No problem, Henry thought. He launched the test again, but this time he asked for an end-to-end link. This approach would prevent him from seeing the intermediate machines used by the cybercriminal, but would give him the entry point of the hacker.

Luca knew immediately that something was wrong. He tried to connect to Millennium's central server with the password that he'd created a little earlier. Access denied. Maybe he'd mistyped the login details. He did it again and got the same message. His computer beeped. By the time he realized what had happened, it was already too late. He'd been spotted. Hurriedly, he removed the RJ45 plug from his computer to disconnect.

Henry smiled, satisfied with his work. His software had just captured the IP address of the hacker. He launched a program that would enable him to visualize where they were located. Probably Chinese or a Russian, he thought. When he saw where they were in reality, he was left utterly speechless. The hacker was nearby, in the very same district of La Défense. Luca was angry with himself at being spotted so quickly. Unlawfully connecting to a highly secure computer network was already something, but doing it without leaving a trace, that required a bit of a genius, which Luca could often be justifiably called. Unfortunately, he'd come across someone smarter, or at least better equipped. He had failed to download the Millenium software. He was going to have to announce the news to Delvaux and finalize their Plan B as quickly as possible, because if one thing was certain, it was that they wouldn't get a second chance.

*
* *

The old abandoned factory behind the Puteaux cemetery was a metal structure with blackened beams, still standing despite the weather and the ill-treatment it had withstood. A whitish light filtered through an old roof made of fiber cement. The redbrick walls, tagged by successive gangs who had appropriated the place as their headquarters, let in the wind that was blowing heartily this morning.

Checkmate?

The cracked facade was falling down and formed heaps of moss-covered rubble on the ground. Next to them lay an old rusty door frame that had been torn out years ago. At the bottom of this dilapidated cathedral were two large blocks of concrete; like a couple of altars used for some type of pagan celebration, between which a fire was still smoking. The floor was littered with broken glass and burnt paper, and an old sofa covered with mold.

One green shrub, the only symbol of resistance and a victorious witness to a silent war, was growing in the center of cement slabs cracked by time.

Kamel, sitting on one of the concrete blocks, recited some verses from a surah of the Qur'an that never left his side. Outside, men on the lookout waited for the arrival of the of rival gang leaders. The young man had the entitled arrogance of someone who took for granted his right to freedom. The leader of the Def Zone gang and its one hundred and fifty urban warriors, he'd made his decision as soon as he heard the announcement of Tarek Laid's assassination by the far right. They needed to reply, to give a voice to and restore some sense of pride within the community, having suffered the ultimate provocation. Kamel had alerted the gang leaders of the territories around La Défense and demanded that they should meet. It was a matter of urgency that they react.

"Kamel, Backo's here."

"I'm coming."

Kamel stood up, put away his sacred book and went to greet the leaders. A large scar marked his right cheek all the way up to his dead eye. To become the leader in a gang was done by respecting the laws of the ghettos. There was no republican front, no election, no court or judges to get in the way here. Power must be seized. The winner became the decision maker, the spokesman and the judge of gang affairs. Climbing to the highest step had cost him his eye, but now he was the leader.

They were all there, the leaders of the ten most important gangs of from the neighborhoods surrounding Paris. Together, they represented an army of more than two thousand young people, ready to fight. Sports pants, sneakers and earrings, long or shaved hair, everyone brought with them the social codes of their own neighborhood. Backo the Serb, Nacer and Souleymane were there. They stood in a circle so that each one could observe all the others.

Kamel was angry. With a quick gesture, he closed his jacket to cut himself off from the cold wind that had picked up, and started to speak.

"Thank you all for coming," Kamel began, taking care to look at each of the bosses one by one.

They nodded in thanks. Silence reigned in the factory.

"These bastard right wingers murdered Tarek Laid. We can not let it go without retaliation!"

"It's none of our business Kamel!" interrupted Chal, leader of the Black Scorpios from Argenteuil.

"Of course it is!" Kamel replied furiously. "For how long are we going to bend our backs? If we act as if nothing's happened, how long before they decide to fuck us again? Destroy our mosques? Shoot us like rabbits in the street?"

"OK, OK... but if we start something it's going hurt," Chal continued.

"And it's bad for business, Kamel!" Nacer interjected. The small leader of the Courbevoie district looked around, seeking support.

"I know Nacer, but it doesn't matter! We're talking about much more than money here. It's about avenging someone who had the courage to speak on our behalf. We're not going to sit back and behave like cowards. There was shooting on the doors of mosques this morning, for fuck's sake!"

"You know that they are hard right. As soon as they can fuck us they'll do it. If it was up to them we should all stay in the ghettos, with no right to vote, with no rights at all!"

"I've seen this before with this in my family in Bosnia." Backo, the Serbian leader of the northern districts of Asnières, was also present.

"Did you see the silent marches in memory of Tarek Laid?" Kamel went on. "Did you hear any voices raised? There was nothing! Nothing at all. So it is us who must answer. We need to send a message. A message that says we are tired of being the ones who have to deal with it and say nothing. We are not fucking terrorists and we must be respected!"

"What do you propose we do?" Soul asked.

"We need to do something big. Show them that we're not just gonna lie down and take this. We'll join forces and march on Paris. We're gonna tear the place to pieces!" Kamel, the charismatic leader of the Def Zone, was evidently angry and not about to calm down.

The faction leaders looked at each other. They were well aware of the fact that they represented the worst of what the system had created. Most of them were born in the very same ghettos where they still resided. They were dealers who worked with whatever they could get their hands on; they brought money to the suburbs in their own way. But with more than fifty percent of the youth unemployed, where were this all really heading? Tarek Laid was a sign of hope. Not for themselves necessarily - they knew it was too late for them to become successful by going straight - but he was a real hope for the kids of the ghettos. The young people needed a future, and this future had just been stolen from them. Even if they did nothing, the hatred that bubbled just beneath the surface, the anger that had built up inside of them for so long, was about to be unleashed upon the streets. It had been brewing since the announcement of Tarek Laid's death. They had to keep control of what was happening. After all, shouldn't leaders lead?

Souleymane, the man who led the gang they called the Smokes, began to speak:

"I'm with Kamel! We need to coordinate ourselves and act. We have to give them back what they gave to us. We've got the goods we need down in in the cellars. AKs, grenades. Shit, it's now or never. I say we blow everything! They'll be begging for us to stop and then we can negotiate on our terms."

"Let's blow up the Quatre Temps mall!" Rach, another gang leader, said breaking his silence.

"Yes Rach, we'll blow up the Quatre Temps mall, then move toward Paris. We'll march under the Arc de Triomphe onto the Champs Elysées." Kamel replied. "We need to hit the capital. Then they'll take notice of us. We need to strike them where it hurts."

The men looked at each other. A gust of wind blew the pieces of paper strewn on the ground up into the swirling air. The wind entered the factory with a sharp groan.

"And it won't end there! We need to join with the other suburbs too. We must be together. By ourselves we can scare them, but together..."

Kamel was standing with his fist closed and his jaw clenched.

"Shall we vote?" asked Souleymane.

"Yes, we'll vote!" Kamel replied. "Who wants to cause mayhem tonight? We have no time to waste!"

Kamel raised his hand, immediately followed by Rach and Soul. The others looked at each other. They needed a unanimous vote. It was not possible for one gang to sit quietly in its suburb while the other gangs were tearing it up just few kilometers from them.

Backo joined them: "I'm in," he said. Now they were four. Still, it was far from the unanimity. Three more hands rose. The others looked at each other questioningly. An eighth hand pointed to the sky. Nacer did not move.

Kamel turned his head towards Nacer. The two men watched each other in an intense non-verbal exchange. They challenged each other in silence. Nacer was the first to tear himself away from the gaze of Kamel's stare. He raised his hand. All faces turned to the last member of the meeting.

"Ok, I'm in."

They had all agreed. Kamel had won them over.

"Everyone meet at 11 tonight. Mobilize your troops. If everyone comes, we'll have a thousand soldiers, maybe more. Everyone bring your heavy weapons. We're done with just setting cars fire. They've declared war on us, so now we're gonna fight back!"

Checkmate?

A fine rain began to fall through the roof of the building, forming thin streams of water that covered the ground. Wind whistled through the metal structure of the plant, carrying with it the smell of wet grass. The men shook hands and disappeared, leaving Kamel sitting on his concrete block. He'd done it. He picked up his prayer book and left.

*
* *

Commander Rougier and Lieutenant Delmas arrived a little early and enjoyed coffee together while they waited for their potential witnesses. They'd not seen each other since the successful dismantling of the gang of traffickers, a terrorism-related investigation three years earlier. That was almost an eternity considering the speed at which work landed on their desks. Delmas knew Laurent, Pauline's husband, and knew how painful it had been for her.

"I'm really happy to see you Pauline. I'm ashamed for not calling you all this time."

"Me too, Francois," replied Pauline, lifting her shoulders. "It's always the same thing: we never take the time to look after our own garden. There's always a thousand other things to do, usually boring, and we forget what's really important."

"How's things at the Counter Terrorist Brigade? Not too many big hairy guys thinking you're some kind of princess who can't handle it?"

"Oh man. I'm the only female Commander there, and boy do they let me know! Can't ever forget."

"I heard about your exploits in the dojo recently!"

"Really? What did they say?" asked Pauline, blushing a little at the memory of her fight against Kowalski.

"Good things. Very good in fact!" answered Delmas, smiling. "You know how well-loved Kowalski is. You know what upset him the most?""

That he lost the fight? No! That he lost against a woman!"

"Nope, not even," said Delmas, laughing heartily. "In fact, what made him really mad was the picture of someone flipping the bird he found stuck on his office door every morning for a week."

Pauline turned her wedding ring around her finger with her free hand. Touching this ring gave her the illusion of closeness to her husband. Delmas thought about the fact that during their last collaboration, Laurent was still alive, which Pauline had probably just realized too. She always puts on that sensual fragrance, he thought. Despite her looks which were not conventionally pretty, Delmas couldn't help but find her attractive. He sympathized with her. He knew what she had gone through. He smiled at her, picked up his cup of coffee and raised it to her as a sign of sharing.

"To you, Pauline! Like the good old times! We have a new case and my sixth sense as a cop tells me that it's a tough one. Maybe even more than tough!"

"I must say that your call surprised me. I didn't expect our career paths to cross again."

"Indeed. Are you sure that Khalid Alzadi is the man identified by Driss Oufik?"

"We can't be sure, Francois! But we're speaking off the record here, right? I didn't tell my boss that we were seeing each other and you know how department heads can be a little sensitive about that sort of thing..."

"Yes, of course! We're absolutely off the record! We can talk about anything."

"Good!" replied Pauline, who became visibly more relaxed. "Driss Oufik has identified the henchman of a certain Al-Naviq. You know him?"

"I didn't know who he was yesterday morning, but now I do, yes. He's a Saudi Arabian billionaire, he has a diplomatic passport and he's the employer of Khalid Alzadi."

"Exactly. So, by establishing that there's a link between our terrorist and Khalid Alzadi, we know in turn that there's a relationship with Al-Naviq."

"And what have you done about it?"

"I wrote my report, and the police chief asked us not to take it any further. Orders came directly from the Prime Minister. Didn't wanna upset the sale of Rafale fighter jets. You understand."

"Yeah, I can fill in the blanks. It's not the hardest puzzle I'll ever have to solve. Except... there are some coincidences beginning to build here. And you know in our business, we don't like coincidences."

"You talking about the bank?" asked Pauline.

"I am. In Malik Aertens' account book there was evidence that they funded the May 1st terrorist group. Went through the Zurich whatever Bank, ZIS, which coincidentally also financed Tarek Laid's campaign," explained Delmas.

"Tarek Laid!" exclaimed Pauline, "whose driver was Khalid Alzadi!"

"So it's pretty clear that this shit show is somehow all connected," Delmas insisted, "so now I'm thinking about Prudot."

"Who's that?"

"Oh, he's a journalist from the 'République Libre', from the extreme right. He told me this morning that they aren't involved in the assassination of Tarek Laid at all."

"So who is, François?"

"Well, I don't know exactly, yet. That could change with Delvaux's call this morning."

"What did he tell you?" She asked.

"Well, he wasn't exactly clear! That's why I asked him if we could meet. He told me that he and a New York Times reporter were being chased by ZIS. Says they're trying to get rid of them. Stop them investigating the bank and Millenium Dust. And that all this had something to do with the death of Tarek Laid."

"And you believe him?"

"I don't know." Delmas answered, somewhat evasively. But we don't have much to lose and he seemed like he was pretty serious."

Checkmate?

Jack and Thomas' taxi arrived in front of the Soleil d'Or at precisely 11.00 am, perfectly on time. Jack had said precisely nothing for the entire journey. He still had an infernal headache pounding in his temples, despite the two 200 mg tablets of Ibuprofen he'd taken, which hadn't had the desired effect. His blood was beating to the rhythm of his regrets. He felt ashamed that he'd fallen off again. Since their arrival in Paris, he'd felt a growing sense of uselessness. Thomas, with the help of Luca and his network of hackers, was developing a program that would be able to beat Millenium in their own backyard but Jack had so far brought little to the party in terms of help. He hadn't even bothered to call the paper for two days now. When the moron Gerry Small decided to come looking for him, not even the editor's support would be enough.

Delvaux had just received a call from Luca, who'd told him that their hacking of Millenium hadn't worked, and Thomas was visibly disappointed.

"Shit!" he said as he hung up. He turned to to Jack, "Millenium's security has just sent us back to first base."

"What did you think was going to happen? That they'd just open up the doors to their vault for you?"

"No, but if we'd managed to get our hands on their AI we could have at least studied it so we'd know what we were up against!"

"But it would have taken days, maybe even weeks, to dissect their program and you you know it!"

"Yes," answered Delvaux, a little too loudly. "Of course I know that! But if we had their precious little toy, maybe we could have saved ourselves some time."

Jack entered the café as Thomas was paying the driver. The noisy establishment was resolutely Parisian, with faux red leather benches and too many customers who stood at the bar repeatedly throwing glances around the room trying to find the free places. The owner behind the bar was lining up the cups under an Italian coffee machine which never seemed to cease noisily grinding beans. Thomas took out his cell phone to call Delmas, who answered on the first ring.

"Lieutenant Delmas? Thomas Delvaux, we're here."

"Perfectly on time! Where are you?"

"You can't miss me. I'm at the entrance of the café, white, thinning hair, round glasses. Oh yeah, and there's a big brown-haired guy who's probably a bit better looking than myself."

"I'll be there in a second."

Delmas had been sat in the back room reserved just for cops. He got up to go and fetch his visitors, whom he spotted easily.

After the usual introductions, they found a table and sat down. The noise was at a more comfortable level than in the main room. One could hold a conversation without having to shout. Jack studied the two policemen. Delmas, in his fifties, was wearing a gray suit and was in perfect physical condition. He carried a sense of seriousness about him. But it was Commander Rougier who caught his eye.

"Mr. Campbell?"

This pretty redhead was not a day over forty, he thought to himself. She smiled at him. Her deep blue eyes seemed to be telling him to move on and look elsewhere; that she didn't want to be noticed. But as she batted her eyelids she revealed a tiny sliver of those eyes, and through this small glimpse one could see a secret garden full of ghosts and regrets. There was a weakness there and Jack knew it. He who dragged in his wake so many alcoholic corpses.

"Mr. Campbell? Can you hear me?"

Jack found this woman, whom he did not know at all, irresistibly attractive. He'd had no one in his life for what seemed like an eternity. The poor opinion he had of himself didn't help things, but when one fought against the bottle, all the rest paled in significance. Just avoiding the bottle day after day was enough to take up all of his energy.

"Mr. Campbell?" Delmas repeated.

Jack snapped out of his daydream. All eyes were turned towards him. Delmas seemed to be waiting for an answer.

"Um, excuse me, I was thinking about something else," said Jack.

"French police are offering to buy you a coffee. That's rare, you know!"

"Well yes, a coffee would be great!" Jack replied hesitantly.

In the main room the machine finished grinding its beans and the sound level went down a notch.

Pauline was staring at the tall, unhappy brown haired boy. He must have been hit pretty hard, she thought, noticing the bruise on his nose now turning purple. It suited him well this broken face, full of bumps. She found him attractive. She could see the confusion she was causing in this man and found herself finding it pleasant. She'd been trapped in the world of police for too long without seeing any new faces. In that world she was only 'Laurent's wife'. Worse still, she was the wife of Laurent, the assassinated cop. To Jack, she was just a woman, pretty and desirable.

The server brought over the drinks and Delmas began to speak.

Gentlemen, Commander Rougier and I thank you for agreeing to meet us.

"It was imperative," answered Delvaux.

"I'm sure that's true," said Delmas. "If I've understood correctly, you have information concerning the investigation into the death of the politician Tarek Laid?"

"In fact, Lieutenant, it's more complicated than that."

"Well, we're listening!" Delmas answered, resting his head on his two hands, elbows on the table.

Jack turned to Delvaux and spoke.

"I'll make it short," he began. I'm not a specialist in finance so I'll keep things simple if that's ok."

"Sure. Go ahead."

"Ok great." He looked into Pauline's eyes and told the whole story from the beginning.

Jack explained how, after receiving Thomas's call in New York, he decided to begin his investigation into Millenium Dust. He told them about the New Haven operational center, and how they'd found a disturbing link between Millenium Dust and ZIS. Then he described the menacing CEO of Zurich Investments &

Securities Bank, Marco Ziegler, and explained how the aforementioned had almost choked when Jack and Thomas had mentioned Millenium and Shuito Pharmaceuticals, which had resulted in them becoming the targets of two murder attempts. He recounted the events of the night when FraNex was burned to the ground as well as their visit to the Miroir with Luca. He didn't mention the 'less official' parts of the story, such as Black Mamba and how they'd managed to identify ZIS in the first place.

Jack tried to paint a detailed picture of the world of finance. He said it was thanks to Delvaux's software that they'd managed to discover Millenium Dust and its manipulation of the stock price of Shuito Pharmaceuticals.

He concluded his presentation by revealing that they had 'kind of' hacked Ziegler's phone, upon which they'd found references to a mysterious BLACKSTONE project. He added that this project was linked to a very advanced market manipulation program, one that was ready to be used on a very large scale.

Jack looked at Thomas questioningly, and asked him:

"Did I forget anything?"

"I think that about covers it," answered Delvaux, "except our theory on the imminence of the threat."

"So you think that whatever is going to happen will happen very soon?" asked Pauline.

"I think that in order for them to launch this BLACKSTONE project, they'd need some kind of imbalance, an instability somewhere. I'm convinced that recent events in France are what they were waiting for. Or worse, what they'd planned. I mean, if you want something to happen, and you need it to happen at a particular moment in time, well then the best thing is to do it yourself, right?"

"So this is where the death of Tarek Laid comes in?" asked Delmas.

"Exactly," answered Delvaux, "if you want to create chaos, what better way than to put communities at odds with each other, create a conflict, especially when the balance is already precarious."

"You think all of this is was planned then?" Delmas was trying to sort through all the information that had been presented to him.

"It's possible. I can't prove anything, but you have to admit that Ziegler's visit to Paris this week is enough to cause concern?"

"Indeed, Monsieur Delvaux. Indeed," said Delmas thoughtfully.

"But who's behind all this? Ziegler can't be acting alone!" asked Pauline.

"He's not, you're right. My money's on individuals or entire states with connections to the super wealthy," Jack added.

"Saudi Arabia? The Russians?"

"That kind of thing."

"So, just to be sure that I've understood you correctly, Mr. Campbell. You think that this whole story is actually an attempt to manipulate stock prices on a large scale?" Delmas' questioning forehead wrinkled with concern.

"Actually, I'm sure of it."

"How much are we talking here? Why are they doing this?"

"They're doing it for the money. Judging by the scale of Millenium's activities on the market, I'd say we're looking at hundreds of billions of dollars."

"That would be the sort of amount that could change the financial balance of the entire planet?"

"If used correctly and with sufficient technical means, this amount of money could change the world in terms of power."

"So we're dealing with a serious threat, to say the least!"

"To say the very least, Mr. Delmas. We're facing a potential financial cataclysm."

"And what can we do about it, in your opinion?" Delmas looked at Jack and Thomas in turn.

"You could perhaps pay Millennium a little visit in La Défense and begin by asking them to tell you about their business activities?" Jack suggested. "That would be a good start."

"We'll try to clear it with the judge, but for now we got nothing concrete on them that we can use," replied Pauline.

The meeting was over. Jack gave Pauline and Delmas his card. He made sure to add to Pauline:

"Call me if you need anything. I'm free…"

Someone turned up the volume on the TV above the bar in the main room. A red banner at the bottom of the screen spelled out names of cities where violence was mounting.

A peaceful march to demonstrate against Tarek Laid's assassination had recently degenerated into fighting in the city of Rennes. The city center was unrecognizable, with dozens of broken windows and pieces of shattered glass lying all over the streets. The camera images showed street furniture destroyed and the inhabitants confused by the speed and violence of the confrontations.

The same scenes played out on a bigger scale in the bigger cities. Paris, Lille, Toulon, Nice, and Marseille all saw conflicts, especially in the suburbs that were traditionally home to immigrant families.

A live feed showed images of a demonstration in one such place; Bobigny, a northeastern suburb of Paris, where a large proportion of the inhabitants were non-white second or third generation immigrants. Gangs were fighting openly in the streets. Shaven white skulls, an unmistakable sign of the hard right, confirmed the presence of the skinhead followers of the Front National who were there to confront the youths. There were the usual scenes of urban violence: burning cars, tear gas, masks on the offenders. The fumes from the grenades mingled with the fires of the burning vehicles that blackened in the streets.

Someone fired into the crowd.

It was impossible to know who was the shooter, let alone from which side the shot was fired. A young man in jeans, a scarf and leather boots collapsed. The stupor was visible on the faces of demonstrators and gang members alike. The riot police charged.

The violence had just been turned up a notch. The country was on the brink of going up in flames.

Delmas and Rougier looked at each other. The images fit perfectly with what Jack had predicted. If they were looking for something that could cause an imbalance, here they had hit the proverbial jackpot.

"Gentlemen, thank you for your help. Commander Rougier and I are most grateful. Given the current situation, I think it's better that we returned to our offices. The next few hours are going to be extremely difficult."

"Do you want to catch up on the situation a little later?" Jack asked.

"We'll get back to you. For now, we need to go," said Delmas.

The group disbanded. Delmas and Rougier walked toward the police headquarters on the banks of the Seine. Jack and Thomas took a taxi back to the Miroir. It was 12:30.

"You know, I heard it was Sunday today," sighed Delmas.

"Tell me about it. I was supposed to meet my mom for lunch, and I'm already late. She hates when I'm late," replied Pauline.

"Ah, the joys of being in the police! I'll call you as soon as I get the word from the judge so we can give this Millenium a courtesy call. Problem is, we got nothing that would justify a search warrant. Not to mention we don't even know what we are looking for."

"Yeah. And we have no idea about the timings of this whole thing, either."

Delmas returned to his desk and picked up the phone. The judge was most likely just sitting down to have lunch with his family. Delmas hesitated. He believed, and was probably right, that if he bothered the magistrate now, with only Jack and Thomas' testimony as back up, the judge would not consider it enough and would refuse to sign off on the warrant. Delmas decided instead to send the prosecutor all the information he had by email, and let him think until Monday.

Delmas decided to contact Captain Erik Thorens at FedPol, the Cantonal Police Office in Zurich. The two of them had met at a seminar on cooperation between the various European police forces. He wanted to ask him for details about the fire at Thomas Delvaux's company and the incidents at the Zurich hospital. The least he could do was make sure that the testimony of his two visitors aligned with the official account.

The seminar had been held in Paris and was set up by Interpol. It brought together representatives from most European countries. The focus was mainly on money laundering and terrorist channels. François Delmas and Erik Thorens had quickly found common areas of personal and professional interest when they met. When Delmas suggested to a few of the colleagues to go and tour some Parisian bars, many had accepted, but Thorens had been by far the most enthusiastic. A little too much, according to some members of Delmas' office, judging by the sight of his arrival at the seminar the next morning. But this boozy evening had at least had the merit of creating friendly ties between the two men, who shared an identical concept of their profession.

He wrote a fax for the attention of Thorens, asking him to call back the next day. After reflection, he added that he would also be interested in information about Zurich Investments & Securities Bank. The Swiss didn't really appreciate people sticking their noses into the business of their banks, but Thorens was able to venture into that field without too much trouble at all.

*
* *

Checkmate?

15. OUT OF CONTROL

Prime Minister du Plessis looked at his watch. It was 4 pm. He was, as usual, perfectly on time for the rendezvous that the President had just set up. The Elysée's call was more than clear: this meeting was not optional. He climbed the steps of the Presidential Palace and met his ministers and their advisers. They were gathered to discuss the ongoing situation with the Head of Government in the Council Chamber.

Communications from the Interior Ministry and the reports from men on the ground in prefectures around the country described a situation which was worsening by the hour. The country was on the brink of an insurrection.

The death of a skinhead around noon had unleashed another earthquake, which the police were struggling to contain. Two mosques had been burned down and very serious confrontations were taking place in many neighborhoods all over the country. Riot police squads were no longer enough to stem the growing popular movement.

The Minister of the Interior ran into the Council Chamber:

"Mr. President, we're losing ground. I've just been informed that two young Muslims from Bobigny have been killed. No more than five minutes ago."

"Do we know how they were killed, and by whom?"

"As always, under these circumstances things are still unclear. But we do know that it wasn't the police that fired. I've requested more details."

"We're heading for a general meltdown. Get everybody in, we have to make decisions. Now!"

Checkmate?

The interior minister's mobile began to ring. He picked up. The other members of the meeting remained seated around the large table. Henri du Plessis saw him turn pale.

"As bad as that?" asked the Prime Minister.

"Um, yes, Henri!"

"We're listening."

"Intelligence has just learned that gang leaders from neighborhoods surrounding La Défense gathered this morning. They're considering joint action. They want to blow up La Défense and set the capital on fire. The suburbs are coming out of their neighborhoods."

The meeting lasted for two hours. They had an in depth discussion about the situation and everyone agreed that there could no longer stand back and watch this happen. Violence would be met by force. The assassination of Tarek Laid had opened a breach in the social structure of the country. A politician who stood up for a community was killed. For Muslim people, his death, although it wasn't officially claimed by the far right, was signed with the blood of their leader. From that moment on, the weakness of government institutions had brought about the disappearance of the rule of law, and in its place the law of the Talion: an eye for an eye. The President understood the way the youth of the country were reacting. He could not allow it to continue or even show empathy, but he grasped its foundation. He would, however, repress it as firmly as possible. The republican ideal did not flourish in chaos.

President Lavalette, after the decision by his crisis council, agreed to speak to the nation at 6 pm. His speech would be firm. A curfew would be introduced from 7 pm and the army deployed where the threat to order was highest, especially around Paris. An armored brigade had been mobilized to secure the district of La Défense.

*
* *

Checkmate?

Füller connected his PC to start the videoconference. He'd told the members of BLACKSTONE to be online at 5 pm sharp. The meeting's objective was to discuss the possible launch of the project. They were now coming to the end of many months of hard work. All of the centers were operational. Ziegler had visited the last three: Paris, London and New Haven. Those in Moscow, Tokyo and Sydney had already been ready for a long time. They'd confirmed their computing power in the Japanese capital via the successful takeover of Shuito Pharmaceuticals.

The connection request notifications began to come in. Small vignettes appeared one by one on Füller's screen. 'Al-Naviq and Dimitri Volkov would like to join the meeting'. Füller accepted the requests and their images appeared simultaneously. Seconds later, Marco Ziegler and Yuchun Lio completed the session.

"Gentlemen, thank you for being punctual! We're all here! We can start what I hope will be our last virtual face-to-face before the launch of BLACKSTONE," Füller said.

"It will be," said Al-Naviq. "Anarchy is spreading throughout France. Disorder is gaining ground by the hour. I believe we've reached our goal. Tomorrow, the Paris Stock Exchange will open with huge losses. The aftershocks of the French protests are being felt in Germany and Belgium. The whole of Europe's financial system will be shaken."

"Sorry to interrupt you, Al-Naviq, but before launching our project, we need to make sure our infrastructure is ready," Dimitri Volkov opined, obviously not wanting to take any chances.

"We are operational," said Ziegler. "Our trial run in Tokyo dispelled any doubts."

"I hold you personally responsible, Herr Ziegler," Volkov replied.

"Storx, our director, has confirmed that we could start the operation at any time. He's been looking forward to this moment for months!"

"Good! You have all of our trust, Herr Ziegler," answered Füller, getting the meeting back on course.

"Gentlemen, we must decide today! The shock felt tomorrow morning in Europe will be tough for the financial markets, and that gives us our window of opportunity. We were looking for something that could provide us with a favorable moment to launch BLACKSTONE. Now I believe we have it." Al-Naviq was convinced that the time had come.

"You're right. I propose that we vote to endorse our decision," said Füller. "Who is for?"

"Me!" The positive response of Fouad Al-Naviq only took one second to arrive.

"Me too!" answered Yuchun Lio, the most discreet member of the group.

"If we're absolutely sure of our Artificial Intelligence, then I am also for," said Dimitri Volkov. "You have not forgotten that my participation is, shall we say... supported by my government. Any failure would be inexcusable."

"I also agree to start the operation as soon as possible," concluded Füller. "Ziegler, what do you think? Will ZIS be ready tomorrow?"

"Yes, without doubt," Ziegler answered, hammering home his words with conviction.

"Gentlemen, in that case, I propose that we launch the BLACKSTONE project tomorrow at 9:15 am New York time, fifteen minutes after the opening of the US financial markets."

Füller made a short pause so everyone had time to take stock of the decision.

"Does anyone have questions before we finish up here?" asked Füller. No one answered. "In that case, this videoconference is over. We'll meet again tomorrow after the New York market closes to discuss the situation."

A notification sounded as each participant left the conversation. Füller couldn't help but smile when the last one disappeared from his screen. BLACKSTONE was going to be a success and there was no doubt that the fall of the American and European stock markets would reshuffle the balance of financial and geostrategic power all over the planet.

Checkmate?

Nobody except these four people knew what was behind BLACKSTONE. This was not some simple insider trading. No; this project would change the influence of nations and would cause a destabilization so sudden that it would the euro area would be thrown into total chaos. It would bring Germany to its knees; but it was worth it. It was the price to pay in order for the country to regain its sovereignty, free from the shackles of the EU. No politician would ever have the courage to do it. Everyone would one day understand what a true visionary he was.

*
* *

Luca was beginning to feel hopeful again. After being disconnected from the Millenium network, it was time to face the facts: neither he nor Thomas would be able to access the BLACKSTONE source code. He'd managed to download about twenty-five percent of the Millenium software but everything was encrypted. He'd been trying for hours to infernal decode the program but nothing he tried was working. Luca Hanser was one of the masters of encryption, however. No code could keep him out for very long. The 'Dark Web' collective to which he belonged often called on him to break through the security of sites they wanted to hack. Always, or almost always, with good reason.

But for the last five minutes, things had cleared up. He had tried a new decryption algorithm and it had just made some significant progress. Suddenly, lines of programming language, source code and files appeared. He still did not know exactly what they were dealing with, but he could at least try to understand how and why the Millenium computer scientists had developed what looked like some seriously smart Artificial Intelligence software.

Thomas, having just returned from his meeting with the police, looked at Luca thoughtfully. He was obviously trying to make sense of recent events. He wasn't able to; it was as if all of this was a huge puzzle but a few essential pieces had been hidden from him.

They continued to work on developing with Thomas back as the lead. While Luca was busy hacking Millenium, Thomas continued to improve upon Black Mamba, all with the support of Luca's virtual friends. With their help he created what he hoped would be a firewall around Millenium. There was no guarantee, but he hoped that with this new version he'd at least be able to block their buy and sell orders. If nothing else, they could attempt to drown the system and paralyze it. The firewall couldn't prevent Millenium from launching its attack, but it could dampen the shock. That's if everything went to plan and they hadn't forgotten anything. They were working blind, especially considering they wouldn't be able to test anything. There are so many unknowns, Thomas thought to himself as he completed the last lines of the code.

"That's it!" exclaimed Luca, "I managed to figure out the source code."

"Excellent," Thomas replied. "Is there anything that jumps out at you?"

"Nothing for the moment... wait! There's a protected file with a password."

"If it's been secured, that means it's probably important. Is the whole file there?"

"Yes, I have the whole structure. I'll run my usual hacking program. It won't be able to keep me out for long, trust me."

Night was falling on La Défense and the two computer scientists were so absorbed in their work that they didn't notice the time passing. It was as if they intuitively felt the urgency of the situation.

"Boom!" exclaimed Luca. "I've just broken through their security! Who's the boss?"

"You are Luca, but we already knew that! So what's inside?"

With a click Luca opened the file. The data contained inside the file displayed on the screen. It was a script and settings that detailed the Millennium project. At first they didn't comprehend the importance of what they were looking at, then suddenly everything fell into place.

In that moment, Thomas understood the purpose of BLACKSTONE.

The stock market speculation, the death of Tarek Laid, the terrorist attack between the two rounds of elections: everything was intertwined. He also knew that their firewall would be of no help to them in view of the threat that was looming.

*
* *

7.30 pm. Jack finally decided to dial the number. He'd put off making the call all afternoon. She won't be available. Or worse, she's not interested. Mustering up all the courage he could summon within him, he entered the ten digits of Pauline's cell phone number.

First ring...

"Commander Rougier," replied a playful Pauline.

"Good evening Commander!" it's Jack Campbell.

Pauline was a little unsure at first, but soon recognized it was the voice of the large, slightly awkward guy staring at her this morning.

"Mr. Reporter! What can I do for you?" asked Pauline in a happy voice.

"Hi! I thought you might want to know some more about the case... I mean, there are still some shady areas you're unclear about, maybe you'd like to discuss them?"

"But it's Sunday!"

"Yeah. I'm sorry I bothered you, Commander! You're right, we'll see each other another time!"

"Having said that... I'm not really up to much today. Is there something important you'd like to tell me?"

"Yes and no... but you know I could... I mean it's..."

Pauline couldn't help but smile. Jack had no new information to give her. No, he called her to spend time with her.

He was trying to flirt! It had been so long since she'd had the opportunity to spend a few hours with a man. How many more times can I refuse? she thought. After all, he's just inviting me for a chat. She made her decision.

"Listen Jack, I don't live very far from your hotel. Are you still at the Hyatt Regency?"

"Yeah I'm still there…"

"Well, I'll meet you there in, say, thirty minutes! At the bar?"

"Perfect, yes..."

"Ok then I'll see you soon!"

Jack's heart was pounding. This woman had an effect on him that he hadn't felt in a very long time. Nothing would happen between them, but he was happy just to spend some time with Commander Rougier, even though he didn't know her at all. But that was also part of her charm. He'd detected within her that fragile sensitivity that just needed to be brought up to the surface.

An hour after her call, Pauline entered the almost-empty bar of the Hyatt Regency, dressed in a blue top, skinny jeans and black sneakers. Jack sipped his Diet Coke, looking at his watch every five minutes before looking up and seeing her walking toward him. He found her beautiful.

He stood up to greet her. Pauline put her handbag on the chair and ordered a non-alcoholic cocktail. A barely palpable embarrassment settled in; neither of them knew how to start the conversation. Jack broke the ice.

"Commander Rougier?" Jack started.

"Call me Pauline!" she insisted. "I'm not on duty tonight!"

"Uh, sorry, Pauline, I wanted to see you because..."

The conversation lasted for over an hour. Jack and Pauline talked about everything and nothing. Once they'd gotten started, the discussion quickly drifted onto more personal topics. Jack now understood why she had a wedding ring, why she had nothing planned on a Sunday, and why a lingering shadow of sadness hovered over her. Pauline appreciated this caring, if slightly clumsy, man. His awkwardness reminded her of her first few meetings with Laurent. But she made an effort not to think about that. Enjoy it, just for you, said a small inner voice.

They decided to dine there. The hotel restaurant was empty. The events of the last seventy-two hours had had the effect of driving tourists and business people away, who had returned home hastily, deserting the French capital. The news shows broadcasting footage of the situation continuously was not going to help reverse that trend.

They ordered a bottle of wine. Jack was happy to see that the monsters were being good tonight. No panicking, no palpitations. He controlled the situation and drank water.

Pauline was on a small cloud. The alcohol was working. She knew she shouldn't drink, but for the first time in a long time she was happy. Or if not completely happy, she felt lighter! That's it. She felt lighter. She wanted the evening to last a little longer. She'd go home soon, back to her normal life, to her dreams that kept her awake in the early morning hours, alone.

Jack smiled. He'd been smiling since Pauline had arrived. This woman gave off a sensuality that troubled him. When she agreed to have dinner with him, he made his little mental dance of victory. He didn't know where it was going to lead them, but he was going to enjoy this little moment of pleasure. The past few days had been grueling and there was no sign that things were going to improve, at least in the short term. He was still in danger after all, a wanted man. Added to that there was the threat of the financial system collapsing and he also had meetings at Alcoholics Anonymous to plan on his return to New York. Not to mention his stellar performances at the bar and in his room only last night.

Pauline couldn't remember how it had happened. However, she did remember kissing Jack first. He hadn't tried to stop her. They were standing up. She was on her tiptoes as he was so tall. After drinking half the bottle of red, he must have supported her, because she was no longer completely in control of her actions. In any case, he had felt her tongue enter his mouth. So he took her by the waist, then put a hand behind her head and pressed his mouth to hers. The kiss lasted a long time before he took her back to his room.

Jack undressed her, at first softly then with ardor. She took off her shirt and they jumped on the bed, naked.

They were one. A fusion of two solitudes. Two wounded beings, mistreated by life. They clung to each other as if they were clinging to a buoy to save themselves from drowning. They lifted themselves up above the nothingness that had threatened to engulf them, perhaps offering themselves hope, no doubt giving them a future.

*
* *

La Défense was being shaken by strong winds and rain that had been falling for several hours. The street lights, battered by the gusts that swept the esplanade, cast flickering halos on the ground. This huge deserted concrete square gave a glimpse of a few pedestrians here and there, nocturnal walkers wandering with worried steps, hastening their pace to protect themselves from the surrounding void.

Thomas Delvaux was thinking about nothing. The window of his office, on the second floor of a modern building, look out onto the open space outside. Directly opposite was the Quatre Temps mall. He looked without seeing, lost in his empty thoughts, at the end of this gray day. The lights of most of the buildings were off, mostly darkness remained, barely pierced by the thin, luminous curtains of a few spotlights.

Still, he saw the arrival of the first silhouettes. He thought at first that it must have been a group of young people crossing the square. There were maybe fifty of them, hoods covering their heads, jogging. Some were carrying backpacks. As they advanced, others arrived. The first group were now in the middle of the esplanade, more and more followed behind. The fifty had become one hundred, then hundreds, maybe even a thousand. An army of anonymous soldiers, puppets suspended by a malicious thread, had just invaded La Défense. The ranks were getting bigger. In the relative dim light of the square, intermittent metal splinters and fleeting flashes were visible. The silent shadows were armed.

The man who was leading stopped his march. The others did the same. He stood under the conical light of a lamppost. He turned in Thomas' direction, staring at the bright window where the Swiss stood with the light behind him.

Delvaux noticed the dead eye and wide scar that blemished his right cheek. Kamel stared at him with his one-eyed glare. Thomas maintained eye contact before admitting defeat and backing off into his office. He got up and turned off the office light, letting the dark hide him from the gang leader's inquisitive look.

Luca and Thomas waited for a few seconds before moving closer to the windows. They could now watch out without being seen. The army led by Kamel had split into two groups. About twenty individuals were heading towards the Quatre Temps; the others continued their progress towards the bottom of the district, in the direction of central Paris. It only took a few minutes before the two spectators could see the twenty men coming back and running as fast as they could. It looked like they were escaping from something.

A few seconds passed before the first strong explosion sounded. The roof of the mall, blown up by the detonation, was lifted into the air. Powerful flames that swelled more and more each second illuminated the sky, while endless debris fell onto the forecourt.

Hell broke into the Miroir's office. Less than thirty seconds had elapsed before two more loud detonations sounded in succession. The intensity of the blast blew the windows of buildings around the central square of La Défense. Their bay windows disintegrated. Luca and Thomas only just enough time to dive under the desks to avoid the falling pieces of glass. The screens of the computers closest to the windows were pulverized by the shockwave, falling to the ground.

Checkmate?

Silence fell upon the forecourt. Outside, the flames grew in intensity, their orange color reflected by the thousands of pieces of glass. Sirens screamed continuously all around them.

Luca and Thomas got up slowly, stunned by the bleak spectacle that was spreading around them. Unsteadily, they made their way to the destroyed windows, walking on the broken shards strewn on the ground, their steps crunching as they made contact with the smooth concrete. Swirls of thick smoke from the mall spilled into the office making the atmosphere unbreathable.

They took their laptops and left the room to go to the server room. In the distance, they could hear the first shots of automatic weapons.

*
* *

16. THE ATTACK

Paris, Monday September 25th, 9 am

The markets opened to heavy losses. Societal problems had dampened investor optimism. The French popular movement had been replicated in Germany, Belgium and the Netherlands, each of which having its effect on the financial markets.

The Paris Stock Exchange had lost ten per cent according to initial reports, Frankfurt eight per cent. The forecasts were reasonably good early in the session, forecasting a return for the CAC 40 to minus seven percent by midday. Things seemed to be getting back to normal.

The attack took place at 3.14 pm, less than fifteen minutes after the opening of the US markets.

Storx was managing all of the Millenium sites. The automation of the process had been a source of endless discussion. Füller wanted management to be totally centralized because activity needed to be perfectly synchronized across the different countries. He'd won this battle and the BLACKSTONE project was now in the sole hands of Storx in New Haven.

Pressing the send key would cause a chain reaction. Like falling dominoes, the first one dropped and the rest followed. For better or worse, there was no way back now.

Artificial Intelligence and the BLACKSTONE program had been created to take control of finance.

As soon as Storx launched it, billions would pour onto the stock exchanges. First in France, where the situation was the most fragile. The shock on the Paris market would be powerful, driving it violently downwards. The shockwave would then spread to the other European markets which would also be severely shaken. As always, the investors with the largest profits to make would start selling first, leaving with a nice slice of profits.

The effect would be to precipitate the movement. Other title holders would take their time, but they'd sell too, eventually. When that happened, total collapse would be near. Everyone would follow. Once losses hit a certain point, the robots that scanned the markets in real time would detect that the levels were falling below limit values, immediately triggering mass sell-offs. Since all the automated software had been programmed in the same way, it would signify the beginning of the hemorrhage. Everyone would sell at the same time.

To avoid this type of domino effect, the authorities had made use of automatic locks since 2008, after the fall of Lehman Brothers. When markets fall by ten percent or more, they're closed for ten minutes. Then they reopen. If the fall continues significantly, they then close for one hour. The objective is to avoid, by contagion, the systemic risks.

But the system is totally corrupt. The existence of the 'Dark Pool' has changed the game. Indeed, the vast majority of global transactions are in the hands of these parallel stock exchanges, subject to none of the regulatory requirements of national stock exchanges. It becomes an exchange by mutual agreement. During stock market closures, the 'Dark Pools' remain open, and the big sell-offs can continue.

If someone rich and/or crazy enough embarks on a large-scale operation, no institution can prevent the bankruptcy of the financial system.

Millenium and the members of BLACKSTONE knew this. What no one could have envisaged was what Thomas Delvaux had just discovered.

The modern era is no longer dominated by process industries. Wealth no longer means owning a steel, concrete or car manufacturing plant. No, the future is virtual. It is the economy of knowledge that rules the world. Power is measured by your ability to manipulate information, disseminate it, and influence its content. Whoever holds the capital of the companies that build this future consisting of social networks, interconnections of systems, search engines and ownership of the Web, they are the ones who will rise to the top of the global pyramid. Here is where the battle will take place. The rest is nothing but ashes of a past in which jobs are becoming scarce and wages are falling. In addition to networks and the knowledge economy are renewable energies and life sciences. Herein lies the winning cocktail of mastery of the world that is looming.

To hold the supreme power, you need the capital of Google, Facebook, Apple, CISCO, Space X, Microsoft or Tesla, giants of the pharmaceutical industry or BioTech, which will ensure the main therapeutic advances of tomorrow. The hands of the politicians are empty. The power is no longer military. It is technological and financial.

The file that Thomas and Luca had opened contained the names of the companies coveted by Millenium, which shed new light on BLACKSTONE's goal and explained why they had created this Artificial Intelligence. It imagined a society in which Web infrastructures would be in the wrong hands, where the contents of social networks would be filtered and only manipulated information would be available.

The BLACKSTONE project sent shivers down his spine.

When they launched their attack, everyone would believe that the financial world was collapsing and panic would bring about the mass sell-offs. They would then use their tools to begin a process that would maintain a sufficient level of crisis so the stock markets continue to fall slowly while they plundered the coveted sectors. The market would lose ten, twenty or thirty percent, but the target companies would be slaughtered, sold at fifty percent of their price.

If everything went as planned, in this finance-ruled world, by the end of the day, the political power would have changed hands. An almost-legal sleight of hand.

Storx's cell phone vibrated. He read Ziegler's message twice.

There was no doubt, the order was clear.

Checkmate?

At exactly 9.14 am from New York, 3.14 pm Paris time, Storx pressed the send button from the Artificial Intelligence control console, propagating the shock wave throughout the networks.

*
* *

At 8 am, Lieutenant Delmas passed through the big wooden door at the Police HQ and greeted the security officer who was screening the entrances. He entered the building and began to make his way up the three floors that separated him from his office. The steps, worn by time and steeped in history, were still not getting any easier to climb. There was talk of moving the headquarters to a new, modern construction, but all the cops in the brigade disapproved of the project. Even though this old building was in many ways awkward and badly designed, it remained the home of the French Police. Nothing could replace a building so full of history.

The exhausted policeman pushed open the door to his top floor office. He turned on his computer and opened up his emails. He was expecting a response from the Public Prosecutor regarding the search warrant for Millenium's premises. It had arrived, and unsurprisingly it was negative. The dossier was too thin to justify the warrant. He was going to have to find more evidence or show some serious initiative.

Despite the ongoing curfew, the evening had been tough and he'd only slept a few hours. All police units had been mobilized yesterday due to the tense situation. Everything had gone awry early in the afternoon with violent clashes in the suburbs, despite the arrival of the army at the strategic points around Paris, and the closure of motorways throughout the area surrounding the capital. The toll of the evening was thirty dead and dozens of wounded, and that was just in Paris. Intense fighting at La Défense had left the business district in disarray, like the rest of the country, which had experienced a night of unprecedented violence. The national count was still provisional, but there were at least fifty dead, many arrests and hundreds of cars burned in the cities. A dozen policemen were dead or seriously injured, but they were still holding out. The police forces and the army, that had been positioned in the places that were under the most severe threat, helped to contain the wave of collective hysteria and keep things calm.

At around three o'clock in the morning, Delmas had returned home to get a few hours' rest.

He noticed a fax had arrived. It was a reply from his friend and counterpart in Zurich. Captain Erik Thorens was not available, but one of his colleagues, Anne Müller, confirmed that Delvaux was an inhabitant of Zurich, he was a computer scientist and his company had been burned down a few days earlier. She sent him an unflattering picture of Thomas, but one that nonetheless proved Delvaux was what he claimed to be. There were also images taken of the accident on Friday. Everything matched the story. Delmas realized that Thomas and Jack were the good guys, and that he'd probably need them if he were going to solve this case.

*
* *

Pauline opened her eyes. She wondered where she was, then she became aware of the hotel room. She felt Jack's presence and the whole evening came flooding back to her. The dinner, the wine, the kiss and the rest. At first she felt a sense of shame, or more one of guilt, then the memories of Jack's skin on hers, of his caresses and the pleasure he had given her, it all came back. She made the decision to accept it. Jack was starting to move next to her. She got up, picked up her things and ran into the bathroom. It was 7.30 am and she was already late.

Checkmate?

*
* *

Thomas Delvaux opened the blinds in his hotel room after taking a hot shower. He hadn't slept much. Their return to the hotel had been chaotic after the explosions of last night. He and Luca were stranded in their office until the army arrived, which had evacuated the entire neighborhood before escorting them back to the hotel under military escort at around 2 am.

The day was gloomy, but at least it had stopped raining. He grabbed his phone to read his messages. Hanna said "hi" and told him that the children sent him kisses. Please let this all end soon, Thomas thought. He wanted his life to go back to where it was just a few days earlier, before all of this had begun. He then noticed that the small icon on the app he had installed on Ziegler's smartphone was blinking. He opened it. Ziegler had sent a message to Storx during the night.

It was easily decipherable: 'BLKSTNE 09/27 - 0915 EST-CONFIRMED'

The attack would take place today: BLACKSTONE, September 27 at 9.15 am Eastern Standard Time. Confirmed!

Delvaux immediately dialed Jack's number. It was time to decide on the program for the next few hours. It was 8.40 am, and according to his calculations, 9.15 pm on the eastern coast of the United States corresponded to 3.15 pm Paris time. That meant it would begin in six hours. He felt the ticking of the countdown that had just begun.

*
* *

Jack didn't hear the door close when Pauline disappeared. She'd been as discreet as she possible could. She didn't want to see him right now. Not yet. Not in this hotel room. She would call him a little later. She had to hurry to go to her Monday morning meeting at the Counter Terrorist Brigade premises. His phone began to vibrate, then ring louder and louder. He managed to get one foot out of bed and tried to locate his pants. He saw them on the floor in a corner of the room. He picked them up and removed the phone that was screaming for him to pick up.

"Hello!" Jack could not hide that his voice was still full of sleep.

"Hi Jack, sleep well?"

"Yes, Thomas, thank you!"

"I have something new! Ziegler confirmed the launch of their project today for 3.15 pm Paris time. We only have a few hours to solve this."

"How long have you known about this?"

"A few minutes. You want to come down and meet me for breakfast? I got some other stuff I need to tell you about."

"I'll be right down!"

Jack, Thomas and Luca met in the hotel restaurant. The gave Jack a summary of what had happened the night before; how they'd discovered what BLACKSTONE was all about and about the attacks on La Défense.

They decided that they should warn Lieutenant Delmas and Commandant Rougier. Thomas was surprised by the slightly reserved reaction of Jack, when it was suggested that he should be the one to call Pauline.

*
* *

Once Thomas had managed to contact Delmas to tell him in detail about their discoveries, they agreed to meet at the Porte Maillot hotel. Traveling through Paris after the night which had just passed was almost impossible. It was much easier however with a police car and sirens. Delmas called Pauline who agreed to join the group.

Checkmate?

Luca, Thomas and Jack were seated at a table in the Hyatt Regency's bar when they saw Rougier and Delmas arrive hastily at 11.30 am. Jack felt his pulse accelerate. He smiled at Pauline who smiled back.

Thomas Delvaux began to explain the urgency of the situation. Judging by the change in their look from curious to outright worry, he knew that they had understood his message.

*
* *

The traffic on the way to La Défense was particularly congested, restricted now to only one lane. Despite the blaring sirens, Delmas had incredible difficulty clearing a passage and cursed to himself profusely. Crossing the Pont de Neuilly proved a particularly fierce struggle. Delmas railed against the drivers blocking the road, preventing his car from passing the line that was now at a complete standstill. The journey dragged on and the minutes lost increased the tension that was becoming palpable.

Luca was glued to his phone, talking sometimes in English, sometimes in German. He was obviously negotiating for help. Delvaux concluded that he was probably discussing with his group of activists and hackers.

As soon as they crossed the bridge, they let the other motorists disappear under the tunnel of La Défense and turned off towards the entrance to the circular, to which access was still closed for civilians. A soldier checked their IDs, then they quickly made their way to the headquarters of Millenium Dust. After a quarter circle on the boulevard, they rounded a big bend and were able to catch a glimpse of the Quatre Temps. They slowed down to take a look at the forecourt. It was like a bombing had occurred. The scene was dantesque. All over the square, scattered debris of deformed metal littered the ground. A few swirls of smoke were still rising from what was left of the mall. Dozens of firefighters were on the scene, assisted by soldiers who ensured the smooth running of operations. Light armored vehicles were traveling at high speed between La Grande Arche and the CNIT building, under the surveillance of a helicopter that flew over the neighborhood with a roar that filled the air with muffled vibrations.

They took a right, leaving La Défense behind them and crossed the junction that connected the circular to the Boulevard de la Mission Marchand. The district of Courbevoie, the district next to La Défense, had suffered heavy damages during the previous evening's havoc. The Engie tower, the third tallest skyscraper in the business district, was another target for the attackers. One of the two explosions that occurred after the explosion at the mall had caused it some serious damage. The GDF-Suez tower, as well as a good part of the surrounding buildings, had also suffered.

Shattered window debris covered the roadway and a roadblock prevented access to the boulevard in both directions. At 1.30 pm, Delmas unceremoniously parked the police vehicle in front of the hastily installed security barriers, and together they all headed for the Millenium premises. Their positions as Commander of the Counter Terrorist Brigade and Police lieutenant opened up their passage without any useless questions.

"There's no time to waste! We've got less than two hours to do this," commented a nervous Delvaux as he got out of the car.

"Here it is!" Delmas pointed to a building at the entrance to the boulevard, opposite the Engie Tower.

Like all the buildings in the perimeter, Millenium's headquarters was in a bad state. It hadn't resisted the explosion and its vaporized windows testified to the power of the shock. Pauline and Delmas headed for the offices and asked Thomas, Luca and Jack, to stay behind to secure the area.

Pauline was looking through the double door that used to have glass within its frames. There was no sign of activity. The lobby was lit, allowing them to distinguish a reception desk and some chairs for visitors. There was no one. Pauline pushed the door, which refused to open. She slipped through the frame, taking care not to cut herself. The glazing on the floor, blown out by the explosion, crunched under her shoes. She stepped forward a few feet.

"Police! Is there anyone here?"

No answer. The silence was disturbing.

"Pauline?"

She turned to see Delmas, gun in his hand, poking his head through the door.

"You got something?" asked Pauline.

"No, I checked everywhere. Everyone who works here was evacuated last night. The area's been sealed off, so there shouldn't be anyone."

"Go get the others, we don't have much time!"

Delmas disappeared. Pauline went through what was left of the door and began to search this part of Millenium's premises. A first door led to a small room that contained an espresso machine that without doubt was used to offer coffee to visitors. No sign of life. She opened the next one. Supplies, nothing of interest. She saw another entrance to her right, just before the staircase which served the floor. She opened it.

Thomas, Luca and Jack saw Delmas running back in their direction, signaling for them to come and join him. They moved toward him, gradually speeding up to a running pace.

"Come on! There's no one in there."

"We're coming," Jack said, leading the group.

With her gun in her hand, Pauline entered the room dimly lit only by the greenish halo emanating from the emergency exit signs. In front of her there was a closed door.

A corridor at 90-degrees then disappeared in the dim light. She stepped forward, positioned herself in front of the door and opened it as she went through.

She squinted, surprised by the brightness that dazzled her and entered the room. At the back was an office, behind which windows destroyed by the explosion were allowing cold wind to flow in from the outside. Scattered papers and scraps of glass littered the floor and covered what was left of a computer. A larger shard of glass, buried into the desk, perfectly indicated the true power of the blast. She moved in closer and found traces of blood. Her gaze followed the small spots that eventually became a pool. A man was slumped under the desk, around him a large puddle of dried blood. Pauline deduced that he must have been working when the explosion blew out the large windows, shards of which had cut his neck. His head was at an unlikely angle to his chest and you didn't need to be a doctor to figure out he'd been dead for a while. She searched him carefully so as not to defile the scene and discovered that he was a certain Henry Dwight.

She heard footsteps, then recognized the voices. She called Delmas' name.

Luca and Delvaux pushed open the door down the hall. A large fingerprint-sensing keyboard showed that it should normally have been secured. It opened. Henry Dwight had no doubt planned to return there, but had been surprised by the explosion. They entered a server room without windows and dimly lit. They gazed for a moment at the immense room. On each side of a narrow passage were hundreds of CPUs, each mounted in large metal cabinets, arranged in single file, flashing to the sound of air conditioning fans. They were in the belly of the beast. There was enough here to send a rocket to Mars, Thomas thought. Jack, who was following them, understood what Allan and Georges, the two friends he made at the Woodbridge diner, meant when they spoke of the power of a nuclear reactor. Within this room was several million dollars' worth of equipment.

Luca was the first to move. He spotted the center console, grabbed a seat and began to boot the computer that ran the local Millennium network. During startup he checked if he had network on his phone. His smile was answered by Thomas Delvaux, who was watching him.

Everything then went very fast. Luca got in touch with his friends online and started the connection sequence. The most essential task was to get into the Millenium network. If they could manage that, they'd have access to all their resources and have some hope of finding a way to block them. Luca looked at his watch. It was 2 pm.

"I'll try to connect to the local network."

"Luca?" asked Delvaux.

"Yes?"

"We can try and use Ziegler's password. You know I still have traces of his last connection from his phone."

"Perfect. Give it to me"

Delvaux went back into the archives of the app he'd installed on Ziegler's phone. Within a few seconds he'd found the username and password used by Ziegler the day before. Luca entered them into the fields on the screen.

"It works!" he exclaimed.

"We're in?"

"We're in. I can see all of their infrastructure."

"You're not worried we'll be spotted?"

"Why? We're using their leader's password. We should be good."

Luca was typing like a virtuoso on his keyboard, tons of lines scrolling down the screen.

"To both of us!" Luca shouted, rubbing his hands, totally focused on his mission.

After a few minutes, he pulled out his mobile phone and called one of his virtual correspondents. His friend then contacted another, who himself got in touch with several other members of the group. An invisible army rose to fight against Millenium.

* * *

Storx's heart began to beat a little faster and his stomach began to feel uneasy. He'd just pressed the key on his keyboard that would inject a quick dose of poison into the veins of the world of global finance.

The strategy initially consisted of flooding the Paris and New York stock exchanges with sales orders. The fall of Paris would cause most other European markets to fall. Simultaneously, they'd launch a fierce strong attack on New York, which would remove any hope that the shareholders might take up refuge on Wall Street. Then just wait for house of cards to tumble. As soon as they saw any signs of it happening, they'd begin the second phase of mass selling. When the robots joined in the fun, there would probably be a momentary closing of the stock exchanges. Artificial Intelligence would then turn to the Dark Pool to plunder the target areas. Upon reopening, BLACKSTONE would send thousands of purchase orders just below current prices to increase the downward pressure. The program determined in real time the price of an asset. If it was $10, it would offer to buy at $9.99. The order would then be canceled because there was no seller, but the price would fluctuate downward to approach the price proposed by the consensus of buyers. The stock would fall to $9.98. Artificial Intelligence would then send out orders at $9.90 and so on, all the way to the ground. All of this happened in microseconds. The success of the whole operation was based on the speed of execution. The panic was going to spread instantly and the sheer power of the attack to would cause the prices to change. But all this had to be managed by automatons, by computers, the Achilles heel of a financial construction built on nothing more substantial than quicksand.

Machines do not think. They react according to what their programs tell them to do. For them, even the unthinkable is acceptable. Everything is a question of limits and thresholds. By the time human operators take charge of things, by referring to their superiors, by the time the decisions to close the markets have been made, an hour would have already passed. In a world that is decided in milliseconds, where the Internet and fiber connections dominate and where the machine has replaced critical sense, one hour meant almost an eternity.

That's how the Dow Jones lost nearly ten percent in nine minutes and one of the world's largest launderers Procter & Gamble had seen its value melt by fifty percent in minutes just a few years ago. Nobody could have guessed that BLACKSTONE had been behind that gigantic mess. But that was nothing, because since then their technology had improved considerably.

If everything went well, in less than an hour the values of the most strategic companies will be decimated, thought Storx. The wand that led the world was about to change hands. He couldn't take his eyes off the screen, which was fluctuating in real time. In a few seconds, the numbers in green would turn red, bright red. He couldn't stop himself from smiling. Right in that moment, he felt like the most powerful man in the world.

But nothing happened.

9.19 am - it had been five minutes since BLACKSTONE had been launched and nothing was happening. The prices remained desperately stable. He was sweating and struggled to swallow.

He probably just had to wait a few more minutes.

Suddenly everything turned off and Storx found himself in the dark. After a few seconds, the lights and emergency generators started up. His cell phone beeped. He'd just received an SMS. He read the message eagerly and his blood froze.

*
* *

Ziegler's phone rang. He picked up as he rolled on his comfortable black leather armchair toward the window of his office, to contemplate the lake, which was rippling with a thousand tiny wrinkles.

"Ziegler!"

"Sir, we're under attack!" the gravelly voice of Zurich Investments and Securities Bank's Chief Information Security Officer showed that he was panicking and was struggling to find his breath.

"What do you mean, Hunter?" asked a Ziegler who'd been caught off guard.

Checkmate?

"We're under attack from hackers!" His watch indicated 3.20 pm. It was precisely the moment BLACKSTONE was due to launch. Surely it wasn't a coincidence! His cell phone beeped. A message. He looked at the photo and realized that the afternoon was not going to go according to plan.

*
* *

Storx immediately recognized the picture on his cell phone. Everyone who works in computing has a respect tinged with fear of one day seeing the face wearing a white mask with an enigmatic smile. Guy Fawkes, 17th century English Catholic, a symbol of armed conflict that arose because of his ideas. With his sculpted goatee and thin moustache, his face was the nightmare of all who worked on computers.

Anonymous, the group of extraordinarily talented hackers who defended just causes, had just launched a massive attack against Millenium.

Luca Hanser, sitting in front of the central console connected to the network led the charge. For years he had been one of the leaders of Anonymous. To be even more precise, he'd been running the collective for two years now. Anonymous needs to be thought of as a collection of autonomous resources, with well-kept identities, and without direct connections between themselves. In the world of intelligence and terrorism, partitioning is the basis for preventing a link from dropping out of the chain. Luca organized the attacks and participated in the development of the targets. He'd been working on a charge against Millenium for several days, but without gaining entry to their network it would have been complicated. Now that they had access, the takedown would be swift.

Behind hundreds of computers around the world, brilliant brains were analyzing and dissecting Millenium's defense mechanisms to focus their attack and eliminate the danger. So far, they'd disconnected all Internet connections for the Millenium operational centers, preventing any information from getting out. The center in New Haven had been entitled to special treatment by depriving it of electricity. They had cut power by attacking the Woodbridge transformer. This morning, residents of the area woke up wondering what had happened to their power supply. Before the energy provider woke up, they'd already had a two or three-hour head start.

Luca urgently needed to do two things, then everything would become much easier.

First, he had to implement within Millenium's system a program that duplicated automatically to create new user profiles, each with a login and password. Every time a user logged out, another profile was created automatically. Luca knew that Ziegler's usurped identity would soon be compromised and he wanted to ensure he had continuous access to the network even when the profile was eventually blocked. He started the program and instantly created a new user profile. If they cut his access from Ziegler's profile, he'd automatically switch to this new user ID and would be able to continue working. Unless they destroyed his virus or cut off the entire network, it would be almost impossible to dislodge him from Millenium's Intranet.

The other task was to siphon Millenium's bank accounts. A taste of their own bitter medicine. As soon as he launched the attack, alarms would be triggered everywhere within the system. He'd just found their account number. The balance made him dizzy. Luca had several accounts in the Cayman Islands, and he knew how to stay invisible. All he had to do was create a chain of transfers long enough and destroy the computer evidence at every step. After passing the money through four or five banks, it would become almost impossible to trace the capital back to the source. He was going to help himself to their riches. He started the procedure.

*
* *

Storx was paralyzed. All of his attempts to regain control of the situation had failed. The central console from which he could control the entire New Haven system was no longer responding. It had completely frozen. His network access was now invalid and he couldn't even connect to the mainframe computer. The hackers had turned him into a mere spectator, condemned to watch his own demise.

From the main screen, he could monitor the activity of the machine, but he couldn't intervene. Hundreds of users were connected. The hackers had gotten through the security filters in only a few minutes. Storx knew what they were after: Anonymous wanted to seize Millenium's AI software.

He made his decision.

"They will not have it!" he cursed between his teeth.

He quickly went to the electric panel. With a furious gesture, he lowered the red lever. All the emergency power supplies were immediately cut off. The flashing lights of the computer cabinets disappeared. The noise of fans and air conditioning went quiet, giving way to a deafening silence. Like a beast that has just finished its last breath, the BLACKSTONE project had just died.

*
* *

"But who?" asked an incredulous Ziegler.

"Well ... actually, sir, it looks like it's you!"

"What do you mean?"

"It's your user profile that's being used!"

"Nonsense!"

"Can you please check?" Hunter's voice was not getting any lower in its pitch, still perched somewhere in the treble frequency range.

Ziegler pressed a key on his keyboard to turn on his laptop. The welcome screen appeared and a message asked him to connect.

"I'm not even in the system Hunter!"

"Then your password has been hacked."

"So what do we do now?"

"I disconnect you! I mean, I disconnect the person who's using your password..."

There was a silence. Ziegler could hear the sound of his correspondent's keyboard keys.

"Sir, are you still there?" asked Hunter, whose intonation had turned to acute anxiety.

"Yes, of course I am!"

"They're hacking Millenium's accounts as we speak..."

"What?"

"I can see that transfers are in progress and alarms have just been triggered."

"Stop them this instant!" shouted Ziegler, who was living his worst nightmare.

"I'll try, but every time I disconnect it looks like another user takes over immediately!"

Hunter hung up right under Ziegler's nose. He had to prevent the pirate transferring the funds and to do this he had to work in absolute peace. His boss was of no use to him. The balance of the Millenium account was being displayed in real time. More than fifty billion dollars. But that was not his problem.

Two hundred million had just disappeared. Hunter was busy patching the breach. A thin sweat now covered his face and his damp hands reflected his level of stress.

Five hundred million dollars. He could not get rid of the intruder. The hacker had created super user accounts and assigned them all system rights. They had the same administrator privileges as himself, so he could not delete them. Hunter launched the lockdown procedure for Millenium's account. It would take a few seconds, but after that no one would be able to access it. For added security, he decided to block the entire system.

Nine hundred million. The account lockout procedure was in progress. Hunter's heart was pounding. The system confirmed that the account had been blocked, then a few seconds later another message prevented any further transfer into or out of the bank.

Luca saw that the transfer progress had just been stopped by the system. He was disconnected. Successive transfers from ZIS to various accounts in the Cayman Islands had proceeded without any problems. They had just passed through the hands of five more or less opaque banks and landed in his particularly well hidden account in the Virgin Islands, another tax haven. He was rich!

*
* *

Anonymous disappeared as quickly as they had appeared. Within a few minutes, they'd removed the threat of BLACKSTONE and relieved Millenium's account of nearly one billion euros. Luca smiled. The operation had been a success. He thought for a few seconds about maybe one day opening an account with Zurich Investments and Securities. "No," he said to himself, "their level of security is deplorable."

*
* *

17. EPILOGUE

Zurich, Wednesday September 27

Marco Ziegler was scared. The anguish hadn't left him since the fiasco of the BLACKSTONE project. He couldn't personally be blamed for Anonymous' attack, but questions remained unanswered. He knew that when nine hundred million euros goes missing, it wouldn't be long before someone came looking for an explanation. The day before, the German newspaper Bild had dedicated a page to the death of Füller, found hanged in his apartment. As economic adviser to Chancellor Konrad, it caused quite a stir. Ziegler knew it was not suicide. This morning it was the turn of the oligarch Dimitri Volkov. His private jet had a serious accident resulting in three dead, including the Russian tycoon. He was not unaware that Volkov had invested government funds, and everyone knew the Russian oligarchy's weak tolerance of failure.

With the scandal of the lost funds that would not end well, along with the discovery of the body of his head of security that would resurface one day or another, Ziegler decided it was time to disappear. He emptied his personal safe at ZIS in which he kept a hundred and fifty thousand euros in cash, just in case. It was always necessary to have a plan B. Nobody knew that he also had a tidy little sum in discrete accounts at HSBC in Singapore, a country which did not extradite. He had to be quick though. His plane was leaving in three hours, giving him just enough time to get to the airport and pass through security.

He relaxed a little once he was in the Mercedes and moving. He turned up the sound of his B & O sound system. He'd be there in less than an hour. The briefcase with the money was in the back, his plane ticket in his jacket pocket. Everything was so far going as planned.

It was then that he saw the two police stationed at the edge of the road, just after the turn. The two men in uniform stood in front of their motorcycles, lined up on the side of the road. One of them faced him, and raised an arm signaling for him to stop.

"Shit!" Ziegler could not prevent himself from swearing.

He slowed down and stopped the Mercedes on the roadside. The place was particularly quiet for a police check. He lowered the driver's side window and smiled. One should always be friendly with the police. The two gendarmes could not have been more different. The one who had beckoned him to stop was chubby and his alter ego tall and sturdy.

"Police check, sir, please get off the vehicle."

"Did I do something wrong?"

"No, don't worry sir, it's just a routine check," smiled the fat little officer.

The big guy was getting closer to the car and Ziegler realized that something was wrong. Their uniforms didn't fit them. Porky pig was too pudgy to be a gendarme, while Muscleman's trousers were too short for him. Even worse, he was wearing a pair of cowboy boots. Ziegler was seized by panic.

"You're not cops!"

"Nope! But we'd liked to have been, right?" replied the imposter, addressing his approaching friend.

Suddenly Ziegler recognized the fake policemen, they were the assassins of Daniel Hassler, the chief of security as ZIS. The two who were responsible for the fiasco at the hospital. The small one with the oversized face pulled out a gun. Ziegler pressed the button to close his window in a futile attempt to protect himself. The shot rang out. The CEO's blood spurted and sprayed the inside of the car. Thin red threads streamed from the wound, spilling onto the dashboard.

Ziegler lay slumped on the steering wheel. Dead, head blown apart. The taller man went around, glanced into the car, noticed the briefcase and opened the back door of the Mercedes. He grabbed the case on the seat. He opened it and a broad smile lit up his face.

"You see," he said, "there is still justice. We get paid for our services, and we get a bonus." "Idiot!" replied Porky. "So, we're done with him?"

"Unless you want to kill him again, I think we've finished the job, don't you?" "Shame about the car though, no?"

"Forget it. Probably not even his... belongs to the bank!"

They continued their discussion as they calmly strode to their motorcycles. Less than one minute later, their taillights had disappeared around the bend.

*
* *

At 8.00 am, the elevator doors opened, emitting their characteristic 'ding'. Jack was happy to be back in his office at the New York Times. For a few seconds he savored the show of the newsroom where a contagious energy still hung in the air. Telephones ringing, loud conversations and lively discussions happening all around. As soon as one sets foot in a newsroom, one senses the positive tension created by the imperatives of getting the latest issue finished by deadline. The publication of a newspaper was a battle against time.

With his Starbucks latte in hand, he took a step towards his office when the voice of Gerry Small, as if by magic, appeared and cut his momentum.

"Mr. Campbell! We're so happy to see you again! Good holidays?"

"Bad Karma," thought Jack. He'd come to meet the editorial director to make a story proposal, and getting stuck Small was the last thing he wanted this morning.

"Listen Gerry, I've just arrived. Give me a few minutes and I'll tell you all about my 'vacation'." He insisted on the word vacation.

"I hope so! Jeez, you go for a week without letting me know what's happening and I'm supposed to be overjoyed?"

"You know, you're actually pretty annoying, Gerry. I left to go do a job with the agreement of the chief editor. If that's a problem, you should go see him!" Jack turned his back on Gerry. His office was so close.

"Shit, who's the boss here?" the voice behind him did not seem to want to disappear.

"Well, there you go," Jack thought, "nothing changes, always the same old BS." Gerry Small's life was summed up in one phrase that he repeated as a mantra: "I am the boss, I am the boss, I am the boss!". Jack decided to ignore the voice that followed him, shouting ridiculously about what it meant to be the boss. "Whatever," he thought.

Sitting at his desk, he took stock of the situation.

This week had been emotional. After stopping Millenium, Jack, Delvaux and Luca, had been interviewed by the Paris police. He'd seen Pauline in action and was impressed. She really had something. They then testified and signed their statements, giving as much detail as possible, and were thanked by the Director of the CTB. There was no doubt that the Paris bombing, the assassination of Tarek Laid and Millenium were linked. One of the sponsors of these atrocities was a certain Khalid Alzadi, who was close to the über-rich Saudi, Fouad Al-Naviq. He didn't know any more than that, but still it was enough for him to draw a few conclusions.

Luca had some trouble explaining the very timely arrival of Anonymous and their collaboration. He had apparently convinced the police that he'd only posted messages asking for help on Facebook. Jack thought they'd accepted this version of events if they weren't able to find anything else more plausible. Luca and Delvaux left for Zurich on the Tuesday.

Pauline and Jack had met again the evening following the collapse of BLACKSTONE. They both knew it would be the last time. Their relationship together was not meant to last. It was something that had allowed them both to turn the page; to direct their energies to the future and to free themselves of their ghosts. They were ready to rebuild themselves.

Jack was now ready to meet the editor of the paper and offer him an exclusive story. He was going to write a book about Millenium, about the danger of the financialization of the world and the fragility of the system. How many other Milleniums might exist? When would the next weapon created to abuse the global monetary and financial system appear? Millenium and their BLACKSTONE project represented an opportunity for him to use in order to denounce the entire system.

But he also had a promise to keep. He always respected his word. He took the beige folder from his desk drawer. Inside was still the contract between Millenium Dust and Ralik, along with Millenium's address in Connecticut. But more importantly, there was a phone number. He dialed the eight digits.

"Good morning, Executive Staffing. Linda speaking, how can I help you today?" replied the secretary, in a neutral tone.

"Hi Linda, I'd like to know if the post of Google CEO is finally available?" A pause. Jack could almost hear the cogs turning in Linda's brain. Then she recognized her interlocutor.

"You need to be in perfect health for this post, you know?"

"I think I'm better."

"Much better?"

"Enough to invite you to dinner anyway."

"Are you serious?" answered Linda's surprised voice.

"I'm serious! How about Mount Etna at the corner of 6th and 29th West? At 6.30 pm, say, Friday night?"

"I'd love to, Jack. See you Friday."

*
* *

Monday, October 2nd

President Lavalette shook hands with the chiefs of Police and the CTB. The two men had just finished their report on the death of Tarek Laid. Lavalette had insisted on being informed personally. They couldn't keep the information about Millenium Dust hidden from the president, nor the possible links between the company and the demented project it had try to carry out: the attack of May 1st and the death of Tarek Laïd. Lavalette felt helpless. Everything reinforced his view that finance had taken precedence over political power.

The head of the government had been very affected by the incredible sequence of events and violence that had seen the country almost go up in flames. The return to a balanced budget that he'd envisioned was now out of the question, dissipated in the smoke of hundreds of burned vehicles and ransacked cities.

The reforms he wanted to implement would have to wait. After what had happened, it didn't seem fair that it should be the people to be the ones who made the efforts financially. The most important task now was to reunite the fractured elements of a society that was on the verge of imploding. The wounds opened by Tarek Laid's death were not going to close again for a long, long time. If they ever closed again. His duty was to breathe new hope into the country. Austerity would only add to an already explosive climate.

The clock was ticking. He had a phone call with Chancellor Konrad in a few minutes.

If Berlin continued to press for the unacceptable reforms that would be rejected by already-estranged European voters, the conversation would be certain to seal the end of any European hopes. The light on his phone was flashing. The Chancellor was online. He hoped that things wouldn't get to that point.

*
* *

Lieutenant Moussa Zalif, Commandant Pauline Rougier's confidant, was crawling over loose ground. He swore silently to himself. The mud stained his jeans and his jacket. Despite all of the precautions he'd taken, nothing would be able to save his new pair of sneakers.

The weather was particularly sullen on this early October day, although there was no rain. The wind was blowing and it mustn't have been more than sixty degrees. Autumn had put one foot through the door and was pushing summer a little further back into the memory each day.

He was in position. Hidden in the grass, he was less than a hundred yards from the disused factory behind Puteaux cemetery. The dilapidated structure planted at the end of this abandoned wasteland stood out clearly in the landscape. Through the lens of his camera, he could see cracked red brick walls and a broken door frame. The wind gave life to the weeds that waved gently in front of him, making shooting a little random. He shivered.

Pauline had asked him to secretly follow Lieutenant Kowalski there. Kowalski had arrived at the building ten minutes earlier and was now stood outside chain smoking cigarettes. He was obviously waiting for someone and he looked nervous.

A car passed Moussa on the shaky road. He stopped breathing for a few seconds, as if it would help him blend into the background. The car stopped at the side of the road and four people got out of the vehicle and headed towards the factory that was just a few steps away. Moussa took the opportunity to take some photos of the visitors.

Kowalski saw the group coming towards him. He greeted them with his hand. Moussa had a close-up of the one who seemed to be the leader. He had a large scar on his right cheek and it seemed like he only had one eye. Moussa continued to take photos.

The group stood aside and the man with one eye began to speak with Lieutenant Kowalski. The discussion seemed tense. All of this lasted only a few minutes. Kowalski gave him a pouch. Kamel took out some documents which he examined thoroughly. The one-eyed man then passed an envelope to the policeman who took it and stuffed it into his pocket. Moussa had captured the whole scene.

Five minutes later, he heard Kowalski's bike start up and the car with the four occupants sped past him. Moussa transferred the photos to his cellphone via Wi-Fi and uploaded everything to his Dropbox account. He removed them from the camera before calling Pauline to let her know that she could now download them. She picked up immediately.

"Commander?"

"Hi Moussa!" Pauline's calm voice answered at the other end.

"I have news from Kowalski. You can download the photos."

"Anything of interest?"

"I believe so, Commander. Maybe even the jackpot. They gave him an envelope."

"Can you see what's in it?"

"No, it's impossible. But it's obvious what was in it."

"Do you know who it was that he met?"

"That I don't know either, but with that face, I'm sure we've got him on file."

"Thank you Moussa. Go back to the brigade and keep all this to yourself. And leave no trace of the photos, ok?"

"Don't worry boss, I've already deleted them."

Pauline hung up. She'd just received the link to download the photos. It only took a few minutes; she studied them carefully. There was no doubt about it: Kowalski had been living a double life. With that and the proof that Kowalski had hacked her phone messages to get the address where the fugitives of the attack were hiding, the screw was beginning to tightened for the lieutenant. She was going to bring him down.

Today though, she had other things to do. She had no time to waste.

She washed her plate and mug, put on her coat, and checked twice that the little box was in her pocket. She went down to the underground parking lot. It would take her a good hour to get where she was headed.

The weather had turned gray by the end of the morning. Her windshield wipers were pushing tiny drops of rain that swelled the small streams of water that trickled down her windshield. She turned up the fans to get rid of the fog that was trying to hide the road and prevent her from arriving at her destination. She parked, walked fifty meters and pushed open the gate. Her heart was pounding. "I should have brought an umbrella," she thought.

3rd path on the right. Number 132. She was there.

The name on the tombstone read: Laurent Rougier

It had been two years to the day.

Pauline took out the little box and removed her wedding ring from inside. She put it gently on the stone.

"I'm sorry, Laurent."

Tears began to roll down her cheeks.

"I know what you think. But I have to move on. Right now I'm drowning, I'm drowning! You know that I tried, but I can't do it anymore. I love you... I want to die. I wish it was me that died. Being alone is too hard!"

She wept convulsively. She was shaken; her tears letting go the sadness that had held her down her for two years.

"I have to try and escape, to rebuild my life! I hope you can forgive me. I love you Laurent!"

She turned her back on site 132 with a heavy step, her gaze fixed upon the ground. The rain soaked her hair and she could feel the icy water creep into her collar and run down her back. She was cold.

When she got back, she took down the picture of Laurent that was stuck on the hallway mirror. She opened the drawer of the little table near the entrance. She looked at the picture with a sad smile. She placed the photo inside, hesitated, and took it back out. She took a breath and for a moment became dizzy. Her head was spinning. She sat down with the picture in her hand. After a few seconds she got up, put the picture down and closed the drawer with a sudden gesture. She wiped her eyes, grabbed her cell phone from her coat and took out the business card.

She dialed the number.

"Paul Revel!" answered the deep voice at the other end.

"Dr. Paul Revel?" asked Pauline, emphasizing the title.

"Yes, to whom do I have the honor?"

"Pauline Rougier, I got your number from Dr. Alexandre Leroy, the Psychiatrist from the Counter Terrorist Brigade."

"Pauline? Yes, nice to speak to you! I was waiting for your call, Alexandre told me a lot about you."

"Do you think we can see each other in the week? Or next week?"

"How about today, Pauline?"

"Today?" Pauline's voice was filled with anxiety. She was scared.

"Don't worry, therapy is something that you work on personally. So you tell me what to do, not the contrary. Do you want to take some time to think?"

"No that's fine... what time?"

"It's 2 pm now, so let's say... 4.30 pm? Do you have my address?"

"Yes, I have everything I need. See you at 4.30 pm, Doctor."

"I'll be here, Pauline. See you later."

She hung up. Her hands, white from the pressure of gripping her phone, began to relax. She felt like she was swimming. Somewhere, buried in her subconscious, a small voice whispered to her that she had just taken the first step on the path toward her future.

*
* *

Thursday, October 5th

The palace of Fouad Al-Naviq, built entirely in white stone, reflected the rays of a burning sun. From his office, decorated with century-old carpets, the wealthy businessman gazed at the pale marble terrace embellished with flowers and arabesques. Four pillars that supported a golden dome surrounded him. The enormous dome hung over the building and was visible even from the outskirts of Riyadh.

Epilogue

His phone rang. It meant that his visitor had arrived. He answered.

"Let him in!"

"As-Salam-u-Alaikum wa rahmatullahi wa barakatuh!" Khalid Alzadi respectfully greeted his master and employer.

"Salam-u-Allium," replied Fouad. "Do you know why I asked you to come?"

"Millenium?"

"Yes Khalid, I just read the depositions that we managed to get thanks to Kamel."

"From the policeman?"

"Exactly! I'm going to need you again."

"A cleaning job?"

"I believe so, Khalid. We have to get Malik Aertens' notebook back. The police haven't yet understood the importance of what they have in their hands."

Al-Naviq paused. He thought a little before continuing.

"That's all?" Khalid asked, taken aback by the silence of his mentor.

"No. Unfortunately. I would like you to question Luca Hanser. He was in Millenium's office when the money was taken and he is the most gifted computer scientist. Have him tell you everything he knows about this subject. I'm sure he's hiding information."

"It will be done!"

"Oh, and Khalid? I'm interested in this Pauline Rougier. The Police Commander. Four years ago she uncovered one of our funding networks, and she's just forced us to abort the BLACKSTONE project. She's the one who found the notebook. Do what you have to do."

END